HIS VIKING CAPTIVE

THE SAXONS OF HYRSTOW

C.A. FRAY

Editor: Tracey Barski

Cover Design: Okay Creations

Published by: CF Publishing

DEDICATION

To the women who didn't know they could until they did.

A NOTE TO THE READER

Thank you for choosing to read *His Viking Captive*.

This book contains scenes of gory violence, a person held against their will, the loss of parents, and the possibility of sexual assault.

If you are sensitive to these topics, please take care of yourself.

THE SAXONS OF HYRSTOW BOOK ONE

HIS
VIKING
CAPTIVE

C.A. FRAY

CHAPTER
ONE

Northumbria
AD 795

"Yrsa, do you want to die? Wait."

A hard tug on the tail of her tunic drew Yrsa Arkyndóttir's attention over her shoulder. Her friend, Vidar, lifted his crooked nose in a snarl. It was intended to halt her from moving forward before the signal. Good Vidar. Always the older brother she never had.

Yrsa issued a curt nod. She may have been eager, but she wasn't stupid. She wouldn't be the one to endanger the rest of them.

The light scent of birch filled her nose, crouched as she was against a white trunk. Watery fingers of sun wove between the tops of the trees, hinting at the upcoming day's warmth. Yrsa's legs trembled with the desire to move, to push through the dense forest as her clan had done when they'd left camp. She dug her toes into the flora-covered soil, so different from the gentle, rolling hills of her lands, and shook out her shoulders.

Ahead, the raid leader and her betrothed, Aric Stealthhammer, knelt behind a bush. Ear cocked to the side, fiery hair tamed with a strap of worn leather, his strong nose peered over the beard that he'd allowed to grow shaggy over the spring. One corner of his mouth curled up as he listened for sounds from the village to the west. The Danish raiders were not to leave the forest until Aric's signal.

Gratitude settled in her bones that such a fearless man would lead her on the path to vengeance. With a breath to steady her thundering heartbeat, she clutched her sword and shield tight to her chest. It was a practice that her father claimed showed weakness. Though what he thought no longer mattered.

A familiar pain lanced through Yrsa with the reminder that he was no longer in the land of the living. She was alone, save for the men raiding with her. And though the loneliness ripped at her, it was chased by the resolution to avenge her father's murder.

Revenge would be the last thing she'd claim for herself before marriage shackled her. As a betrothal gift, Aric had vowed to show her the coward that had killed her father during his last raid. Blood and victory before her wedding.

In the span of one breath, the sun reached around Aric's outpost and fitted itself among the figures that sat in wait like black flies on a carcass. Aric's gaze snapped to the warriors. The grin that stretched his lips did not reach his eyes. As he swung his sword in an arc overhead, the raiders sprang from their nests among the trees. Blood roared in Yrsa's ears as she jumped up. Being that it was her first raid, Vidar suggested she be stuck behind the others. Aric agreed. Yrsa had ground her teeth and said nothing against the slight. She'd honed her training for an entire winter, and she wouldn't let pride wash that hard work away.

The Saxon village of Hyrstow was sleepy. Chickens wandered about the perimeter of the collection of wooden huts. A few women carried baskets or children through packed dirt pathways, greeting one another with smiles. Rectangle in shape, the huts squatted in a haphazard latticework among small swaths of rambling land, each with animal pens, a fire pit beside the door, and a pile of logs stacked alongside. Reaching to the sky, the village church stood proudly among the huts that made up the village square. A Roman king's remains were rumored to be buried beneath the nave, along with a longboat's worth of treasure. Riches and glory were what her father had sought on his last raid, and Yrsa was determined to gain what he had lost.

The warriors wove between the huts like hungry wolves spilling through a herd of sheep. Aric stalked past a woman as she stepped out, her hand raised over eyes against the sun. Those eyes widened as she froze before she looked beyond Aric and saw the rest. The shriek that careened from her set off the chain reaction Yrsa had anticipated.

Aric punched the woman in the teeth with a gloved hand. She buckled in pain, collapsing in the door's threshold. Yrsa winced then immediately steeled herself. She'd see much worse by the day's end.

One by one, men opened doors and stepped into the daylight. They pulled tunics overhead and blinked stupidly at the sun while screams of terror rose as the raiders made their way to the village center. Most men disappeared into their homes, then reappeared with spears and axes. A few had swords. It was too late. These Saxon scum would pay for what they did to her father.

Her hands were steady as Yrsa strode through the bush and into the village proper. Thatched roofs, wood paneled walls, cook areas surrounded by small fences were calm amidst the patter of feet, the rush of people coming to join the fray. A bald, burly man burst from a door in front of her. She did her best not to startle at his hulking frame. She was sure he could swing the ax in his hands with enough force to remove a leg despite the implement's dull appearance. His muddy eyes widened at the sight of her.

She'd braided her golden hair tightly against the sides of her scalp in rows that were secured into a knot at the crown of her head. The rest fell down her back, the tendrils messy from her sleep on the forest floor. Though Yrsa didn't usually adorn herself with makeup like the women of her class back home, she'd run her fingers through the blood of that morning's sacrificed goat and swiped it over her forehead, down her left eye and her cheek. With her father's sword and her shield, she imagined she looked terrifying. As her muscles tensed to deliver a blow, she *felt* terrifying.

"A woman?" the man exclaimed. His brows rose with his ax as if he wasn't sure what to do with the weapon now that he knew she was female.

Yrsa bit back the sigh that itched her throat. She'd heard that Saxons were strange about their women. Tales had traveled among her people of Saxon women being chained to the duties of cleaning and birthing. No matter. Soon they'd see what a warrior woman could do.

The man's hesitation cost him. Shoulders tense, heart racing, Yrsa plunged her sword forward. She was ready for her training to guide her. The weapon drove toward the man's heart, aim true. He gathered his wits quick enough to swipe his ax in an arc. It blocked the blow.

Determined, Yrsa side-stepped, striking a second time. The blade opened the man's upper arm, spilling blood.

"Which of your men fought in the last Viking raid?" she demanded. Getting answers from the enemy during battle likely wouldn't work, but if she could glean any insight on the raid during which her father had died, it would be worth the effort. Aric hadn't been forthcoming. In the face of her questions, he'd told her that the Saxons of Hyrstow had overtaken them, they'd fought their way free, but not before a large, dark-haired Saxon slit Arkyn Ironsword's throat.

Rather than answer, the man swung his ax to the side, aiming for her middle. Yrsa blocked with her shield, the impact reverberating up her arm. She grit her teeth, dipped low, and jabbed her sword into the man's thick leg.

His enraged bellow of pain engulfed them while the metallic tang of fresh blood filled Yrsa's nostrils. As she rose, she yanked the weapon back, but the tip of the blade remained stuck in the man's bone for a moment too long. It allowed him to shove the ax handle against her raised shield.

Yrsa fell back into the dirt, pain shooting through her buttocks and legs. Fear was a sliver in her side. She had to rise. Yrsa yanked at the sword and, as her blade stripped out of him, the man's keening shout rose among the cacophony of noise growing in the village.

Too quick, he drew the ax overhead. Yrsa rolled to the side, hefting her shield up. The edge of the ax etched along the wood and thudded to the ground beside her hip. She sprang up as the man slapped a meaty hand over the blood that gushed from his thigh.

"Who killed the Danish leader that raided last fall?" Yrsa shouted.

Without a word, the man's lips curled above his stained teeth as he swung his ax at her, one-handed. Yrsa easily deflected it with her shield, once, twice. Frustration prowled in her chest. She had to discover who killed her father before her clansmen laid waste to the village. Her blood feud was hers to settle, hers alone.

"Which of you killed the Danish leader?" She tried again. Sweat slipped between her shoulder blades.

"What raid?" The man's brows bent down in confusion. Liar.

Blood singing in her ears, she shoved at the man with her shield, knocking him backward. Yrsa was glad for her height. Her strike pressed the man toward his hut, and he swung his ax in a desperate arc overhead to reach past the shield. Yrsa spun to the side and darted behind him. It was then that she caught a view of the center of town. Vidar fought two men. His moves were swift and sure, cutting and maiming with precision. She spat an oath under her breath. Vidar had no sense of self-preservation. He'd take on all the men in Hyrstow if it meant showing off for Aric. Yrsa couldn't fault him. The desire to prove herself flared to life inside her. It made her envious of the way Vidar had run farther into the fray. She needed to be there. And, while the man before her could be her first kill, restlessness that she wasn't with the others tugged at her.

With all her might, Yrsa threw the butt of her sword into the back of the man's head. He fell like a bundle of straw from a loft, the thud dulled by the packed dirt.

As she stepped around the sprawled body, she felt the prickle of someone's gaze against her neck. She brought her shield and sword up as she turned and came face to face with a girl. The slip of a thing glared at Yrsa, mallet in hand. The tangles in her auburn hair and the bare feet beneath her wrinkled wool shift revealed how hastily she'd dressed. She looked from Yrsa to the collapsed man. However fearsome she found Yrsa, she stood her ground.

Yrsa hesitated. Long days training with Vidar had not prepared her to face a child. She had only imagined harming bloodthirsty killers. The girl must have been no older than ten or eleven, though the stubborn tilt of her chin betrayed a toughness earned by hardship.

"Get out of here or you will meet the same fate as your father," Yrsa growled. She didn't have time for children.

The girl's big eyes snapped from Yrsa to the man on the ground. Her tinkling voice was flat as she said, "My father's dead."

Yrsa had to keep pushing forward with the rest of her clan which meant killing the child or taking the time to run around several huts. Heart hammering in her chest with frustration at her own indecision, Yrsa lunged forward, baring her teeth. The girl let loose a scream and disappeared through the weather-beaten door behind her. Yrsa didn't give chase. There was no honor in hunting people.

Screams rose over acrid smoke that drifted from somewhere to her left. Male shouts of fury mingled with the clash of metal. In the distance, Aric shoved his shoulder against the hulking mahogany door of the church. The towering stone building stood sentinel over the people scurrying like rats to fight or flee. Her clan fought off a circle of Saxon men who thrusted spears and axes. Yrsa ran to the square, arms pumping with an energy that buffered her from the fear she should have felt at the prospect of injury.

A bellow of pain cut through the crowd. Aric's second, Magnus, lay at the feet of a tall Saxon. Blood pumped from Magnus's stomach. His meaty arm flailed, ax swiping blindly at the hulking man that stood over him. The Saxon's face was dotted with crimson, the spray reaching into his dark hair. His chest muscles heaved as he drove his sword downward into Magnus.

Yrsa slowed to watch. She'd not yet witnessed death in combat and a warrior of Magnus's skill lying dead caused her pulse to quicken and her stomach to churn. The man drew his sword from Magnus's sprawled form and danced backward, his mouth arranged in a grim line within his short beard. His movements were smooth as water over rocks as he swung at another of the advancing Danes with his long blade.

Excitement and fear caused her to halt beside a hut close to the square. He could have been the beast that ended her father. Many of the men she'd seen were tall and dark haired, but this one was a near-giant. A man of that size wouldn't think her a threat. If she could surprise him, slay him before he suspected her, she would garner the respect of her clan. She had trained well and she was quick. And, buried deep, was the thread of ambition that ran alongside her revenge. She could be wife to Aric and be valued as a raider. She wouldn't be relegated to simply bearing children and doing chores. If Yrsa could prove herself to her betrothed, maybe the marriage wouldn't be as dismal as she foresaw.

Shoving a deep breath through her nose, Yrsa took a step forward but halted when she realized that she stood alone beneath a deep straw overhang. Though the urge to cut through the crowd of Saxons was great, it dawned on Yrsa that she was at an advantage.

Aric had broken into the church and had not yet emerged. Her clan hadn't known what fortifications the stone church had, and Aric needed time to look for treasure. If Yrsa could find another entry, she could help search. And the opportunity to help with the bounty would prove her use. Perhaps more than killing a man she couldn't be sure killed her father.

As if sensing her presence, the bearded Saxon looked up across the square, skewering Yrsa to the spot. His brows rose and fell in a blink, eyes narrowing, lips folding into a grimace. Everything slowed as Yrsa stilled beneath his stare. The giant took a step over Magnus's body at his feet, eyes glued to her.

Heat flashed through Yrsa. The intensity of his gaze pierced her. Not one to back away from a challenge, she stared back, unabashed. Before he could get close, another Dane jabbed a spear in his direction.

Yrsa bristled at her own stupidity. The urge to maim the Saxon was as sharp as the lick of a blade through flesh, but Yrsa couldn't be sure if he'd done the deed she suspected. With an oath, she cut to her left, choosing her future.

Ducking low, Yrsa dipped around the rear of the hut. Each home was built of boards driven deep into the earth. Chickens ran loose, clucking amid the chaos. A child's wooden doll lay across the deserted path. Guilt plucked at the back of her mind. The village reminded her of home, Inivik. And yet it housed the man that wrenched her father from this world.

Yrsa skirted the last few huts and darted into the protection of the thick woods that flanked the square's northern border. She skimmed along the tree line until the rear of the church came into view. Yrsa had never beheld a structure so tall. The stone façade pierced the sky, standing at least three stories in the tower. There were different parts that branched off the main body of the building. One of these held a wooden door overshadowed by a lone, thorny bush.

With quick breaths, Yrsa ran from the safety of the trees to kneel under the dappled cover of the bush. A lock of rusty iron barred the church door's handle. With a glance behind her to ensure solitude, Yrsa threw her shield arm up and brought the weight of the solid lindenwood across the U-shaped shackle. Pain, fierce and angry, coursed up her arm and into her left shoulder. The lock rattled, undamaged, though the wood beneath chipped away enough for several bugs to scuttle out. Her way in.

Hefting her shield up, Yrsa brought it against the door three times in quick succession. Each blow to the rotten boards jarred Yrsa from elbow to shoulder. The apprehension that she'd be found had her peeking behind her too often as the wood steadily chipped away. Soon there was a hole large enough for Yrsa to squeeze through. A male shout from inside caused her pulse to roar in her ears. She tucked her shield behind the bush and crawled into the black abyss.

C ool air swept along her cheeks as Yrsa pulled herself through the door's wooden jaws. There were no windows; the only light came from the hole she'd stolen through. Damp, stale air laid heavy on her chest like strips of wet wool. It took a few moments for her eyes to adjust and when she stood, she found she was in a moderately sized, stone walled storage room. Shelves lined the left wall, barrels were to the right. Huge lumps of cloth were piled in the center of the room like giant loaves of bread that had decided to spring up wherever they pleased. Yrsa pulled a hunk of cloth from one. Beneath, the cool grains of carved wood betrayed the bowed shape of a chest.

Victory caused her breath to quicken. Chests! The treasure her father had long sought was beneath her hand! And all at once, the pain of losing him formed a fist in her throat. She could only hope that he would have been proud of her discovery.

A thump startled Yrsa from her grief. It came from behind the inner door. Her hand flew to her side to grip her sword. She'd be captured or killed if found alone. A man's low whine drifted under the heavy planks followed by Aric's muffled intonation. Relief grew like a vine inside her.

Another, larger blow, as if a body had been shoved against the door, blasted through the quiet space. Yrsa strode forward to open the door from her side. A simple bar of iron with a wooden handle was set into the locking mechanism at the wall. Yrsa took hold of the handle to see how far she could pull it. The bar moved then halted when it met with resistance from the other side.

"Aric?" Yrsa yelled. She banged the side of her fist against the door.

"Yrsa?"

Satisfaction curled through her at the hint of disbelief in Aric's tone. Whoever was with him began to wail.

"Aric, I've gotten in. Join me on the other side of the church. There are chests in here and I'll need help to haul them out."

There was a muffled struggle and deadly words from Aric.

"No! No! I'll open it!" the other man sobbed. Keys jingled, then the zing of metal scored through wood. Within seconds, the door opened inward.

Aric's silhouette loomed in a short hallway. One of his ruddy brows was cocked while a grin played at his lips. He clutched a stocky man by the back of his robes the way a mother cat would hold a wayward kitten. He appeared to be one of the Saxon holy men, his head shaved on top with a circle of dark hair sprouting like a ring of mushrooms around the bottom of his skull. A long talisman dangled from around his neck, the centerpiece crafted of wood crossed by another in the middle. The man's bulbous features flowed with tears and snot.

Yrsa backed away to reveal the chests illuminated by the light peeking in from the church hall. There were six in total, each with a brightly colored tapestry draped over top. She threw the cloth off the nearest to show Aric. The bald man shouted in objection, his accent shaving his words. "You defile the church!"

"I can't believe it. Well done," Aric said. It was the highest compliment he'd ever paid her. Despite their recent betrothal, Aric had yet to show any warmth to Yrsa, instead treating her like something to be tolerated. She suspected it stemmed from his bedding the ship-master's daughter and Yrsa's thorny disposition. Whatever it was, it was fine with her. She didn't expect his affection, but the surprise at her capabilities stung. She took small comfort in the fact that they didn't have to pretend with one another. Marriage need not have affection, but Yrsa hoped it might contain respect.

Aric shoved the sputtering man to the packed dirt floor so that he could examine the chest. Yrsa trained her sword on the discarded blubbering mess to ensure that he didn't try to escape.

"You cannot remove the Lord's property," the man

said, his voice stronger now that he faced Yrsa rather than Aric.

"Hush," Yrsa muttered. Deliberately, she drew the tip of her sword from the center of his rounded belly to his neck. The blade kissed the clammy flesh. As he flinched, the man's lips settled into a line of hatred.

"We'll take the chests out the front. The rest should have dealt with the Saxons by now. I'll get Leif and Harald," said Aric.

Yrsa felt her grin of triumph falter at the prospect of Aric retrieving the others. For some reason, she expected something more from him. A word of encouragement about her value as a raider, or even a confirmation that her father would be proud. Anything other than the cold smile of victory that curled Aric's lip as he strode from the room.

As she waited, she surveyed the man at sword point. Heavy jewels glinted on his pudgy fingers. He glared at her with lips set in a mulish line. She grinned.

"Give me those," she said, tipping her chin at his hands.

The man's eyes narrowed, his mouth pursing in refusal. He slid his hands into the sleeves of his robes.

"I said, give me your rings."

Yrsa flicked the tip of her blade along his sleeve. The man gulped.

Through the church hall, a male grunt and clipped shout was followed by a heavy bang. Metal clashed.

"They've overridden you!" the clergyman burst out. His muddy eyes sparkled.

"Oswald?" a deep Saxon voice carried down the hall.

"Ridley! In here, brother!"

Yrsa drew the blade back to the man's neck to prevent further speech. Sweat made her palms slick. It would not end well for her if the Saxons rushed in with her sword on one of their holy people.

Shouts and the clattering of wood against stone echoed from the main area. Yrsa couldn't make out if Aric was alone or if Leif and Harald were there to help. Worry slipped a finger down her spine. Aric was the most skilled fighter Yrsa had ever laid eyes upon. He'd raided with her father and had the spoils to prove his worth. But the deep voiced brother of the clergyman sounded alert. Her stomach churned. She considered running the clergyman through so that she could assist with the fight, but a man of his standing could be valuable. The sudden clang of metal against metal was accompanied by an oath from one of her clansmen. It turned the tide of her contemplation.

"Get up," she commanded. The bald man glared at her but obeyed, hefting his bulky form. Swiftly, Yrsa pulled her father's gilded dagger from her belt. It was one Arkyn had always worn. Until his last raid. When Yrsa commented that he left it behind, he'd bestowed it upon her with a twinkle in his eye. As her fingers fit along the handle, she ducked behind the clergyman, looping an arm around his shoulders to press the blade into his neck. The grip of her sword in her left hand made her feel unbalanced but she wanted to be in control of the dagger with her right.

"Walk."

The man obeyed. She could no longer see his face, but for an odd reason, she felt as if he was smiling. It made her shoulders feel tight within her tunic and leathers as they proceeded through the short hallway.

Yrsa swallowed a gasp as they entered the main room. Pristine stone reached to the sky and came together in huge beams of rich, gleaming wood. The hall that they'd emerged from bisected the main room. To her right, a long section of stone floor gave way to a table draped in a delicate cloth. It held various chalices and candles, screaming of wealth not yet disturbed by her men. Behind it, a wood structure of the same design as the clergyman's talisman stood against the far wall. It was nearly as tall as a man. To her astonishment, inlaid into the wall above the wooden shape was a circular window made of coloured glass. She'd never beheld such a thing. The church must have been wealthy indeed. To Yrsa's left, row upon row of benches sprawled to the large front doors. What Yrsa saw at the room's center made her blood ignite.

The huge, dark-haired Saxon from the village square fought Aric and Harald. Leif lay on the ground between a row of benches, unmoving. The Saxon held a sword in one hand and a short, bloodied blade in the other. He moved like liquid silver against the advance of the two Danes. His long arms pumped back and forth against their blows, striking, and defending in a powerful dance. The threads of his beige tunic had been sliced across the shoulder, though only a scratch had marred the round muscle.

Suddenly, Harald struck a blow meant to maim the man's leg, but he threw his ax too low and missed. As the Saxon blocked a strike from Aric with his blunted blade, he thrust his sword upward. A soggy, rushing sound ricocheted around the chamber as the sword lodged in Harald's chest.

A strangled roar wrought from Aric as he stilled, eyes wide, unable to do anything but watch his friend sink to the ground. Aric and Harald had fought alongside each other since childhood. Only the slip of metal through flesh could be heard in the cavernous space as the Saxon withdrew his weapon from Harald's body. The silence was broken by the triumphant squeal of her hostage. Aric and the Saxon's gazes ripped to where Yrsa stood.

"Brother," the Saxon said. His voice was deep, the inflection strange. He'd appeared tall when she'd spied him across the village, but in person, he was a beast. The breadth of his shoulders was nearly as wide as the benches around them, his forearms taut, corded. Eyes the color of a young fawn examined her beneath the dark mop of his hair.

Yrsa tipped her chin upward as those eyes flitted over her. She prayed she looked fierce. The thought of the brawny Saxon thinking her a helpless female made her want to punch something. The muscles in his throat worked as he finished his assessment. Then he nodded, jaw clenched, as he lifted his sword. A thrill spun through her belly. He would fight her as if she were any other warrior.

Aric grinned; his teeth smeared with red. "We have something of yours."

"Ridley. Kill that one, then we will have this witch whipped to death. She disrespects the church. They have defiled the House of God. Ridley, they must be stopped. She's…"

"Enough," Yrsa snapped. Her mind raced with what to do. Killing the holy man outright would incite the rage of the beast before her. Keeping the insufferable hostage alive would be a better choice if she needed to get away. Her left hand longed for her shield.

"Release him," the Saxon commanded.

Yrsa tightened her grip on the dagger at the man's throat.

Rather than heed her warning, the man in her grasp writhed as he spouted insults. "You heathen! Bitch. I will have your carcass…"

Yrsa's upper lip curled in a sneer as she lifted her sword and bashed the pommel into the back of the man's head. Knocking him senseless was impulsive, but Yrsa couldn't listen to one more word. The gasp he released as he slumped to a heap made her grin.

Without her bargaining chip, she kept her eyes locked on the Saxon as she stepped around the body. The Saxon remained still, weapons up, tightness bracketing his mouth. Yrsa's gaze skittered to Aric. Dried blood matted his hairline. Closer, she could see that his pallor had turned ashen. A dark stain marred his side. Injured.

And while her body thrummed with energy for a fight, panic tightened her throat. She and Aric had sparred together but had never fought side by side against an enemy. Especially not one of such ability as this Saxon, whose hold on his weapons was relaxed, his toned body ready. She swapped her sword to her right hand, holding tight to the dagger in her left.

The man, Ridley, lifted both of his weapons higher. He would not back down. Well, neither would she. She knew that she should be wary. For some reason, facing off with the rugged male made something low in her twinge.

"Surrender," Aric barked, "and we'll give you an honorable death, despite the harm you've caused our clansmen. I will spare your brother."

Yrsa couldn't help her brow from jerking up in surprise. Aric was lying. He would kill Ridley, and his death would be anything but honorable. The fact that he was negotiating with the Saxon made her think his injury was serious. He didn't want to risk a fight. And even though some of the commotion outside had quieted, Yrsa was aware that time was running thin since their clansmen were not entering the church in victory.

A laugh clapped from Ridley. Straight, white teeth were folded in his smile. "You can't possibly think that I will accept that dismal offer."

Yrsa's eyes widened at the man's elevated speech. He was no laborer or simple fighter. He spoke with the confidence of a learned man.

"Very well then. You shall die your way," Aric spat as

he swung deeply with his sword, the blade aimed at Ridley's torso.

The Saxon snaked backwards, throwing a blow with his short sword to deflect. It gave Yrsa the perfect chance to jab with her sword. The movement caught Ridley's tunic, ripping the fabric along the bottom and exposing ropes of muscle along his stomach. He glared at her, as if annoyed that she would strike when he was engaged with another opponent.

"What, Saxon? You don't want to face a woman?"

Ridley swung upwards against a downward attack from Aric, the metal of the swords clattering around them like a blacksmith's hammer.

"Normally, no, though it appears you are more demon than woman, so I have no issue fighting you." The corner of his lips twitched upward. It enraged Yrsa that he had the audacity to mock her. Just like with the boys she'd grown up with, she would have to prove herself.

Yrsa bared her teeth and thrust her sword toward the man's neck. The move was one handed and, therefore, not as powerful as it should have been if she'd had both hands on the hilt, but she didn't want to give up her dagger quite yet. If she had to get in close, a few quick jabs would do the trick. Ridley ducked and twirled toward her, his short sword aimed at her arm. Her dagger clattered to the ground as blood, hot and stinging, rose across her wrist where the metal had taken a bite out of her skin. Yrsa grit her teeth against the smirk that marred Ridley's mouth.

In the same moment that Ridley danced back, Aric moved to cut the Saxon's legs from beneath him. Ridley twisted toward her, his great body shifting back to avoid the blow. Before she could jump away, Ridley crashed backward into Yrsa, taking her down to the floor between benches. Pain shot through her bottom as she hit the stone. Ridley's sprawling weight overtook her. He was built like an ox. Her breath whooshed from her. Yrsa tried to buck him off, but the movement only thrust her hips into the small of his back. The scents of straw and sweat and something woodsy invaded Yrsa's nostrils.

As she struggled to draw a breath, Ridley dropped his short sword to the steps. Wrapping a long-fingered hand around her thigh, he pushed himself upwards. His hand-print was like a hot iron against her leg—searing, then gone. Yrsa was left panting as he rose to thrust his sword against Aric's descending one. Aric swung his weapon down wildly close to them, but Ridley deflected it. Her betrothed's arm flung back with impact, pain etching his features. The slice along his left side drooled blood.

All at once, the doors to the church burst open and Saxons appeared, axes and pitchforks in hand. Dread took wing in her chest. She and Aric had to get out. They could escape the way she entered. But she had to get to Aric first. With a grunt, Yrsa propelled herself upward toward Ridley to deliver at least one severe blow.

As she shoved upright, the cold kiss of metal slid through her back. Blinking stupidly, Yrsa looked down at the tip of her dagger. It protruded from the flesh below the bone that swept along her upper chest. Chasing the recognition, pain, like the fire of a funeral pyre, shot through Yrsa's back and shoulder.

"Ridley! I got her!" the shrill voice of the clergyman rose over the thunder of her heartbeat in her ears.

Despite Yrsa's intention to remain upright, she swayed forward into Ridley. He caught her with one arm while blocking Aric's advance with his other. The vibration of metal on metal rang through his body into hers.

"Yrsa!" Aric shouted. Yrsa tried to push herself out of Ridley's grasp, but her good arm was pinned beneath his, and her other had begun to numb. She was merely able to lay a hand against Ridley's stomach. He growled at her touch on his bare skin.

"Release me!" Yrsa shouted.

Several Saxon men charged through the line of benches, allowing Ridley to rear back. Pain shot from Yrsa's shoulder to the tips of her toes at being handled like a sack of straw. He held her to him as her legs gave out. She needed to get to Aric. Black stars winked at the sides of her vision.

"Get out of here, Oswald! You have no weapon!" Ridley barked. His voice was muffled. Yrsa couldn't force herself to focus. A metallic tang coated her mouth and all she could smell was Ridley's straw and forest scent. She knew she should have been afraid, but indignation gripped her instead. Failure sowed itself deep in her bones.

The last thing she saw before darkness shrouded her was Aric, sword raised, running to the horde of Saxons.

CHAPTER
THREE

The woman in his arms was dead weight. One arm hung limp at her side, sword still loosely in her grasp; the other lay trapped between their bodies. Her long legs had buckled beneath her, and Ridley had instinctually crouched to cushion her fall. Blood wept from her shoulder wound, the hilt of the dagger sticking out of her back at an awkward angle. They were stuck behind a large, overturned bench just past the crossing, near the ambulatory.

Ridley wasn't sure if his men could see him, shielded as he was behind the bench and a pillar. The red-haired Viking's face had twisted when he beheld Ridley holding the female raider, then he'd turned and ran down the aisle, sword raised at the approaching men. Ridley had seen the determination to die in battle before. A mark of honor for some.

Shouts and heavy footfalls clambering up the aisle heralded the arrival of his men. He needed to kill the woman and help them. There could still be a countless number of raiders in Hyrstow.

Thick, hot rage snaked through him. Shadows flickered at the corners of his vision, his limbs quivering with the urge to lay waste to any raider in his path. The Earl of Deircia hadn't called him the Hangman of Hyrstow for nothing. Not that he'd hung that many people in his days as a knight; it had just been one, and the bastard had earned it.

He tensed his legs, preparing to push up from the cold stone when his gaze tripped over the woman.

Riotous golden hair fell in a curtain past his arm. Her shapely bottom lip curved too easily into a grimace for him to think it simply from pain. It seemed natural, as if a scowl always crowned her mouth. What appeared to be dried blood darkened one side of her face, contrasting with the pale skin beneath. He knew some tribes painted their faces during battle. Her speech had a layered, lyrical quality. Combined with the red-haired male's clear death wish caused Ridley to suspect them to be Vikings.

He'd heard whispers of the terror they'd inflicted on Lindisfarne a couple summers back. There had been murmurings across the north of long-haired, pretty men that killed like demons and stole anything valuable. If the woman he held was a Dane, she deserved whatever pain she felt. She had raided his village, had intended to harm his brother. Had mocked him.

Ridley pushed back the memory of her tart retorts. Of the mischievous glint in her blue eyes as she thrust her sword at him. He'd admit the sight of her—slender, sinew layered with a swiftness gained from practicing with a sword—had caught him off guard. Even stabbed through the back, she had struggled against him. Had demanded he release her as she dipped into unconsciousness.

The woman's neck tipped, exposing the milky column of her throat. It would be all too easy to slide a blade along it.

He could do it. He'd slain innocents before.

Ridley blocked the memories that clawed to the surface of his mind. He shut them away before he could break into the cold sweat he knew too well. He was better than the man he used to be. His quiet life as Hyrstow's chieftain had proven that.

A man's guttural moan pierced the air as the wet sounds of metal through skin mingled with the thud of clubs. Heavy breathing and blood. Pungent scents held only during the cradle of battle brought Ridley back to himself. Even if his men were here, the Vikings overrun, there would be people hurt, dying. *His* people. Ridley had to keep moving.

The sword in his hand was heavy, and he gripped it tighter to distract from the reluctance he felt as he raised it. To have the woman's slim throat butchered by such a large instrument would be a pity. He could choke the life from her just as easily. He put the sword down, though every battle instinct shouted at him not to, and placed his palm against her airway. Slowly, he squeezed.

As if sensing her death, yet unable to wake, the woman's body shuddered against him, eyelids fluttering, breaths halting as his palm pressed. It would be over soon.

And Ridley's soul would meet hellfire at the time of his judgment for slaying a helpless woman in a church. It made him no better than the men that destroyed his life years ago.

The thought made him want to heave up the contents of his guts.

No.

He lifted his hand from the Viking's throat. The breath that stole through the woman was like the sun breaking over the horizon. Ridley's vast relief should have indicated that something more was at play; however, he simply dismissed it as not wanting to be a death dealer.

His life in Hyrstow was not to be stained with blood. It was the reason he'd taken the charge that winter. Fealty to his earl's command that he return home, which was a kindness gifted from old friendship, had Ridley working himself to the bone to prove he could shed his warrior title and take up the charge of chieftain. This raid proved his efforts were not enough.

A small moan spilled from the woman's lips.

Ridley's gaze snapped to the small group of men that loomed down the aisle. His friend, Branton, was pulling his ax from the prone body of the large, fire-haired Viking. The others were checking the other fallen men. They hadn't spotted Ridley.

They would soon. Or Oswald and his band of priests would come out from hiding. And when they did, they would expect the Viking woman dead. That, or seek it for themselves.

A strange pang stung Ridley's chest at the thought of the men turning to find her in his arms. Ridley had seen what bloodlust could do. He'd felt it thundering through his own bones, beckoning for more violence. If the people of Hyrstow found her now, after the Vikings had destroyed homes and hurt their kin, her death would not be a quick one.

It made him want to bare his teeth, to cover her with his own body. Possibilities roiled through his mind. He'd decided she wasn't to die. But she couldn't be found, and he couldn't set her free to raid again. Plus, the blade in her back would be a death sentence if left untreated. If he could rouse the female, he could learn if there were more raiders to come.

Ridley's head ached. She wasn't to die but he wouldn't cart her through the village to be ravaged. Branton had turned back to the doors, his ax dripping crimson. The others had picked up the red-haired Viking's body and were dragging it out to the village square. If there were any raiders left, the body was proof their leader was dead.

Sweat slipped down Ridley's brow. The air in the church was rich with incense. He needed to draw a proper breath, but the woman's torso was pressed to his, her legs sprawled before them. Without knowing she did so, she still invaded him.

Ridley's head whipped back to the main altar for an escape route. There was a door at the north transept and another at the south. A short hallway joined the south transept to the cloister where the priests were likely hiding. It connected the small storage room at the rear where the woman, Yrsa, had come from. He wouldn't risk the priests seeing him.

With gritted teeth, he grasped his sword and pushed up with his legs, cradling the woman to his chest with one arm. Her head hung back, legs splayed, a dead weight against his movement. The knife in her back protruded out her front, the blood coating her shoulder as he shifted. Back and stomach muscles tense, he held her chest to his, slung his sword into his belt and hefted her into both arms. She sucked in a thin breath as he moved, despite his effort not to press on her injury.

"Hold on, woman," he muttered.

Shoulders hunched against the prospect of being seen, Ridley moved around the overturned bench and through to the aisle. He made his way to the north door as quickly as he could. Heart hammering, he paused at the closed door at the end of the hall, shoving it open with his back. He peered over his shoulder through the narrow gap.

Smoke billowed from the west, closeting in the church's woodhouse a few yards to the north. The wood-house stood solitary and hadn't burned, which Ridley took to mean that the fire was in the village proper. He swallowed around the stone that settled in his throat. Shouts from the southwest tugged at his ears. Instead of the alarm of invasion, they were tinged with glory.

Like good wine, victory loosened Ridley's limbs a

little. He wasn't sure how much coin or silver the raiders made away with, assuming that's what they came for. Hyrstow's wealth was in land and sheep and crop. The church held the village's few precious items, and Ridley had halted that attack.

Suppressing a grunt, Ridley shoved the door open with his back and made for the tree line behind the woodhouse. He didn't know what he would do if someone caught him. If there was a scream of someone in need. His singular thought was to get to the trees. Get to his hut. Stash her there and go back to help his people.

If he was caught on the way, he'd give her up even if anger surged within him at the prospect.

The woods welcomed him with open arms. Yrsa was an awkward burden as he tried to maneuver between trunks. Her wound wept. Ridley paid no mind. Roots and broken twigs seemed to twist from the ground to hinder him. He found himself panting by the time he rounded the west side of the village where his hut stood at the edge of everything.

The short fence around his home had been damaged, the door to the hut itself kicked in. Anger made him squeeze Yrsa's arm and thigh hard enough to punish. She deserved much worse.

Between the forest and the hut, the expanse of grass was empty. Distraught female voices rang from deeper in the village. The men must have deemed it safe enough for the women to come back home. Cries of sorrow and frustration rent the air. Ridley clenched his jaw against the loathing that he felt for himself with a Viking in his arms. He shoved it down to the pit of his stomach and ran across the grassy stretch to his hut. Inside, he kicked the door closed with the heel of his boot.

The bed had been tossed, the cups and cutlery from the cabinet thrown to the floor. The books that Oswald had lent him were sprawled like flying birds across the tabletop. Clothing was strewn about as well, but the advantage to living like a near-monk was that he didn't have much to sack.

Ridley strode to the bed and dumped the Viking onto her front. A groan passed her lips that Ridley refused to let himself feel bad for inflicting. He was done with her. He'd gotten her to safety and the itching guilt that crawled over his skin for helping her was enough to drive him mad. He'd leave the knife in her shoulder to keep her incapacitated.

Sweat slicked his brow. Urgency tugged at him. His people needed him.

Quickly, Ridley shoved away the straw that covered the floor in front of the table and yanked open the trap-door beneath. Relief flooded him when he saw that his things were still intact. Whoever had been in his hut hadn't found the cellar. Shoving aside his father's sword and the small box of trinkets from his childhood, he dug out a large spike, hammer, and length of rope. Carefully, he closed the door and covered it with straw then tied the rope to the spike.

Eyes set on the task so as not to drift to the female on his bed, Ridley pounded the iron into the ground at the side of the bed. Once embedded deep in the dirt, he scooped up the free end of the rope, sunk to a knee on the bed and tied it to Yrsa's left wrist. Her bones creaked under his quick knots. He didn't care.

A pain-laced groan parted her lips. One side of her face was pressed to the mattress, the other facing him. Ridley stilled, hand on the knot at her wrist. Suddenly, the hand beneath his splayed on the mattress, finding purchase. Yrsa emitted a strangled growl as she shoved herself upward, which morphed into a sharp intake of breath as she collapsed back down.

Something akin to pity threatened to settle in Ridley. Rather than entertain it, he rose from the bed and made for the door. She was a raider. One he didn't kill in the moment, but still may have to once he had a better handle on the village.

"Tell me who killed him," the body on the bed croaked.

Ridley stopped, lips tight together. Her words tangled in the bedclothes, half muffled. It was a wonder he could understand her speech at all.

With a breath that rattled, the woman shoved up with her good arm again. Blood leaked from her wound as she moved. Heedless, she tried to right herself, eyes unfocused.

"Was it you?"

The words were like a slap. He'd saved her and here she was, safe on his bed, accusing him of killing someone.

Her teeth were a white slash in the dim light as she ground them together, pain etched on her angular features. She tried to push herself higher, looking down at the blade that protruded from her chest. Blue eyes shot from it to him, pinning him to the spot. They burned with anger and hate and something raw that made him want to go to her. To place a comforting hand on her back and let her lean into him.

Ridley shoved the feeling aside like it had attacked him. Before she could distract him again, Ridley ducked out the door and secured it behind him.

The hot, rippling pain inside Yrsa's shoulder needled her awake. Her eyes felt as if they were coated in gritty fleece as she forced them open. She lay in a bed. The unfamiliar wood walls of a hut greeted her.

Yrsa sat up, too fast. Agony etched its way along her shoulder, down the bones of her right arm. It took everything in her not to retch. Her leather vest was gone, her tunic ripped down the center, then fastened with a thick leather belt. The unfamiliar weight of it pressed against her middle. A sweet-smelling bandage wound around her neck and over the upper part of her right arm which was cradled in a makeshift sling. When she lifted her left hand to inspect her injury she found it bound to one end of a rope. The other end was tied to a stake in the floor. Her lap was heaped with woven blankets. The scent of oak lingered in the bedclothes.

Hastily, she scanned her prison. The bed she

resided in jutted like a buck tooth into the center of the room. To her left, was a small stool and, beside it, a wooden chest. Against the adjacent wall stood a table with two chairs, across from her was a cabinet, and the right wall housed the door. Or, what she assumed was a door—the skin of a deer was hung over it which Yrsa assumed was for insulation. In the center of it all was an unlit pit of firestones. Everything else was blank. Walls lacking adornment of any kind stared down at her.

So, she thought. *I am still in Hyrstow.*

It wasn't encouraging. Her memories were a jumble of images and sensation. Of Aric, exhausted and with his sword drawn, then the bite of cold steel sticking from her chest. Her dagger! It had been removed from her, which meant it could still be nearby. Before she had a chance to search for her blade, a tall figure entered the hut. Yrsa froze. Though her instincts screamed at her to move, defend herself, do *anything*, she sat there staring at the dark-haired Saxon she'd met in battle.

He seemed equally surprised that she was awake. Dark brows rocketed to his hairline then descended just as quickly. Stubborn jaw hardened beneath his beard. In his hands he held a bowl and a knife—*her dagger*.

The fear a downed deer must feel when it is about to be slaughtered flooded Yrsa. She had to get away. Acting on instinct, she twisted to her left, reaching for the cup that stood on a stool beside the bed. Her singular thought was to break the clay into a shard. Pain like a piece of cinder in her shoulder made her want to scream as her fingers brushed the flat of the stool rather than the cup.

"No," the man growled. Footsteps thumped against the ground and then he was everywhere. Long fingered hands wrapped around her waist and tossed her to her back. Yrsa grunted. In an attempt to shove him off, she swung out with her injured arm, fist connecting with the Saxon's torso, but pain like fire through her chest weakened the blow. Before she could cry out, his hand descended on her mouth, his body blanketing hers.

"Stop," the man said. His warm breath cupped her cheeks.

Yrsa tried to respond but her words were blocked by the heavy hand at her lips. The scents of fresh bread, forest, and male flooded her. She grit her teeth against the intrusion.

"You will injure yourself." The words were folded in a stern grimace that made Yrsa want to snarl.

Her lip curled with an insult as she became aware of the rugged nature of his face, inches from hers, and the way his arm banded around her middle. His eyes had turned into the golden slits of a wolf watching its prey. Both of them glared at the other, chests heaving. With a toss of her head that made it swim, Yrsa freed her mouth from the grip of his palm and sunk her teeth into the meaty side of his hand. The man released a grunt, pain stripping his features raw.

"I will not hurt you!" he hissed. "However, I cannot promise the same of my people. You must remain silent, or someone will hear you."

The petty triumph of the bite didn't last. Yrsa didn't know whether or not it was the assurance that he wanted to keep her secret, but the surge of energy she had felt at the man's arrival drained from her bones. She slumped back into the softness of the bed. It was everything she could do to keep her eyes open. As she blinked hard, the man removed his hand from her mouth. Fresh, sweet air flooded Yrsa's throat, causing her to wince as her chest expanded. Satisfied that she wasn't going to try to escape, the man crawled off her, stripping her of warmth, and stood. She yearned to lay there and recover. It was not what a warrior would do.

Yrsa hated that her head spun as she forced herself into a sitting position. Silent, the man moved to the doorway and bent to retrieve the items he'd been carrying when he entered. A substance that looked like oats sat in a wet, gray pile beside the upturned bowl. He did his best to scoop the muck from the straw covered ground and replace it in the dish. A tinge of red settled amidst the gray as he scraped it from his hand.

"Breakfast," he said. A lock of dark hair fell over his eye as he straightened. He tossed his head to move it, but the curled hair settled back into place.

Yrsa narrowed her gaze at him, suspicious as to why he would feed her, though her mind was too cloudy to sort through the details. The man placed the bowl on the stool next to the bed then slung her dagger into the loop of his belt.

Yrsa wet her lips, her tongue feeling like it was coated in sand. "That is mine."

"It is a fine blade. After I took it out of you, I decided to keep it." He stood at the end of the bed, hands on his hips, one side of his mouth curling upward. His dark brown tunic hugged his powerful frame.

"I need it."

The ghost of a grin remained as he shook his head ruefully. His eyes narrowed, the skin beside them crinkling in a way that made Yrsa think he spent most of his time in the sun. It was strange. He was imposing but did not incite fear as he stood before her.

"Put the knife from your mind and concentrate on your wellbeing. You lost much blood. I don't have the skills of a healer, either. It was difficult to remove the blade and not have you die in my hut."

Yrsa's eyes widened as questions crowded her mind. He saved her. To what end? Where were her clansmen? The fighting had subsided some time ago if this man had time to heal her. She drew a breath to calm the webs of thought that tangled together.

"Where am I?"

"Away from the others. You are safe."

Yrsa snorted. Could he be more vague?

The man stalked to the table that stood next to the left wall, took a chair in hand and placed it at the end of the bed. As he settled into the seat and stretched his legs in front of him, it struck Yrsa that he was a man built for the outdoors, not confined to the trappings of a home.

"What are you to do with me?"

It occurred to her that she should have perished in battle like an honorable Danish raider. Yet she'd succeeded in a disastrous series of firsts: first raid, first true combat, first war wound, first time captive. She had no doubt that this man would not simply let her go. The dark feeling of self-pity yawned around her. She should be in Valhalla among her ancestors, but she had failed at dying with honor. The man leaned forward, forearms to knees. Golden-brown hair dusted his sinewed forearms.

"Where are the rest of the raiders?" he asked. His voice, deep and rich, was one that was used to commands.

The man had a name, but Yrsa could not remember. It had been shouted between brothers in the heat of combat, falling through the clang of swords.

"What are you called?" she demanded. He wasn't the only one who was used to commanding others.

The chair creaked as he sat backwards, broad shoulders testing the limit of the woven chair-back. He rubbed a hand across the back of his neck.

"This is going to be more difficult than I thought," he muttered. "It was easier when you were sleeping."

"And how long have I been asleep?" Yrsa shot back.

"Two days."

Days. Not hours, but entire days at this man's mercy. Panic rose like the flapping wings of a caged bird within her chest. Mentally, she took inventory of her body—if there were any aches or pains to indicate she'd been violated in any way. There were none.

"Where are my people?"

"Fled. Dead. You're the only one left."

Fear like a lump of ice struck her middle. Dead or fled. Aric. Vidar. Were they alive?

"Because you brought me here!" she shouted. Yrsa had to clench her teeth against the pain that sprouted in her shoulder from the outburst.

Tawny eyes flicked to the bandaged portion of her arm then back to her face. He bit his bottom lip as he thought, the pink flesh denting beneath white teeth. Yrsa glared for all she was worth while trying to listen for any hint of activity beyond the timbered walls. An ax fell on wood while birds chirped. The murmurs of voices mingled with footsteps revealed lack of conflict. It was well and truly over. The clamp of captivity pressed down on her.

"Where was your camp?"

Yrsa's brow tented in confusion. She didn't know why he wanted answers from her, but she wouldn't give any.

"What are you to do with me?" she snapped back. She hated the sudden power the man held over her.

He leaned forward, elbows to knees again, cracking his big knuckles as he stared her down. "Tell me where the rest of your filth has fled," he repeated. The words held an edge, one that warned her to heed him.

Yrsa pursed her lips in refusal. She would not reveal the camp where her clan had started their journey. Instead, she looked around the room, pointedly not at him. Wood planked walls greeted her on all sides. Light shone through the hole in the straw-thatched roof to allow smoke from the center fire pit to escape. The only thing remarkable about the room was the stack of books that sat on the table.

The man's movement was so swift, Yrsa barely recoiled before his fingers wrapped around her left arm. His knee shoved between her legs to prevent her from moving. Those golden eyes were filled with a burning cold that threatened a fate worse than death.

"Tell me where your people fled!"

Yrsa's intake of breath was the only thing that betrayed her fear.

Abruptly, the Saxon looked to the space above her head, his entire body tensed as he straightened, listening. Sure enough, a male voice crept from outdoors, the echo of it forming a name.

"I must go," he replied, standing. "Do not call out. No one will help you. Your people are gone. You are alone."

"Wait!" Yrsa demanded, the lack of control fraying her mind. "Who are you?"

"Ridley Ward. Chieftain of Hyrstow."

Without anything further, he disappeared through the hide covering the door.

The shaking started as she strained to hear the direction of his retreating footsteps. It rattled her arms and legs, undeterred by her attempt to stifle it. As if her body knew how dire her situation was even before her mind could reconcile the danger.

She was alone, at the mercy of a man who wanted answers she wasn't willing to give.

After too long, the quaking stopped, leaving exhaustion in its wake. Yrsa grimaced at the snarl of pain in her shoulder. She tried to look at it, but the angle of her neck spiked fire into the wound. The bandage had remained in place during the scuffle for a weapon, though a minty scented brownish ooze seeped out from beneath the cloth.

She'd had to attempt escape. Ridley could want her for anything. Sacrifice, slave, whore; the possibilities of her subjugation swirled in her mind. She would sooner die than serve a Saxon. She was Yrsa, Daughter of Arkyn the Ironsword, fierce in her own right. She would not allow herself to be at anyone's mercy.

Her stomach churned at the sight of the bowl of mush on the stool beside her. She knew she had to get away but felt too weak to leave the bed. Gingerly, she laid back to regain herself. Within moments, she disappeared beneath the blanket of sleep.

CHAPTER
FIVE

"Ridley! Will you pay attention?" Oswald commanded.

Ridley shook his thoughts back to the present as he and a small group gazed at the rear door of the church. He could barely focus on the hole that had been rent in the aged panels, presumably smashed by the Danish shield discarded beside it.

Ridley drew a slow breath through his nose to ease the ache that grew in the back of his head. Three men had been killed in the raid, two of them family men, the third the only son of the village weaver. Worse, two sisters, Isolde and Sigrid Tanner, had been stolen by the retreating Danes. Ridley didn't want to imagine what atrocities were being inflicted on them, though he knew all too well what young women had to face at the hands of raiders. The morning after the raid, after speaking with each family member of those killed, he'd set up search parties to scour the countryside for the females to no avail. Much to Oswald's complaint, those tragedies and the near constant repair of Hyrstow in the days since the raid had demanded all Ridley's time.

"Yes, Father. Please, continue. I was just considering what could have done damage such as this," Ridley said.

"It was the witch that I stabbed. I know it. She must have broken in when I was being assaulted by the leader."

Ridley bit his lip to stop himself from reminding his older brother that he was hardly assaulted. Shouted at, manhandled, yes. There had been many others who had sustained worse injuries. However, the buzz of his irritation didn't have to be aired in the company of others.

Impressed, Ridley examined the hole. Most people would have tried to break the lock or the bar that secured the door. The she-devil was clever, he'd give her that. And stubborn as a mule. Even after he'd returned late that night, feeling like his soul had been sucked through his teeth, she'd refused to die. Once the fires had been put out and the dead carried to burial sites, he returned to his hut to find the woman still alive. Nearly delirious from the come-down of battle, Ridley had sat on the bed, his hip to her stomach, to examine her wound. The blade had gone clean through her upper shoulder and glanced down beneath the bone that swooped from her neck. He didn't think the wound was fatal, yet the rot could be.

Ridley pulled the blade from her shoulder and doused the wound with hot water. She'd woken long enough to screech then pass out from the pain. He'd applied a poultice and wrapped the wound with the strips of a clean tunic. The bite mark on his hand would be a reminder of his charity for days to come.

"I believe it was her," Ridley muttered as he bent to inspect the boards. His first thought was to have a new door built, but with a multitude of repairs required throughout the village, he'd have to settle for a few roughly hewn panels bolted across the hole. The door could be replaced at the church's expense later, when there weren't new homes to build.

"Did ye find 'er among the dead?" Old Joseph Builder asked. He'd been part of the group that had rushed into the church at the end of the battle.

"No. She wasn't among any of the dead I found."

"Strange. I woulda noticed a woman like that amongst the pile 'o limbs. She was handsome, fer a Viking."

Oswald scoffed as he clasped jeweled fingers together within the long sleeves of his brown robe. "For a pagan, you mean. I am too glad to have been the one to kill her. A woman like that could only have been sent from the underworld to cause salacious thoughts in pious men."

His words chafed Ridley. The thread of desire that had so disturbed Oswald was something Ridley had steadfastly shoved to the back of his mind. Her beauty was not something he could let himself dwell on. He'd saved her life, but she'd earned it by fighting tooth and nail for it. He just had to figure out what he was to do with her.

She'd been his secret for two days. While she slept,

Ridley justified her capture by telling himself that she would know where to look for the Danish camp when she awoke. He'd make her tell him where the raiders would have taken the Tanner sisters. Plus, she'd been the only female. She must have been valuable. If the Vikings returned, he could use her as leverage.

Aside from killing her, the right thing would be to make her a slave. Possibly give her to a family that needed another hand on their farm. One that could afford another mouth to feed. His friend Grahame came to mind. His family held more wealth than all of Hyrstow combined. Though the thought of handing the spirited Viking over to his jovial, handsome friend made Ridley's muscles clench to his bones.

There was also the possibility of selling her at the Eoforwic market in the summer. Though, if her attitude during the raid was any indication, she would make a poor slave. She seemed to know her way around a weapon. The only female in a band of raiders, he could only imagine how hardened she was. Ridley didn't know if he'd have the heart to break her or give her to a man that would. He didn't enjoy keeping slaves in the village. A man was a man to Ridley, no matter what luck had dealt them.

"Well, let's get on with this. I have to 'tend to Emma Baker's home," Ridley said.

The men returned to the discussion of the amount of lumber needed. After more debate than Ridley had patience for, it was decided to patch the hole for the time being. Oswald also had Ridley agree to send Joseph's son,

Ewan, up to the church's roof in order to assess any damage.

Unnecessary, yet Ridley knew the Reverend of St. Paul's would continue to pitch fits until appeased. His elder brother had never possessed a penchant for the strife of others, even after serving as a priest most of his years. It was yet another reason the Earl of Deircia had given Ridley charge of Hyrstow. His brother was ambitious for a priest and had a good hold on the ear of the village. Ridley was to ensure that influence didn't turn the people away from their earl.

Joseph walked with him to the charred remains of Emma's home.

"Have ye heard anything more on the Tanner lasses?" Joseph inquired as he limped along. His old hunting injury must have been acting up. His weathered face looked like he'd aged ten winters since the raid. Ridley was relieved Ewan was old enough to take over the bulk of his father's calling.

"No. We've searched all the way to the Eadric's borders."

Joseph stroked his long, gray beard, nodding. "And the men? There were blood feuds sworn. I can't imagine they are pleased not to chase the Vikings past the borders."

Ridley hissed out a breath. He pasted on a small smile for several children, letting his face fall only when they'd passed. "They aren't. But you know the decree and the price of trespassing on Bernira land."

"Aye, death. How else will you satisfy them then?"

"I wish I knew. I've sent word to the earl to request an ease on the border restrictions for the purpose of searching for the raiders. By the time it comes through, the Vikings will already be gone or will have rallied with more forces."

Joseph clapped him on the back as they approached the burnt remains of Emma's hut. "Chin up, lad. I knew yer doing yer best."

Next to the timber shell stood Emma, her luminous brown eyes focused on what remained of the blackened floorboards. Her chestnut hair was bundled beneath a burgundy kerchief swathed about her neck. It snagged Ridley's attention, causing him to wonder how much she'd been able to grab from her hut as the flames enveloped it. An elderly woman put her hand on Emma's shoulder as she walked by. Emma clasped it for a wordless moment then let go as she saw the two men approach.

"Hullo Emma," Joseph said.

Emma shielded her eyes against the sun with her hand, offering a soft smile. "Greetings Joseph. Chief Ridley."

The little curtsy she gave to Ridley in acknowledgement of his status made him uncomfortable. It shouldn't have. It simply delineated that she thought of him in high regard, though his friends would insist it was because of her feelings for him.

"Emma," Ridley said with a smile, quick to dispense with the formalities. "How are you?"

"Oh, as well as I can be. Merthe is excited to be staying with her cousin, which is a blessing."

"Well, let's see what we can do ta get yer home remade." A kind grin poked out from beneath Joseph's beard as the older man set to work examining the jagged edge of burnt wall. The hut's straw-thatched roof had been completely devoured by fire. It was a miracle that two of the walls stood upright at one corner.

"Were you able to retrieve any of your belongings?" Ridley came to stand beside Emma, his height towering over her delicate frame.

Emma's doe eyes scaled the remains of what she'd lived in her entire adult life. Something wistful tugging at her mouth. "I grabbed most of Merthe's clothing and the chickens out back. I tried to go back for Jon's sword, but the hut was aflame. When it cooled off enough for me to look through it, the sword was gone. Stolen maybe."

Ridley nodded, his mouth adopting its familiar grim line. "He wouldn't have wanted you to risk yourself for a sword."

Emma looked up at him, freckled nose wrinkled. "I suppose you're right. 'Tis a shame, though. I would have liked to give it to whoever my new husband will be. A nice piece of steel like that should have been used by someone in my family."

Though straightforward in their interactions, Emma had never spoken of taking a future husband with Ridley before. She would inevitably remarry—Emma could still bear children and would need to be cared for. Even the two harvests since her husband's death was a long time for her to raise her daughter alone.

Ridley swallowed the goose-egg sized lump that formed in his throat. His eyes locked on Joseph inspecting the edges of the floor. Emma had lost her husband, Jon, to illness. Ridley figured she must have well and truly loved Jon for her to not have remarried yet.

Ridley rubbed a hand over the back of his neck to release the tension that had mounted there. His parents had loved one another as well. Because of their example, growing up, Ridley assumed everyone who married was in love. Not until he was on his own did he realize that love was like a rare jewel.

"Well, I'll take a look and see what can be done," Ridley remarked, stepping away from Emma and into the hut's remains.

The damage was extensive. If the material was available, Ridley wished to build something nice for her. She'd been through enough as a widow. The bed had been reduced to heaps of charcoal and the thought of Emma and Merthe, waking up to a fire above their heads made his skin crawl. Not for the first time, Ridley cursed the raiders. More specifically, he focused his hateful thoughts on the blue-eyed woman inside his own hut.

Too soon, Ridley was required at the blacksmith. They bid goodbye to Emma, then Joseph walked with him through the center of town even though the older man had enough work for a fortnight.

"Y'know, Emma is a fine woman," Joseph started.

People milled about, helping one another complete repairs to their homes and animal sheds. Despite it not being Sunnandæg, the day of the weekly market, a few people had set up stalls to trade goods and procure needed items. Cured meat mixed with the scent of spring roses lent to the illusion of normalcy. Women called to one another across the stalls while children scampered beneath the carts. It didn't distract Ridley from the bloodstains that marred the ground. He couldn't wait for the sun to bleach them.

"Not you too," Ridley grumbled. He swept a glance around to ensure no one could hear them. "Grahame and Branton have already shared their thoughts that I should court her."

"Now, now. Ye've not shown any interest in courting anyone since ye came here. Unless ye have a woman afar at the earl's castle. It's no good fer a man to be alone. Especially a chieftain."

Ridley rubbed a hand over his mouth to hide the grimace he could barely suppress. "There isn't a woman at the castle. It doesn't matter. I need to focus on Hyrstow."

"Aye, but a wife gives a man purpose. Helps you get through the hard times."

"Been through plenty of those so far," Ridley said.

The skin around Joseph's eyes crinkled with the deep grooves of pent-up laughter. "Aw, sonny, don't get too bent up about yer station. With the raids that've been goin' on in the other villages these last coupla years, ye've done as well as ya can. And, even if ye don't want

Emma, ye should have a woman to care fer ye. A good wife won't stop ye from dallying with other ladies, if ye so choose. And it is nice to come home to a warm meal and house full 'o children."

The thought of coming home to a good woman, a roasting meal, and a crowd of rambunctious children wasn't new to Ridley. It was one that often warmed him on countless nights alone. He was old for not taking a wife. There had been women, though none had caught his interest enough to settle.

As a knight, he'd been a near nomad. Traveling through the country didn't lend itself well to marriage. And he refused to leave a woman by herself in a home where she was forced to defend herself against God-knew-what. His was a lonely existence; Ridley knew he could remain unmarried and serve Hyrstow. The village and the people in it demanded much of his time, even prior to the raid.

"It's not that I don't think highly of Emma...and I wouldn't be going 'round with other ladies if I were married."

They'd made it to the blacksmith, thank all that was holy. Joseph held his hands up in surrender but gave Ridley a wink before he strode off, a slight limp in his gait.

Ridley could barely focus on his discussion with Aeon Smith regarding the lock Oswald ordered forged for the church's main door. Instead, his concentration continued to swing to thoughts of the female in his hut. Fear of her shrieking loud enough for others to hear competed against images of her injuring herself trying to escape. His mind had been calm all the days that she remained asleep; he'd told himself that he'd done a noble deed by saving her. Now, dread was like an ax to his gut at the possibilities of what could befall her.

Finally, as the sun burned past the tree line, Ridley made his way back home. Several goats walked alongside him, seeking the warmth of the village hearth-fires for the evening. A group of children giggled as they kicked a ball into his path. Grinning, he kicked the ball back. The rich scent of meat, onions, and bread carried on the wind and, for the first time that day, Ridley was satisfied with the sun-drenched, hungry feeling of a job well done. His village was safe. Those that relied on him would eventually have their homes repaired and their lives rebuilt. He would find the Tanner women. He had to. His people were all that mattered, and he would give all of himself to them.

As Ridley rounded the neighboring homestead, a crash bounded through the walls of his hut. With his heart lodged in his throat, Ridley ran.

CHAPTER
SIX

"You fell."

Ridley stood beside the bed, a small glass cup in one hand, the other on his hip, eyes narrowed at her. He appeared wild, hair in disarray, as if he'd been tugging at the ends. Shadows haunted the area beneath his eyes.

Yrsa pulled at the threads of herself to come together. Her mind felt thick, her tongue dry. Hunger was a hollow anchor in her belly.

"Drink this."

Ridley shoved the cup under Yrsa's nose as she eased herself into a sitting position. She grasped it with a shaky hand, the rope heavy where it pulled against her skin. Her fingers brushed Ridley's as she took the drink, the warmth of them mocking her. She had the wherewithal to glare at him over the rim of the cup as she brought it to her lips and drank the cool liquid. Water. She'd half expected poison, but the way Ridley tracked the movement of her throat as she swallowed caused her to wonder if he wanted her to live.

"I found you unconscious on the floor." The words were spit at her as if he was incensed that she would try to gain her freedom. His arms were crossed, mouth folded within that dastardly beard, shoulders hunched. As if she, alone, was the cause for every one of his problems.

"Let me go." Yrsa infused the command with steel. Despite the throb in her shoulder, she straightened her spine.

"No."

"Yes." The vehemence with which she spat the word caused her head to swim. She tried to hide it by taking another large gulp of water. The freshness of it soothed her throat.

"No," he growled. The deep sound reverberated down into Yrsa's bones.

Ridley turned from her. He strode to the other end of the hut, grabbed kindling from a small pile beside the table, and set it inside the fire stones at the room's center. Next, he tucked a large handful of old grass between the spaces of wood, then withdrew a flint from his pocket. As he worked, he resolutely ignored Yrsa. Pig-headed man.

With a scoff, Yrsa twisted herself toward the stool so that she didn't have to face him. Her mind turned over what he could possibly want from her.

"Who are you?" Ridley asked over the small flames that began to lick the kindling. Even crouched, he was big, the fabric of his tunic stretching across his shoulders, eyes set on the task at hand.

Yrsa brought her knees to her chest and, with her teeth, began to pick at the heavy knot holding her wrist. Untying it with one injured arm had proven impossible. She'd tried for most of the day.

"Woman, I am someone who is answered. Your name."

Yrsa ran her tongue over her teeth. Her name was one of influence in her home country. Depending on his plans for her, if Ridley knew of her status, he'd have more power over her. His scheme could be to hold her for ransom. Or sell her to a merchant. She was able-bodied and young.

"I am Yrsa. I carry the last name of my master's house. He cares not if I return, so you will not be able to barter for my life."

Ridley glanced up at her over the flickering flames, mirth in his ochre eyes. "Do you take me for a simpleton? You are no slave."

Yrsa's stomach plummeted. She had never been a good liar. Her brows pinched together with her scowl. "I am. You don't know the ways of my people."

Ridley stood and walked to the cabinet behind him. From it he withdrew an onion, several carrots, a hunk of bread, and something wrapped in rough beige cloth. "The way you use a sword says otherwise. No slave would show the same skills you possess. It was a fine bit of steel you wielded during the raid. Pity it's gone."

"My skills have nothing to do with it," she spat. Yrsa

flexed her right hand as she spoke. She longed to feel the weight of a weapon in her grasp. A dull throb in her neck sharpened her attention back to her injury.

Ridley moved to the table and began chopping the onion and carrots into strips with a cooking knife he withdrew from a shelf in the cabinet. Her mouth watered. It had been days since she'd eaten, and even the pungent scent of onion claimed her attention. She'd tried to reach the shelf earlier, but the short length of rope wouldn't allow it. Still, Yrsa tried to avert her gaze from where he'd stored the knife so as not to appear satisfied to know of its placement.

"Ignoring the manner in which you hold yourself—I doubt a slave would jab their nose in the air the prissy way you do—you seemed quite familiar with the leader of the raid."

A pang of guilt made her wince. What had happened to her betrothed? Dead or fled. Yrsa didn't think that Aric would flee but a small part of her hoped that he had. True, she harbored no real affection for him, but he was a strong leader. Her remaining clansmen would need him to chart the way home.

"We've got all night, princess. I am a patient man. You can tell me about yourself now or later, but you will tell me." Ridley didn't look at her as he spoke. His focus was on the chopped items that he placed in a small iron pot. He plucked up a dram of something white from the table and scraped in a spoonful. Beneath the mid-length sleeves of his tunic, the muscles in his forearms flexed as he worked.

His ease about the room surprised her. If unmarried, the men in her village lived together and had meals cooked by a gaggle of women made up of mothers, sisters, and friends. This, a single man, living on his own was an entirely new animal to her. And she hated that she was fascinated by it. She hid her curiosity with a snarl.

"I am Yrsa, Daughter of Arkyn Ironsword, the great Danish raider. You would do well to let me go, Saxon. Or my betrothed, Aric Stealthammer, will set upon your village a wrath that you have never known." Haughty pride rang through her words. If Ridley wanted to know of her, so be it.

Ridley stilled. Through the veil of smoke that traveled upward through the roof's hole, Yrsa saw his lips twitch downward. He stared into the tabletop for a moment, his gaze unfocused. The gnawing unease in Yrsa's belly stretched. He wasn't telling her something. Just when she was about to demand an answer, Ridley straightened. Placing the pot inside the hot firestones, he stood before the flames. He kept his eyes averted as he gave her his back.

"Are you scared, Saxon?" Yrsa challenged. She propelled herself from the bed and took a step toward him despite the screech from her shoulder. The floor felt unsteady beneath her feet. She'd been recovering for too long. It had just been a shoulder wound; it shouldn't have caused her to sleep for days. Unless Ridley kept her down somehow. There was no telling what a Saxon monster like him would do.

"I doubt your betrothed will come for you." The words were quiet, muttered more to himself rather than her. A broad hand gripped the back of his neck and massaged the muscle there. Yrsa's own gaze fixed on the long, strong looking fingers, her cheeks heating at the thought that he'd opened her clothing to treat her wounds.

Indignation itched the base of her skull. Her mind kept reaching for missing pieces and coming up short.

"Why?" she shouted. He'd demanded answers as soon as she'd awoken earlier. Now he was subdued, caught up in his own thoughts. Well, she had questions of her own.

Ridley turned so swiftly that Yrsa nearly fell back on the bed. Her breath caught in her throat as his large body crowded into her space. The scent of forest and sweat pushed against her defenses.

"Keep your voice down," he ordered. His lip curled as he spat the words.

Yrsa had grown up in the presence of intimidating men. She knew that posturing was about imposing threat, and if the man was large, size would help cultivate the risk. Usually, the peril of a fight was enough to turn the other person away. But there was an edge to Ridley's intimidation that hinted it was barely used and, therefore, deadly.

Yrsa still handled him the way she handled the boys she'd grown up with: she hiked her chin high and stared directly into his icy amber eyes. "Or what?"

"Or my people who remember their homes being

destroyed and their women stolen will come. I promise they will not be so kind to you as I have been." Ridley's breath fanned over her cheeks as he gritted the words through his teeth. His chest was a hairsbreadth from where her arm was cradled to her. A murky memory of being pressed to the heat of his body, sheltered against the roar of battle caught her off guard.

Yrsa fisted her left hand at her side, infuriated he was right. She had no idea how many people in the village had been injured or killed by her clansmen. What she did know was that she had better luck evading Ridley than an entire angry mob. She cut him a curt nod.

"What are you to do with me, then? If your intent is to keep it a secret as to why I am here, what is your plan for me?"

"An eye for an eye," he snapped, glowering at her. The veins in his forearms bulged as he crossed his arms. The weight of his glare was enough to make a man quake. It was a good thing Yrsa had lived long around insufferable men.

She hiked a brow. "What is the meaning of *that*?"

"It means that until the maidens that were stolen are returned, you will remain here as a bargaining chip."

"Stolen maidens?"

Ridley's mouth moved around unsaid words. He nodded, fingers clutching his upper arm. "Don't appear surprised. I'm sure your kind is used to taking unsus- pecting women from their homes."

Yrsa opened her mouth to retort then snapped it shut. The raid's mission hadn't been for slaves. It was for the church's treasure. For revenge against the murderous Saxons that had butchered her father. Death and dismemberment were the punishments. Her clan knew that.

"Where is the Viking camp?"

A demand, not a question.

Yrsa pressed her lips into a line. Her stomach churned over the possibilities of what would befall two Saxon women in her camp. Even if she told him, whoever remained would likely have moved on by now. Unless...

There was a possibility Vidar would convince the others to return. He had sway. He was a friend as good as a brother. There was no way he would just leave her here. And Aric wouldn't lose face by abandoning her.

"Tell me where your men took the women," Ridley commanded, his gaze burning into her own. His body was like a bow strung taut, ready to snap.

Yrsa swallowed around what felt like a stone in her throat. "No. Now release me. I will return and free the women."

A loud, spiteful laugh cut through him. Yrsa hated it. "You expect me to believe you would do that? And that your clan would listen? You're likely their whore. Brought along to be passed around."

Before she knew what she did Yrsa threw her tethered hand up in an open-palmed slap. As if she were a fly, Ridley caught her wrist, his strong fingers circling around the slender bone. Yrsa yanked her arm back, but the Saxon's grip was that of an iron manacle.

"I am no whore. And I will not be yours either," she

rasped. Oak leaves, straw, sunshine and male stole up her nostrils. She resolutely shoved it out with a breath.

Ridley's amber gaze was like a rough-palmed hand chafing her skin as it roved from her face to her chest, then hips, to toes and back up again. The evaluation wasn't lewd, though it certainly wasn't innocent. It made Yrsa's pulse throb, warming her neck and cheeks.

"I do not want you to be."

He released her with enough force to send her bottom to the bed. Weakness made her unsteady, damn it. She sunk into the softness of the blankets, thankful to be away from Ridley's angry heat.

"What are you to do with me then?"

"You will tell me where your people have taken our women. You will heal."

"Why heal me just to use me against my people? I will not help you hunt them." She had to assert herself despite the panic that tightened in her chest like a band. A captive could easily be sold or raped or killed. Ridley could do anything he wanted to her, and no one would be wise to it. It chafed that there were other women, even Saxons, in her same predicament elsewhere.

"Oh princess, you will do as I say. And you are smart enough to not take your chances with the people of Hyrstow."

Referring to her as royalty rubbed against her pride like sand in an eye. Indeed, her family name afforded her a certain level of comfort, but she wasn't some female that was waited upon.

"What am I to do here? You are gone all day. Am I to be tied to your bed to await your return?"

Ridley's brow dipped, his features falling into the grimace that Yrsa was becoming familiar with. Running a hand through his wavy hair that crept past his chin, he turned from her and strode back to the fire. Now that there was space between them, Yrsa felt she could draw a proper breath.

Ridley did not answer, the infuriating man. It was like asking questions to a wall. He stirred the concoction in the pot with a diligence that seemed unnecessary. Yrsa perched on the bed and tried a different tactic.

"Have you no wife or children? Or is this a separate hut where you keep captives?"

Ridley shook his head before she finished speaking. "No wife or child. This is my home."

"Your home?" Yrsa took an exaggerated look around the hut. Barren walls stared back. It was merely one room. The only items of extravagance were the few books on the table. Danish homes were spacious, with beams reaching to the sky. All who were kin could share the warmth and companionship around the great central fire. The longhouses were adorned with rich furs, colorful tapestries, long tables with metal goblets, knives, and jewelry. Swords of a family's ancestors were displayed on the walls. Even after her mother's death Yrsa remained in her family home with her aunt and cousins. "This is a barren cell. How long have you lived here? Does your kind not live in a longhouse?"

Ridley ignored her as he stirred the contents of the

pot. The aroma of onion, herb, and carrot made Yrsa's mouth water. Involuntarily, her tongue slipped across her lips. Ridley's gaze snagged on the movement. When caught staring, his frown deepened. He stood, removing the pot from the coals.

Surprisingly, he prepared two bowls of food and brought one to Yrsa. She accepted it with her good hand, eyes locked on him as he quickly stepped away. It was as if he thought she would throw the hot food in his face. The thought that he was wary of her made her want to smile in victory. She didn't.

"I don't trust you with utensils," he said with a barely perceptible twitch to the side of his mouth. He retrieved the cup from the bedside stool, filled it with liquid from the jug on the table and plopped it back where she could reach it.

Yrsa remained seated, battling with her pride as to whether she should take a bite. As far as she could tell, Ridley hadn't poisoned the meal and she was starving. Mindful of the heat, Yrsa plucked out a chunk of carrot and popped it in her mouth. Savory flavor exploded on her tongue. She scooped the food into her mouth, barely tasting the morsels.

They ate in silence. Ridley sat at the table, chewing his food methodically as he watched her. Though she should have gone slow lest her stomach revolt after so much time without food and drink, Yrsa finished her cup of what turned out to be watered ale in three gulps. Despite the humble nature of the meal, it restored her. Begrudgingly, Yrsa was grateful. Ridley didn't have to share his food, and she wanted him to continue to do so.

"Thank you."

Ridley's brows shot to his hairline as he stood, and Yrsa cursed herself for saying anything at all. He took her bowl and cup, placed the items on the table, wiped them with a wet cloth and returned them to the table to dry. The simple acts made him seem so...self-sufficient. Curiosity ate at her as to why he wasn't married. Widowed, perhaps? He was obviously strong and capable. His swordsmanship was something to envy.

"You must be tired," he said.

Yrsa could tell by the lack of light through the hole in the roof that night had fallen some time ago. She looked around the hut for anything like a privy but found nothing.

"I need to..." she tapered off, gesturing around the hut, hoping he would catch on. Her hope died as he cocked his head at her as if she was from Francia. "I must make water, you idiot," she snapped.

Ridley's frown deepened before he replied. "Right. Well, there is a chamber pot on the other side of the bed. You are free to do as you please, and I will remove it."

Her hackles rose at the thought of humbling herself in such a way before her captor. "I will not. You must take me outside."

"No chance of that, princess. You'll scream your head off or try to run from me."

Yrsa folded her bottom lip between her teeth. It wasn't wrong of him to expect her to escape, however, she hadn't yet entertained a plan of breaking away from him that evening.

"I will not. I need some time to relieve myself and wash. There is a river nearby."

The muscles worked in Ridley's jaw as he mulled over her proposal. He crossed his arms over his chest, hands at his biceps. They were strong hands, tanned and veined from work.

"No."

Yrsa scoffed and clenched a fist against the feeling of helplessness that mounted within her. She'd never considered being unable to satisfy the most basic of needs. Heat climbed her neck that she had to beg to relieve herself. "I swear to you that I will not run. And I will not seek help as you have advised none will come. My hair is matted, and I am dirty." After a heartbeat, she added, "Please."

Ridley's gaze snapped to hers at the entreaty. He seemed perplexed. Yrsa couldn't tell if he had simply not planned for this obvious need of hers or if this was a tactic to show her how vulnerable she was. He paced about the hut, a bear within a cage. "Swear on your betrothed's life."

"Done."

A grunt of a laugh escaped him. "You agreed to that too easily. Do you not love your betrothed?"

Yrsa worked to steady her features, but Ridley caught the flash of annoyance in her eyes.

"Ah, princess. You'll have to swear to me on something that you hold dear. If it is not your man, then what will it be?"

"Marriage has nothing to do with love," Yrsa retorted. "Respect and admiration are fine reasons to wed. I respect my betrothed. He is the greatest fighter I've ever seen."

The grin that cut across Ridley's mouth didn't reach his eyes. He stalked around the fire, gaze never wavering from her, and leaned down to place both hands on the bed in front of her feet. She tried not to fidget under his derisive stare.

"The greatest fighter you've ever seen?" he asked, his voice like silk.

Yrsa's heartbeat pounded in her ears. The non-threatening tone made the hair on the back of her neck stand. She nodded.

"You are lying." The words were flat, unimpressed, as if she was a wayward child that disappointed him.

Despite the tickle in the back of her mind that Ridley was goading her, Yrsa narrowed her eyes and lifted her chin. His face was so close she could make out a bump along the ridge of his nose that hinted at a break long since healed. "I speak the truth."

"No, princess. For you witnessed me fight on the day of the raid. Did I not impress you?"

Yrsa balked. She couldn't help it. Of course, she thought Ridley was impressive. The strength and speed with which he swung his sword would be etched upon her mind forever. Though her pride would never allow her to admit such a thing.

"You fought well enough."

A mirthless laugh rumbled through his chest, the warm breath of it coasting over her. "Well enough? I slaughtered five of your men in the town square before entering the church. I fought off three raiders while listening to my brother squeal as you held him at knife-point. I defended myself against you as well. Pray tell if your betrothed could do the same."

His words had teeth. And Yrsa couldn't deny their truth. She remembered her desire to fell the tall Saxon at the start of the raid and, in her current state, recognized that she would never have been able to do so. Ridley fought as if he had done so a thousand times before. He was an excellent warrior, and worse, he knew it.

"Fine. You are skilled."

The mattress caved under his weight as Ridley leaned closer. Yrsa's pulse quickened as a lock of hair fell across his forehead. She was torn between wanting to brush the strand away and punch him in the jaw.

"More skilled than your betrothed?" Ridley's bronze eyes pierced hers, determination shining in their depths.

Yrsa rolled her eyes heavenward. This was about his self-admiration. Why did he care what she thought of his swordsmanship? "Yes. You are an excellent swordsman."

"The best you've seen?" he pushed. The fingers of his hand were close enough to her bare ankle that Yrsa thought he would grab it to yank her off the bed if she didn't give him the answer he sought. Rage burned inside her bones.

"Yes, the best I've seen!" Yrsa hissed.

Ridley's lips twitched again, and a sliver of warmth seeped into his eyes. Yrsa was annoyed that she noticed they were flecked with hazel, the lashes around them sooty. Satisfied, he pushed off the bed, reaching down to untie the end of the rope where it was secured to the floor. She hadn't been able to pick at that knot earlier, and the fact that he could untie it so easily spiked resentment through her. Her helplessness in the face of the enemy knew no bounds.

As Ridley worked, self-loathing for her betrayal of Aric tightened her throat. But she had tussled with boys as a child and honed her combat skills as a woman. Everything was a pissing contest for a man. Despite her inner guilt, she had to remain unaffected, if she was to survive. Once she escaped she'd never have to humor him again.

Yrsa stood as Ridley tied a slipknot at the end of the thick rope and secured the rough fiber around his own wrist. Yet she wouldn't allow him too much pleasure at her forced answer. She propped her left hand on her hip and in a taunting tone said, "You may be the best I've seen, Saxon. But that is because I rarely fight in front of my reflection."

The laugh that clapped from Ridley was so unexpected, it made her jump. The sound was rusty but hearty, as if he hadn't had a good laugh in a long while. She scowled at him.

"Oh, you are a fiery one, aren't you?" Laugher cushioned the words as Ridley made his way across the room, winding the rope around his wrist so that there was only a foot of slack between them. Next, he retrieved her boots from beside the cupboard and placed them on the floor in front of her. Before Yrsa could move to slip them on, Ridley had gone to one knee. Her mind stumbled as his hand encircled her ankle, the other gripping the cuff of the boot. His calloused hand was warm against her cool flesh. Yrsa didn't let him lift her foot as he tried to coax it up.

"I can do it, Saxon," she said, her tone lethal.

Ridley's face turned up, one brow raised in question. Objectively, his face was rather pleasing. Yrsa wanted to shove her fist into it.

Setting her jaw, Yrsa bent at the waist, her shoulder groaning in protest, and gripped the top of the other boot. Ridley sat back on his heel to watch her wobble as she struggled.

Carefully, she cased her foot into it, forcing the leather up around her ankle before she reached with her right arm and had to drop the boot as pain shot through her wound. Yrsa gasped.

"Come now, princess. Let us not be all night with this," Ridley said.

Yrsa scrunched her nose, infuriated with herself that she was forced to rely on the man. She nodded.

Ridley tipped his balance forward, hand encircling her leg below her knee, and drew the leather up. She felt like a newborn fawn as she swayed on one foot. Tentative, she placed her tethered hand on Ridley's rounded shoulder. He flinched under her touch. It made Yrsa smile. When he'd slid both boots on, he stood, avoiding her gaze. He picked a blanket from the bed and handed it to Yrsa.

"Put this over your hair. It shines like the sun."

Yrsa did as she was told, though her movements were awkward. Her bound wrist felt heavy with Ridley's arm attached to the other side of the rope. It didn't help that her right shoulder protested in pain with each movement. Finally, she settled the material over her head. Her palms felt clammy at the prospect of going out into a village that she'd raided.

Ridley looked down at her, mirth still crinkling the corners of his eyes. It was a strange sensation, this hulk of a warrior standing so amiably close. As if remembering his hate for her, he schooled his features into a frown.

"You are not to shout. You are not to run. We will go to the river; you will do what you require. If you think to evade me, you will die."

Yrsa nodded. Ridley must have believed her, for he drew back the hide, opened the wooden door behind it and stepped outside. Yrsa followed.

CHAPTER
SEVEN

Yrsa hunched down beneath the blanket as she stepped out into the warm evening. There was no telling who was walking about. She needn't have worried. Ridley's hut squatted on the western ring of the village, set apart from the more populated tangle of homes toward the village center. To her right, in the distance, the church loomed against the inky night. The bones of a small fenced area yawned under the moonlight, empty of animals. She shuddered as a breeze cupped her cheek, bringing with it the faint scent of fresh greenery and ash.

As they crossed a wide strip of grassland to the forest beyond, Ridley's solitude struck her as odd. Did he not display his status in the community? Was there not a longhouse for him to remain with his men? Yrsa thumbed through her memories of the raid but couldn't picture anything grand. As they skirted the village, more questions bloomed about the man beside her.

Ridley remained close, moving like a shadow as he led them through the bushy stand of saplings that separated the village from forest. The air was clean and crisp and Yrsa took a deep, thirsty breath of it. The open air, if only temporary, was something she didn't think she'd take for granted again. Thin trees gave way to oak and pine. Their footfalls were engulfed by the spongy layer of leaves and twigs that blanketed the forest floor. The trickle of moving water echoed through the branches. Yrsa no longer worried about the noise she made as she moved. Ridley too, straightened a little, more comfortable amongst the trees.

She didn't speak, her focus on the uneven ground as it dipped down to wherever the water rushed. Ridley seemed to sense her unfamiliarity in the dark. He remained two paces ahead, his body turned to the side, roped arm up, as if ready to catch her if she tripped. The dappled moonlight kissed his powerful silhouette. Inwardly, Yrsa cursed herself for noticing the broadness of his shoulders, the line of his neck as his dark hair brushed against his nape.

Abruptly, the trees halted. A strip of mossy ground descended to the banks that met the river's edge. It was followed by a shallow lip of sand that cradled the lapping water. Wide oaks and towering pines ringed the inlet, their roots humped around large stones. The clear scent of water beckoned Yrsa to the shoreline, though not before she attended to the urges of her body.

Ridley loosened off a length of rope to give Yrsa privacy. Without hesitation, she disappeared to relieve herself behind the weathered gray trunk of a wide tree. The task was difficult with an injured shoulder and bound wrist, but eventually she was able to right her clothing. As she did so, her thoughts scattered to her predicament.

Escape was her only hope. What was most important was finding her people. If Aric and Vidar were alive, she sensed that they would be back. To save his reputation, Aric would need to recover the treasure from the church. She was sure Vidar cared enough to look for her if they returned. And the remaining men may want more women.

The thought gripped her like a steel band around her chest. Taking slaves had never been the plan. She knew it was done, but Aric had never brought female slaves back to Inivik from his other raids.

Unless he took them and used them and left them to die.

Yrsa shook her head against the thought. It was too harsh to wrap her mind around. Not when her own captor stood a few feet away. Yrsa had to escape. Then she could see if what he said about the stolen females was true. Her honor would dictate she kill Ridley as well, for keeping her captive. That, however, was a slim possibility.

Her head throbbed with worries as she undid the knotted mess of her hair. The blood-matted braids that bound her head felt frizzy beneath her palm and the leather holding half of it up was like a gnarled fist clutching the strands. With one hand, it was impossible to unwind. The need to wash herself, to inspect herself and her injury, was overwhelming.

Tears pressed behind Yrsa's eyes. She was alone, injured, in the care of a man who would not reveal her fate, and she was so helpless she could not even undo her own hair. One thing was certain: she could not cry. She bit down hard on her bottom lip to quell the frantic swell of helplessness that rose within her. As she drew a deep breath, she heard Ridley stir in the distance. The scent of silver birch and wildflowers greeted her. It reminded her of the copses of trees that she and Vidar would play hide and seek in as children. Yrsa exhaled heavily. She would survive. And she would need Ridley to do that.

Straightening her shoulders, she emerged from behind the tree and walked to him. She didn't know what she was about to do, exactly. Yrsa was not one for seduction and did not want to set a precedent for it when she was most vulnerable. Ridley had already seen her body—it was just limbs and a torso, after all—and had not violated her. All the better if he did not think her comely. Though some part of her preened to think of Ridley looking upon her with lust, it did not serve her escape if he desired her.

He appeared taller, more powerful in the darkness. Gods, he was appealing. Begrudgingly, she had begun to accept that fact. He stood with his back turned, unlike so many others would have done, to give her some semblance of privacy. The lightly woven tunic he wore showcased the contour of muscle in his shoulders. His trousers hugged his strong backside, and Yrsa found herself eyeing him longer than she should have. Disgust with herself chastised her. It didn't matter what he looked like. He was a murderous Saxon that kept her against her will.

"Saxon," she whispered. "I require your assistance."

Lines of weariness bracketed his mouth as he turned to face her. His arms were crossed against her entreaty, the grooved muscles of his forearms etched in moonlight.

"What, princess?" His voice was a quiet snarl among the trees.

Pulse hammering at the base of her throat, Yrsa stepped close, leaving a mere gap between their bodies. Warmth and tension radiated from Ridley as he held himself still.

"I need help untangling my hair. The leather strap holding it is caught and I need to wash away the blood."

Ridley's eyes narrowed at her sudden meekness. Yrsa cursed her previous, impulsive self that had taught him to be on guard. Only now did she realize that everything would have been easier if he trusted her to be scared and timid.

He looked at the mess of her hair, then toward the river. "Are you sure?"

Yrsa forced herself to not roll her eyes at him. She did not understand his sudden reluctance to put his hands on her. He had done so to heal her. "Yes. It is difficult, and I doubt you will allow me a chance to bathe again."

Ridley's eyes widened at the word 'bathe' but within a second, he steeled himself.

"What would you have me do?" his warm breath fanned over her cheeks as he spoke, caressing her lips.

"Just unwind the leather and release the braids, if you can."

"Just," he muttered. His mouth formed a sour line as he lifted his hands to pick at the leather strap at the crown of her head. Yrsa gritted her teeth, expecting him to wrench the thing from her tresses, but Ridley's fingers were gentle in their exploration and careful as he unwound the strip.

As he worked, Yrsa became aware that she was eye level with his chin. Ridley's arms boxed around her head as he picked at the leather, and for the first time in her life, she felt petite. Back home, Yrsa was the same height as most of the men. She was built of slender muscle but was certainly not small.

Her attention snagged on where the bronzed skin of his throat met his padded chest, eyes trailing along his collarbone to the rounded muscle that joined his shoulder and neck, the same spot where she'd been stabbed. The scent of oak and straw and male filled her nostrils, luring her in with a sense of comfort that should not have been afforded by her captor. She grimaced.

"Does it hurt?" Ridley asked. The vibration of his voice rumbled through the slip of space between them.

"No," Yrsa said. Inwardly, she cursed herself for relaxing her guard. She contorted her features into a frown.

"There," Ridley said, bringing the offending leather

before her eyes. She snuck a hand between them and snatched it before he tossed it away.

Instead of backing up, Ridley lifted his arms again. Yrsa fought the urge to step away. In her mind's eye, she pictured all manner of things he could do; grasp her hair and hit her skull with his own, encase her neck in his large hands to choke her, yank her hair until she was brought to the ground. She flinched and hated herself for it. But when Ridley sunk his fingers into the braids at her scalp and began to gently unknot them, Yrsa's eyes widened with surprise.

If Ridley knew she was torn between sprinting into the bush and melting into a puddle because his hands in her hair felt so decadent, he gave no indication. He focused on working his fingers between the tangles, lightly massaging the strands apart. Yrsa's eyes fluttered closed. If the man was to kill her, at least she wouldn't see it coming.

She had always loved having her hair caressed. When she was little, before her mother had given up efforts to make her into a proper woman, Yrsa would sit for hours while her mother wound her hair into all sorts of designs befitting a great warrior's daughter. Looking back, those had been the best times they'd spent together before her mother's death. They were the only ones not fraught with her mother's disappointment.

"Does it feel good?" Yrsa's eyes flew open to find Ridley staring at her as the pads of his fingers worked along her scalp.

Yrsa commanded herself to think of a clever retort,

but her mind came up as blank as a starless night. With Ridley sifting through her braids, his scent pressing into her skin, eyes lit from within as he stared down at her, she suddenly could think of little else than what his lips might feel like against hers. As if he could read her thoughts, one of Ridley's hands dipped down to cup the base of her skull. Dazed, Yrsa tipped her head back into the comfort of his palm. The other trailed down her neck, around her good shoulder to settle on her lower back, drawing her closer. It had been so long since she'd been touched in any affectionate manner. Her hand came up to rest on the solid muscle of his chest, the heat of his skin through his tunic so pleasant, she wanted to wrap herself around him to steal his warmth. Her lips parted as his eyes locked on them.

"Yrsa," Ridley breathed as the distance between them disappeared.

Her name was like a cold pail of water overhead. What was she doing? If anything, *she* should seduce *him*. And he was doing a good job of subverting that intention. Hard and fast, she shoved at his chest, breaking the spell. Ridley dropped his hands as if she were made of fire, while she stumbled backwards, almost tripping into the water.

"Don't," she commanded, bringing herself to her full height.

Ridley's jaw snapped shut. The flame in his eyes had disappeared. All that was left was cold disgust.

"I – I must wash."

"Of course," Ridley's voice was smooth, unaffected.

As if having her in his arms moments ago was less than nothing. He turned toward the trees and did not glance back. For some reason, Yrsa expected him to disagree, like he did earlier when she spoke of Aric's fighting skills. But who was she to assume anything about this man? The icy grip of embarrassment wound about her pride at his complete change in demeanor.

With the relative privacy of Ridley's turned back, she toed off her boots, shimmied out of her trousers, and undid the belt around her middle. It took an aggravating amount of time. Her shoulder throbbed from all the movement and her heartbeat wouldn't calm. When it came time to discard the tunic, she was stuck. The right sleeve had been cut, brought up under her arm, then knotted around her neck overtop of the bandage. It allowed her arm freedom while the sling held it steady. The left sleeve was intact; the rope that bound her left wrist rendered her incapable of sliding off the garment. If she hadn't been covered in blood and filth, she would have given up. But she was so close to the fresh feeling of a clean body that she couldn't deny herself this indulgence.

"I need you again," Yrsa bit out. She was glad for the darkness around them because her cheeks were aflame.

Ridley bowed his head but didn't move. It was as if the weight of the heavens shoved his shoulders downward. When he turned, in the dimness, Yrsa could see his fingers clench his upper arm. "What?"

"You must help me undress. The tunic is tied to me."

A mirthless laugh passed his lips. "God is certainly punishing me for something."

Despite his annoyance with his God or her, he came to the water's edge to stand before her. Hands on his hips, he glared down at her as if it was her fault that he'd secured the tunic in such a manner. His gaze skittered over the material, then down to the ground. It was too dark to see if his cheeks had ripened to red as Yrsa's had.

"On with it, Saxon. It seems as though you've seen me naked enough already." Yrsa's voice was strong even though her heart had lurched into her throat.

"I wasn't looking at your body parts when I was saving your life," he growled.

"Even so, I lived on a ship full of men for days. Modesty isn't a luxury I've been afforded as of late."

His nostrils flared but the words seemed to do the trick. With deft fingers, he untied the piece of material at her neck, leaving the bandage intact. Without further comment, Ridley pulled the tunic free, unknotting it then tugging the left sleeve along the rope until it was gathered around his wrist so that there was enough slack to bathe. As soon as the material unwound from her body, Ridley snapped his gaze away. Yrsa was glad. Even if her lower belly quivered with the prospect of Ridley seeing her nude.

Wind picked up, scraping along her bare skin, spreading gooseflesh as she bathed in the frigid water. She washed quickly, though it was difficult with one hand while at the same time trying to keep her bandage dry. She imagined she did a very poor job of it, but she did feel refreshed when finished.

Ridley held the blanket out to her as she emerged from the water, keeping it at arms length for her to grab. He faced away, resolute against the sight of her as she dried off and wrestled on her trousers and boots. He did not go to one knee to assist her as he did in his hut. Whatever had made him dip his head to kiss her had passed as if it had never been. Yrsa told herself she was glad for it. A flirtation with the Saxon scum that held her was not something she wanted to add to her list of regrets.

Her tunic still in his hand, he strode up the incline as soon as she had fastened her pants. Yrsa had to wrap the blanket around her upper body to scramble to keep up with her captor.

He did not slow as he approached the village. He must have decided to have her found out after all. Hackles up, Yrsa coiled her muscles for an attack. She wouldn't be able to do much with one injured arm and the other secured, but she thought she might be able to loop the rope around a perpetrator's neck if need be. She could kill at least one man in a last show of rebellion. Bile coated the back of her mouth. But no attack came. Hastily, they made it back to his hut where Ridley untied his wrist and secured the rope to the stake that jutted from the floor. He doused the smoldering fire with the last of the watered ale. Without a glance at her, he strode from the hut, leaving Yrsa alone. He did not return.

CHAPTER
EIGHT

"Come on, Rid. Put your back into it!"

Ridley hefted the ax overhead before bringing it down in a smooth arc. The newly sharpened blade sank into the center of the wood at his feet with a satisfying *thunk*. The impact rattled up his arms and into his shoulders, tickling the edge of tension he'd been carrying there since the raid.

"You could help," Ridley said to Branton as his friend came to stand beneath the overhang of his hut. Crows cawed to one another from the depths of the forest that butted up against the nearby meadow dotted with sheep.

"And rob you of your relaxation time?" Branton raised an eyebrow at the growing heap of chopped wood. His easy grin disappeared behind the cup of ale he lifted to his lips, then reappeared even wider. The sleeves of his dark brown tunic were rolled to his elbows and the leather vambraces he wore when felling trees, discarded.

The strings at his neck were loose, hinting at the muscled chest beneath. He must have finished the day's labor.

"I would hardly call this relaxing." Ridley's sour mood bucked at his friend's joviality. He'd hoped the mindless task of chopping wood would distract him from the jewel-eyed woman in his hut. His enemy. A fact he had to constantly remind himself of.

Ridley's muscles ached as he hefted another log and brought the ax downward. He deserved the pain. After instructing battle exercises with half the village men then attending the funeral of Alder, a farmer injured in the fighting that had succumbed to the fever, Ridley's sense of helplessness was soaring. Alder's wife would require help with their crops, though, thankfully, her two sons were strapping young men who could shoulder much of it. The funeral had been filled with their grief. Alder had been a beloved member of the village; he had always been full of stories around the community fire and a wealth of knowledge about crop rotation.

Later in the day, the prospect of returning home to the woman with a body of a goddess and tongue like a demon did not appeal to him. Or, rather, it appealed too much. He'd sought out Branton's hut to distract himself with mindless chopping. As Hyrstow's woodcutter, Bran had stacks of wood a plenty. While the sun tracked across the early evening sky; he'd begun to realize how futile his effort was. He couldn't keep Yrsa from his thoughts. All day his mind and body had warred between roiling hate and unfettered desire. He disgusted himself.

"If you're looking for a job, too bad. You already have one," Bran called.

Ridley tried for a smile that formed more of a scowl. "I'd give it up in a heartbeat if it meant if I could be head cutter of Hyrstow."

Bran's laughter boomed from beneath the overhang. "I'd love to see that. A traveling soldier turned wood cutter. Very prestigious. Though this is the most relaxed I've seen you since the raid."

Branton toed his way through the scattered logs to stand beside Ridley. He remained silent as Ridley placed a new log on the chopping stump and squared up with the ax. The thick, cheery heat of the day was finally abating, though sweat trickled down the center of Ridley's naked torso.

Branton rocked back on his heels, arms crossed over his wide chest. He stroked his dark beard, then with a shake of his head, he strode back to the hut, placed his mug on the ground and retrieved the second ax that leaned against the wood wall. "You look tired."

He placed a log, thicker than Ridley's, on another stump and heaved his ax up. The wood gave way beneath the blade, clean and fast, the sound of the cut echoing into the meadow beyond.

"I'm fine." Ridley didn't need a lecture. After a sleepless night in the forest, Ridley had returned that morning, took Yrsa into the trees near his house to relieve herself, then prepared a slice of bread and cheese for her. All the while he peppered her with questions about where her clan would take prisoners. She remained sullen as she sat on the edge of the bed, chewing. At least she hadn't thrown the food on the floor. It was an improvement. As he'd removed his tunic to shake it out so as not to reveal that he'd slept in the woods, he felt eyes on the skin of his back. When he turned, Yrsa had looked anywhere but him.

It rankled that she'd had no questions. No demands for freedom. He'd expected to be bombarded, to be flayed by her sharp tongue. Instead, she pursed her lips in a mulish line any time his gaze fell upon hers.

Ridley had no idea how he'd become such an idiot in such a short amount of time. Seducing him must have been her plan at the river. Those same lips had been pillowed and parted, her head tipped between his hands as he untangled her braids. She'd been so pliable beneath his fingers. The errant thought that he was the only person in the world that could make her soft had flitted through his mind. She'd shivered as his thumb had skimmed her neck just below her hairline, the skin there like velvet. And he'd been under her spell. He'd stooped to kiss those pink lips—a blatant misstep.

And then she'd needed help to undress.

Ridley gnashed his teeth together as he split the next log. The thing wrenched in half, one of the pieces skittering into Branton's leg.

"Christ! Watch out," Branton said. His inky brows pinched together.

"Don't stand so close," Ridley barked, stalking over to rip the offending wood from the ground. He hocked the thing in the direction of the wood pile that stood against the hut. It hit the dusty ground in front of the pile with a dull thud.

"I know that you're overseeing a lot, but I am not the person you take that out on," Branton said. A silky warning underlied his tone. It was one Ridley was barely familiar with. The distance, he knew, was born of choosing different paths that converged again with Ridley's appointment as chieftain. They'd been the best of friends as boys then, swallowed by his own grief, Ridley had gone off to fight for the Earl of Deircia.

Ridley shoved a breath through his nostrils. He knew that none of this was Bran's fault. His friend had been cutting trees from the allotted section of forest near Hyrstow as fast as he could. He'd overseen the rebuilding of a grain storage shed and had even helped Ridley ensure the men of the village were in fighting shape in case the Vikings returned.

"Forgive me. Haven't been sleeping right since the raid."

"I can tell." Branton shoved his ax through another piece of wood. "You're not skilled at covering your plight."

Ridley grimaced. He hoped his friend was wrong. Yrsa's life and his reputation depended on his ability to keep up the belief that he was in control. If he was found out for harboring a raider, he could only imagine the retribution Hyrstow would demand. Not to mention the ruckus Oswald would strum up. He already thought Ridley too unskilled for the role of chieftain. As much as Ridley cared for his brother, he held no illusion that

Oswald wanted him there. And after the previous rocky years under chief Fredrick's reign, Ridley couldn't risk his people's wellbeing.

"Why not sup with us tonight?"

The suggestion was not unexpected. Ridley often dined with his friend's family. Freda, Branton's wife, was a wonderful cook. But, even as the thought of enjoying a meal and a tussle with Branton's children crossed his mind, he knew his worry would be constant. His own hut was on the edge of town, separated by what used to be his father's meager farmland. It was more secluded than other homes, born from the simple truth that his parents had been peasants, barely scraping by. He could have taken up residence in the hall where the single men of the village stayed. Instead, Ridley opted for privacy. For the home of his parents, whom he'd failed all those years ago. However, others passing into the woods could still hear Yrsa if she made a ruckus.

"Another night."

Branton propped the head of the ax on the scarred stump and draped his heavy forearms over the butt of the handle. The hair on his arms had lightened in the sun from always working outdoors, making the scars there easier to see. "Why?"

"I'm busy," Ridley replied.

Branton heaved out a sigh and looked to the sky. He gentled his tone. "With what? Rid, you did your best by the village during the raid. You can't keep working yourself to the bone to make it up to all of us."

Ridley grunted as he let his own ax fall to his side.

The words were a kind offering that wasn't deserved. He was responsible for his people's wellbeing. If he had done better, trained the men when he'd first arrived in Hyrstow in the new year, he wouldn't have a Viking in his hut.

"Thank you, Bran. Really. There is a lot of work. And I want to ensure everyone is settled enough to put this behind us."

"Raids happen, Rid. It is a way of life. If not the Vikings, the Britons. Or those sacks o'shit of Eadric's."

Ridley nodded, his mind sharpening on the name. The Earl of Bernira's land butted against Hystrow territory. There had been conflict for years when he'd been a boy, culminating in the raid that ripped his parents' lives away. A bitter taste coated the back of his throat. "But one hasn't happened in a long while. Maybe too long. It's made Hyrstow soft."

"Just because you are used to a life on horseback, protecting, and fighting in the name of Lachlan, doesn't mean we're all useless."

"My life as a knight gave me the skills to prepare us. Something I should have done better."

"Where's this coming from, eh? You get appointed and think there won't be time to learn what makes the village tick? You've given up combat, sure, but why? To turn us into soldiers? We're simple people, Rid. Not your forces to command."

Ridley gripped the handle of the ax so tightly his knuckles ached. He hated the assessment, though he recognized the truth in it. He'd been a warrior for years.

Yet finding peace in his homeland was something more difficult than battle, it seemed. Instead of offering a reply, he stacked another log.

Branton's blue eyes rolled skyward. Dusk coated the sky overhead in a robe of violet. The long grass beyond their wood piles swayed with the tune of the breeze, reminding Ridley that he'd need to get an early start in the north field with Grahame the next morning. The raid had not only stolen lives but days critical for sowing crops.

Bran gave him a hard look. "You need something, Rid. Freda asked me the other night if you were courting anyone. When I told her no, do you know what she said?"

Ridley could barely suppress the grin that threatened to escape at the thought of Branton's iron-willed wife's opinion. Freda, sister of Grahame, had grown up being badgered by her brother's friends. She'd heard the worst language from the three rough and tumble boys and had been teased mercilessly by them her entire life. Until one day, when Freda had had enough and told Branton he'd better kiss her or never speak to her again. Grahame had laughed but Branton had stood there, the color draining from his face, as if the prospect of not speaking to Freda was a fate worse than death. He kissed her then and there, sealing their fate together, much to the dismay of the eligible ladies in the surrounding villages.

"What?"

"She said you were worse than all the royalty in

Eoforwic, like a princess waiting for the perfect prince to sweep you off your feet."

Ridley snorted as he bent to retrieve the chopped wood. The jagged grain of it bit into his forearms and stomach but Ridley welcomed the sensation. Arms full, he carried it to the woodhouse beside Branton's hut and piled it inside. The scent of oak and birch calmed his raw nerves as he stacked the pieces.

Princess. The dig wasn't lost on him. Yet his own use of it was to taunt Yrsa. The question of why a woman of worth was thrown in with a bunch of raiders was something that still bothered him. Ridley hadn't known women to fight or raid. It wasn't that he thought it impossible; he'd known many strong willed women and respected them. Yet a female Dane coming all this way just to raid Hyrstow didn't seem likely. Did her affection for her betrothed run so deep that she wouldn't allow him to raid alone? An ugly feeling sat on Ridley's chest at the prospect.

When he emerged from the woodshed, his friend was staring at him with narrowed eyes.

"What now?" he griped. Bran was worse than a woman. The man had it so good with his own family that he couldn't imagine anyone suffering a life alone.

"We weren't prepared, Rid. You can feel guilty about that all you want. Believe me, I do. I know that raids are part of life, but seeing my children scrambling about the hut, looking for weapons to defend their mother is something I swore to myself I'd never let happen."

Bran let the words trail off, captured by the wind that

stole through the meadow, reminding the men of the time. Ridley swallowed the lump that had formed in his throat. The early night wound around them, peaceful with the echoes of crickets. He clasped Bran's shoulder in a rough embrace. The raid had scared them all.

"I'm sorry, friend. It had never been my intention to leave your family, or any for that matter, in the jaws of such a terrible foe."

Branton nodded, blinking away unshed tears. He patted Ridley's hand on his shoulder and sniffed.

"Ah, look at me, in my old age, just bein' a sop." Branton laughed at himself.

Ridley bent to retrieve his tunic from the ground and shrugged it on. Next, he settled his belt around his waist.

"My point is, we're all torn up. But there isn't any point in wrestling with it longer than you need to. We'll plan better for next time."

The words made Ridley's hackles rise. There wouldn't be a next time. He should have had sentries posted at the outskirts of town. He should have up-kept the younger men's combat training. He should have had a better evacuation procedure for the women.

"Tell Freda I'll be by later this week," he said.

Branton nodded.

With that, Ridley took his leave. The restless unease of returning to his hut grew in him like a beast with every step forward. Maybe his friends had a point—he needed a pliant body to lose himself in. He hadn't been with a woman since being stationed in Hyrstow. As chieftain and fresh meat for the single women, too much expectation was placed on his commitment to wed. Of the women he'd known as a boy, most were married. A new crop of young women had sprung up in his years away, but Ridley felt nothing other than a paternal affection for them as chief. His own hand did the trick to slake his desire. That was until the she-demon Yrsa appeared. Ridley's desire for the flesh of a woman had grown the moment he'd set eyes on the wilding. And with it his own self-loathing.

The village had quieted during the dinner hour. Many fires burned outside with iron pots set atop to boil. Older children stirred the contents while the younger ones added logs. Woodsmoke and sun, broth and bread scented the air. His hut came into view, stoic and dark, nestled before the forest a little way behind. Nod was slinking around the door when he arrived. The dog sniffed the wall, as if scenting something in the hut, then loped around to the woodpile and shoved his nose into the dirt where the wall met the ground. His ears perked up as soon as he saw Ridley.

"Hey, Nod," Ridley murmured. On a frosty morning he'd found him, a black three-legged thing with huge, pointed ears, huddled against the shelter of his woodpile. Ridley wasn't sure if the dog's back leg had been hacked off at some point or if he had been born that way. Despite the absence of a leg, Nod didn't seem to have any problem walking. Ridley had taken pity on the scrawny thing, and tossed it some scraps. For months now, he'd been feeding the lanky animal whenever it came around.

Nod stood taller as Ridley approached, then dipped

his head low. Ridley put his hand out, palm up and waited for the dog to sniff him. Nod took a searching whiff of his palm, pressing his wet nose to Ridley's skin.

"How've you been?" Ridley asked, softening his voice to the pitch he used only with Nod. The dog thrust his head into Ridley's hand and yawned. Ridley couldn't help but grin as he gave Nod's coarse fur a good scrub.

"Hungry, boy?"

Nod leapt to the side, tongue lolling out of his mouth in a wide, doggy grin.

Because of Nod's arrival, Ridley forgot to brace himself as he entered the hut. In the dim light, he could make out blankets and hides swamping the floor, the bed barren. One woolen blanket had been wound around the spike in the ground, as if used for leverage to yank the heavy iron. The stool was overturned, deep grooves etched into one of the legs. His pot, two bowls, the chest that housed his clothing were all upended. In the center of it all was Yrsa, sitting with her legs tucked under her, buttery hair cast around her shoulders like a net, dark blue eyes locked on him as he entered.

Ridley sighed. She was worse than a puppy.

"Saxon, take me to wash," the words flew out of her mouth before he could step into the chaos. Her lips were pursed in the scowl that made Ridley want to kiss her bottom lip to see if she tasted as sour.

Instead of heeding her demand, Ridley moved about the perimeter of the room to the table. It and the cupboard where he kept the kitchen supplies were the only items that did not look like they'd been used in an escape attempt. He picked up a cup, filled it with water from the jug and took a long pull. The liquid was warm but welcome.

"Saxon. I need to relieve myself. Take me outside."

Ridley briefly considered a time when he lived alone. Had it only been four days ago?

"Saxon, take me..."

Ridley dipped his head to cover the rusty chuckle that escaped.

"Not on your life, princess. Not after all of this."

He placed his mug on the table, tucking his chin to his chest. Exhaustion beat him over the head. All he wanted was a good meal and a cup of ale and sleep. His talk with Bran left him feeling worn to the bone. Yet Yrsa's scowl was as deep as a fissure in a mountain. There was no doubt that she would murder him if given the opportunity. Her upper lip drifted toward a sneer as she straightened to spit her fury at him, then sunk downward in a grimace of pain. Alarm prickled the back of Ridley's neck as he picked up the metallic scent of blood.

"What happened?"

"Nothing," she said, drawing her knees inward. Her features slid from angry to impassive. Ridley didn't know which was worse. At least when she was spewing hate at him, he knew where she stood. Her good hand, the one tied to the rope, was half clasped against her stomach.

"Tell me," he commanded. Annoyance snaked through him. When he'd saved her, he thought that, maybe, she'd be thankful. Gracious even. Or fearful. Most women would have cowered under the glare of a beast such as he. But no. This one snapped her gaze to the empty fire rocks before her, intent on ignoring him.

Ridley felt the woven threads of his patience fray. He'd buried a good man today because of her raid, was behind with the crops, and had to find the missing women. She was the reason he couldn't even return home to get a goddamn moment of peace. And the set of her chin, slightly tilted up, snapped something in him.

Ridley loomed, using his height to scare her. A shadow of fear dashed across her pretty face. "For the love of God, woman, tell me what you've done!"

CHAPTER
NINE

Rather than obey, Yrsa tucked away the fear that had played across her face and curled her lip in a snarl. With a growl, Ridley sat on his haunches and wrenched her wrist up to discover what she hid.

Thick welts marred the smooth flesh on the inside of her palm. The edges were ragged, smeared with crimson. Rage that she would be so stubborn as to harm herself burned through him. It didn't take a moment for him to piece together what had happened. Desperate to escape, attempts to pull the spike from the ground single-handed hadn't worked. The cuts weren't deep but there were many. As if she didn't give up for a long while. Surprisingly, his anger was flocked by begrudging respect for her spirit.

Yrsa expelled a breath through her nose as he manipulated her hand in the dusky light.

"Why do this?" he demanded, easing his tone. He

released the silky skin of her wrist despite the urge to swipe his thumb over it. "You won't be able to pull the thing from the ground."

"I had to try," she shot back. Her navy eyes glistened.

Of course, she did. All she did was 'try'. Try to challenge him in battle. Try to tempt him at the river with pillowed lips and her wild, juniper scent. Try to escape him and maim herself in the process. Guilt roiled in his belly.

Ridley rose to retrieve the jug of water from the table, picking his way through debris, stepping over the rope that laid on the floor like a snake. Methodically, he retrieved the iron pot that had been tossed beneath a chair, poured water and set it on the hook that stood above the fire stones, one of the few intact items in the room. Yrsa watched in silence as he disappeared outside to retrieve wood, ignoring Nod as he did so, returning to kindle a flame. Once the fire licked at the wood, Ridley looked for a scrap of cloth from his upturned chest that could serve as a bandage. An old tunic did the trick and, with the knife at his belt, he rendered the material into strips and placed them in the water to boil.

"Where do you go all day?"

Ridley kept his eyes on the pot of water. Everyone had so many questions as of late, and he was tired of always having to think of an answer.

"To work."

"You tie me up and leave me all day long. What am I to do?" she demanded. Contempt layered her words.

"Not bloody well wrench your hand off trying to get

away," he muttered. Ridley cast a glance in her direction then regretted it. Her pale skin glowed in the flickering firelight. Desire snaked through him. Even with her face twisted into a scowl, hate rolling from her, it was there. He knew he shouldn't feel her pull. She was a Dane, a Viking raider, and his captive.

It didn't matter how his body called to hers. He'd never allow himself a taste of her. Yrsa would likely bite his tongue off anyway.

"Let me wash my hands by the river."

Ridley raised an eyebrow at her. "No."

"Heimskur," she spat. Ridley didn't know the word but could deduce an insult when he heard it.

"The river won't help. The water needs to be hot."

She looked at him as if he'd grown a second head. It rankled. He was accustomed to others trusting him. Even in disagreement, respect was given. Ridley pinched the bridge of his nose. An ache had bloomed in the front of his head and threatened to grow.

"The water needs to be clean to help. That's what happens when you make it hot as soup. It's something I learned the hard way."

"Why should I believe you?" Her blue eyes narrowed at him as if he were a speck of dust to be brushed away.

"Because I've had injuries a plenty and the times boiled water was used, the better I've fared. You'll see. It's what I did to your shoulder."

Yrsa shook her head. Suspicion tugged at her brow. "You're trying to hurt me. To torture me for being a Dane."

Ridley gave her a flat look as he poked the flames. "Then why save you in the first place?"

"Because you want to make an example of me! Perhaps you thought me an easy target..."

"No part of you being here has been easy!" Ridley bellowed.

Yrsa's flinched back. He didn't care. Red hot rage snaked along his muscles, charging him with the urge to slip his knife along her throat to end both their suffering. "You demand and you glare, and you make a mess of my home! You don't listen and you lie. All this after I helped you. You've made my life a living nightmare!"

A high-pitched whine from outside caught their attention. Ridley let loose a sigh that brought his shoulders down from around his ears. He'd forgotten about Nod. Abruptly, he retrieved a couple of strips of dried meat from the cupboard—and left the hut without a word.

Nod waited in the shadow of the doorway. He whined when he saw Ridley, prancing to the right then left, tail wagging in anticipation of the meat in Ridley's hand. His heart softened toward the animal. "Sorry I'm late, boy."

He laid the strips of meat on the ground in front of Nod. The beast set upon the food as if he hadn't eaten in days. Ridley knew that likely wasn't the case since spring was rife with rodents and small animals for Nod to catch.

The darkening sky overhead called Ridley back to himself. The man that shouted and raged at Yrsa seemed an imposter. Ridley had built his life upon the foundation of doing the right thing with a steady hand. Now, he was spitting mad at a woman that *he* captured. His emotions hadn't been in such upheaval since he'd told Lachlan he wanted to retire his command and return home months ago. Ridley let out a long sigh and scratched behind Nod's ear before heading back inside.

Yrsa was still on the floor beside the fire, cradling her hand, staring at the flames that danced beneath the pot. Ridley was surprised she didn't attack him with the hot water or a fire stone. He ignored her and crouched at the other side of the fire. The water was just about to crest to a boil.

"You have a dog?"

Ridley pressed his lips together.

"Saxon." Her voice was pointed.

It centered him, brought his thoughts back to the task ahead. Her hand needed healing. The water frothed in the pot, cloth tumbling through the bubbles. Ridley dipped a spoon into the water to draw out a strip of the material. He let it hang in the air to cool for a moment, then crossed to stand in front of Yrsa.

"Hold out your hand."

Rather than listen, Yrsa wrapped her right hand around her left, holding it protectively to her stomach. The gesture caused Ridley's chest to tighten with unease. She was at his mercy and knew it. And he'd been thinking that he'd slit her throat to solve the inconvenience of her. What kind of monster did that make him?

One he recognized all too well. A man intent on extracting vengeance against whoever rose up against his earl. One who could barely recognize that slaying innocents was wrong if it meant sending a message to his enemies. Ridley wasn't that man anymore. He'd chosen to pull the knife from Yrsa. The choice set into motion events that he would now have to navigate.

Ridley softened his command as he knelt in front of her. "I will not harm you."

Steam rose in wisps from the strip of wool dangling in the air between them. Eyes narrowed in suspicion, Yrsa huffed a breath. Then, without a word, she held her hand out.

Gingerly, he cradled her palm in his own. Though slender, her hand was strong and calloused and warm within his.

Yrsa let out a low hiss as the hot wool kissed the angry welts. Ridley allowed the material to sit against her skin for a moment as he placed the spoon in his lap and leaned forward to take her hand in both of his. With light fingers he swiped the cloth across her palm, clearing the dirt that had settled into her flesh. She made no complaint as he cleaned, though he felt her eyes on his face. He was about to ask where the Danish camp was, where the female captives would be. But her previous refusal made him think she either hated him so deeply she wouldn't tell or that she simply didn't know. He'd have to break down her barriers to find out. How he'd be forced to do it made the pulse throb in his neck.

Her eyes felt like a brand on his skin. Briefly, he wondered what she truly thought of him, a grin cracking his lips with the knowledge that he wouldn't have to wonder long—from what he knew of Yrsa, she had a problem holding her tongue.

"What?" she demanded. Her eyes were narrowed, full lips downturned as always. An image of them wet and parted and wanting stole through his memory.

Ridley simply shook his head, his grin deepening with her annoyance.

"Why are you smiling?" Yrsa asked again, though this time she tried to draw her hand away from his.

Ridley held fast, causing her to yank harder, then he let go. She nearly toppled backward. Her mouth gaped open, eyes wide. Ridley gave her a wolfish grin.

"I only thought that I have no need to wonder what you are thinking since you'll surely tell me."

Yrsa glowered at him while Ridley's smile widened. It was fun to pester the woman.

"You wonder what I think of?" she snapped, righting herself with as much dignity as she could muster with her arm in a sling and an injured hand.

Ridley ignored her. He plucked the wool from her hand, grabbed the spoon, then stood. He felt Yrsa's eyes on him as he tossed the wool onto the table and dipped the spoon into the bubbling water to clean it. It took him a moment to wrangle another wool strip onto the spoon, and the entire time, Yrsa remained mute, though the line of her mouth moved over unsaid words.

"Here." Ridley knelt beside her, closer than before, taking her hand before she could retract it. Her fresh, midnight scent caught him by the throat. He didn't know if he'd ever become accustomed to it. It was like the thrash of the ocean against cliffs, hounding and relentless.

Ridley swallowed hard against the sudden dryness in his mouth. Yrsa kept silent as he wound the strip around her palm and tucked the tail end into itself to secure it. His heart beat too fast at the feel of her skin against his. The reaction was unbecoming of a chieftain, a warrior, as if he'd never touched a woman before. And this one wasn't available or susceptible to his touch.

A light knock on the door caused him to start.

"Ridley?" Emma's muffled voice punctured the skins he'd hung above the door to prevent sound from carrying.

Ridley's head snapped up. The thought of sweet, kind Emma finding the wildling in his hut made his guts turn to water.

The effect on Yrsa was equally surprising. Rather than scream down the place, she scrambled to the right side of the bed and tucked herself into a ball so as to not be seen by whoever entered.

"Stay quiet," Ridley commanded in a hushed tone, though he needn't have.

Yrsa's hands were tucked into her chest, knees to her chin. Her eyes darted from the door to him, fury and fear swirling in their depths. The look sobered him more than the threat of Emma.

Outside, Emma stood beneath the cover of a heavy cloak, a bundle of cloth in her hands. Her hair was swept into a long ponytail, yet some strands had escaped the sides, curling around her heart-shaped face. She eyed

Nod warily as the beast lounged by the woodpile, showing his teeth.

"Nod," Ridley scolded as he came out and saw the look on Emma's face. The dog stood, shook out his coat and slinked away into the forest.

Immediately, Emma's mouth lit with a smile. "I didn't realize he still came around."

"He hasn't for a while. Caught me by surprise today. Though I am glad he's alright. Looks healthy," Ridley said. He ran a hand through his hair to disband the tingle of worry that pricked at his scalp. If Yrsa wasn't tied up in his hut, the visit would have been welcome.

"To what do I owe the pleasure of your visit, Mrs. Baker?"

Emma's smile faltered around the corners at her married name. Generally, Ridley was friendly enough with the people in the village to call them by their given names. However, Emma appearing at his home with the soft look of shyness in her eyes had Ridley's instinct jumping to formality.

"I wanted to thank you for all of your hard work as of late," she said, taking a small step forward.

Ridley had to tilt his head downward to hold her gaze, slight as she was. "You don't have to. It is my duty." He suddenly became aware of the light scent of lavender that wafted from her.

She grinned prettily, showing neat, white teeth. "I wanted to. You've been so busy helping others this week. This is a small token of thanks." She held out the bundle in her hands, the scent of honeyed buns wafting from the cloth. Emma was a superb cook. She'd prepared many hearty dishes at village gatherings, and he always had a coin to spare for her baked goods at the weekly market.

Ridley accepted it, his fingers brushing hers as he did so. There was no jolt of awareness, no rush of concern for propriety. "You are too kind. Thank you," he said. As much as he appreciated her gesture, the sooner Emma was gone, the better.

Emma gave a derisive snort. "It's not simply kindness. You don't have a wife or sister or mother clucking after you. You live all the way out here on the edge of everything..." Her eyes touched on the looming forest behind his hut then softened as they came back to his face.

"Aw, well. I get on just as well as any man. Thank you for thinking of me."

A breeze tickled Ridley's cheek as silence stretched between them. He had no idea if Emma wanted an invitation to share the buns or not. He shifted from foot to foot, trying to work out something to discuss other than her rebuild. A tightness thickened his throat. Time was passing, and Emma was standing there with her hands threaded together, big eyes staring up at him, waiting for *something*.

"Shall I...walk you home?" he guessed.

Emma's smile brightened. "I would like that," she replied.

Ridley nodded. He held up one finger to indicate she wait for a moment, then he dipped through the door to place the buns inside.

Yrsa stood next to the bed, head pushed up against the wall, listening. Her arm was extended as far as it would go against the rope, her legs tucked under her. When he entered, she drew away to stand at her full height. Ridley raised his finger to his lips in a gesture to remain silent. Eyes narrowed, lips curled into a sneer, Yrsa gave him what appeared to be a Danish vulgar gesture without saying a word. The urge to grin at her tugged at his lips, but Ridley didn't have time to waste. He strode around the fire, placed the buns on the table, and left, hoping Yrsa didn't burn the place down in his absence.

As he and Emma departed along the path, Ridley drew a steadying breath. Yrsa had been right there. If Emma had peered into the hut at the right angle...

Yrsa would be found out. She was too unpredictable. She would make too much noise. During the walk, beneath the cover of conversation about Emma's rebuild, Ridley's mind chewed the disastrous possibilities. What should have been a nice time with a neighbor was soured with worry over Yrsa. She was his curse. His source of strife in a beautiful, insolent package.

He had to find where the Danish camp was, where the Tanner sisters were taken, then he would rid himself of Yrsa. One way or another.

CHAPTER
TEN

Ridley's gentle snore caught Yrsa's ear. Alarm flooded her, shaking her awake. She'd been in a deep, dreamless sleep. One that held her under, making Yrsa second-guess if what had woken her was Ridley or a dream of him. Other than her body, which had traitorously stretched out in peaceful luxury, the bed was empty. Silent, she leaned to peer over the side. Ridley was stretched out on the straw floor, a thick blanket drawn over his hips, head resting on his palm. Sleep had smoothed away the ever-present crease between his dark eyebrows. Soft, steady breaths flowed through parted lips, his bare chest rising and falling in a hypnotic rhythm that Yrsa could almost feel. Her blood pulsed hard in her throat. To her knowledge, it was the first time he'd slept in the hut with her. She found it absurd that such a miser of a man could be rendered so peaceful, boyish even, in sleep.

Something inside tugged at her. A sense of curiosity,

perhaps, though she didn't dare look too hard at the feeling. She'd seen plenty of men with fine, battle honed bodies spar in Inivik. She'd bedded down on a ship between ranks of warriors wrapped in their cloaks. Shirtless men did not impress her. But Ridley...he was a different animal than any of the men she'd known. His broad chest, padded with hard muscle, tapered into a stomach that boasted hard swells and valleys. It was as if he'd been carved by the Gods themselves, each placing a bit of brawn or a slice of definition. Old scars covered him like rivers on a map. Yrsa wondered how the chieftain of a nothing village near the Northumbrian coast came to have all those nicks. Yrsa clenched her thighs as she wished for a blade to slide across his throat.

Without warning, Ridley's eyes snapped open.

Yrsa froze, not wanting to be caught staring but knowing it was too late to withdraw. Ridley did not move. He simply stared into her as if he knew he'd wake to find her looking at him. A flush threatened her cheeks. She clenched her teeth at the challenge in his gaze. He'd been the one to lay beside the bed. It wasn't her fault she'd been caught staring.

From one breath to another, the moment shifted from challenge to something Yrsa couldn't name. It pricked, warming her insides, causing her to shiver. Ridley's icy stare melted as it trailed down, landing on her mouth. Of its own accord, Yrsa's tongue darted out to lick her top lip. Ridley's gaze flared. Something akin to *want*, raw and insistent, swam in its depths. Yrsa's breath caught, anticipation curling inside of her as she waited to see what he would do. What she suddenly *wished* him to do.

In a blink, he shifted, breaking the spell. Without a word, he rose from the floor, stretching his hands to the sky, muscled back contracting as he did so. As if she wasn't there, he released a hearty yawn and scratched his chest, fingers running absently over the dusting of dark hair. Then he strode to the table, withdrew two buns from beneath the cloth cover, held one out to her and stuffed the other into his mouth.

Glaring, Yrsa snatched the proffered bun from his fingers. Their sweet, yeasty scent had wafted from the table since Ridley had placed them there the previous night.

Ridley had not returned late after being out with the other woman, though he hadn't been in a mood to put up with Yrsa's demands. The tenderness he'd displayed while he cleaned Yrsa's hand had been used up. When he returned, he'd taken her to the tree line to relieve herself, then brought her straight back. He'd tidied the hut she'd so effectively destroyed then made a bed for himself on the floor. Yrsa had been ignored then forgotten.

Now, he plucked the water jug from the table and took a long pull. A dribble leaked out the corner of his lips, tangled in his short beard, and traced down the strong line of his throat. Was his beard soft or coarse? Did the woman from last night find the look of it pleasing?

Wiping his mouth with the back of his hand, he

issued a satisfied grunt then held the jug out to her. Despite her thirst, Yrsa scowled in refusal.

"Have a sip, princess. You must be thirsty." Ridley's gravelly voice made Yrsa's insides knot. Shirtless, with his trousers slung low along the V of his hips, the musky scent of sleep clinging to him, Yrsa found it difficult to focus on his orders. His body was hard and strong, and it caused a flutter in the lowest part of her. The only thing she could draw on to protect herself was hate. She crossed her arms, forcing her gaze to the door.

"Fine. Suit yourself." Ridley placed the jug on the stool by the bed then gave her his back. He donned his tunic, the material molding itself to his chest and shoulders. Next came boots. Her dagger was taken up from the table and slung into his leather belt.

Ire shot through her. Ridley carried her father's blade as if it were a gift from the man himself. It brought to mind that he was as likely to be Arkyn's killer as anyone else in Hyrstow.

With all her time in captivity, she'd decided that her only chance of escape was if she softened Ridley to her. She needed to return to the river. To distract him and flee through the forest. Which meant she had to endear Ridley to her enough for him to heed her request. Despite the sliver of desire she thought she saw that morning, Yrsa didn't delude herself into thinking she stood a chance at seduction. As her mother had repeatedly pointed out over the course of her life, Yrsa was no prize. She'd been too busy climbing hills, too chummy with the boys, too forceful with her opinion. She was skinny and muscular and didn't sit still. And Ridley didn't seem the type to fall simpering at her feet anyway. If he had any interest in bedding her, he would have forced the issue already. No, Ridley seemed to have the singular focus of Hyrstow. And, perhaps, the woman with the soft voice. Still, Yrsa couldn't stare at the bare wooden walls any longer.

"I need something to do when you are gone," Yrsa blurted.

Ridley moved as if she hadn't spoken. He unwrapped the cloth package on the table, withdrew another bun and took a giant bite. As he chewed, he came to stand before the bed, brow arched in question.

Yrsa's words tripped over themselves to get out. "You leave me here until dusk. I am tied like a common animal. I am bored."

"Bored?" He swept the back of his neck with his hand, as if he'd never been bored in his life and didn't know what to do with the information.

Yrsa seized her chance to convince him of her value. "I could...prepare food for you whilst you are gone. Chop meat or peel vegetables."

Ridley's mouth twitched. "And leave you with a weapon for you to saw through your binding with?"

"What about grinding grain?"

"And give you a pestle to club me with when I return? What do you take me for, Yrsa?"

A smirk wound its way along Yrsa's lips. He rarely called her that. Only princess and the occasional grunt indicating she was a woman. It was a surprise in a room that had little to reveal. Absently, she toyed with the bun in front of her as she tried to think of other tasks.

"Don't waste that roll. It's delicious. And made by one with more kindness than you." Ridley stuffed the rest of his own roll into his mouth, his scruffy jaw working as he chewed.

Yrsa scoffed. The woman he referred to had a light, straightforward voice that held her words in a smile. Yrsa wondered what she looked like. Was she a plump, fresh young thing? Or was she petite and thin, soft as a petal? The thought of either made something in Yrsa's middle fold into knots. It was difficult to imagine the rough warrior within the delicate embrace of such a woman. "Kindness has naught to do with it. If she's sweet, it's because she wants something."

"Not true. She's just not a heathen like you."

"A heathen like me?" Yrsa placed her hand to her chest in mock offense. "That woman wants something. Why else would she bring you food? Does she need protection? No, she seems to be getting along fine. Maybe she wants to bed you. She—"

Ridley moved so quickly, Yrsa couldn't stop him as he plucked the bun from her hand, pried off a chunk and shoved it past her lips. Golden, honeyed bread melted against her tongue, mixed with the warm hardness of him. Her shock prevented her from biting Ridley's finger, and by the time she thought to do so, he'd withdrawn.

"Why," she demanded around a mouthful of the sweetest food she'd tasted in months, "would you do that?"

Ridley shrugged, shoving his palms down his thighs as he straightened. The sliver of a grin parted his lips. "You didn't know what you spoke of. I thought I would save you the indignity of your assumptions by distracting you with food."

Yrsa snorted. Ridley's stupid mouth and cocky words caused a flipping sensation in her middle. It made her want to shock *him* the way he'd done to her. If she could, she would wrap her hands around his neck and squeeze...

Unbidden, an image of her arms around his neck, fingers running through his hair came to mind. It rankled. The man held her against her will. Worse, he was a Saxon. Yet she'd never had such thoughts about Aric. Not once did she have cause to blush when in the company of her betrothed.

Yrsa was so defunct that she lusted after the man that kept her prisoner.

"Get away from me," she sneered, steeling herself against the heat in her cheeks. Ridley straightened, the slight grin that played at his lips disappearing.

"My friend, Grahame, has sheep. I'll see what wool I can find. You can clean in or spin it or whatever he needs. That should satisfy your boredom."

Yrsa gaped at him. "I will do no such thing."

"Let me guess, you had servants."

Yrsa forked her hand into her hair to keep from strangling him. "To the dismay of my mother, I wasn't skilled in womanly duties. My father indulged me by allowing me to play with the boys. To train with them, too."

"Did they train you in kidnapping and torture? Because I am sure that is what is happening to the Tanner sisters."

His words fell like arrows, each one piercing. Yrsa edged to the side of the bed, straightening her back against the unwelcome imaginings of what her clan was capable of. They were a good group of men, yes, but the women were spoils of a raid. If they were taken...Yrsa could only hope that the women had been able to flee or had been killed swiftly. Much like she planned for herself.

"I know nothing of their whereabouts."

Ridley's lip curled with contempt. "Liar." He stalked forward, big hands fisting at his sides as if to stop himself from choking the life from her. "Tell me where they are. I want to return them to their family. They are innocents."

Hatred burned in her chest. For Ridley, for her clansmen, that she wished to tell him knowing that she could not. Ridley seemed to sense her warring thoughts. His lips softened at the corners, hands uncoiling as his shoulders fell. She nearly thought he would fall to his knees before her.

"I do not want more bloodshed. I want the females returned."

Yrsa choked on her own self-loathing at the entreaty. She could not give away the location of her men. If they were still at camp, or if they ever decided to return one day, the river's finger that ran half day's ride south was the perfect place to shore their mighty ships.

Yrsa licked her dry lips. She had no stake in the Saxon women. She told herself they were not her worry. "Maybe they went willingly. Danish males are far more beautiful than you Saxons."

"You cannot believe that to be true. Women never go willingly in raids."

"You speak as if you know that well."

Ridley's jaw clenched so hard Yrsa thought he would crack teeth. His gaze darkened. She'd touched on something. A soft spot in his past. And, like a good warrior, she struck again, swift and true.

"Your body speaks of battle. The way you fight. It makes me think that you are no stranger to raiding villages. Taking women against their will."

He bared down on her before she could bring up a fist to ward him off. Large hands clenched around her upper arms like bands of iron. Rage, pure and cold, twisted his mouth into something ugly. Yrsa forced herself to pin her glare to his when she wanted nothing more than to cower.

"You know not of what you speak." Icy fury coated each word.

"Don't I, Saxon?" Yrsa said, then allowed herself to cave into her fear, to twist her face to the side, eyes clenched shut in preparation to take the hit he would surely knock her down with.

Then his hands were gone, his tall frame backing to the table. A strange mix of regret and horror slipped across his features before he shrugged on his usual impassive glare.

"I will bring back something to occupy you," he said as he retrieved the jug of water. He poured a cupful and placed it on the stool beside the bed. As he straightened, his eyes landed on the rope staked in the floor and said, "Little good your father's training did you."

Yrsa growled low in her throat. In half a heartbeat she was on her feet, left hand throwing a punch to his jaw. Ridley dodged the swing but didn't back up enough. Yrsa's foot made solid contact with his thigh, wringing a grunt of surprised pain from him.

Swearing an oath, he backed away. A crooked smile wound the corner of his mouth upward, as if pleased for the distraction. Well, she'd give him a distraction. She reached for the jug and threw it. The new scars on her hand screamed in protest as the jug struck the door, but her target had already darted from the room.

CHAPTER
ELEVEN

"What do ye need all this for? Are your nights so boring that you want to spend your time like an old woman, is that it?" Grahame cut Ridley a broad smile as he passed him a bundle of cleaned fleece.

Ridley took the burden in both arms, water dampening the front of his tunic before he dumped it into the large basket he'd brought with him. Ridley returned the grin, widening it for the sake of Grahame's mother, who stood in the doorway of her house. She waved, squinting against the sun at the men who stood outside her wooden gate. Fiona had been all too happy to accommodate Ridley's polite inquiry to assist with combing her harvest of fleece. She'd allowed him to borrow a set of combs, laid carefully at the bottom of the basket.

"I'm going to take it over to Merthe, if Emma will allow it. She's been idle as of late."

"Ah, getting on well with the new missus, are you?"

Grahame waggled blonde brows as he gave Ridley a friendly elbow to the stomach. Ridley had to flex his muscles to soften the blow, Grahame now being much stronger than when they were young.

Ridley cut Grahame a roguish grin that was a lie. He knew gathering supplies under the guise of giving them to Emma's daughter was a risk. He needed to give a bit of the fleece to Merthe and and keep some for Yrsa. Though presumptuous, he hoped Emma would think him kind for occupying her daughter. Let his friends talk. If it occupied Yrsa, Ridley would do almost anything.

Finding her staring at him over the side of the bed that morning had caused his blood to stir. Her curious, dark blue eyes had raked over his torso. He didn't know if she'd noticed the way she'd sucked in a breath, licked her lip, as if he was a sweet treat to devour. That blood that had been stirred? It shot straight to his cock. He'd had to feign indifference, stretched in the other direction and adjusted himself so that the evidence of his arousal wasn't at her eye level when he rose.

"Get off it. You and Bran are as bad as a crone with your gossip."

Grahame just tossed his golden head back and laughed, teeth bright in the sun. He clapped Ridley on the back then bent and hefted the basket.

"You're a poor sport Rid. Been gone so long you don't realize all we have to do in Hyrstow is gossip. I should know, it's usually about me."

They walked along the path that curled down the hill to the fields. Sheep dotted the grass, naked-looking after having been sheared. In the distance, Grahame's father held up a hand in greeting from where he clipped wool from a sheep, his apprentice at his side. Surprise at the vast amount of animals on the land coloured Ridley's features.

"I can't believe how it's grown," he said as they walked.

Grahame shrugged big shoulders, as if amassing such wealth wasn't a result of hard work. "God's been good these last few summers. Lots of lambs. Lots of interest in wool in the markets. The Earl of Deircia himself sent his steward last spring with a request to increase the amount we harvest. With it a handsome sum to buy more animals. Though I almost think that someone with the earl's ear may have turned him to the idea." Grahame eyed Ridley suspiciously.

Ridley ran a hand through his hair. "When the Lachlan had need for more wool, I only told him where to find the best."

"Well, my parents certainly appreciated it. We've got to go to Eoforwic by the end of the summer to sell off the extra once we meet the earl's due. There'll be plenty."

A boy appeared at the top of a rolling hill. He ran toward them, his chest heaving as if he'd covered a long distance. Alarm raced through Ridley, his legs readying to leave the fleece and run to the village if need be.

"Wonder what's about," Grahame muttered, his shoulders tensing.

"Sir! Sir Ridley," the boy panted as he came up. It was one of the church's acolytes, John. He gripped a piece of parchment which he passed over to Ridley as he caught his breath. "This came for you. His Holiness said you are to read it right away. I looked for you, but couldn't find you until now. My apologies for being tardy."

Rather than concern about the contents of the missive, Ridley's attention sharpened on where the boy might have looked for him. "And where did you search? My duties take me all over the village."

John startled at his sharp tone. Grahame put down the basket, brows narrowed toward Ridley. Ridley ignored it, his entire focus on the young man's pimpled face. The shadow of a cloud passing overhead darkened the day.

"I..uh...I asked around. You've been helping with rebuilding and Joseph didn't know so I went to your hut..."

"You did?" Ridley cut in. He plucked the outheld parchment from John's hand.

"Y-yes. But I didn't hear anything from inside so I thought you'd be out ridin' with the guard but then I saw Freda, and she told me she'd seen you trekking up this way."

Ridley could feel Grahame's stare burrow into the side of his face. He ignored it as he drew a breath to even out his heartbeat. The prospect of a young man stumbling in on Yrsa had not occurred to him. He wasn't sure what she would do to the youth to gain freedom.

"Thank you, John."

The boy nodded then turned back in the direction of the village. Ridley noted the lack of tie as he opened the parchment. He buried the annoyance that rose from Oswald's invasiveness. Tension ratcheted through his neck as he read the short note from Lachlan. The news brought him back to a place he'd worked hard to forget.

"Well?" Grahame asked. He couldn't read, nor could most in the village. Luck had shone down on Ridley the day that Lachlan took him as a ward and squire. His literacy was a kindness, though not one without merit. The earl had been shrewd to ensure that those who would do his bidding could also read his correspondence.

"Before I came here, I commanded an outfit that reclaimed the land to the northwest of Hyrstow's territory. Past the woods that border your father's fields."

"You took Bernira land? The Earl of Deircia allowed it?" Shock drained the color from Grahame's tanned face.

"The Lachlan ordered it. We claimed farmland on the other side of the forest, just short of the village of Guston. It was bloody work. The people there did not want Lachlan's rule."

Grahame swore. He ran a hand through his curly hair, pacing one way then back to Ridley. "Bloody work? Jesus, Rid. Where? Whose farms?"

Ridley ran a hand over his mouth to halt the confession that threatened to spill forth. Grahame didn't seem to notice. He paced away, then back, one hand on his hip, the other wrapped around the back of his neck. He drew a harsh breath through his teeth, face tipped to the sky. "Why didn't you tell me sooner?"

"I was ordered not to."

"You were ordered? In the name of God, Rid! My parents...we've been living with a target on our backs since, and we didn't even know it. We're on the other side of that forest and Eadric is a filthy bastard. He'll have no qualms over cutting us down!"

Ridley raised his hands in a gesture of calm. "It hasn't happened. The land was stolen by Eadric years ago. Taken when Hyrstow was raided when we were young. Before I went to Lachlan's keep."

Grahame swung around from his pacing, a tightness bracketing his mouth and eyes that rarely made an appearance. There was only one raid to which Ridley referred. The one that had changed Ridley's life forever. He pressed on, willing the memory of his mother's screams away.

"The Earl of Bernira did wrong. It has always been Deircia land, and it is again. That is what the letter says. Lachlan has bestowed the land to us and we are to farm it this summer. It comes a little late in the season but we must make due."

Grahame scoffed. The bitter sound did not suit him. "Is this to be common knowledge? Can I tell my parents?"

Ridley nodded. The news would spread fast. He bent to pick up the basket that Grahame had abandoned. "Yes. They should be aware."

Grahame gave him a flat look. "Can I have some men to guard our border?"

"There isn't a threat, Grahame. Believe me, we took care of those who would have come after you."

"Aye, but people's memories are long, and revenge holds longer. You know that better than any of us. I'll stand watch every night on the border if you won't allow a guard."

Ridley felt his shoulders slump a little under the weight of his friend's distrust. "I will appoint Travers and Ewan and anyone else who can be spared. Those boys are spoiling for a fight after the raid."

Ridley didn't say what else he thought: that the men would be bored on the edge of Hyrstow's lands since there hadn't been a disturbance from Guston territory since his men had laid waste to it. He wasn't ignorant enough to think the threat had passed for good, but the contestation of lands was in the hands of the earls that battled over it. All Ridley could do was believe the man that had given him purpose and a home would do what was best.

"I'll take my leave." Ridley said as he turned down the path back to Hyrstow proper. Grahame barely looked at him as Ridley turned away. "Grahame. I..."

"Stop, Rid. Whatever you are about to say, don't. I know you were only doing what the Earl of Deircia ordered." Grahame forced a grin that didn't meet his eyes. "All is well, eh?"

Ridley nodded. Shame crept up the back of his neck as he walked back to home with the fleece. He should have told Grahame when he'd moved back to Hyrstow in the winter. But Lachlan had ordered him to speak no word of it, and Ridley obeyed his command.

He hadn't been in the right mind to discuss the

matter, either. What had happened near Guston had spurred him to return home. He knew he was a pawn in the greater workings between the lords of the land. Returning to Hyrstow had been his only play to gain any semblance of a good, simple life.

Ridley looked down at the basket, his mouth downturned. His mind cast him back to the way Yrsa's blue eyes had widened when she'd beheld his shirtless body. Like daylight shining on the shallows of the sea. A simple life? How wrong he'd been.

YRSA HAD long since put the fleece aside by the time Ridley entered. She'd combed the entire bundle, albeit poorly. It sat in straight tufts in the bottom of the basket, awaiting Ridley's approval. Her right shoulder ached beneath the sling. Yrsa knew she should take better care of her body. The only way she'd be able to escape was if she was well enough to do so. Yet, when Ridley had stormed into the hut, cold and distant, as if she were a mere speck of dust in his mind, she'd vowed to herself she would comb all the damned fleece.

Ridley held a candle aloft as he entered, the soft glow illuminating the high blades of his cheekbones. Darkness had stretched into the corners of the room hours ago. Yrsa had nearly gone mad with it. She'd tried to sleep. Tried to run her mind ragged with thoughts of how to kill the mysterious Saxon that killed her father. How to escape Ridley. How to find her people. She'd been unsuccessful. Hunger and thirst and the need to relieve herself clamored for her attention.

"Where have you been?" she asked, not bothering to keep the poison from her tone.

Ridley's eyes skittered around the room until he spied her among the shadows, sitting on the floor, her back to the bed. The candle cast a golden glow as he secured it to a holder in the center of the table. In his hand was a small, savory scented bundle. Yrsa's mouth watered.

Without reply Ridley passed the food down to her awaiting fingers. A bowl was warm and welcome in her palms, a swath of homespun buffering the heat. Yrsa carefully lifted the bowl's covering. Tones of rosemary, carrots, and parsnips rose on the steam. The growling of her stomach made Ridley's lips curl upward as he straightened, removed some wood from the pile that squatted near the table, and readied the fire pit. As sparks caught the bits of kindling, the shadows lessened around Ridley's face revealing lines of fatigue that had settled beneath his eyes.

"There is a hunk of bread layered in the cloth. Be careful."

Indeed, a thick strip of dark bread lay overtop the pottage. Yrsa dipped the bread into the thick broth and ate. The vegetables were softened to perfection and the bread was fresh. Yrsa moaned.

"Thank you," she said around a mouthful. Though she wanted to strangle the man for leaving her so long, Yrsa forced herself to continue niceties. Ridley nodded as the flames devoured the small logs he'd placed on the fire, bathing the hut with cool amber light.

"I didn't have much to do with it. Emma, the woman from last night, asked me to sup and sent me home with more. Lucky me, I don't have to cook for you this evening." He stood and dropped his big body onto a chair. The back of it groaned beneath his weight.

Yrsa ate in silence, words burning her throat as she swallowed mouthfuls of the delicious broth that felt like an elixir from the gods. When she couldn't stand his distant silence any longer she ventured a question about the woman that was so kind as to feed him.

"This Emma. Are you courting her?"

Once the words were out, Yrsa wished she could suck them back in. Who was she to ask about who he courted? All she knew was that no woman simply cooked for a man for no reason. Especially not a man that looked like Ridley. It surprised Yrsa that every unmarried woman in the village wasn't knocking on his door to bring him food or steal bits of his time. If sheer powerful brawn wasn't appreciated by Saxon women, his apparent concern for his people and the kindly way she'd heard him speak to others should have been.

Thankfully, Ridley ignored her. It was just as well. Yrsa wasn't sure if she wanted to find out about Ridley's women. Instead he toyed with one of the books on the table, running a finger down the spine, then opening it, closing it. For a slip of a moment, Yrsa wondered what it would feel like to have those fingers caress her in the same way.

"You appear...tired," Yrsa ventured. Usually, Ridley was insistent on peppering her with questions. Or telling her to keep quiet. There was something subdued about him. Something that pulled at his shoulders, his mouth. Yrsa hated herself for even noticing.

A low gravelly laugh escaped him. The sound twisted her belly.

"I am. But I have a Viking taking up my bed, a village to rebuild, the threat of future raids, and a hundred other things on my mind. So, forgive me, princess, for not being your plaything tonight."

"My *plaything?* You dare say that *I* play with you? When you keep me locked up like an animal..."

Ridley's hands were raised in surrender before she could finish her rage-coated sentence. "How did you make out with the combing?" He eased himself from his seat and approached the basket beside her.

Yrsa pressed her lips together as he sifted through the straightened fleece. She couldn't help but catch Ridley's scent of wilderness however, there was something else too. Earth and air and something flowery. Feminine. It caused the hair on the back of her neck to itch.

"You did all of this?" he asked, his voice betraying his disbelief.

"I did."

"With your injured hand?"

Surprise was so entrenched in his voice that Yrsa dared peek up at him. Ridley towered above her, both hands holding a swath of her work. For a frozen moment, he stared down at her as if she were something to behold. Yrsa felt a sliver of pride. She nodded.

So quick it made her jump, Ridley dropped to a crouch and took her left hand in his. Gently, he turned her palm up and unwound the bandage that bound it. The welts had scabbed over well. Ridley nodded, drawing his lip between his teeth. Brow furrowed, he skimmed the pad of his thumb over the welts. The reverence against the backdrop of her pain sent a jolt of warmth through Yrsa.

"You're even more stubborn than I've given you credit for." The words were light, cradled in awe. He sat on his haunches, knee a hairsbreadth from hers. Something other than scorn bathed his features. It made him appear younger, softer. But this close, she could feel the heat that radiated from him, could tell that his top lip was thinner than the bottom yet shaped in a way that made her wonder how it would feel.

Abruptly, Ridley dropped her hand.

"Come," he said as he slipped the dagger from his belt and bent to cut the rope from the stake. Again, he made a slipknot and looped it around his wrist. Yrsa stood as he wound the binding around his veined forearm to keep her close.

"You are not to make a noise. Grab that blanket for your hair. Now come."

Yrsa did as told though the cold root of fear coiled around her ribs and tightened. They took the same path as the first time they traveled into the forest. The earthy pine scent almost overwhelmed Yrsa once past the tree line. She practically gulped air, grateful for the small token of freedom despite not knowing Ridley's plan.

If he decides to end me, let it be in the forest.

Thoughts of her own death weren't new. Especially since being captured. There were so many ways that she could suffer. And though Ridley didn't seem to be one to inflict that sort of damage on her, indeed he'd done the opposite by healing her and feeding her, Yrsa couldn't fathom when the ax above her neck would drop. But she felt it coming.

Rather than stop at the river's edge where she'd bathed, Ridley struck further north, through a dense flock of trees. Yrsa did her best to keep up across the unfamiliar terrain but her feet caught on several roots and mounds of dirt. Ridley was purposeful in stride yet seemed to understand that Yrsa's feet had never traversed that land. He remained close, keeping an attentive eye on her progress lest she trip. Finally, the woods opened to a wide clearing.

The white glow of the moon was high among the stars. Beside her, Ridley took a deep breath for what seemed like the first time that evening. His gaze cast over the long-grass field, lips set in a neutral line rather than his familiar grimace. Though she should have been scanning for ways of escape, her eyes locked on Ridley. The slight lines that bracketed his mouth had softened, and the light breeze toyed with his dark shaggy hair. Something about the way his shoulders unhitched made Yrsa ache with yearning. She wished she could experience such a sense of carefree contentment.

"Why are you staring?" he asked. "I would think you've seen enough of me over the past few days."

He glanced down at her out of the corner of his eye, a smirk playing at his lips. For once he didn't seem to mock her. Yrsa didn't respond and, instead, allowed her eyelids to flutter closed, trying to enjoy the moment she knew wouldn't last. She drew in a deep breath, letting the clean air fill her lungs all the way down to her belly. Grass, soil, and water mingled with the scents of stew and flames that hung on them from the hut. When she opened her eyes, she stared into the expanse overhead. Stars were glittering jewels nestled among the dark violet sky. The river babbled to their left as if to remind them of its presence. Yrsa hadn't noticed how accustomed she'd become to the background clatter of the bustling village. Footsteps, friends calling to one another, children laughing, people chopping wood were the constant backdrop of Yrsa's confinement. The freedom promised in the open breadth of the meadow nearly brought a tear to her eye.

"Why are you staring?" Yrsa retorted softly, keeping her gaze ahead. She felt his eyes on her like a hand against her cheek. It thrilled her. As much as she hated him, his attention was intoxicating. When she gathered the courage to glance up at him, Ridley cut her a rueful grin.

Yrsa's hands went clammy. Her skin ached with a need that she couldn't entirely name. And she couldn't help the feeling that her fate and Ridley's were twined together like ribbons of smoke in the night.

"I'm staring because you confound me."

Pleasure rushed through her and, all at once, she loathed herself for enjoying his words. It stank of betrayal. Her father had been killed by one of these Saxon monsters. How dare she feel any warmth or desire toward the man who had foiled her plans and kept her tied up like an animal? How could she relax in the beauty of the night when Vidar and Aric were out there, possibly hurt, waiting for her return?

She had failed her people and herself. She would never bring honor to her family. If she couldn't escape, there was only one way. The way of steel and blood and honor. Her mother had always called her impulsive. It was true. And it was a cold, dark reality that drove her to make a simple request of her captor.

Staring out at the grasses, she spoke the words that tasted like ash in her mouth. "Please kill me."

CHAPTER
TWELVE

Ridley wasn't able to pull his eyes from Yrsa while she took in the meadow, her eyes glittering. Earlier, with her hand in his and the scent of juniper around him, he'd been sorely tempted to pull her into his arms and show her with a kiss just how thankful he was for her hard work. Now, under the blanket of stars, a lump lodged in his throat at her beauty, his own mind tripped over itself trying to think of something to say. Their relationship was so tenuous, he knew that whatever he uttered would be cause for sharp retort. But the moonlight caressed tendrils of her golden hair where the blanket had fallen back. The way her face had cleared of worry as she closed her eyes to take a breath had rendered him mute.

Death was the absolute last thing he would give her.

Yrsa implored further when he hesitated. "If you have any tenderness in your heart, killing me would be a mercy."

She moved in front of him, barring him from the scene of tall grasses and flowers, her brows pinched together. Ridley's mind bucked. He had no idea what made her think that he wanted her dead. He'd *saved* her.

"Do you want to die so badly?" he asked, crossing his arms against the line of questions.

Yrsa's eyes were wild, her words quick. "I do not want to die. But I cannot continue living without knowing my fate. Am I to be a slave? Are you to sell me? Make me someone's whore? Will you have me beaten? Killed by your villagers? Have..."

Each question cut. Of course, she wondered what he planned to do with her. But her ugly assumptions that he would have her raped or beaten after he'd taken the care to heal her was like rubbing sand into an open wound. He'd not been raised to be this man. A man who steals from a woman her dignity.

Ridley stepped close enough to feel the warmth coming off of her body and placed his hand against her mouth to stop the barrage questions. Yrsa stilled, quiet as a deer ready to bolt. Her lips were slightly parted against his palm, shallow breaths tickling his calloused skin. With his other hand he circled her upper arm applying a gentle, steady pressure that he hoped would not earn him a punch to the jaw.

"I plan to sell you in Eoforwic," he said, his tone gentle. He lifted his hand despite the desire to keep touching her.

Yrsa's shoulders bent inward like a leaf cowering against the wind. He hadn't decided to sell her until pressed, but as he said the words, he knew them to be true. She couldn't stay in Hyrstow without the threat of death or worse looming over her head. Too many in the village carried haunted memories of Viking raiders. And after having kept her secret, he couldn't claim her as his slave. She'd dug under his skin with silken claws. His body yearned for hers, which was a danger for them both.

"Come," Ridley said, taking her elbow and steering her to walk through the field. He needed to clear his head, which was impossible with Yrsa standing before him, her eyes empty with resignation. To distract himself, Ridley caught her free hand in his and wrapped it around his outstretched arm. Yrsa jerked in surprise and attempted to withdraw, but he settled his other hand atop hers. When she saw that he intended nothing untoward, she followed.

The tall grass swam against their legs as they made their way around the perimeter of the clearing in silence. Hundreds of frogs croaked in a rising cacophony, and underfoot small, unseen animals weaseled away from their steps. Ridley remained silent. Yrsa's request tugged at him. It shouldn't have. He'd heard men and women beg for death, though none in a position as able-bodied as Yrsa. She was so vital, so full of fire, that Ridley could not reconcile the thought of her *not* living.

As they crossed the expanse, Yrsa opened her mouth, then closed it. Moonlight bathed her, giving the high planes of her cheeks an ethereal glow. She pursed her lips, then glanced at her hand on his arm. Her fingers flexed, shooting little jolts of pleasure through him.

"What do you want to say?" Ridley asked. If it had more to do with her death, Ridley's impatience would win out, and they would likely have a shouting match in the middle of the meadow.

Instead, she gave him a sidelong glance, as if calculating whether she could trust him. "When will you take me?"

Ridley bit back a grin at her shrewdness. He wasn't destined to go until after summer harvest. It was an event farmers completed once per year, when the bounty of harvest had shown itself. Whatever they didn't keep for themselves was brought to the Earl of Deircia for payment of taxes, then the rest taken to market. Ridley would visit Lachlan's keep on the journey, a happy respite, then continue to the large city. He'd been a few times, though not as chieftain.

"I travel to Eoforwic in the summer and again after autumn harvest depending on the needs of the town and how the crops are growing."

"That is a long ways off."

"Do you want to go sooner? No telling who I will find to buy such an impetuous item."

"I am no item!" she huffed. Ridley began stroking the soft skin at the top of her hand to sooth her. He agreed. She was not a mere item but a righteous banshee cloaked in a princess's skin.

After a sweep along the west bowl of the meadow, he

unwound the rope and Yrsa took her leave to attend to her bodily needs. Ridley faced away, as always, skin tingling in anticipation in case she tried to strangle him with the length of rope.

"How did you become chieftain?"

Ridley turned as she emerged from the bush, her step springy. Those long legs of hers, clad in trousers rather than a dress, beckoned his stare. She'd allowed the blanket covering her hair to fall to her shoulders. Rather than advise her to lift it, Ridley kept his mouth shut. The strands fell below her breasts, tangled, and were so golden they were almost white in the moonlight.

"You seem young for the task, is all," Yrsa allowed when he didn't offer an answer right away. Her eyes were openly curious, lips braced in a neutral line as if she expected him to disregard her.

His heart quickened. Gone was the rebellious sneer and tense caginess that she wore like a mantle along her shoulders. Ridley suspected that this curious, thoughtful Yrsa wasn't afforded to just anyone and therefore he answered her in truth.

"I am. But my brother is the Reverend of St. Paul's church. That carries some weight for my family name. I believe you met him in the raid," Ridley said wryly. Yrsa's gaze drifted to the meadow though her lips rounded upward. "I also owe my earl gratitude for this station. I fought for him for years, and he favored me by bestowing me with Hyrstow. I grew up here. It is my home."

"Skill in battle is the same as running a village?" Yrsa arched an eyebrow.

They turned along the far western point of the clearing and came to walk along the trees that hinted at the river's edge. The rope around his wrist had begun to chafe where it rubbed the skin beneath Yrsa's hand, but he didn't loosen it. Speaking with Yrsa without argument or worry of being found out was a pleasant surprise. One he enjoyed too much.

"It does. Battle is more than fighting skill. You have to organize your men, strategize your attack, depending on your resources." Ridley shrugged when he realized he was spouting things Yrsa likely already knew.

"You say that your brother gives weight to your family name. What of the rest of your kin?" she asked.

Ridley considered not telling her. She likely didn't care to know and was stalling to figure out a plan of escape, but the slight tilt of her head caused him to think she was listening. He'd never shared his story with someone who didn't already know of it, and therefore someone who didn't pity him.

"My parents were killed in a raid on Hyrstow years ago. I have no siblings other than Oswald. He is all I have in this world."

Memories of being cared for in a small cot at the back of the church were clouded with the heavy scent of incense, the taste of sour wine on his lips and poker-hot pain. He'd taken a sword to the leg during the raid. The wound had coursed deep through the meat of his thigh, and luckily, Oswald had found him before he'd bled to death.

Instead of replying, Yrsa kept her gaze ahead as they

walked. Sweet grass and the musk of juniper wafted toward him, settling in his lungs.

"How old were you?"

"Nine," he replied. When she didn't say anything further, he continued. "I don't remember much of it. I know that there were men that breached the village and were sacking houses. My father was called away to defend. Oswald was fourteen, so he went as well. I wanted to go but could not on account of my age."

"You would have been in the way. You were only a child."

Ridley had been staring ahead as he spoke but felt the pull to look at Yrsa as if he were powerless to do anything else. She peered up at him through her silvery lashes, eyes narrowed with conviction.

Ridley nodded around a sheepish grin. "I know that now. At the time, t'was not so easy to accept. But it wasn't long until I got my chance to fight. I tried to defend my mother when the time came."

The man that had broken into his family's home hadn't expected them. Ridley recalled his coal-black eyes widening with surprise inside his pockmarked face when he saw Ridley and his mother hiding beside the bed. Ridley wasn't sure if the man's surprise had spurred him to strike her down or if he would have done so anyway. It had all happened so quickly that Ridley didn't have time to think. He'd launched himself at the man, the scent of fear and blood in his nostrils. He'd failed his mother. Failed so miserably.

Yrsa's grip tightened around him, bringing him back to the present. His breathing had become shallow. A cold dampness beaded his forehead. All these years later, his reaction caught him off guard when he was faced with the memory of his mother being clawed from the earth. Suddenly, he needed to get the words out. To tell this woman of the chaos that formed in the wake of a raid.

"I was glad to be there for her last breath. It was something my father wasn't afforded. He was slain defending the village, which was for the best. My parents...they loved each other. If just one of them was left, I don't think the other would have been able to go on. The feelings they had for one another blotted out the sun and the moon. It was like magic, growing up in a household with parents so devoted."

Yrsa snorted softly. "You speak of love as if it is a living, breathing thing."

"Is it not?" Ridley asked, eyes locking on Yrsa's features. He thought he spied mirth behind her mouth.

"No," she said slowly, as if he were dull. "Love does not exist. It is a fairy tale told to children to ensure that little girls obey their husbands and little boys consider their woman's feelings. It is the stuff of our great legends, not found in the real world."

Indeed, Ridley did not think he would find love himself, yet he believed it to be real. "But you were betrothed."

"Not that it is your business, but Aric and I share no such tender feeling. Neither did my parents. Marriage is for alliances. You speak of your parents' death? Well, my mother married my father then hated him for leaving. He was always gone on raids. He became a great warrior, one who brought back gold and jewels and fabric and weapons. My mother benefited greatly and yet was not happy with him nor me. When she learned I wanted adventure, she decided to quell the urge in me by beating me. Only when he was near did she treat me well. Love is not something to behold. To think otherwise is to live in the clouds."

Rage iced his limbs at the mention of her being beaten. Though he couldn't picture Yrsa cowering to her mother.

"Tell me you fought back," he said, voice gruff. His tongue felt thick at the thought of the woman beside him being hurt.

"I did no such thing. She was my mother. The crown jewel of our village. I heeded my lessons, and bruises fade. Still, I did not listen."

A wide grin spread Ridley's mouth. She hadn't cared for her Viking betrothed. Her mother had not broken her.

Yrsa took one look at his smile and wrenched her hand from his grasp. Quick as a striking snake she dove for the dagger that hung on his belt. Indeed, she was able to draw the thing nearly out by the time his hand closed around hers, his grip punishing.

"Let go!" She tugged her hand but Ridley held fast, pinning her arm between them as he shoved against her with his chest. Clear midnight and silken hair and the warmth of her clouded his senses.

"What were you going to do? Stab me then cut your-self free?"

"That plan sounds as good as any!" Yrsa snapped, baring teeth. Rather than flinch at him crowding her, she drew herself to her full height, eyes piercing. Damn him to hell, he liked it. She didn't cower. Didn't pretend to be anything other than the dangerous woman she was. And it made him want to pull her to him for a taste.

A laugh rumbled from deep within him, rusty and combative. He knew was depraved to enjoy his captive's struggle. During the raid, he'd remained merciful yet Yrsa uncovered the feral part of him he'd buried deep.

Thoughts of the raid had him doubting himself all over. He'd not brought back the two missing sisters. "Where is the Danish camp? I need to find the Tanner women. Tell me where it is."

Yrsa's nostrils flared. She was cornered, her grip on the dagger strong, but his was stronger. Her injured arm pressed against his chest, legs locked, pushing back so that she wouldn't topple. He should have anticipated her reaction to being trapped. Instead, he stared into those eyes of such deep blue, entranced by the fury in them, not at all prepared for when she bent her head and sunk her teeth into his shoulder where it joined his neck.

Pain, sharp and brutal, dug in around her teeth, burrowing into him. Somehow he had the presence of mind not to throw her off. She would undoubtedly take a chunk of him with her. Before she could, he wrapped his free hand around the back of her neck, pushing her into him so that her mouth had to widen around his flesh.

Yrsa bucked against his hold though her teeth loosened on his shoulder. The pain lessened, becoming a dull ache that changed to something else as she relaxed her jaw.

Her mouth on his muscle, her wet lips, the pain, the press of her body against his; it made him feel alive for the first time in years. Ridley fought the urge to lift her against him, to take her mouth with his until they bit and licked each other breathless.

As if she were made of flame, he released her. Panting, Yrsa stumbled backward, hand empty. Ridley heaved out a shaky breath. His shoulder throbbed. He shoved the dagger back down into the safety of his belt. Yrsa's eyes narrowed at him.

"I hate you," she spat.

"Likewise," Ridley hissed. He took a step toward her with half a mind to carry her like a barrel over his shoulder. She could claw and scratch at his back like a wildcat for all he cared. He would deserve it, but so would she. At least, it's what he told himself because the need to put his hands on her again was madness.

Before he could get a hold of her, she darted to the side. Her good hand was fisted, body ready to fight. It reminded Ridley that he was the one stalking an injured woman. He rounded on her so they stood face to face.

"What made you come to our shores? Try to hunt our people?"

"My father was killed by Saxons last fall. I've sworn a blood oath to avenge him."

Ridley stopped short. Truth rang in the words. Suddenly, her presence in the raid made sense. Why she hadn't tried to make off with valuables from the church. Why she hated his kind. Why she looked at him like she thought him worse than death.

"A blood oath?" He demanded, sucking in another breath. It settled too shallow in his chest. He shouldn't care if her father died. People died all the time.

"You likely did it! Or any one of the savages in your village."

It was a seduction, the pull to wrap her in his arms. He knew of loss, the need to cling to a blood feud after a loved one's death. The impulse was a warning. One that dictated he not lower his guard. She'd been about to kill him with her teeth a few moments ago. There wasn't any way he would pity her after that.

Yrsa would say anything to make her escape. She was a raider. Murderer. That was all he could allow her to be.

"It is time to go back."

Before she could argue, he threaded his hand in hers, the scratches on her palm grazing his skin, and pulled her toward the forest. She dragged her feet against the sudden change of direction. He continued, ready to yank her forward if she made him. Both of their breaths sawed through the air, rough and angry. Finally, Yrsa followed in petulant silence, trying to drape the makeshift hood around her hair with her bad arm.

Soon, the milky moonlight revealed the edge of town. Ridley slowed as he circled the path to his hut. He tried to ignore the feeling of her hand in his, strong and supple and entirely too distracting. Yrsa's steps whispered beside him, her warmth a constant reminder that any noise she made could have them found out. His muscles clenched to his bones in anticipation of her scream. But it wasn't Yrsa's voice that made his blood freeze.

Through the lattice of huts, a male voice called, "Ridley? Is that you?"

CHAPTER
THIRTEEN

Yrsa crashed into Ridley's back as he stopped short. If panic didn't have him by the throat, he would have savored the feel of her lithe body pressed to his. On instinct, he snaked his hand backward, securing it around her waist to hold her in place.

Oswald's stout form appeared from behind a hut a ways back. He was far enough away that he likely couldn't see Ridley's features, however he knew his brother's stature. Ridley was the tallest in the village. Without thought other than protecting Yrsa and himself, he turned, gripping Yrsa about the waist, his hands settling on the slight flare of her hips. He nuzzled his face into her hood, lips grazing the shell of her ear as he spoke.

"My brother is coming up the path. He will raise the alarm and you will be found out. Do exactly as I say, and I will try to keep you alive."

Her entire body stiffened beneath his grasp and

Ridley could feel her work her arms between them to lessen his hold.

Yrsa growled low in her throat. "Get your hands off of me, beast."

"Pretend you and I are being intimate," he breathed.

"No," she hissed, pressing her hands to his stomach. His muscles jumped under her touch. "I will not..."

"Ridley!" Oswald called again, his approach swift.

Yrsa shoved at Ridley and tried to turn. Her breath came out in little bursts of panic. "Let me go. I will not be caught..."

Oswald's footfalls beat the dirt behind them, announcing their time was up. Damning the consequences, Ridley yanked Yrsa to him and stamped his mouth upon her lips. She froze like a deer right before it bolts into the underbrush. But then those pillowed lips he'd been gazing at for days scored along his own. She tasted of woodsmoke and warm broth and cool sky. He stifled the groan that threatened.

"Ridley, answer me."

Yrsa fisted her hand in his tunic at the words. Tension racked her. Ridley could taste the fear in the insistent press of her lips. But they would get out of this, he would see to that. Gently, he ran his hand up and down her lower back, reveling in the slow way she leaned into him.

Back in the meadow they'd wanted to tear one another to pieces. Ridley must have been out of his mind from it because he dared to slide his tongue along her bottom lip. Her mouth tilted upward beneath his in the ghost of a smile. It was dangerous, if only to keep her hidden in plain sight. Yrsa's free hand tucked up on his chest, skimming up to his neck where it rested against the base of his throat.

"Ridley! What in heaven's name—oh!"

Oswald was directly behind them. Yrsa flexed the pads of her fingers around his neck. It sent a jolt of desire through Ridley so strong, he clasped her to him tighter, aligning their bodies so that his legs pressed hers. He needed more. Suddenly he was a man in drought and Yrsa was water that would slip through his fingers. Momentarily, he dragged himself away from the heat of Yrsa's mouth to grumble, "Some privacy would be nice."

"Privacy! Far be it for you to talk to me about privacy! Look at you, gallivanting around the village with a female companion!"

It sounded as if Oswald had stopped a few paces away. There was no telling how much he was able to make out in the moonlight. Ridley made himself impossibly taller, broader, curving his shoulders into Yrsa to keep her out of sight.

He nuzzled Yrsa's cheek to block Oswald's line of vision and hoped to God that all of Yrsa's hair was covered. She let loose a breathy little laugh that tickled his ear. Something in the sound caught hold of Ridley and tugged. He released her waist to clasp her chin, drawing back slightly to look into her eyes. He had to make sure she was still with him. Had to confirm that the racing of his heart wasn't all one-sided.

It was too dark to see anything other than the

shadow of a smirk, the faint arch of an eyebrow. As if she found the whole thing hilarious. Of course, he could rely on Yrsa to have no regard for the danger that lay behind them. Her body had softened to his, molding to him. On impulse, he stole another kiss. It was swift and urgent and left Ridley yearning for another. Blood rushed through him, hot and insistent.

"Ridley, let this gentle woman go and face me," Oswald commanded. He infused pious authority into his tone that he didn't normally reserve for Ridley.

"There isn't anything gentle about her," Ridley murmured and Yrsa gave a little snort in response. "Sorry brother, but I am busy. We can speak tomorrow."

The shuffling of feet on the path told Ridley that Oswald was moving about, reluctant to leave without having been obeyed. Ridley dipped a kiss to the corner of Yrsa's lips, intent on ignoring Oswald.

"You will come see me on the 'morrow," Oswald snapped before storming away, muttering to himself about irresponsibility and loose morals.

Ridley would be in for it. Oswald loved nothing more than to lecture, and heathen impropriety was a favorite topic. With his hand tracing dangerously close to Yrsa's backside and her scent wrapped around him, Ridley couldn't bring himself to care.

The skin of her neck taunted him. He told himself that he was trying to protect her before he dipped his head and skimmed his lips against the column of her throat. Her skin was paradise. She tasted like sunshine on the salty rocks of the coastline. Ridley suddenly wanted to rove her entire body with his mouth. Her sharp inhale denoted her surprise, the sound causing all the blood in his body to rush to his groin.

Instead of shoving him away for taking liberties with her virtue, the hand on Yrsa's injured arm curled into his tunic. She tipped her head back. It was an invitation to yank her closer, to feel the press of her curves against him. Then her hand at his throat threaded itself into the hair at his nape, pulling him to her. It took all of his willpower to not feast on her mouth again.

Calling on every shred of self control he possessed, Ridley dropped his hands and took a step back. He couldn't cave to what his body screamed for. He refused to slake his thirst for his captive. He could not compromise her for his desires. She was still the enemy.

Yrsa stood tall, yet her features were a wash of confusion.

"Come," he commanded. She issued a noise of annoyance but obeyed. Quick, they made their way through Ridley's door and secured the hides behind them.

"That was close," Yrsa said through a breathy laugh as she drew the blanket from her head. It tumbled around her shoulders, the gold strands of her hair gleaming under the faint light of the fire's embers.

"'Thank you' are the customary words of gratitude," Ridley said dryly as he loosened the rope from his arm. He needed to sever her tie to him, to gain distance before he pulled her to him and sought her mouth again.

Yrsa crossed to the bed and sat down, leaning back

on her hand, as if she owned the room. It irked him. She was everywhere. All the time. He could not get a break.

"Thank you," she said tartly, shoving her nose in the air. "I am forever grateful to you, oh chieftain of Hyrstow, for saving me from that dreadful priest brother of yours."

"That priest brother of mine was the one that stuck a blade in your back," Ridley said through clenched teeth. "You should be wary. He tried to kill you once."

Yrsa scowled and curled her knees to her chest as if to protect herself from his words.

As he came to the end of the rope, Ridley stopped, examining the coarse fibers as a suppressed memory pushed itself to the forefront of his mind.

"Why didn't you kill him in the church?" he asked, almost to himself.

Yrsa pursed her lips, causing her cheekbones to sharpen in the dim light. She clutched at her bound shoulder, as if to remind herself how she wound up there.

"Answer me, witch."

Yrsa just glared at him with refusal. His words were harsh, but the lust and frustration that swam inside him, harsher. He wasn't in the mood for Yrsa to toy with him. Instead, he focused on her offenses.

"You could have killed him in the church. You had a knife to his throat, and I would not have been able to make it across the floor to save him. Why did you not kill Oswald when you had the chance?" Ridley demanded. Her stubbornness sparked something primal in him.

"Go away, Saxon."

His patience snapped as anger surged through him like a bear striking a death blow. He was across the room in seconds, hand gripping her upper arm and yanking her to her knees on the bed. Yrsa yelped in surprise but it morphed into a growl as he got in her face.

"Answer me!" he nearly shouted, the rage inside twisting back in on itself and eating him alive.

"Why should I have?" she hissed, her voice a knife in the darkness. "I already told you. I was there for my father's vengeance. For treasure."

Her words crashed upon him like a rock to his thick skull. He'd expected her to admit she'd meant to. Not to insist that her intent in the raid was different than everyone else's. The wiry softness of her in his hand made something inside of him crumble. Ridley sneered and let her go. She remained on her knees on the bed, ready for a fight.

"Earlier in the meadow, you left so quickly I couldn't tell you. Now you demand information. What is it you're after, Saxon? Because it appears that you do not even know."

Ridley bit back an oath he wanted to fling in her face. Instead, he ran a hand through his hair and pulled at the strands. The pain helped. Soothed his mad urge to hold her, to scream at her. What did he want? Because this man that lied to his brother and yelled at women was a stranger.

Shoving himself from the bed, he strode to the fire but the rope still tied to his wrist tugged. It yanked him back to himself. He and Yrsa were connected. Whether he hated it or not, he'd done this. Shame rose, heating him from the inside out.

"I didn't want to kill you," he said. He put his hands on his hips, let his head fall back as he clenched his eyes closed. He couldn't bring himself to look at her. "Even though you were a raider, I didn't want to see what would happen to you."

When he dared turn to face Yrsa, she'd sat on the edge of the bed, legs braced over the sides as if ready to spring up and fight at any moment. Her eyes tracked his movement.

"And now I am *safe*."

The venom in her words flayed him, as intended. He was normally a patient man. One used to the ups and downs of life. But something about Yrsa wrought sense from him and flung it to the dirt. He was trapped, just as surely as she. The night had twisted him into someone he no longer recognized. What started as a walk turned into an unburdening of his soul to a woman that hated him.

Though her kiss hadn't felt fuelled by hate.

"Indeed, you are safe."

"Not from you," she said, though the words sounded hollow.

She was right, and Ridley had no retort against it.

"I am tired." Yrsa cast him a flinty look then settled herself into the bed, scooping the blanket over her as if to warn him away. She was finished with him for the evening, yet he still wanted to argue. The long tether of his patience had worn to a thread, and yet he still craved

Yrsa's sharp tongue, her lip curled in a snarl. She was too damn beautiful as a hateful, wild thing that he knew he had no business taming.

Sudden as a joust strike, exhaustion swamped him, settling behind his eyes. He wasn't made for the deviousness that this task required. His body ached for the comfort of soft blankets rather than the hard coldness of the forest floor. He had to go, needed to get away from Yrsa and all that they had shared that evening. But instead of turning to the door, his feet brought him to the bed. Without a word, Ridley unsheathed the dagger on his belt and tossed it lightly onto the table, out of Yrsa's reach. He removed his boots, dropping them like heavy stones to the floor.

He was so damn tired. From hiding Yrsa. From Grahame's frustration about the border. From cleaning up the raid and helping his people rebuild. The ache of not being enough for this duty caused his soul to sag.

He just wanted one night of good sleep to get his head straight. Even if it was next to the she-devil that kissed him like he was a piece of honeyed candy. He could claim the bed. Though it wasn't chivalrous of him to kick her out, she could take the floor. For one night.

Ignoring Yrsa who watched him like he was a predator circling his prey, Ridley crashed down upon the mattress, closing his eyes against the last few hours. He stretched out. The softness of the straw and blankets reminded him of how sweet his life had been prior to the female's arrival.

"What are you doing?"

"Going to sleep."

"I see that, but shouldn't you be on the floor or in the forest or in someone else's bed? Anywhere else?"

Ridley cracked an eye to find Yrsa, arms crossed, mouth twisted into a delectable frown. Resolute, he shut his eyes, though his lips twitched upward at the thought that he at least irked her as much as she irked him. "I've slept in the forest and on the floor since you've been here. And, unfortunately for me, I've not shared someone's bed since before I came to Hyrstow. I am tired. I want to sleep in my own bed for once."

He could feel her contemplating. Could sense the murder in her gaze, the tightening of her fists against the mattress. He knew she'd rather be dead than share a bed with him. His lip curled upward as he thought of her making a show of taking up residence on the floor.

"You big Saxon brute, move." She pushed his shoulder. Hard. Shoved at his leg with her foot. He didn't budge. Eventually, he heard her shove out a breath and the mattress dented beside him.

Surprise prickled his skin. He didn't anticipate she would degrade herself by lying with him. The mattress could fit two, he was lucky in that regard, but Yrsa's upper arm bumped his unceremoniously due to lack of space. He refused to open his eyes and show her his shock. She didn't need to see the current that he felt where her arm scraped his, the way her thigh warmed his own.

Ridley frowned. He could almost smell the stubborn hate that rolled off her. It mingled with the straw of the bed and the female musk of her skin. She always wore her feelings on her face, and he would bet his best sword her supple lips were creased with disgust. That, or she was eyeing the rope to see how much length there was so that she could strangle him with it as he slept. Curiosity gnawed a hole in him.

Finally, he peeked out the side of his eye to find Yrsa on her back, eyes pinched shut. Her hair, fanned on the pillow, was dangerously close to tickling the side of his face. Ridley shut his eyes and crossed his arms over his chest, the fabric of his tunic stretching against the tension in his muscles. It would drive her mad if he remained there all evening.

"No floor for you, princess?"

Yrsa snorted, flicking her wrist to make the slackened rope between them jump. It landed on Ridley's upper leg, dangerously close to his most sensitive parts. His eyes flew open as he jerked in delayed response. Yrsa grinned sweetly beside him.

"Not calling me 'witch' anymore?"

Ridley turned his head to glance at the impossible woman that confused him more with each word. Her top teeth had sunk into the full flesh of her bottom lip as she stared back, daring him to speak. He'd shared with her about his family, kissed her to save her, wrenched her from the bed in anger, and the fact that he called her a witch was what irritated her? Ridley felt as if he was swimming against a tide of expectation that he had no idea how to get through.

"You didn't like that?"

"I don't mind the term. But it was the way you said it," she said.

Ridley didn't bother covering the laugh that rumbled from his chest.

"What is funny?" She smacked his arm with the back of her hand.

"Oh, princess, of all the things that happened tonight..."

Twin spots of heat painted Yrsa's cheeks as her straight nose crinkled to combat the smile that sought freedom.

"You are strange," he said, unable to fight the grin that spread his mouth.

"I am what I am," she shrugged, as if she knew fully of her oddities. "And you are a confounding, idiot man."

His smile widened. He'd never been accused of being anything but forthright, a rule follower. He shrugged, the action causing their shoulders to graze. A dull pain had taken up residence where she'd bitten him. Though she didn't appear to have broken the skin, the ache would remain for days. It would remind him not to fall into the lull of her beauty.

"Don't know that I've ever met a woman that made me as mad as you have."

With a scowl, Yrsa turned away from him. As Ridley settled into the satisfaction of his own cleverness, his mind wandered back to the kiss they had shared and the way her fingers had curled into him.

Against his will, his lower half swelled with the renegade thought of her wet mouth. She was warm and solid next to him and all he'd have to do was roll her over and...

Ridley stifled a moan and rolled away from the temptation that he couldn't rid himself of. They lay like that for a long time, both awake, trying to outlast the other. Eventually, Ridley felt Yrsa's breathing deepen, and he willed himself into the restless sleep of a man hard as rock for one that he could never have.

CHAPTER
FOURTEEN

As the gauzy bands of sleep fell away, Yrsa realized her cheek rested on a hard, warm chest. Ridley's heavy arm draped about her, his hand gently curved around her bandaged shoulder. One of her legs was tangled overtop his, locking them together. The woodsy, sweet male scent of him surrounded her. It was enough to make her flush.

Yrsa's heart skipped as she conjured the feeling of Ridley's hungry hands around her back, pulling her to him while his lips took hers so completely. Her kissing experience was limited, yet she had no doubt that Ridley had been exceptional. She burrowed her head down into Ridley's body to escape the blush that scored her cheeks.

"Mornin'." Ridley's gruff voice rumbled through his chest into her ear. The hand that had been draped around her lifted so that he could gingerly unearth his body from hers. As he moved, he ensured the blanket tented over his raised knees. Without a glance her way,

Ridley scrubbed a hand through his hair, letting loose a shaky breath.

He seemed to want nothing to do with her. And though she assured herself she wanted nothing from him, the rebuff stung.

"Sleep well, Saxon?" Yrsa infused her voice with petulance.

Instead of answering, Ridley shoved back the hair that had fallen across his eyes then untied the slip-knot from his wrist. Without word, he dropped the binding, stood, shoved on his boots, and stalked out of the hut.

It happened so quickly that Yrsa's entire body locked up. She was free.

It had to be a trap. Something that Ridley had laid out in his mind last night, trying to further ensnare her in this game he played.

Trap or not, she had to escape. With a jolt upward, Yrsa threw off the remaining blankets and stalked to the table across the room, dragging the rope behind her. Sunlight poured in from the roof's vent, illuminating the simple room. The worn wooden tabletop was filled with various objects; clay bowls, an iron pan, books, a jug of water...nothing that would aid in her escape.

Yrsa's limbs shook as she searched for anything to be used to defend herself with. The firestones were large but unwieldy. She already knew the chest near the bed contained blankets, some skins, a carved toy horse, clothing, and jars of herbs. The short cupboard that squatted to the left of the doorway housed a few bowls and cups.

Too long. She was taking too long. She felt as if she was trapped under a blanket, unable to get free. Her fingers flew along the items carefully stacked inside until, finally, she unearthed knives held in a tidy little box. They were light and thin, meant for slicing food. Yrsa withdrew all three. Fumbling, she tucked one into the bandage that held her arm to her chest, one in her belt. The last she gripped in her left hand. It felt odd. She fought with her right and held her shield with her left. No matter, she planned on escaping without the need to use the blade.

Her skin prickled as she felt time shrinking around her. She had no idea who else might be about. Escape in daylight was risky. Her shoulders hitched around her chin as she stood. In the same breath, Ridley stomped back inside.

Yrsa's blood shot through her, fast and hard and ready for a fight.

Ridley's honeyed eyes tracked across the room in search of her. Yrsa swore she saw relief in their depths when he spied her...until they locked on her hand clutching the knife.

"Still here, princess?" There was a sardonic twist to his lips that made Yrsa want to slap him.

He must have run to the river to bathe. His wet hair was nearly black, the ends curling around his neck. The mouth of his tunic hung loose, as if he'd pulled the material on in a rush and hadn't properly settled it across his shoulders.

With a curl of his upper lip, he strode to the chest,

withdrew a brown tunic and dark trousers. His eyes locked on her as he threw the items on the bed. Yrsa's heart beat furiously beneath his stare as he undid his belt, then stripped off his damp tunic and tossed it on the floor.

Ridley was...magnificent. Dark hair covered his chest then delved into a V that kissed his navel. The roped muscle of his stomach damn well *glistened* with dampness from the river. Yrsa gulped at the way the muscles in his chest bunched as he unfastened his trousers and pushed them down his thick, defined legs, the juncture of which was covered by a tan loincloth that did little to hide his endowment. Various scars were enmeshed in his skin, the largest of which climbed from the center of his right thigh around his hip, disappearing beneath the cloth at his waist.

Yrsa had known Ridley's body was battle built from seeing him without his tunic, but this damp, god-like figure before her was too much. Unbidden, her thoughts dragged back to their kiss. The seed of desire that had been planted the previous night sprouted. Yrsa knew she shouldn't feel anything but hate toward the Saxon that held her captive, but in that moment, it was difficult for her to care.

By the time her eyes raked back to his face, a smug smirk cut his lips.

"Found the cooking utensils, I see," he said.

The grain of the knife's handle ground into her palm as she tightened her hold. "I needed weapons," she said, slowly.

"I thought you'd be tearing through the forest by now."

Unhurried, Ridley reached for his clean trousers. The sinewy muscle of his shoulders flexed as he bent forward to pull them on. Yrsa hated that she couldn't tear her eyes from the muscles on the sides of his stomach where the pants settled.

She licked her dry lips. "I needed something to defend myself with."

"Defend away, princess." Ridley made a rolling gesture with his hand, beckoning her to continue with whatever she planned.

Yrsa had no idea what to do with Ridley's change in demeanor. Last night he had been a bear. This morning he seemed carefree. It was like the lash of a whip that Yrsa couldn't brace herself against. Worry caused sweat to break out along her hairline.

When she didn't reply, he continued. "There is a small cellar on the floor beside the cupboard. You'll find some preserves and bread. Bring them out, and we shall break our fast."

Yrsa's jaw fell open. Anger tightened her spine. How dare he be so indifferent to her as a threat?

"I am not to be ordered around," she snapped, taking a step toward him, holding the knife out at her waist. She doubted he cared but had to assert herself.

"Apparently not. I practically order you to escape by giving you time to get away and here you are, ready to make breakfast!"

Yrsa grunted. What was she to have done? Run from

the village with nothing to defend herself? It would not take long for Ridley to find her and drag her back...but would he have? After last night, maybe he'd decided he didn't want the trouble of her in his life any longer.

A cold sensation settled over Yrsa at the thought that he was done with her, just like that.

"You had ample time to run, princess. Even as I dress, you make no move to leave. Though, I will admit that I am glad you find my naked form pleasing enough to ogle at. It makes me feel less like a rogue for wanting to bed you this morning." Ridley ran a hand through his wet hair as he stepped closer, the movement emphasizing the round muscle of his upper arm. Unashamed of his bare chest, he leaned in, his tunic dangling between his fingers.

Yrsa's jaw flapped up and down. "You should not speak to a woman in such a manner."

Ridley donned his tunic, a grin peeking out the hole as he pulled the garment over his head. "I wouldn't dream of speaking to a lady like that. But, as you've constantly reminded me, you are a Viking."

A little scream worked its way up her throat. Yrsa choked it back. He was so infuriatingly condescending. But then his words registered.

"You wanted...to bed me?" she asked. Thankfully, she kept her voice strong even though the thought of Ridley rolling his big body over hers made her insides quiver.

"What can I say? I am a man—one who has not had a woman in a long while. And you were cozying up to me quite nicely this morning."

He was a man, and she, a woman. That was all. Though Yrsa had never been with a man before, she'd been around enough to know that they enjoyed their time between a female's legs.

"You took the bed! Where was I supposed to sleep?"

Ridley shrugged, stepping close enough to make her back up. He smelled like fresh air and clean water. Holding her gaze, he wrapped his fingers around her outstretched wrist and pried the knife from her grip. There was no malice in his golden stare, only curiosity hugged with humor. Yrsa felt herself flush from her hair to her breasts. It made her want to punch him in the throat.

"The floor is always a good choice. It's one I've partaken in this week, princess. It was your turn." Slowly, with his thumb grazing the sensitive skin of her wrist and his warm breath fanning her cheeks, Ridley crept forward. Yrsa yielded ground until her back met the hard plank of the wall.

Her breath hitched. She was utterly trapped. Though, instead of his usual grimace of frustration, Ridley looked at her as if her features were crafted of glittering jewels and he was a thief.

"How is your shoulder?" he murmured. With his free hand he clasped her bandaged arm, inching his palm from her elbow up to her shoulder. A small part of her knew she should worry he would find the knives beneath the bandage and in her sleeve, but another, dangerous part craved the touch of his calloused hands on her skin. As his fingers roamed upward, Yrsa tensed, waiting for the dull throb of pain to which she had become accustomed, but it eluded her. Rather, her skin was alight with heat beneath the constraints of the bandages, firing wherever Ridley's strokes scored her. As his fingers worked around the knotted sling at her neck, his thumb lingered on the skin there.

"Let's take a look," he said, his voice gravelly as he brought both hands up to untie the material.

The cloth was stiff with dried poultice, and Yrsa immediately regretted not having taken the bandage off herself during her time in the hut. The scent of it was tinged with old blood, sweat, and wood smoke. Ridley seemed unbothered. With a gentleness unimaginable of someone his size, he peeled back the cloth from her shoulder. Reflexively, Yrsa tightened her arm against her chest where the knife lay, but Ridley refrained from pulling the wrapping free.

"The wound looks good. Clean," he said.

Yrsa craned her neck to look down at her shoulder. The flesh throbbed as she twisted her head, though it wasn't the sharp spike of pain that she experienced when she moved too quickly. The sight of angry welted skin snarled at her—dark pink in the center, tinged purple and yellow at the sides where the skin folded over on itself as if in self-preservation.

Yrsa knew she should have been proud of the scar. It proved that she'd beaten death. And yet, under the weight of her own failures, the crudeness of it cracked open something in her.

"It's so ugly," she whispered. She hated herself for the tears that pricked the back of her eyes.

So swiftly she gasped, Ridley had her chin between his fingers. His tone was layered steel as he said, "No part of you is ugly."

He did not look away. It caused her palms to sweat at the truth that hung between them. That he thought her pleasing to behold. For once, Yrsa couldn't keep his gaze. Her heart felt so tender she wanted to wrap her arms around Ridley to glean some of his strength. It was something she could not afford herself, so she turned the topic back to her shoulder.

"How did you heal me that night? You said before you used hot water?"

Ridley drew a finger over the wound, his touch as light as the brush of butterfly wings. His lips turned downward. "I poured boiling water in it then stuck a hot poker in the end."

"You what?"

Ridley had the grace to wince. "I didn't like you very much. You were passed out. Well, that is, until I did *that*. Then you screamed like a demon."

"Of course, I did," she snapped, though deep down, she knew she wasn't that angry with him. The wound was too high to kill her, but rot easily could have. Ridley's decision, though brutal, saved her from torturous pain and possibly delirious death.

Yrsa rolled her shoulder to test its flexibility. Her skin felt tight, the muscle beneath stiff. Pain came and went, but she would eventually be able to use the arm to its full capacity. Ridley kept hold of her elbow, supporting the arm while she tested it.

When she looked up, he was staring at the bare skin that dipped below the wound, hunger glimmering in his gaze. She shivered. To halt her own craving for his lips, she commented on something that had snagged her attention.

"You didn't like me then? Does that mean you like me now?" Yrsa asked. Lusting after her was one thing. It didn't seem so uncommon for a man to do that. But to gain the esteem of someone after they hated you was something else entirely.

Ridley's fingers pushed her hair from her shoulder, grazing her puckered skin. "I don't quite think that is the word for it, princess," he mused.

Somehow their bodies had drifted closer, aligning like boats shoring together. The sheer size of him, dwarfing her tall frame, caused her to curl toward him until her bandaged arm met with the solid muscle of his stomach.

At that moment, Yrsa had to admit that she didn't hate Ridley all that much either. Especially when his hands had drifted to her hips to press her against him in a way that ground her lower half deliciously against his growing hardness. Her nipples tightened beneath the fabric of her tunic, becoming painful points begging for Ridley's fingers.

As if scenting the change in her, Ridley dragged his bottom lip through his straight teeth as his gaze settled on her mouth. To push him away or pull him in, she wasn't sure, Yrsa tucked both hands against his chest. The feel of him, hot and hard and hungry, made her want to bite him and lick him all at once.

Yrsa knew she should shove him, make a run for it, but it was as if she were in a trance, her lips begging to mold to his. Big hands scraped along her hips to her ass, then back up the sides of her ribcage as if trying to memorize the feel of her body. Yrsa hummed deep in her throat at the hurried, reverent feel of it. Of their own accord, her fingers curled into his chest.

It was enough encouragement for Ridley. Ever so softly, he dipped his head and grazed his lips along hers.

"Rid!" a boisterous baritone clapped through the hut. The door slammed.

Yrsa and Ridley jumped apart as if burned. Before them stood a rough-hewn, black haired Saxon whose shoulders swallowed the entryway. Blue eyes the shade of a cloudless winter sky pierced her. They were set in a wide, heavily bearded face. The sleeves of his forest green tunic strained against bulging muscles, the material pushed past sinewy forearms that he settled across his chest. A well-used hatchet hung from the belt slung along his waist. Though shorter than Ridley, the sheer broadness of the man reminded her of a demon. Dark brows shot up in surprise as he took in the sight of Yrsa.

"Well, well Ridley. What have you got here?"

CHAPTER
FIFTEEN

Branton surveyed them with a shrewd look of humor. It absorbed every detail yet left the person that he stared at with the sense that all would be well. Ridley had seen it before. Right before he'd thrust a blade into the chest of the man that had killed Ridley's father. At the time, Ridley was glad for it since he'd been holding his sword to the neck of the man that killed his mother. But when directed at Yrsa, that stony, narrowed gaze set atop curled lips sent a shiver down Ridley's spine.

"Bran," Ridley said as his body screamed at him to position himself in front of Yrsa, "what has happened?" He tried to keep his voice cool. Though the strain of very nearly having Yrsa pliant in his arms only to be interrupted by a man that would kill her made it very difficult to remain calm. His cock had been like rock that morning. The way she'd burrowed into his side, as if she'd belonged there, had him itching to roll over and ply her mouth open with his. To rut her into the mattress like an animal. The frigid dip in the river should have quelled his body's demands, but what he was starting to realize was that it wasn't only her body he lusted after.

Bran's eyes widened upon Ridley's movement, his smile curling upward. "I have news from the Reverend Father. Though I see you're otherwise occupied. Hullo there, miss..."

Yrsa stiffened beside him. She didn't answer though that felt like answer enough. Her white-blonde hair, sharp cheekbones, and pointed mouth gave away that she was not from Hyrstow. Even if it wasn't clear that she was of other ilk, her subtle shift to balance her weight on both feet, good hand fisted at her side, back proud and straight, betrayed that she thought Bran a threat.

Ridley rooted his feet to the floor so he didn't step fully in front of Yrsa as his friend's biting stare roved over her.

The tilt of Bran's head as he dropped his hands to his hips signaled the moment he reasoned it all out. "Since when did you have a penchant for Viking, Rid?"

Ridley's shoulders hitched around his neck as his mind scrambled for what to say. Branton was his best friend. He could trust him. Rather, would *have* to trust him if there was any chance of bringing Yrsa to Eoforwic later in the year.

For some stupid reason, Ridley hadn't expected anyone to find Yrsa this way. When she didn't scream the place down after the first couple of days in his hut, he almost expected that they could keep the secret. They had to be quiet, but folks didn't go barging in on one another's homes, though he should have expected it from Branton. In his few months back home, he'd stressed that Bran and Grahame were always welcome.

"Bran," Ridley began, hands open and outstretched, "she's my captive. I caught her during battle and have been holding her here." Sweat beaded at his temple.

Bran smirked, the bastard. "I see that you've been *holding* her."

Yrsa released a grunt of frustration. Cloth rustled. Ridley assumed she was trying to rewrap her bandage. It made Ridley want to curse.

"Listen, Bran. I need you to not say a word of this. Oswald stabbed her in the church during the raid. She looked of importance to the Viking leader, so I smuggled her back here. I was planning to keep her as a bargaining chip if the Danes came back. That is all." Ridley stepped forward, pushing conviction into the words even as he sensed the wrongness in them.

Branton's genial smile firmed. "They won't come back. Their leader is dead."

"Yes, but there could be a second in command. Or there could be another wave to come." Bran gave him a flat look as he scratched his head. He knew Ridley was reaching. The Danes would have thrown all their power at Hyrstow right from the start. They didn't seem the kind to hide in wait then try to take a weakened village days or weeks later.

The echo of metal hitting the ground claimed Ridley's attention. He and Bran both turned their attention to Yrsa whose bandage had come fully undone, falling off her shoulder to reveal the angry red welt of her injury. Two knives lay on the ground at Yrsa's feet. Yrsa's stormy eyes were wide.

"Dead?" The word slipped between her lips and watered the seed of dread that Ridley had buried there since the raid.

Bran looked from Ridley to Yrsa, his mouth falling open in a taunting smile Ridley knew from long nights of drinking when Ridley was able to visit. "The big red-haired Viking. He was your leader, no? Did you not know he was dead? I slipped the blade through his heart myself. Saw the light leave his eyes."

Before anyone could react, Yrsa flew past Ridley, swinging her closed fist at Branton's face. Bran couldn't block it, and Ridley was too slow to grab her. Yrsa's fist met Bran's jaw at the same time her fingers curled around the ax on his belt. Bran's eyes widened as he sucked in a short breath. Swiftly, Bran's hand clamped over hers before she could yank the tool out.

With a shriek of frustration, Yrsa's knee flew up into his thigh. It earned a low grunt. As she tried to yank her hand from under his, Branton wrapped his other hand around neck. Blonde strands tangled between his meaty fingers as he began to squeeze.

"No!"

Ridley's shout was loud enough to halt an ox. It caused Bran to hesitate just enough for Ridley to wrap his arms around Yrsa's waist and wrench her out of Bran's grasp. Bran must have seen Ridley's determination because he let her go. Thrashing, Yrsa's back strained against Ridley's front as she threw out another jab while Bran backed away, hands up against the onslaught.

"Christ, Rid, you didn't tell me you were keepin' a damn banshee!"

Ridley threw him a look of severe annoyance as he tried to keep hold of Yrsa's middle. He was stronger, but she used her height to an advantage, shoving her ass into his waist as she clawed at his arms.

"Let go of me!" she shrieked. When he didn't she snarled, kicking back into Ridley's knee in an attempt to free herself. Pain shot into his leg. He clasped her tighter, thinking he'd break her in half if she kept at it. All the while, Bran silently watched, mouth agape.

"Stop, princess, you'll hurt yourself," Ridley growled into her ear. She didn't heed him. He managed to catch her right arm then held it to her chest to prevent more damage to her shoulder. As it was, she'd ache later.

"Yrsa, stop," he commanded.

Bran stared at them with the grin of a jester. As if he'd never seen anything so ridiculous. Bran had seen a lot in his life. Ridley wanted to strangle him. And the woman he held, for that matter.

Muttering an oath, he turned them so Yrsa faced the fire pit, not the man that she wanted to kill. Her buttocks thrust into Ridley as she tried to free herself. Damn him to hell, he *liked* the fight in her and the curve of her ass against him.

"Princess," he said, his cheek against the side of her

head. Her hair was soft against his mouth. Her entire body went as stiff as a wooden board. Ridley could smell the scent of sweat and rage that coated her skin. He couldn't let her go until she understood she could not fight Branton. She would lose. After what felt like an eternity of Ridley standing between his old life and something new, Yrsa sagged in his arms.

"Aric is dead?" The question was hollow, punctured with disbelief. It reached inside Ridley, crushing something in him.

"Yes."

A silent sob wracked Yrsa's body. He held her, forcing himself to refrain from dipping his nose to her hair and offering platitudes of comfort. She would want none of that from him. When she took a step forward, out of his arms, he let her go.

Yrsa did not turn to face him. Her straight-backed resolve screamed at Ridley worse than her words could have.

The silence in the hut suddenly swamped Ridley like a wave against a teetering ship. He released his pent-up frustration on the rope, the end of which lay beneath the straw. He secured it around the stake in the floor, yanking the knots with every ounce of his strength so that Yrsa couldn't pull them apart. Bran toed it with the tip of his boot when Ridley finished. He opened his mouth but Ridley growled "don't" in a tone that left room for nothing but obedience and picked up the knives on the floor. He didn't meet his friend's gaze as he marched out of his hut. Branton followed.

Wind clawed at Ridley's arms as he strode to the forest. Clouds pressed from above, darkening the sky, their swollen purple underbellies threatening rain. A couple of women walked with buckets toward the trees. He nodded in greeting but kept moving to the northwest, through dense underbrush and past reaching oak sentinels. Not until Ridley was deep in the forest did he stop and release the breath that strangled him.

He'd veered away from the cut of the river, plunging deep between birch and poplar to prevent anyone from overhearing. A few moments later, the crunch of flora halted as Bran came to stand beside him. They stood in silence for a few moments, both facing the swell of trees before them, though Ridley could almost feel the simmering anger in Bran. Absently, Ridley noticed he still held the utensils Yrsa had dropped. Their slender metal seemed such pathetic implements with which to defend oneself. He heaved a sigh.

"You've been keeping a raider? Rid—"

"Yes," he said, cutting Bran off to stanch the flow of questions he knew were coming. Ridley shook out his shoulders to loosen the tightness in them. "I fought her in the church. Right before you and the others came in and dispatched the leader. Aric, I guess his name was. Her betrothed." He spat the last word.

Bran merely raised a heavy brow, remaining silent so that Ridley could go on. Bran would have made a great soldier if he'd had any inclination to fight. He'd listen, execute a plan.

"Before I returned to Hyrstow, Lachlan had us sack

land near Guston, in Bernira," Ridley paused when Bran's mouth made an 'O' of surprise. "It used to be his, and he wanted it back." As if the explanation could sum up the stony look in Lachlan's eye when he'd given Ridley the order. He disregarded Ridley's protest to keep peace between the earldoms of Deircia and Bernira and had dictated Ridley to not poke his nose into matters that didn't concern him.

"Aye, I recall it was long ago. But Grahame's land is on the other side."

"I said as much to Lachlan. Though I have the Earl of Deircia's favor does not mean I can fathom his intentions. He had us take the farms, order the people who lived there to accept Lachlan's reign. Some did. Most didn't."

"Rid, what does this have to do with—"

"There was a woman. Yellow haired, young. She hurled her refusal at me knowing full well the ramifications. My men butchered her animals. Burnt a field. By that time, Eadric's knights had heard of our encroachment on the territory. We'd battled some of them that morning. It was bloody, but we won. And the woman's homestead was the last we needed to conquer. I told the men to push through, to finish the job, so we could return home. She thrust an ax into the back of one of my younger soldiers. I'd been fighting for days, and I saw this young man, just a little older than Neil, go down. I grabbed the woman and ran her through with my sword."

Bran had the decency to flinch. But he did not offer

platitudes. Unlike those offered by his men as Ridley stared down at the crimson that decorated the woman's pale skin. She'd stared up at the sky as life drained from her, not meeting his eyes. She didn't give in to her killer's demands even in her final moments.

"The day I killed that woman, I told myself I would no longer be a death dealer. Months before, Lachlan had mentioned my return to Hyrstow. I brushed it off at the time. But when I came back, I requested it. I no longer wished to kill innocents in the name of territory. That's all my life has been since my parents were slain.

"I tried to kill Yrsa in the church." The memory of his hand on her throat chilled him. "I couldn't do it. She reminded me so much of that yellow-haired woman. Full of fire and resentment. I didn't want to have another innocent's blood on my hands."

"She's not innocent, Rid. She's Viking," Bran said, crossing beefy arms over his chest. He began pacing between tree trunks. The breeze changed direction, as if snaking around Bran's legs in agreement. How could Ridley begin to explain something he could barely fathom himself?

He plowed his fingers through his hair, releasing a short breath of impatience with himself. "She is that. She's also mine."

Bran halted to shoot Ridley a sardonic grin.

Ridley tapped the small knives against his thigh. "I don't mean it like that."

"No? You just claimed a woman. In all the years I've

known you, you've refused more than a single night's entanglement."

"I mean to say she's under my protection. She's my secret for now."

Bran shrugged. He bumped the side of his fist against the trunk of a birch as if to ground himself with it. "No wonder you're acting so strange. You've been doing repairs like a man on fire. Then not leaving your hut. People are starting to think you hate them."

Ridley winced as the truth cut. "I had no idea what to do with her once she was here. I don't want her a slave. Can you imagine what the others would do to a female raider living in their midst? Yet I can't set her free...I didn't think..."

Bran snorted. "You, not think? You're always ten steps ahead of everyone else. It's what makes you a good knight. And a better chieftain."

"Not any longer. I've been so worried that Yrsa would scream and be found out that I haven't been able to put more than a couple of ideas together this week. It's why I agreed to sup at Emma's cousin's last night. Yrsa's in my space, sneering at me, making demands—she is not cooperative, in case you hadn't noticed."

A hearty laugh escaped Branton. He clapped Ridley on the back and squeezed his shoulder. Blue eyes crinkled at the corners, buffering the smile he offered. Ridley sometimes wished it was so easy for him to be genial. "So, the Viking woman has made you so miserable you're finally coming to your senses about Emma?"

"I accepted a meal. That is all." Ridley tried to temper

his impatient tone. The evening had been nice. Though it had been crowded with Emma, Merthe, Ingrid, and Paul and their four children, they had all enjoyed a good supper, well prepared by Emma. Ridley suspected Ingrid wouldn't want Emma's cooking skills to leave once her new hut was ready.

Branton's snort confirmed he didn't believe Ridley for a second. "She'll make a fine wife. She's a beauty, can manage a household, is kind...for some reason, she has the patience to wait for the likes of you. Hell, if I weren't married she'd be my first choice."

A crash in the bush behind them had Ridley whipping around, knives palmed. Nearby, a grouse flapped its wings beside a stretch of bush. Ridley released a shaky laugh at his own surprise. When he turned back to Branton, his friend was staring at him with narrowed eyes.

"You look like you're about to jump out of your skin, Rid."

"I'm fine. Just a bit skittish."

Bran put his huge hands on his hips and bit his lip, considering Ridley. "Have you been bedding her?"

Ridley knew his face twisted into something ugly but couldn't help it. To have his best friend think that he would take advantage of a woman in his care, even though that is what his body had been begging of him as of late, stung. He straightened to his full height. "I have not."

Branton gave his shoulder a shove. "Rid. I'd understand if you were. She's not sore to look at. But she *is a*

Viking. You can't trust her. She had weapons hidden in her clothing for God's sake."

"You came in at the wrong time. She found some *utensils* and wanted to keep them to defend herself if the time came. She's been stabbed and held captive."

The look Branton leveled was one of steel. All mirth disappeared from his countenance. He stomped a few feet away, spat, then turned to face Ridley head on, hackles up. "Do you hear yourself? You're defending her. A Viking! You may not have bedded her—yet. But I saw the lust in your eyes when I entered."

"It's not your business Bran. I plan to sell her in Eoforwic in summer. If I can keep her existence a secret until then..."

"That is weeks away!" Bran shoved a finger in Ridley's face, anger radiating from him. "You think she'll just let you keep her until you deem it time for her to go? What are you, God? She will try to kill you at every turn."

"Well, she hasn't yet," Ridley muttered, attempting to turn away. Branton caught his upper arm and gave it a shake. His friend's thick fingers dug into his flesh. Ridley had lithe height over Bran, but Bran was sheer brawn.

"She's Viking. She will. Or others will return for her. Maybe one of them saw you take her back to your hut. She must be of value if she was the only woman in the raid—could she be a prostitute? She seems too feisty to be a priestess."

Ridley snorted. "There is nothing holy about that woman other than the number of times she asks her gods to strike me down."

Bran let go of his arm with a shove. "Rid. You're not thinking."

"I am!" Ridley thundered, frustration with Bran and himself boiling over. "I couldn't kill her, I admit that. But just as you said earlier, the Viking leader is dead. She was his betrothed. That is why she was part of the raid." Ridley halted as the reality of what they'd revealed to Yrsa sunk in. He rubbed his hand over his mouth to tamp down the sense of unfairness that Yrsa had to find out of her betrothed's death in such a manner.

"If they return, I will use her as a bargaining chip. Lure them in, and we can make a kill. If they don't, I'll sell her at Eoforwic. She might know the whereabouts of the Tanner sisters. Either way, the only one inconvenienced is me." Ridley rushed the words, his tone earnest. He had to make Branton understand. He could handle Yrsa. He had so far, even if he'd been dangerously close to letting her go that very morning. And maybe it would have been for the best if she'd taken off through the trees. He'd no longer have to worry about her, and she could return to her people, if they were still on Northumbrian soil. Though, now that Bran knew of her, that couldn't happen.

Bran paced away, then back, hands flexing at his sides like he was doing his best to not hit Ridley. "You said you couldn't kill her *then*. What about now?"

"What about *now*?"

Branton held up resigned hands to beckon Ridley to stop speaking. "I'll do it. You won't even have to go back to her. I'll do it now if you want."

Ridley stared, dumbfounded, at his friend. The thought of Bran entering the hut, knife in hand, ready to end Yrsa's life charged Ridley's limbs with deadly power. She was tied to a stake with nothing to defend herself. She was no helpless woman, but she would not win a barehanded fight against a bear such as Branton. A feeling like ice forming along cold water took hold of Ridley's insides. He'd felt the sensation in battle when it was time to execute a plan. And later, in combat when he had to slide a blade through a man's ribs.

He was in Bran's face without conscious thought. "If you lay a hand on her, I will chop it off."

Branton's lips formed a flat line though his eyes were aflame. The strangled growl of the threat wasn't a tone that Ridley had ever used on Bran. They grew up together. Fought together. Were brothers in every sense of the word. Ridley had just drawn a line in the sand, and they both knew it.

"You will do nothing," Ridley ordered. "You will keep quiet. You will help me sell her at the market. For I am your chieftain, and I am doing what is right."

Bran gnashed his teeth as he leveled Ridley with a look that told him he wanted to smash his face. They glared at one another, nose to nose, fists clenched. Ridley sized up Branton's destructive power against his own skill with a blade, which he had in hand, meager as they may be. It would be an even match if it came down to it. Finally, Bran gave his head a shake, stepping back.

"Aye, you are my chieftain, and I will heed your order. I will not utter a word of it and give you what assistance you require. But I want it known, Rid: I do not trust this. If anything happens to you or Hyrstow because of her, I will show the Viking no mercy."

Before Ridley could reply, Bran delved into the forest, striding back the way that they'd come.

The tired sigh that wrenched from Ridley made his shoulders sag. What was he doing? He scrubbed a hand down his face. What Bran had said was true. The prospect of the Vikings' return was an excuse Ridley used to justify Yrsa's captivity. There had been no breach of the sentries since the raid; nothing had been found by the hunting parties he'd sent out to search for traces of them.

And where did that leave him? Keeping Yrsa in home for weeks until he could sell her? She would be found out —she already had been. And Bran's immediate offer was to kill her. Ridley turned back to the village proper, not bothering to step clear of the short branches that would whip his legs. He deserved a good whipping for how he'd treated his friend. For what he was putting Yrsa through.

As twisted as the suggestion to slay Yrsa was, Branton meant well. He saw what Ridley could not do for himself. Ridley should have tenderness in his heart for such friendship, but all he was left with was a block of iron in his chest. One thing was for certain: he had to ensure Yrsa's cooperation for the coming weeks. And he doubted she'd go easy on him.

Ridley came up short as he met with the first scattered huts. People milled about, readying for the day ahead. Chickens clucked, and the scent of pottage wafted. Clouds hung low but maybe the rain would hold long enough for Aiken Thatcher to finish repairs to the last couple of roofs.

A sinking sensation pulled at his gut when he looked toward the church. Branton had come with news from Oswald. Ridley had been too caught up with Yrsa to find out what it was. Oswald would expect him immediately. Ridley's brush off last night and his tardiness in response to whatever Bran's news was would put his brother on edge. And Oswald was not a patient man.

Ridley strode forward, barely stopping for pleasantries along the way. He'd returned to Hyrstow to start a new life, though Lachlan had his own reasons for appointing one of his men to the village with one of the most powerful churches in the earldom. If the news was something from his earl or raiders, Ridley needed to be privy to it. Worse, those clouts from Guston could have done something to Grahame's farm. How could he have forgotten?

Frustration with himself was a tightening noose. As he entered the hushed church, Ridley braced himself for the verbal lashing his brother was about to deliver.

CHAPTER
SIXTEEN

Yrsa froze at the sound of the door opening then closing. Her muscles coiled, ready to defend. She needn't have worried. Ridley stalked in carrying a pile of firewood, which he dumped onto the floor in a heap beside the firestones. Without a word, he made the fire, building the kindling into a sturdy pile then using a flint to strike the flame. Through it all he ignored her, intent on his task.

With a grimace, she took up her project of gnawing at the rope's fibers. It was thick and hard and after an afternoon of chewing at it, her teeth hurt. She stared at Ridley all the while, daring him to tell her to stop. He didn't. His presence was like a black cloud. Tension had bracketed his mouth, only relaxing when he blew on the sparks. The flame wrestled against being caught, going out twice before igniting the tinder. Once the fire had grown, he came to stand before her, hands on his hips.

Yrsa kept her gaze locked on the worn leather of his boots. She burrowed her teeth in the rope to keep her tears at bay. This man had kept Aric's death from her. What was worse was that deep down she'd known he'd spoken in half truths.

Dead or fled.

He'd stated it simply during their first encounter. Ridley had known Aric was dead when he'd questioned her about his fighting skill. He'd spent evenings with her, knowing that the man she was to marry had been slain. He'd shared with her about his mother's death, had *kissed* her and not once revealed the truth.

He'd allowed her to hope for a rescue. One that would never come.

"Yrsa."

Her name was heavily wrapped in Ridley's deep voice. She didn't care. Any energy she had for confrontation had dried up her earlier tears of frustration and hopelessness.

"Look at me," Ridley demanded.

She pulled the rope from her mouth, revealing how few of the fibers were damaged, and bared her teeth at him.

Ridley released a long sigh and turned away, crossing to the table. Hands shaking, she shoved the rope to the side, her failure at escape tunneling its way into her.

"Bran will not say anything of your presence."

Intent on ignoring him, Yrsa allowed her head to fall back against the bed. It stretched the muscles of her neck in a pleasant way. Not for the first time, she wondered how quickly it would take to finish healing. The flesh had sewn together yet a crusty scab remained. After her crying spell, she'd removed the sling and slid her hand through the tunic's sleeve. It still was a chopped mess of material but it would have to do.

"There is to be a gathering tomorrow night in cele-bration of Hyrstow's repairs."

With an unsteady breath, Yrsa took up the rope again and began to chew as the silence between them grew into a monster that Ridley couldn't conquer with the pleasantries of conversation.

Finally, he gave up as he prepared the evening meal. Yrsa only peeked up at him when she thought he wasn't looking. She couldn't help but notice the corded muscle in his forearm as it tapered into the tanned skin of his hand while he sliced bread. Or the way his dark lashes fanned his cheeks as he concentrated on his task. Or the curve of his lips downward. It drove her mad that she was so aware of his smallest movements.

When the meal was ready, Ridley placed a bowl and cup beside her on the floor without comment. She refused to look at him or the food. Starvation seemed like a better way to die than remain within the confines of the hut for the rest of her days. Or be found out and slain like Aric.

Ridley remained crouched in front of her. Yrsa expected him to shout, to demean her, but he merely covered her hand with his. The warmth that eased from his grasp made her realize how icy her fingers were.

"I am sorry that you found out about your betrothed

that way," he said, voice gruff and soft all at once. "And I am sorry that I kept it from you."

Her lip trembled at the crash of emotion that flooded her. Aric had been a good match, though she'd never truly wanted to wed him. But he'd been a strong leader and, without him, Yrsa had no idea how the rest of the men fared.

In an instant, she was in Ridley's arms. Foregoing her dignity, she curled into the safety of his chest, shutting her eyes against the onslaught of fresh tears that brimmed along her lashes. Scents of soil and oak and the sweetness that she now associated with Ridley held her just as strongly as he did. For a moment, Yrsa yearned to turn her face up to his and have him devour her mouth to wipe the pain of abandonment from her soul.

But the comfort only lasted as long as her mind stalled with grief. The man whom she wanted so desperately to kiss her was a Saxon. He kept her captive and was one of those that had killed her father. Shame, hot and violent, made her straighten within his grasp.

"Take your hands off of me, Saxon." Though she knew them to be right, the words felt heavy, misshapen. Slowly, as if unsure if he'd heard her, Ridley released her.

"Yrsa..." he began warily.

"What?" she demanded, adding ice to her tone. "You are sorry, and I should bow down to you for your graciousness?"

Ridley glowered as he reared back on his haunches, hands dangling over his knees now that they weren't filled with her. "I merely thought you wanted comfort."

"From you?" she spat. Resentment for her situation coated her in confidence. "The man keeping me captive? Who will sell me at market?"

"I saved you," he hissed.

Yrsa shook her head against his words. He wasn't the victim. Shooting to her feet, she fisted her hands to her sides. She glared down at him, her mind only slightly tripping on the view of him at her feet, his face level with her most intimate parts. The heedy desire that struck her caused her to straighten her shoulders, welcoming the anger that steeled her spine. Her right shoulder pained her and she used that pain to inject poison into her next demand.

"Tell me of the others that are dead. A dark haired one with a crooked nose? Did you strike him down?" Yrsa knew he likely didn't know of Vidar. But the thought of her friend, the only person she cared for, dead, threatened to break her.

Ridley rose to his feet, his handsome features shrugging on the impassive look he adopted when he wanted to disengage.

"I do not know of whom you speak. I did not see him among the dead." It was a small kindness, this acquiescence to her demand. Somehow, it was the last thing she wanted of Ridley. She needed to hate him. Needed to quell the growing desire for this man who lied to her, who kept her. She felt her eyes burning as she gave him a little shove, enough for her to feel the hardness of his muscled chest, and to make him take a step back.

Without comment, Ridley gave ground. He strode to

the fire and added several logs, the set of his shoulders betraying his annoyance.

"Now that your friend knows I am here, what am I to do? Hope no one comes during the day to slit my throat?"

Ridley flinched as he stirred the coals, gaze set on the task at hand. "I have his word that he will tell no one."

"Oh, his *word*." Yrsa crossed her arms. "The word of a Saxon is as good as dirt."

Ridley came around the fire, finger pointed at her. "Branton is one of the most honorable men I've known."

"Was he so honorable when he was sliding a blade into my betrothed?"

"He was!" Ridley gritted through clenched teeth, his golden eyes demanding she listen. Their glinting beauty held her captive just as much as he. "Your people invaded mine. What else were we to do? Branton defended the village. Do you love your betrothed so much that you cannot see the truth? I am sorry for your grief, but you cannot lay the blame on me or my people."

Yrsa couldn't help the scoff that escaped her. Ridley always circled back to the ridiculous topic of love. Beads of sweat broke out along her collarbone from the heat of her anger. "I care nothing of love. I care that my leader, who was to be my husband, is dead. A fact which you did not tell me, even though you knew!"

"Keep your voice down," Ridley warned. His chest heaved with the quiet order.

"I won't," Yrsa shrieked, "because your beast of a friend has probably killed my father!"

A theory had formed in her mind as she stared at the

hut's blank walls. A dark-haired Saxon killed her father and her betrothed. Did it matter if she thought it Branton? Or even Ridley? They were all the same.

"Impossible. You know not of what you speak..." Ridley stomped over and got in Yrsa's face. He was a liar. Anger, boiling hot, fought for a way out.

Yrsa balled her left fist and threw it at Ridley's face. He dodged at the last moment, though her knuckles grazed the side of his jaw. Pain shot into her hand but it was like a savage kiss that kept her going. Ridley blinked in astonishment for a fragment of time before his brows dropped in fury. Deftly, he caught her wrist and twisted it behind her while pulling her into the line of his body. Like an iron band his other arm went around her middle, trapping her injured arm at her side. The movement pulled at the puckered skin of her shoulder. Yrsa couldn't help her strangled gasp of pain. Every part of their bodies melded, their faces a thumbs-width apart.

Ridley breathed through his nose, searching her face —for what Yrsa didn't know. When he finally spoke, his tone was feathered like butterfly wings made of steel. "Branton did not kill your father. His wife bore a child last year, and she grew ill. He did not go with any hunting parties or travel to other towns while she recovered. He was too busy caring for his children and praying that his wife would live."

The press of Ridley's body against hers was a distraction. Yrsa squirmed, unwilling to give up. She spat, "It could have been any one of your people! Even you!"

"Would you believe me if I told you I did not kill him?

Because I didn't. I've been a knight to the Earl of Deircia for many years. I'd taken up residence in Hyrstow in the New Year. The only Vikings I've killed were part of your raid."

It was said with such conviction, without a blink or hesitation, that Yrsa knew the words to be true. She felt it in the way he pulled her tighter to him as he spoke, in his wild look that begged her belief.

"But you lied about Aric," she said, voice cracking. She squirmed more and tried to wrench her wrist free but Ridley tightened his grasp.

"Is that why you hate me right now? I lied?"

Yrsa didn't give him the satisfaction of an answer, even though the question struck true. For some reason, his mistruth hurt her more than the news of Aric's demise. Instead, she tried to stomp on his foot.

"Would you stop moving, woman!" Ridley growled. His nostrils flared, hips flexing into her ever so slightly.

Yrsa was suddenly aware that her body was layered upon his and strung like a bow. His chest, stomach, thighs pressed hers, while the blunt ridge of his cock strained against her lower belly. She stilled.

Ridley went on, ignoring the flush that suddenly met her cheeks at the sensations the promise of him elicited. "I am sorry I did not tell you about Aric. You've reacted just as I thought you would. I didn't want a wild, heart-broken Viking to tear down my hut."

The words were soft and gravelly. Ridley searched her face as he spoke, warm amber eyes feasting on her lips. It stuck like a bramble in her mind that he didn't reduce her to an emotional woman. He acknowledged her as a Viking. The sheer respect in his voice, and the hard length of him against her was a heady mix. One that she didn't think she could resist for much longer.

His gaze traveled from her lips to her neck, fixating on her pulse at the base of her throat. Those lips of his on her skin, she knew, would do wonders. Yrsa panted as she steeled her gaze, though her traitorous nipples pebbled against the harness of Ridley's chest. His eyes drifted to half-mast, trance-like, then he straightened, his features turning to stone. "If you remain quiet, I will release you."

She clamped her mouth shut dramatically, pressing her lips into a line, though she squirmed to show him that she would not obey all instruction. The hardness of him set aflame the spark that had been kindled the night before. For some reason, baiting Ridley, causing that smug, confident beast to fight his own desire caused languid heat to unfurl inside her.

Ridley's features settled back into stone, as if the hardest part of him didn't strain for the softest of her. Another lie. She affected him more than he cared to admit. He'd taken so much from her over the last few days, she wanted to wreck him the same way he was wrecking her. And, by the way his gaze had turned molten with her squirms, she knew just how to ruin him.

Yrsa pushed herself up on her toes and pressed her lips to his.

This kiss was different from the first. Ridley didn't move and, for a moment, Yrsa thought he'd drop her from his grasp like a piece of cinder. She pressed harder, opening her mouth, demanding his attention. Then a groan worked its way up his throat and passed into her. His rigid body crumbled, hands gripping her, not to contain but to pull her into him. Finally, Ridley caved to the kiss, opening to her.

Yrsa darted her tongue against his teeth, the inside of his mouth. As if to corral hers, Ridley's tongue curved along her own, guiding it in a rocking rhythm that had Yrsa pulling her arm from his grasp so that she could secure it around his shoulders. As if the burning need to touch her overrode his sense, Ridley skimmed his hand along her waist then anchored her against him with a heavy arm across her lower back. It felt too good. His strength, his size. Yrsa couldn't help but caress the hard jaw beneath his springy beard.

A heady thrill spun through her as a growl vibrated through Ridley's chest. It was intoxicating, being the reason for desire in such a powerful warrior. Need clenched low in her belly, tossing aside any plans Yrsa had to gain the upper hand.

"Yrsa." Her name escaped him as he sought the tender skin of her neck. His beard scratched in the most delicious way. She couldn't help but wonder how the hair would feel against her throat, her breasts, her stomach.

The turn her thoughts had taken was like playing

with fire. Ridley's hands were as hungry for her as his mouth. While his tongue scraped across hers, his other hand roamed from her shoulder to her back, then up to cup her breast.

Yrsa reveled in the feel of his craving. She knew she shouldn't. But the urge to push him away before it was too late was quelled by her need to claim him. To bite his skin and lick it and have him ravage her. She knew she shouldn't desire a Saxon, especially her captor, but in the same moment she rationalized that she could allow herself *this*. This tugging, primal need for Ridley. Surely, she deserved some reward for what she'd been through. And if the reward was Ridley's body, she would gladly take it.

As if to prove it to herself, she shoved her fingers into his hair, pulling at the ends. Ridley groaned against her neck and palmed her backside, fitting her to him harder. It shot slippery pleasure through her bones.

"That feels good," she whispered before claiming his mouth once more. Her words were tattered, breathless things that she didn't recognize. Ridley's wandering fingers found her nipple and rolled it between his fingers, eliciting the most decadent curling in her breast; she hissed in pleasure. Ridley swallowed the sound. She needed more. Like an animal, she rubbed her core against him, seeking release from the pent-up energy that had overcome her.

"Christ, princess, you will be the end of me if you keep that up," he warned, his voice hoarse.

Heedless of his words, she delved her hand down to run it over the hard length that prodded her. The thick ridge was hot and insistent and Ridley growled low in his throat when she touched him. Emboldened, she ran her hand up and down, over the material of his trousers, fascinated at the size and hardness of what she felt. She knew what it was for but the thought of such a thing tearing into a woman made her insides clench with a mix of fear and longing.

"Yrsa," he warned, clasping her hand over his shaft. Though he meant to still her ministrations, Yrsa rebelled. She gripped him tighter, eliciting a deep grunt that made her laugh.

This was power. If she could tempt and tease this beast of a man, she could control everything. Yet Yrsa's tether on her own faculties cut as Ridley dipped his lips to her ear, breathing against her, "I have dreamed of your skin against mine."

Then he was gripping her ass and lifting her, seeking the cradle of her legs. It put an end to her exploration but the flick of friction against her most sensitive parts made up for the loss. A tightness was building low inside of her, like a spark that reached for kindling.

"Ridley, I need...I don't know..." The words disappeared from her tongue when she realized she wasn't versed in carnality. She only knew that she wanted more of his touch, his lips, his weight against her. He sucked in a breath when she rolled her hips, the movement grinding him against her core. Pleasure shot through her, beckoning her to do it again. Lost to sensation, she wrapped her arms around his neck and took his earlobe between her teeth as she rubbed herself against him in an attempt to chase away the hollow feeling of need that grew in her lowest parts.

Slowly, as if it took great willpower to freeze each limb, Ridley stilled. He pulled back from her mouth, big hands still clutching her ass, though his brows were drawn together as if in pain.

"Have you been with a man before?" he asked. The words grated out of him, as if the cost was almost too great to bear.

Yrsa bit her lip, not sure of the answer he wanted. Her lack of answer was enough. Ridley locked his muscles, eased her down his body, removed his hands from her. A soft oath escaped his lips.

"Ridley, I want to continue..." Head hazy, she clung to him, the warmth of his chest and thighs pressing through her clothing.

"As do I, princess, believe me. But I cannot be the man who introduces you to being a woman."

The rejection was like the slap across the cheek of a wayward child. Yrsa dropped her hands, fisting them at her sides as she sucked a breath through her teeth. She forced herself to take a step backward, the space between them making her shiver. Rejection and scorn at herself for being so stupid caused her to lash out with her words.

"What does it matter? I am stuck here. You plan to sell me. The one who owns me will likely take that liberty for himself anyway."

The desire to mold herself to Ridley's frame was overwhelming in the face of what undefined lecherous man would steal her innocence in the end.

Ridley's gaze widened as his brow crashed downward. "I will ensure you aren't given to someone with ill intent." His words carried a hollow finality that she knew he couldn't guarantee. He merely said them aloud to convince himself. More lies. To himself this time.

Yrsa shoved down the thrum of desire that coated her. She crossed her arms against the doom of possibilities that lay ahead. Her gaze drifted to the straw floor, the worn table, the bed heaped with blankets where she'd likely have the last comfortable sleep of her life. Her shoulders deflated under the weight of her future. She could feel the heaviness of Ridley's gaze.

"Look at me, princess," he said, and his voice was tender. He drew the back of his fingers along her cheek then down her neck to the jagged scar that marred her flesh. His reverent touch made the ache in Yrsa's heart bloom. Softness wasn't something she'd ever been afforded. It seemed cruel that Yrsa would encounter it in her captor's hut, of all places.

She kept her gaze on the fire, afraid that Ridley would see the fear in her eyes at the prospect of starting a new life as a slave.

"Yrsa," Ridley said, insistent as he reached for her.

She drew her arm away before he could grasp her. His touch would send her tumbling into the seductive lure of his arms. Something that he clearly didn't want. Why would he? She was a Dane, a raider, everything he detested.

All at once, she wished to be sold right away. She would have an easier time escaping a fat old man than Ridley.

"May I make a request?" Her voice was stony, eyes still locked on the fire. The flames danced with her erratic heartbeat. "Can you sell me to an old man? Someone I'd have a chance to fight off? Even if I have to submit at first, could you ensure my owner is someone I could get away from?"

Ridley's features turned thunderous.

"I won't let anyone force themself on you," he said through clenched teeth. "I promise. You won't have to worry about ill treatment."

"You can't promise that," she shot back. "Now that your friend knows of me, you won't get away with selling me to some nice widow. I'm a raider. Someone to be put in her place. The only way I get out of this is if I put a knife in the man who owns me."

Ridley clasped the back of his neck with one hand and squeezed. The action made his muscle bulge, and Yrsa had to tamp down the liquid heat that ached inside her at the sight. His gaze skittered over her collarbone then back to her face. The moment hung between them, pregnant with loathing for the future.

Finally, his heavy sigh ricocheted around the hut. "I can't sell you to someone knowing you plan to kill them. But I *will not* give you to someone who will abuse you."

Yrsa infused steel in her spine and prayed that Ridley

had softened to her enough to hear her out. She looked Ridley straight in the eye. "Then let me go. Because you know enough of me that I will not cow to an owner. I will get away eventually, Saxon. Or meet my father in Valhalla trying."

CHAPTER
SEVENTEEN

"Let me teach you to fight." The words flew from Ridley's mouth before he could form a coherent plan. He felt like he was slipping in mud uphill, unable to grip. The iron grasp he had on his sanity had been wrenched and tossed away by the woman in front of him. His body was hard as stone for her, his mind tripping over the feel of her against him, and here she was speaking of killing the unsuspecting man he sold her to. Or provoke her death by escape. He had an insurmountable need to protest both.

Yrsa was beautiful and able-bodied. She would garner excellent coin in Eoforwic. And thoughts of her thrown to the floor, struggling against the weight of a huffing pig on top of her gave Ridley an unholy craving for violence and blood. Then she'd mentioned her own death, and he'd had to lock his muscles against the nausea that stole through him.

Yrsa's perfect lips dipped downward. They were still

swollen from his kisses. Those eyes that were a blue flame for him moments ago had chilled to slate. "I know how to fight."

Fuck. He'd insulted her. He'd learned that if there was one thing Yrsa couldn't take, it was a slight to her competency. He hadn't meant that.

"Not with an injured arm. Even after you heal fully, you'll favor it." The words rushed out, thoughts tumbling forward. "I will do my best to sell you to someone honorable. But I would sleep better knowing that you can defend yourself."

Yrsa's left hand pressed the gnarled flesh at her shoulder. Ridley nearly shook with the need to run his tongue along the groove to show her how beautiful the scar made her. It meant she'd survived. "Think, Yrsa. You hold your sword in your right? Earlier, you could not break my hold."

"Maybe I did not want to," was her sharp retort.

It prodded Ridley that the words pleased him.

On impulse, he drew his finger up her arm to the yellowed bruise. Reverently, he ducked to place a quick kiss upon the skin before Yrsa could push him away. When he drew back, her mouth curled upward, something like yearning filling her gaze.

"Fine. Since you are the best warrior I've ever seen..." Ridley grinned, glad she had moved on from talk of death to tease him.

"Alright. We can start with the basics. With the celebration tomorrow, folks will be busy preparing food and decorations. The night after next, we'll venture into the meadow and train."

Yrsa nodded as she drew her right arm down to her side then rolled it into a curl, testing its use. She winced slightly at the stretch. Ridley slipped the dagger from his belt, cut the length of rope at its base and tied a slip not to loop around his own wrist. He contemplated getting a new rope since he was constantly cutting this one down.

"It's alright. I'll likely be fighting off my owner in their home, so close quarters are better."

Every muscle in his body gripped his bones in protest. He didn't want her to have to fight at all. And yet, he couldn't just let her go. She could be caught by someone else with worse intentions or return with her people to slaughter the rest of Hyrstow. He didn't want to see her harmed by his people, and yet he couldn't bring himself to trust her to leave and never return. And, if he was truthful to himself, the thought of never again seeing Yrsa ate a hole in his chest.

"Right." Yrsa's chin was tipped up with resolve. He couldn't help it—he traced a knuckle, feather-light, along her jawline then stepped back, closer to the space near the door, away from the fire. Yrsa followed, hands fisted at her side, brows and mouth twisted downward in concentration.

Before Ridley could ready himself, Yrsa launched herself at him, fist flying at his face. She certainly knew to use surprise to her advantage. Reflexively, he caught her fist in one hand and snagged her wrist with the other. In a flash, Ridley had twirled her, her back to his front, his arms locked around her, holding her in place. She struggled, shoving her backside against him in protest. Ridley rolled his eyes heavenward.

"First lesson, princess: don't shove your ass into the man who wants to have his way with you," he said against her ear, his lips grazing the sensitive shell. Yrsa stilled, breaths sawing out of her. Ridley was tempted to nuzzle past the mane of her hair into her neck, she was just so delicious in his arms. He shook the desire from his mind with the knowledge that he was just like the men she had to fear.

"Good. If a man is intent on having you, your struggle will only incite his lust."

Yrsa craned her neck to look up at him, a smirk playing at her lips. She gave a thrust backward and wiggled against his still-obvious arousal. Ridley grit his teeth. The woman would drive him mad.

"I know," she said, eyebrows raised in superiority. Lightness spread through him despite the heavy tone of the lesson. This teasing, superior Yrsa was quickly becoming his favorite thing. He smiled, showing teeth, scrunching his nose at her know-it-all attitude.

For a heartbeat, she giggled, the sound tinkling, then stepped away. Ridley let her go, adjusting himself in his trousers as she faced away. When she turned, her face was wiped of flirtation, hands ready at her sides. Immediately, she moved to throw her arm which Ridley easily dogged.

"Why are you advancing?"

"Because I don't want to be taken off guard."

"Well, stop. I know you're going to come at me. It's more likely that the man will advance on you. You may have something in your hands if you're preparing food or doing chores. You can use it to harm him, but remember that anything you use against him can be used against yourself."

Yrsa nodded. It was then, when she'd calmed, that Ridley rushed her, wrapping his hands around her waist, and tossing her to the mattress. She thrust her knee upwards to block him from descending and rolled. As she did so, Ridley grabbed hold of her hair. He didn't pull, he just held the strands taut. Yrsa stilled. She knew when she'd been bested. Without a word, Ridley released the honeyed strands. He expelled a long breath to steady the guilt that weaved through him. She was learning how to survive.

Yrsa turned to face him, her face and neck flushed. "Again."

Ridley nodded, moving to wrap his hands around her. She bolted to the side, streaking to the table, hands scrambling for anything to use to defend herself with. Settling on the half full jug of ale, she clutched it in front of her. Ridley came hard at her, one hand ready to grasp the jug, the other open to wrap around her. The liquid swished a dollop over the rim as Ridley halted, hands up in surrender.

"Can we at least drink the ale before you destroy me with the jug?" he asked.

Yrsa's eyes hooked on the jug in her hands. With a sheepish grin, she set it down. Ridley stole his chance, catching her arm by the elbow and yanking her to him. Yrsa swore at the trick. She attempted to drive her arm back to wrench her elbow free, but the motion only succeeded in shoving her breasts into his chest.

"If I have you by your good arm, what do you do?" Ridley demanded.

"I smash you with the jug in the first place," she snarled, bringing her knee up between his legs. Ridley closed his knees together just in time.

"Wrong. You take the heel of your hand and smash it into my nose or windpipe."

He grabbed the hand of her right arm, flattening the palm and exposing her wrist. He then guided it up to below his nose and showed her where to push.

"Remember to focus all your power into your wrist and shove upward. That will give you some time to get out of my grasp."

Yrsa made the motion several times to get the hang of it. He then reiterated with a blow to the throat. When Ridley was satisfied that she understood, he let her go.

This time, he grabbed at her with more of his bodily force. Yrsa couldn't run, trapped as she was against the table, and Ridley easily looped an arm around her shoulders. There was murder in her eyes as she struggled, completely against his order. Her breasts crushed against his chest, the friction from her taut nipples testing Ridley's hold on himself. She was sluggish in her attempt to shove her hand up while she held his gaze, a storm brewing in her eyes. With no small amount of annoyance, Ridley reached for her wrist to bring it up like he did before. The snick of metal through leather made him freeze.

A smile tweaked Yrsa's lips as she secured the dagger from his belt beneath his chin. The blade was cool against his throat.

"If you move, I will slit you open." Her tone was ice, her limbs supple and relaxed in his grip. Ridley dared to breathe, staring into eyes that had morphed to slits of stone.

"Well done," he hissed.

"Thank you," she smirked. "You were too busy focusing on my chest to notice my hand at your belt."

Ridley allowed a wry chuckle. "Princess, are you going to finish the job or release me?"

His words pushed the metal edge into his throat. A good flick of Yrsa's wrist would render him useless. She could cut herself free as he flopped around on the floor then wait until an opportunity presented itself to escape the hut. She knew it too. Her eyes darted to the door and back to his face, her grin of triumph wavering.

Ridley didn't want to die, but he appreciated the irony that they were practicing Yrsa's escape from her captor, and she'd done it. Since their kiss, Ridley could think of little else than the feel of her beneath his lips and hands. His lust for her while in his care made him just as bad as any man who would try to mistreat her. And because of the rage he felt at the thought of Yrsa being forced into relations with her future owner, a small amount of pride swelled within him if she did decide to end him.

It wouldn't be a bad way to go. In the warmth of his home, at the hand of a beautiful woman. Yrsa would make it quick. He didn't think she had it in her to make him suffer.

A pang of unexpected regret hit him. He'd led a solitary life; he wouldn't abandon anyone with his death. Except the woman that would strike the blow. A selfish need to see her to safety bloomed inside him, growing with the vine of attraction he had for her. She was so strong, so confident, and yet vulnerable. Her bravado was borne of a life of having to prove herself. And he suspected that if she killed him, it would be another burden for her to carry. Yrsa stared, blue-gray gaze unflinching. And all at once, Ridley didn't want to leave her.

"Well?" he asked.

With an inclination of her head, Yrsa tucked the knife downward and stepped away. She released a ragged breath through her teeth, dagger hanging at her side. Ridley had to stop himself from reaching for her again.

"Why didn't you finish me? You would have gained your freedom."

Yrsa twirled the knife between her fingers, the gold inlay on the handle glinting in the firelight.

"You saved me," she said, as if it was as simple as a life for a life.

Ridley knew different. She'd gotten under his skin. And, despite his capture of her, he held a sliver of hope that he'd gotten under hers.

He held out his hand for the dagger, doubtful that

she would give it up. He tensed, readying for an argument. There was no way he would trust her with a weapon.

Not for the first time, Yrsa surprised him. She held the dagger in both hands, staring at the edge of the blade, then laid the handle on his palm.

"When you sell me, be sure to give that back. That was my father's."

Ridley nodded, astonished that she trusted him to do so. And he would. It was hers.

"It's getting late." Night had fallen long ago and the following day would be busy, preparing for the evening's celebration. He had to speak to Oswald regarding the collection of the King's tithe on lands near Guston. There was one more thing he needed from Yrsa, though.

Ridley slung the dagger into his belt, his shoulders tensing under the weight of what he had to ask her next.

"Yrsa, the Danish camp. Where is it?"

Yrsa avoided his gaze, dragging her lip through her teeth as she did so. When she didn't say anything, he pressed again.

"Princess, please. I beg you now. The Tanner sisters were taken by your men. They face the same threat that we've discussed all evening. Do not let them suffer at the hands of your men any longer."

Yrsa had the decency to flinch. She scraped a hand down her face. "They are probably not even there. You had said the men died. That Aric died. He'd be the one to lead them away and if he's gone..."

She blew out a frustrated breath. Her eyes were locked on the floor. "You ask me to betray my people."

Ridley caught her elbow in his hand, bringing her close. She tensed but allowed him to drape his arms around her shoulders and put his forehead to hers.

"Please. I want them home safe. Or to find them so that their families are afforded a proper burial."

Yrsa leaned back, away from him, eyes scoring as if searching for the truth in him. Then she pressed a kiss to his lips, so quick he wasn't able to reciprocate.

"Southwest. Near where the mouth of the sea joins with your river. It's where we shored our boats. About a days' trek."

Gratitude and sorrow were twins in his heart. They'd already scoured that land. There had been no boats, only evidence that people had slept there. However, that Yrsa gave the information freely was not a boon he didn't appreciate.

"Thank you," he breathed.

She nodded, brows tenting together with doubt. Ridley knew she would war with the guilt of telling him. He tried to convince himself it was not his concern. As if to remind himself of that, he loosed a breath and stepped away from her, even though his body called for him to wrap her in his arms once more.

Though right then, Ridley wanted nothing more than to crawl into bed with his arm draped over Yrsa. Which was something he shouldn't want. She wasn't his.

"I will stay at Branton's tonight."

Yrsa pierced him with her narrowed gaze, a frown

marring her beautiful mouth. She crossed her arms. "Why?"

Ridley grated out a breath. "Because, Yrsa. I am tired. We've just been through ways to kill your captor, and it has not escaped my attention that I am he..."

"Is it because I bested you? I won't hurt you if you do not give me reason to."

Ridley drew his hand across his brow to erase the lines of incredulity he knew were forming. "I don't want you to feel unsafe. You are under no threat from me, but I don't want you to doubt that fact."

She took a purposeful step forward. Her shoulders were thrown wide, sharp chin tilted upward.

"I do not doubt it."

"Even so, I am aware that even if I keep you for the good of my people, it is to the detriment of you."

Yrsa's scowl deepened. Her gaze remained locked on him, demanding. Then she surprised him by reaching out to brush a stray piece of hair from his forehead. The tender gesture caused his heartbeat to quicken. Next, she placed her warm palm along his cheek. The small scars from where she'd tried to wrench free of the stake felt like small threads against his skin.

"You do not have to go," she said. Her tone was rich as silk. "If you stay somewhere else, will there not be questions? Will others not wonder why you are not sleeping in your perfectly fine home?"

Yrsa's thumb stroked down his face, smoothing across his bottom lip. Ridley felt his resolve caving. The softness of her reasoning after the rush of their mock fight caused every bit of him to strain against his decision to leave. Even if she did not fear him, it was not an invitation to stay and bed her. And Ridley knew his sleep would be restless with Yrsa pressed against him.

"Yrsa..."

"Ridley," she shot back, "you know how I can be. If you are as tired as you say, do you really want to fight me on this tonight?" Taking a step into him, she curved her hand around his waist. Her scent pulled at something primal in him. It was a siren call. "Stay."

He laughed as he dropped his forehead to hers. She had him. He did not want to leave. Their noses touched, and he was sorely tempted to plant his mouth on hers.

"What am I doing?" he asked himself.

Rather than reply, Yrsa stroked her hand down his neck and rested it on his chest. For the briefest of moments, she brushed her lips against his. Need punched him in the middle. Then she stepped back and strode to the bed. Ridley watched the sway of her hips as if he'd go blind if he looked away.

Could it be that Yrsa was feeling the same tangled web of craving that he was? That she fought against the same desire that clamped Ridley's muscles to his bones whenever he was around her? His cock jumped at the thought.

"Ridley," Yrsa commanded and he was compelled to follow. His feet carried him to the bed where he sat to pull off his boots. Yrsa was doing the same. It was the first time he'd witnessed her without them, since those first few nights when he'd taken them off after healing her. She kept them on, he knew, ready to run if the opportunity presented itself.

"Do you..." she paused as she pulled the blanket back, settling herself in the center of the bed. Ridley's heart squeezed at the sight of her there, so full of promise.

"What, princess?"

Her cheeks turned the color of a ripe apple. She swallowed, stilling, and became the self-possessed woman he knew. "I would like a new tunic. You've cut mine down the middle and it is hard with blood. Might I use one of yours, if you have one to spare?"

Guilt threatened to swamp him. Yrsa's chin remained steady, shoulders back, as if steeling herself for his denial. To have to ask for something as basic as clothing...

"Of course."

A lump formed as he searched the bedside chest for something appropriate. Everything would be too large on her but she could belt it. He pulled out his softest piece, the wool a rich burgundy spun by Grahame's mother and gifted to him years ago when he'd stayed for Winter Solstice. The cuffs were stitched with fine black thread, the holes at the neck tightened with softened leather. He'd barely worn it since, having no need for such finery.

Yrsa's eyes widened as she felt the garment. "This is... I can wear something else. This is much too elegant for me."

"It's yours," he said, looking away to bar further

refusal. He untied the slip knot at his wrist so that she could pull the length of rope through the sleeves then remained facing the fire to afford her some privacy.

Ridley grit his teeth and thought of dunking himself in the cold river as the sound of cloth rustled behind him.

"Ridley."

He tensed at the sound of his name from her lips.

"You may turn."

Yrsa wore nothing but her trousers and a smile. The tunics sat in a small pile beside her. Ridley felt his jaw unhinge. The firelight licked at the column of her throat, the delicate bones at the base, the curved orbs of her breasts, her taut stomach. It was as if the light itself was alive, stroking the expanse of flesh before him. Ridley hardened, his cock a slave to the sight of her.

"Yrsa." Her name barked from him, sharp with shock. He'd seen her nearly naked. He'd felt the softness of those breasts but the sight of her, sitting like a queen before him, made him want to kneel. "What game is this?"

Her grin spread a little wider. "No game. It is as I said before. I wish to choose who has me. And my body craves yours."

Ridley swore. He shoved a hand through his hair. "I do not want you to feel as if you have to do this with me. I am not a good man, Yrsa. Nor do I wish to be seduced only to be tricked."

The wince at his rejection was slight, but Ridley saw it. She rallied though, steeling herself against it. With a shrug she said, "Think what you want. Right now, good or bad makes no difference to me."

Ridley felt his resolution fray beneath her stare. Christ, he wanted her. Wanted to run his tongue along her skin until she begged for him, as a man, not just as a ploy to free herself. He wanted to ram himself inside of her until he couldn't remember his own name. Wanted to make her knees shake and walls clench as she came for him, over and over.

He ran an impatient hand along his front to assuage the desire that seemed to yank him closer to the bed. Yrsa's gaze flared at the motion. Somehow he'd come to stand at the side of the bed, hands fisted. Without hesitation, she reached out, her hand curving overtop his clothing, around his cock. The touch was tentative, exploratory. Ridley's eyes fluttered closed as he swelled under her. God, he wanted this. Wanted her. Yrsa had brought something out in him—a sense of life. When she made an appreciative noise in the back of her throat, he caught her wrist, eyes flying open.

There was no way he would have her think him a brute. Someone who would shirk the responsibility of chivalry and take her while she had no choice. But he could assist her with her own pleasure. He could show her how tempting he found her, how beautiful. Even if it made him sport a hard on for a month.

Ridley climbed onto the bed, finding his way beneath the blanket. He shucked off his shirt but left his trousers on, as Yrsa had done. The way her eyes gobbled up his torso made him want to blush. Ridley knew he wasn't bad to behold. His body was well muscled. But the sheer hunger in the gaze of such a breathtaking woman was one of the highest compliments he'd received.

As he crowded in beside her, she shivered. It wasn't from cold, he knew, because when he wrapped an arm around her lower back, her skin burned. Ridley swallowed hard. His cock strained against the confines of his pants. With a steady breath inward he leashed his lust, praying that he could see his plan through.

EIGHTEEN

Yrsa thought he'd be greedy. That Ridley would aim for her breasts. But he'd wrapped his arm around her back, pulling her to him, then brought it up to her shoulder so she could use his arm as a pillow. The unexpected tenderness confirmed that she was making the right choice. With his other hand, he caught her chin and kissed her, deep and slow. It made something in Yrsa's chest purr.

"Turn for me, princess."

Ridley moved to his side and she followed suit, so that her back was to his front. The hardness that she'd felt with her hand prodded her behind as their bodies fell in line. An urgent heaviness had settled in her nether region, one that hummed against the clenching of her legs together. Yrsa couldn't help pushing her bottom into him.

"Are you to have me like this?" she asked. Her heart

beat erratically as she tried to remain still. She had no idea what men liked or how they took their women.

Ridley pressed a kiss to her hair as one hand cupped a breast. He squeezed it gently then dragged his finger around her peaked nipple. The lazy scrape of it was like a bolt of lightning between her thighs. "Tell me, Yrsa, did you and your betrothed share any intimate moments?"

Yrsa stiffened. She did not want to speak of Aric.

"Shhh, it's alright," he said against her ear, breath tickling. His finger moved to her other nipple, circling at a maddeningly slow pace. "I do not wish to discuss him, only to ask if you've been pleasured by a man before."

Yrsa twisted her face to peer at him, to see if he spoke in jest. His eyes were like liquid gold as they watched her, his mouth tipped upward.

"You know I haven't lain with a man."

His fingers skimmed down, over the plane of her stomach. He met with her trousers, which he undid the laces of, then pushed them gently down. Yrsa helped shimmy her hips to move the material along, eliciting a harsh pant from Ridley as she nestled her bare ass into his front. Once the barrier was removed, he grazed his fingers up her leg to tangle in the soft hair at the apex of her thighs. He tugged, ever so gently. Yrsa gasped.

Ridley's grin spread. It made something in her chest clench with yearning. She had the silly urge to be the cause of more of his smiles. "There is a difference between being pleasured by a man and lying with one."

He kissed the tip of her nose as his fingers drew a circle around the inside of her thighs. Yrsa sucked a breath through her teeth as she laid her head back on his arm. If he wanted to talk, she would.

"And what difference is that?"

Ridley's fingers splayed along her thigh, then hooked her knee over his in one smooth motion. He widened his legs, baring her. Yrsa could not stop the gasp that escaped her mouth.

"Laying with a man," he murmured as his fingers wound their way around her opening in wide circles, "means having that man's cock inside you." He pushed the thick ridge of him against her back.

Yrsa panted at his words. She'd heard them before, thrown in jest between men in the village, on the ship. But Ridley's voice so close to her ear, dark and silky and full of promise, sent a thrill through her. His fingers moved upward, teasing, stroking until they crested the bud at the apex of her thighs.

"Pleasuring a woman feels like this."

Ridley pressed down, sending an exquisite shock through Yrsa. She didn't try to hold in the moan that parted her lips. Ridley caressed the bud with steady pressure then his fingers danced away, circling the area as if to gather all the feeling in her body and focus it on the singular point.

"Ridley," she hissed as something built in her. A sensation like water building at the bottleneck of a river, pushing and pushing, ready to burst.

Yrsa felt his smile against the back of her head. Then he dragged his fingers downward teasing her entrance, moving back and forth, upward over the bud then down again, and again, nearly breaching her until Yrsa thought she would go mad. When her hips began moving of their own accord, chasing the feeling that she feared would disappear if he stopped, Ridley pushed a finger into her. Yrsa sucked in a delighted breath of the feel of him filling her. She bit her lip as she adjusted to the sensation. Pure, pent-up pleasure fixated around his hand.

"Ridley," she gasped, a silent plea for more.

Ridley unearthed his other arm from her head to prop himself on his elbow so that he could have more leverage to capture her mouth. His finger began to move in her, gently at first, then faster as she kissed him with tongue and teeth. As she gave way to the pull of his heavy weight all around her, he flexed his hips into her ass, as if trying to curb his own desire.

In a steady rhythm, he withdrew his finger, swirled it around the bud between her legs, then thrust his finger back into her. Each time, her body mourned the loss of feeling full, but a delicious spark of heat curled out from the press of his finger. Behind her, Ridley began to pant, the sound guttural, as he pressed his cock into her backside. Yrsa was practically splayed across Ridley and she loved every desperate moment of it. His mouth on hers, his thrusts growing harder. Yrsa rocked her hips into his hand, greedy for the sensation that she wanted to drown in. It was as if her body was the sword in Ridley's hand as he swept and parried in some final battle.

With a shudder, he shoved his finger into her as he pressed his thumb at her juncture, and the dam broke, the battle that was her body, won. Yrsa moaned as she cracked open. Warmth cascaded through her, made her dizzy as her inner muscles clutched Ridley's finger over and over. He kept moving inside her, coaxing out her release. Then Ridley stiffened, his groan guttural, as a warm liquid met her back.

Panting, Ridley touched his head to hers. He eased his fingers out of her, settling his hand on her hip which Yrsa covered with her own. Too soon, he cleared his throat and sat upright. Gently, he pushed her onto her stomach. Yrsa, her body completely relaxed, flopped forward to obey.

"Here, princess," Ridley said.

She felt a cloth at her back, where the warmth had spurted. Vaguely, she knew she should ask about it, if it was blood or something she should be aware of, however Ridley didn't seem bothered and her mind was in the clouds. When he finished, she turned her head to watch him through half-closed eyes.

Ridley tugged on his shirt, eyes cast toward the door. Worry pulled his features downward. It tweaked something in her heart. She didn't hesitate when she reached out to drag her hand down his forearm.

"I don't think we were too loud," she murmured.

He glanced at her, his face softening. "Aye, I think you're right."

Something still haunted those tawny eyes, though, and it sent a chill through her. As it should have. He was not hers. He was Saxon and her captor and though her bones felt full of water, she should hate him. It was difficult to bring herself to do so.

"Lay with me, Saxon."

Yrsa said the command with as much strength as she could muster. Ridley looked as if he was about to say no, his gaze ravaged with something akin to guilt. She wouldn't allow it. Though he was her keeper, she held onto her own resolve. To show that he need not carry the weight of her choices, she circled his wrist with her hand and tugged at him until he obeyed. Ridley settled down next to her, his great body hard and warm beside her own. Pleased enough to have gotten her way, Yrsa drifted to sleep with her hand tucked over the heart of her enemy.

CHAPTER
NINETEEN

The bustle outside lasted from dawn until just before the supper hour. Initially, Yrsa had thought the footfalls to be an intruder. The scuff of feet against the dirt paths that weaved through Hyrstow would come close, then fall away. Ridley had mentioned a celebration, but after their evening together, Yrsa didn't recall many details.

Curiosity piqued, she searched again for a gap in the boards to peer out of. After nearly an hour, she found a sliver of space between boards beside the bedside chest. If she pulled the rope and crouched on her knees she could look out. Villagers moved to and fro, hands filled with food or fabric or tools. Though Ridley's hut was on the outskirts of the village proper, the path directly in front of his dwelling seemed to be a shortcut down to the river. Women and children carted clothes into the trees and came back with soggy items that would be hung to dry closer to their homes.

As the sun climbed to the top of the cloudless blue sky, the scent of roasting pork permeated the air. Fresh baked bread, roasted apples, and stewed herbs wafted. Yrsa's mouth watered. She knew she wouldn't receive a morsel of what was prepared. Not that she deserved any. The celebration was for the repair of Hyrstow. Of anyone, she was the least entitled to it.

That morning, Ridley had woken her before dawn to take her to the river to relieve herself and wash. He'd kept her leash long and hadn't said much. Yrsa didn't blame him. They'd awoken tangled in one another, their scents mingled. Ridley had been stiff against her leg and Yrsa's belly quivered with the hope that he would pleasure her as he did before. Instead, he kept his gaze from her while they dressed and did not speak much as they trekked to the water.

His resolve against her injured her more than she wished to admit. They'd both been caught up in one another, but when it mattered, he was the one to put an end to their growing closeness. And she was the Viking who threw caution to the wind to lie with a Saxon.

The deep rumble of Ridley's voice outside caught Yrsa's attention. Mingled with it, a woman's quiet laughter. Yrsa had taken a break from abusing her knees in favor of practicing how to perfectly position her hand to break a nose, but Ridley's voice had her scuttling to the crack in the wall. She pressed her eye to the rough wood, the fibers itching her cheekbone.

Ridley spoke to a petite brunette, a wide smile plastered across his face. It was a true smile with crinkled eyes and a wide breadth of teeth. It transformed him. Curiosity snagged Yrsa and held her in place. The woman's heart-shaped face was sweet-lipped and open. She held the hand of the young girl Yrsa had encountered on the day of the raid.

Though she couldn't hear their words, the cheerful tone of the conversation was apparent in the trio's nods and grins. The woman's thick-lashed, brown eyes were paired with a dimple on one cheek when she smiled. Which was a lot. A tunic the color of butter complimented a sage skirt that ended at her ankle. An ivory apron hitched the fabric becomingly around her tapered waist. If she had to guess, Yrsa placed the woman as Emma. Next to the woman, the girl, who must have been around age ten, spoke. She gestured exuberantly and had a tinkling laugh that rang through the nearby huts. Ridley's eyes softened with kindness as he nodded along with what she said. They were a picture of familial bliss. Yrsa's heart stuttered.

As the three parted, Emma's hand skimmed Ridley's forearm. Yrsa bit her lip to stay the urge to chop it off. When Ridley entered the hut a moment later, he wore the remains of a smile.

"Hello," he greeted, his upturned lips turning neutral at the sight of her kneeling on the floor, her back to the wall. The rope was taut, her wrist at its limit.

Yrsa nodded but didn't move. After seeing him so happy with another woman, she wasn't in the mood to be generous with words.

Ridley took an exaggerated look around the hut.

Finally, he came to stand at the fire pit with a handsome smirk that caused her stomach to flip. "You haven't destroyed the place today."

The hut was put together as it had been the night before. Chairs were neatly tucked under the table, cookware stowed in the cabinet, books stacked. True, in the past she'd made a mess searching for weapons or trying to get away, but she resented the implication that she was the cause of all disaster.

Remaining tight lipped, she stood and scooped up the cup of ale Ridley had left for her that morning. Ridley's eyes were on her as she took a long pull.

"Thirsty?" Without waiting for a reply, he turned to the cupboard and withdrew the brick of cheese and a loaf of bread wrapped in muslin. He went to the table, plucked the dagger from his belt and cut several hearty slices of cheese. Next, he made quick work of the dark bread. Slapping the items together, he crossed the room and held the food out to her.

Yrsa placed the cup on the stool and took the food from him. She wasn't starving, but she wasn't exactly feeling charitable. She eyed Ridley over the bread as she took a bite. The cheese was sharp and the bread soft, melting in her mouth. A part of her wished she could hate it but the taste danced on her tongue.

"Ah, and I found something else for you," he said. From the small leather pouch on his belt, he procured a small handful of dark berries. Yrsa glanced from his hand to his face, confusion swelling. Ridley nodded for her to take them and she did, accepting the little pile in the center of her hand. Stupidly, she sat with the berries while he returned to the table to clean up the cheese and bread, barely looking her way as he did so. As if she was so easily forgotten.

Yrsa popped the entire handful into her mouth. Sweet, cheery flavor burst on her tongue. She chewed and swallowed, wishing for more. Ridley didn't bother to ask if she enjoyed them.

"You're in a good mood," she accused around a mouthful of bread and cheese.

"I guess I am," he said with a shrug. "I'll be out this evening and not sure when I'll be back."

He slung the dagger into his belt, the motion drawing Yrsa's eyes to his lithe hands. Hands that had explored her last night. A blush pricked at Yrsa's cheeks, though Ridley was oblivious.

He was in a hurry, and Yrsa was petty enough to keep him longer.

"What do your people do at your celebrations?" she asked after swallowing another bite.

Ridley strode to the chest near the bed and withdrew a fresh tunic and set of trousers. He laid them on the end of the bed and began to strip. Yrsa stared, unabashed. They were past the point of modesty, yet it irked her that he felt comfortable enough to undress in front of her. As if she were kin, not someone he'd had his fingers inside the night prior. The muscles in his chest rippled as he yanked up the trousers. Yrsa's hands itched to run over the valleyed skin of his stomach.

"There is a feast. My brother will bless the meal.

There's been a pig roasted and Emma has been baking delicacies all day. There'll be ale and dancing. We usually have a feast once all the planting has been completed, but with the acquisition of new lands, we're not there yet. It was decided to celebrate most of the planting and the repairs anyway. Everyone is looking forward to it."

The sinew of his shoulders flexed as he brought the tunic down over his head. Ridley caught her staring as the material slid down his chest and over the ropes of his stomach. He smirked but said nothing.

Yrsa's cheeks set aflame. Apparently, she was much more affected by Ridley than he was of her. She bit the inside of her lip to quell the urge to go over and plant a kiss on those idiotic upturned lips.

If only to keep him talking she asked, "New lands?"

Something darkened in Ridley's eyes as he tightened his belt. "Yes. We'd have them plowed and planted by now if not for the raid."

Guilt shot through her, Ridley having aimed the bow of his words well.

"Where are they?"

"North. I claimed them for the Earl of Deircia prior to the New Year. It was my last order before coming back home."

The last word was full of affectionate nostalgia. As if he'd never thought to truly see home again. The bread and cheese were gone so Yrsa twisted her hands together as she stood. Her injured shoulder felt stiff, yet she'd been able to stretch it throughout the day.

"And you plan to stay? Not fight for your earl any

longer?"

"Yes, Yrsa." The words were quick, cut with impatience. He prowled back to the table, his shoulders tighter than a few moments ago. "I will fight when required. When he commands me. But for right now, I plan to start enjoying my life here."

He claimed the water jug, poured the liquid into a bowl and splashed it on his face. The droplets clung to the planes of his cheekbones.

"With people like the brown haired woman you were just speaking with? Or do you have a gaggle of women trailing you around for affection?" Yrsa pressed. She'd intended to lace the words with humor. They tumbled out snippy instead.

Surprise overtook Ridley's damp features. He paused to wipe his face on his sleeve, brows descending as he thought of how Yrsa could know of a woman, then ran both hands through the unruly wave of his hair. The wet strands were tamed momentarily then sprang back to fall over his forehead.

"I was just speaking with Emma...wait, how do you know that she has brown hair?" Ridley ran his hands through his hair again then placed them on his hips, looking down at the stake in the floor to ensure the rope was properly tied. When he found Yrsa still secured, he cocked an eyebrow.

"There's a gap in the boards." Yrsa jerked her chin behind her. She didn't see the point in lying.

Eyes narrowed, Ridley inspected the boards. His sleeve brushed Yrsa's arm as he stepped close, his now familiar scent surrounding her. He dropped to a crouch to eye the gap. "Hmm, something I'll have to remedy before winter comes." His discerning stare didn't seem to care that Yrsa fumed at his side, arms crossed, bottom lip secured between her teeth.

"It looks as though she's excited to see you tonight."

Ridley shrugged as he stood, his gaze locked on the gap, distracted.

"It is possible. I told her I'd save a dance for her later, if she was still there. She has a daughter that she will need to send to bed at some point, then I might be able to ask."

Yrsa took a step back, so that she didn't reach her hands around Ridley's neck and squeeze. The fact that Ridley was looking forward to a night out, away from her and with the pretty little Emma, made her insides writhe like a barrel of snakes.

Was this what her life had been reduced to? A few kisses from rugged Ridley, and she'd forgotten her vengeance? A celebration was being held to showcase her people's failure. She was a Saxon's captive, jealous of the woman Ridley wanted to dance with.

"Well, I hope you enjoy yourself." The words had the bitter taste of an apple seed.

"I shall," Ridley replied slowly, her tone catching his attention. The pensive curve of his mouth dropped into a frown as he turned fully to her. He reached for her elbow, but she yanked her arm away.

"Yrsa..."

"Don't bother. Have a wonderful time with your

Emma..."

"She is not mine. I do not have time for a petty spat with you today. I must be there to start the festivities."

"Indeed, I am sure you do, *chieftain.* Gods forbid you spend more time with your captive than necessary. Go. Go enjoy your precious Emma and your food and your merriment. I'll be here, in the dark."

Ridley stepped to her, a slight grin curling his damned handsome mouth. He ran his knuckles along the front of her shirt, eyes like those of a hungry cat. "If I didn't know better, I would think you jealous."

"Of course I am!" Yrsa exploded, throwing up her hands, inciting protest from her shoulder. "I am stuck here in this infernal hut all day! I should be with my clan. Not waiting here for a Saxon to return home!"

Surprise coated his features but he shoved it down, recovering enough to murmur, "A Saxon? Because I'm just like all the rest in your mind?"

"Of course you are! I am captive here, while my source of entertainment is leaving for a celebration!"

Ridley flinched as if she'd struck him. He stepped back, turned, strode to the door, then came at Yrsa, palms outstretched at his sides. The sheer magnitude of such a tall man barreling at her had Yrsa pressing her back to the wall.

"Your source of entertainment? Is that all I have been to you? I thought..." he thundered. As if surprised at what he was about to say, he forced his jaw closed, trapping the words inside the cage of his teeth.

Yrsa held her breath, wishing he would hurt her with

words. She wanted the reminder that they were different. That Ridley hated her. She wanted what he said to carve its way into her soul to show her how stupid she'd been.

"No. Do not concern yourself with what I thought."

So fast she flinched, Ridley yanked the dagger from his belt and plucked the rope tied to her wrist. Despite her desire to be brave, she closed her eyes against the slash of Ridley's blade. After the kisses, the soft touches, even the taunting, she hadn't thought he would kill her. And in her last moment, her mind's eye conjured a picture of Ridley grinning down at her, the glow in his eyes making her feel like the most precious creature in the land.

Then, her arm was lighter. She opened her eyes.

Ridley had sawed through the rope. His chest heaved as he glowered at her, daring her to rush him or run. When she stood there, mouth agape, he threw the end of the rope at her. She didn't even have the wit to catch it. The length of it hit her leg with a dull thud.

"There. You're free of me. Leave after dark and do not dare hurt the people of my village or, so help me, Yrsa, you will wish that I let you die in the church." His words were sword strokes, each one a painful slice. Before she could retort Ridley turned on his heel and left the hut.

Yrsa could barely fathom it. She was free. It was so fast. With Ridley so angry.

It was all she had wanted. But instead of triumph, she felt like a stone settling at the bottom of a lake, never to feel the warmth of daylight again.

Oswald had begun the blessing by the time Ridley made it to the village square. His preacher's voice rang out over the bowed heads of the crowd, amplified by the obedient silence. Oswald's small yet pointed grabs for power hand rankled Ridley since his arrival in Hyrstow. Tonight, Ridley could barely bring himself to care.

His chest felt too tight. A light sweat broke out on his skin and his pulse throbbed in his neck. Ridley knew he'd have to be jovial with his people tonight. His friends. They'd barely seen him over the past two weeks, and they would know something was wrong. Because it was. All wrong.

He'd set her free. Had practically yelled at her on his way out. Yrsa would no longer be a burden. Ridley could concentrate on his responsibilities.

He winced as he strode forward. She called him her

"entertainment." As if none of it had mattered. He sucked in a reedy breath to steady himself. It didn't work.

Oswald finished his prayer and a buzz of voices murmured 'amen'. People stood from the dust covered ground where they knelt, various conversations rising through the early evening. An assortment of tables, several taken out of the hall where the fighting men slept, had been pushed together to make two long tables along the central space. Cut branches were woven together to decorate the tables' centers. Spiced pork, fresh herbs, butter and bread should have made him hungry. Instead, he felt as hollow as when he'd killed the woman from Guston.

"There you are!" A hearty slap on his shoulder brought Ridley from his brooding. Branton and Grahame flanked him, their cheeks flushed, as if they'd already gotten into the ale.

"Rid! What took you so long?" Grahame said, his green eyes skipping between Ridley and the crowd. Always on the lookout for a woman, not that he needed to be. He was the pretty one of the three with his bronze hair and lack of scars. People from surrounding farms had flocked to Hyrstow for the feast. There would be plenty enough women for Grahame to tangle with.

"Been busy," Ridley said. His clipped tone caused Branton to raise a black eyebrow, which Ridley ignored. He wasn't in the mood for a lecture.

"Daddy!" Branton's daughter, Ginnie, ran to him as Freda approached with a baby on her hip and their son, Neil, in her shadow.

A wide grin broke out on Bran's face as he scooped Ginnie up. He tucked her unruly chestnut hair behind her ear as he lifted her.

"I thought you were going to let Mum braid your hair for the feast?" he said.

Ginnie smiled, showing the gap where her two front teeth used to be.

Freda rolled her eyes as she approached. The baby, Æfflead, cooed at the sight of her father, pumping her chubby legs against Freda's rounded stomach. "And pigs will soon fly, I'm sure. Too headstrong. Hello, Ridley. Brother."

"Hmmm, sounds like her mother," Bran teased.

The men greeted Freda with a hug and kiss on the cheek.

"Hey, hey, back off my woman," Branton scolded good naturedly as he took hold of his wife around the shoulders with his free hand. Freda's porcelain features broke into a wide smile, the freckles across her nose wrinkling.

"Ridley need not be warned away when I have three young in tow and another in the belly! I'm sure he'll have women lined up to greet him tonight!" she teased, swatting at Bran's arm. Branton looked down at his wife, eyes full of mirth.

Ridley tried for a good-humored smile, but it felt brittle. Their casual happiness gnawed at him.

"Ah, but you do not know the allure of that ass of yours."

"Father!" Neil chided, his face stern. The boy swept

his gaze to the crowd around them to ensure nobody overheard.

Grahame belted out a laugh at his nephew's embarrassment as Branton's hand wandered over Freda's backside. Neil's face reddened.

"Oh, enough of you scoundrels. Let's go eat," Freda commanded the lot.

Grinning, the group sat at the food laden tables. Huge chunks of carved ham were surrounded with dishes of roasted carrots, potatoes, beets, and various greens. Unlit candles were set at intervals, awaiting the fall of night. The scent of fresh, yeasty bread permeated the air from the loaves that graced each table.

As the others settled, Ridley disengaged himself and walked to the smaller, central table set for the chieftain and reverend. Regret that Ridley could not eat with his friends poked his already irritated mind. He felt it a silly tradition that, as chieftain, he had to sit at a special table denoting his station. He swallowed his distemper about the arrangement, knowing that Oswald preferred it.

As the highest ranking priest, Oswald was the only clergyman to join the gathering. The others sustained themselves with pottage and prayer. Oswald had settled in a sturdy wooden chair, busying himself by glaring at Ridley as he cut open a dinner roll.

"Greetings, Father," Ridley said, infusing his voice with a heartiness he didn't feel. He settled himself on his own stool, ignoring Oswald's stare.

"It would have been nice if Hyrstow's chieftain had

been standing beside me as I conducted the opening prayer."

"You could have waited."

Oswald took great care in slathering another roll with golden butter as he spoke, his eyes on the crowd. "You could do what was needed, for once."

Ridley let the slight slide. He didn't have the fortitude to engage in one of Oswald's petty squabbles. People all around had begun to dig into the meal. Relief tugged Ridley's shoulders downward. But it was nearly done. The people of Hyrstow deserved an evening to relax. Even if he couldn't. The tightness that wound through his bones made him think he'd never relax again.

"My apologies, brother. It looks as if you had everything under control. Your blessing was superb." Ridley reached for the pile of meat on their table and snagged several slices of ham for his plate. The meat was a rare treat. The pig had been purchased by Grahame's family for the village. It was another reason was grateful for his friend. Grahame's family was the wealthiest in Hyrstow and the most generous.

"Truly, Ridley, you can't guide these people well if you are not willing to show up for them. Plus, all the gluttony and merriment of this night will undoubtedly loosen inhibitions. I'm considering an extra tithe so that I may pray over the souls of those who become wayward tonight."

Ridley's jaw hardened against his brother's words as he chewed. Oswald's greed for the church never failed to surprise him. The salty flavor of the ham turned gamey in his mouth. "I forbid you from seeking further restitution from these people after they've worked so hard."

"Restitution! Oh, don't be dramatic, little brother. I merely meant a donation..." Oswald's jeweled hand fluttered to his neck. A line of sweat peeked from the collar of his brown robe. He was a picture of surprise until his eyes hardened like chips of polished wood. He spoke under his breath. "Do you think I do not know why Lachlan sent you? He doesn't see the good I am doing with Hysrtow."

"With your many requests for 'donations'?"

Oswald's lip curled. "Indeed. All for the benefit of the church. We've had more people flocking here for prayer over the past two years than ever before. St. Paul's needs new construction. It all goes back to the patrons in some way, and yet the Earl of Deircia does not envision how beneficial a close relationship with the church would be. He's stuck in the old ways of power."

Ridley sipped from his ale, not in the mood to discuss politics. Lachlan had charged him with turning the people's hearts from the growing threat of the church. A heavy task and one that Ridley didn't think himself suited for. He'd just arrived back in Hyrstow. He didn't want to sway people from their beliefs. As unhappy as Lachlan might be about it, the most he'd done was keep track of Oswald's various donations.

"Oswald, these people have been through enough. Though I respect the church's concern for their souls, I do not wish to burden them with anything else this night."

Oswald's shrewd eyes narrowed. He was rarely, if ever, told no. However, he hated making a scene, and Ridley knew that if he opposed the tithe in front of others, Oswald would not make a ruckus about it.

"Aren't you in an excellent mood this evening," Oswald drawled. It came out stiff. Sarcasm didn't suit him.

"You need not worry about my mood."

"Would this have to do with the young lady I saw you carousing with? Has she deemed your intent as less than noble and rebuffed you? Or perhaps her father is not accepting of your possible union?"

Oswald was fishing, but the questions dug past Ridley's defenses. He ripped a piece of bread from the loaf between them. It reminded him of Yrsa's rebuff of the sweet rolls Emma had given him. Of her mouth around his fingers. Pain, as real as any sword point, lanced through him.

"Have no fear, brother; you've taught me well. My intent is noble when it comes to the woman in question. And her father is dead so there is no anger there."

The words weren't entirely true, but Oswald would never know. After keeping a woman captive, honor was not something he considered himself high on. Not that it mattered now. Yrsa would be gone when he returned. His anger dissipated at the thought. In its place was an emptiness that nearly stole Ridley's breath.

Oswald's brows pinched together as he chewed a spoonful of sweetened carrot. He turned to Ridley. "Father is dead? Was it Miss Merthe Baker?"

"Merthe? Christ, Oswald, have you no shame? She is a child!" Repulsion that Oswald would suggest such a relationship rocketed through him. Marriage to a young woman was done throughout the kingdom, but Ridley was not a man such as that.

"She is the only one without a father that came to mind. She is attractive, for a young lady. In time, if her hips widen, she could bear you many children," Oswald stated as he looked sidelong at Ridley. There was confusion in his gaze, as if Ridley was a puzzle to be solved.

"It's not her," Ridley ground the words through his teeth. He turned fully to his plate, disbelief and disgust coating the back of his throat. He knew that Oswald had never been with a woman due to his vows, but he wasn't so out of touch that he thought courting a child was acceptable, did he?

Oswald continued stuffing chunks of potato into his mouth, chewing noisily while he slurped at his ale.

Ridley could eat no more.

Finally, the meal ended, and Ridley excused himself before Oswald could utter anything further about donations. He made his way down to the long bench where Grahame, Branton, and the children had been joined by Emma and Merthe. The children laughed at one of Grahame's jokes while Freda's fingers moved up and down Bran's back. It warmed Ridley's heart to see everyone enjoying themselves. They deserved it. Despite what Yrsa believed about the Saxons, they were hardworking, honest people, every one of them.

The hollow feeling in Ridley's chest grew at the

thought of Yrsa's pert nose poking the air as she degraded him for being Saxon. Her lips had always drawn back in a snarl, as if having to assert her superiority was the only way she knew how to live. And maybe it was. But then his thoughts gave way to the memory of her smooth breast in his palm, the warmth of her curled into him at night.

Ridley had been a fool. She'd thought him mere entertainment, and she was right. He'd never be anything but Saxon scum to her. Not that it mattered any longer.

"Ridley!" Branton snagged him from his own thoughts, shaking his arm heartily. "Looked like you and your brother were having a wonderful chat up there."

Ridley scrubbed a hand across the back of his neck, sheepish that others had seen their disagreement. "Was it that obvious?"

"No. Of course not," Grahame amended, with a toothy grin, sandy curls ruffled lovingly by the breeze. "You just looked like you'd rather be boiled in oil than listen to whatever Oswald was on about."

A chuckle escaped Ridley. "Sounds right."

Thankfully, Freda passed Ridley a mug of ale from which he drank deeply. "Well, that's done now. After all your work this half fortnight, you'd better be ready for a good time." She nodded over to where a cluster of women stood near the great fire.

Ridley cut Freda a smile that he was sure looked grim. The last thing he felt like doing was dredge up flattering words for women he had no interest in.

"Get in line, Rid!" Grahame shoved at his shoulder, wiggling his eyebrows at the group. One of them, pretty, with hair like an autumn leaf giggled something to her friends. Grahame's grin widened, his dual dimples cracking his cheeks.

"I'm sure you'll have no want for attention, brother. Let Ridley have a go at them first. You can tell me about how the calving went. Are you up to your arms in lambs?" Freda said.

Grahame rolled his eyes. "Aye, I am. Pa is not inclined to get his hands dirty in his old age."

"Well, if you'd settle down, I think he'd start letting you do more at the markets. Plus, you'd have sons to help."

Grahame made a face as he waved Freda's suggestion away. "I'll be saddled with all that soon enough."

Freda rolled her eyes at her brother and settled herself on Bran's lap. He snaked an arm around her waist, placing a hand over her swollen belly. She leaned into him. Ridley's heart became an open wound at the sight. Such easy love between his friends. Their children around them. A new babe in Freda's belly.

An image of Yrsa flashed to mind, her arms around him, lips tilted upward. Her glorious stomach swelled with his child. The rush of pain he felt twist his insides nearly knocked the breath from him.

"Well, lads, I'm going to make the rounds. Isla Dunn is looking mighty fine this evening." Grahame winked at them as he made his way to the central bonfire south of the tables.

A flute rose over the conversation and, moments later, a drum joined. At the other end of the table, Ridley noticed Ginnie pull at Merthe's sleeve. Merthe, holding Æfflead beneath her chubby arms, bounced the baby on her knee. The two girls excused themselves, Merthe passing off the baby to Freda, then ran off together toward a larger group of children that danced in the light of the fire.

"How much longer do I have, do you think, before she starts noticing boys?" Emma remarked wistfully. She appeared beside him holding a mug of ale in one hand, the other across her middle, cradling her elbow, amusement in her eyes. The top half of her hair had been tied back, somewhat like Yrsa's had been the first time he'd seen her, though Emma didn't sport the intricate braids that Yrsa once did.

"I'm sure it's too late," Ridley replied.

Emma shoved his arm with her shoulder as she turned to watch the revelry around the bonfire. Many groups congregated around the blaze, while other folks enjoyed games of dice at the tables. Older women flitted about, filling jugs of ale and snatching slices of meat. The crackling of the flames and scent of woodsmoke had Ridley on edge.

"I think you might be right," she groaned, tipping her cup toward where Merthe's gaze was locked on Grahame, who had made good on his promise to find Isla Dunn. The pair were dancing in a large crowd that moved to the drum's beat, kicking up dust, laughing.

"At least she's chosen someone too old for her,"

Ridley amended. "Grahame has other women in mind. Namely, any grown woman with two legs and a heartbeat."

Emma's lips twisted upward, and she nodded. "I'm sure one leg wouldn't bother him." Ridley coughed a laugh around a mouthful of ale.

"He seems young, compared to you and Branton."

"Are you calling me old?" Ridley asked in mock offense.

Her smile crinkled the corners of her eyes. She was pretty. Ridley knew it. If Yrsa hadn't barrelled into his life, he may have found happiness with Emma. As it was, he couldn't stop thinking about the blonde Dane. Was she already gone? Did she care that she'd left him?

Ridley had been an idiot. The surprised ripple across Yrsa's features as she climaxed was something that would be imprinted on his mind for the rest of his days. He'd wanted to give her pleasure in the middle of the night, then that morning, then again in the middle of the day and when he'd caught her spying on him. He wanted her mouth on him, his on her, bringing her to the tipping point in every way imaginable. His grave mistake was finding his own mind-blowing release with Yrsa.

It had made him want to keep her. To think of ways he could convince her to stay when he knew she never would. The shame of it drove him from the bed early and made him avoid her throughout the day.

"Certainly not! You're no older than I," Emma retorted.

Ridley was shaken from the memory of Yrsa. He'd

been completely adrift and Emma was polite enough to not say anything. He looked at her over the rim of his mug as he took a drink. Emma was kind, unrelentingly so, when he didn't deserve it.

"Would you..." She turned her face up to him fully, her easy grin tentative.

"Yes?"

"Would you care for a dance?"

Ridley felt as if he'd run off a cliff face and was caught in mid-air. He didn't want to share a dance with anyone other than Yrsa. Couldn't fathom holding another woman in his arms after he'd had her in his the night previous.

But she was gone. And he, a fool, had fallen so completely in love with her, he didn't see it until it was too late. The realization was a blow that threatened to knock him backward.

He cleared his throat as he placed the mug on the table.

"That would be nice," he lied.

Emma looked up into his eyes, the smile tugging her lips wider than he'd ever seen it, and nodded.

Ridley forced himself to smile as he took Emma's hand in his. It was easy. As easy as it should have been with a woman. He imagined Yrsa's reaction if he'd politely asked her to dance. She would have tried to claw his eyes out. If he was honest with himself, he would have enjoyed it.

"Are you happy?"

"Pardon?" Ridley asked.

"You're smiling. You must be pleased with the turnout." Emma said. She had to crane her neck backwards to peer into his face.

"Indeed," he answered, though the grin dropped from his mouth as he guided Emma through the dancers, past the looks of those speculating why the chieftain and the widow were sharing a dance.

Ridley cast his gaze about the people around him, at the happiness and love, and felt like he'd never feel that warmth again.

CHAPTER
TWENTY-ONE

Yrsa wished the grinding of her teeth could drown out the sounds of merriment in the central square. From where she crouched inside the line of trees she could clearly see the spectacle that unfolded before her eyes. Ridley twirled with Emma in a group dance that left them both breathless and laughing. His friend, Branton, joined with a fair skinned, midnight-haired beauty that must have been his wife. She did her best to jaunt through the line of people with a baby on her hip. Various children streaked through the group, giggling. Other villagers weaved in and out of her line of sight, sometimes blocking Yrsa's view of Ridley's friends, then moving away to reveal him chuckling at a joke with Emma. She'd never seen him so jovial. And here she was, unable to tear her gaze from the man that stepped all over her affection. Impatience with herself needled her. She had to focus.

After Ridley unceremoniously freed her, Yrsa had stood there in shock for far too long. Her mind had felt fuzzy, trying to reason out Ridley's abrupt change in attitude. His expression betrayed something she couldn't fathom he would feel: hurt. It made her want to snatch back what she had said, which didn't make sense. She was at his mercy, not the other way around, so she shouldn't be the one to feel guilty.

Wreathed by the glow of the fire, Ridley spun Emma then pulled her to him for a slower dance. Jealous indignation simmered in Yrsa's blood. Ridley had awakened a carnal desire in her so potent, she practically salivated when she saw him. Instead of feeling the same, he freed her and sought out pretty little Emma.

She'd never be good enough. For anyone. Frustrated with her own stupidity, she shoved a tear from her eye with the heel of her hand. Loosing an unsteady breath, she slunk through the trees surrounding the east side of Hyrstow.

Yrsa needed something of value. If she was to trek her way across Northumbria, she'd need coin or gold or things to barter. Ridley had nothing in his hut, barring some fine leathers and his kitchen wares. It was too large for her, too much of a burden to carry. His swords were nowhere to be found and any money he had must have been kept in the pouch on his belt. She couldn't risk time raiding the other huts. The only place she knew held treasure was the church.

In the darkness, she could make out that the church's

rear door had been hastily repaired with some half-hewn planks secured across the hole. It was a sore disappointment, though not unexpected. The back of the church was cloaked in shadow, but the celebration nearby made her jittery. Quickly, she ran to the door, then smoothed her hands over the new wood. With a silent curse, Yrsa wished she had more in her possession than the eating knife that she'd retrieved from the cupboard in Ridley's hut. Yrsa prodded the rough edges of the jagged hole around the boards. Above the fresh pieces, the old wood chipped away into darkness beyond.

Her heart sped up. She could be the one to succeed. Even if she hadn't found her father's killer yet, she would show the others that she could do what they could not. And if her people had deserted her, she would need that treasure to buy her way out of Northumbria. Palms sweaty, she gripped the knife and began to work the blade into the wood.

She froze at the sound of footsteps approaching. Yrsa scuttled behind the safety of the bush just as a man and woman came around the corner of the church in search of privacy. Crouching as small as she could make herself —gods, she cursed her lanky frame—Yrsa hoped against all else that they would move on.

"Ridley," Emma's voice was as light and wispy as a falling feather. "It is a rare treat that you and I find ourselves alone together."

Ridley shifted from one foot to another. He scratched the back of his head. Yrsa couldn't make out his features in the dark, but his tone was buffered with good humor when he said, "Joseph is an old busybody. He only insisted I check his handiwork on the church door so that I'd have an excuse to be by myself."

Emma's laugh was tinkling. "Indeed. I particularly liked his reason that I should accompany you 'for a woman's perspective' on the repair."

A small snort escaped Emma as they laughed together.

Yrsa's breath fisted at the base of her throat. Ridley had pleasured her in a way she didn't even know was possible. He had held her as if she were a precious gem. Betrayal slid through her like a blade between ribs.

"I must admit, I did enjoy having you for supper the other night. You spend so much time alone. I am pleased you decided to join us." Emma clasped her hands in front of her, as if to stop herself from reaching out and touching Ridley's body.

"As am I. Your company has been appreciated." Yrsa could hear the grin in his words. He turned to Emma, head tilting down to look at her. Yrsa's legs tensed, ready to jump up to shove Ridley away from her.

"The home for Merthe and I is truly wonderful. Do you have the time this week to 'sup with us again?"

Ridley hesitated.

Yrsa shut her eyes. It was too much. A dark rage bloomed in her mind. It blocked out sense. Before she could witness any more of their dallying, Yrsa darted into the trees. A surprised gasp flew from Emma at the disturbance, but Yrsa did not stop.

Branches grasped her clothes. Leaves smacked her face as the dim vermilion light of the bonfire faded. As much as she wanted to run, roots and trees tried to trip her. The only way forward in the dark was to take careful, sweeping steps through the underbrush. Her pounding heartbeat made it hard for her to listen for sounds behind her. When she heard the snap of a twig, she glanced back, though saw nothing but silvery trunks. Distracted, a fallen limb caught her toe. She fell heavily to her knees, the pain shooting up her legs. Yrsa forced herself still. She tried to quiet the breaths that sawed in and out of her.

She'd run straight east. The cool scents of earth and leaves and saplings surrounded her. Damn her haste to get away from Ridley. She didn't know the lay of the land well enough to push forward. Her people had raided from the southwest. If she looped north where the foliage was thicker, she could make her way past Ridley's to the river on the west side of the village. At least it would join with the inlet where her people had shored their boats. There was a slim chance her remaining clansmen were still there. If they weren't, she'd have to find a village to steal supplies from, weapons and food, if she was to be stranded in this infernal country.

Decision made, Yrsa crept through the bush, stepping carefully so as not to fall again. As she moved toward the church, she noticed Ridley and Emma were no longer against the wall. A grin twisted her lips at the thought of them breaking apart as she rushed by. They deserved the surprise.

The crack of a twig behind her was like a blast. Yrsa froze mid-step. She stretched her hearing for all it was worth but the merriment of Hyrstow's celebration drowned out the sounds of the forest behind her. Ducking low, she made her way to the north. Each crunch of twig and leaf beneath her feet blared but she kept moving. Finally, she came around to the west, far enough that she could scent water yet still close enough to Hyrstow to see flickers of the village's light.

Something sentimental pulled at Yrsa's feet. Without meaning to, she found herself turned toward Ridley's hut for one last look. It remained simple and stoic, cloaked in darkness, alone at the edge of the village, just like its owner. Yrsa wished she could hate it, her prison. But she'd healed there. Learned that her heart sought the gruff laugh and biting words of the man who had kept her, that she craved more than the hollow promises of a betrothal to a man like Aric.

Suddenly, a figure rushed her, clamping a hand to her mouth, and clocking an arm like an iron band around her arms and middle. Yrsa twisted like an eel to break free, but whoever held her tightened their grip. Oak and ale and the sweet scent of straw shoved up her nostrils as she fought for a breath. The man was a wall of muscle that Yrsa's own body seemed to recognize even before her mind did.

"Yrsa, stop. It is me. Do not make noise; there are others nearby," Ridley breathed into her ear.

Her bones wanted to liquify at the deep timbre of his

voice, but she forced herself to remain tense like a rabbit caught in the claws of an owl, ready to bolt if given the chance. She nodded.

Cautiously, Ridley lifted his hand from her mouth, bringing it around to splay it on her lower back, his smallest finger fitting itself precariously close to her backside.

"Unhand me," she bit out, tone hushed. There wasn't a breath between their bodies. The heat from him seeped into her. If he hadn't flirted with Emma mere minutes ago, Yrsa would have enjoyed it.

"You must vow not to run away. I will not harm you." His voice soaked into her skin. She wanted to bathe in it.

"You say that now, until you tie me up in your hut."

His sigh was deep and long. It made her body rise and fall with his, eliciting such unwanted desire, Yrsa had to clench her teeth against the urge to kiss his neck.

"You are right to think that, but I promise I will not."

Yrsa peered up into the shadows of his face. There was no way for her to tell if he spoke the truth. The only thing she did know was that Ridley was not someone to take an oath lightly.

"Fine."

Ridley squeezed her body once then unlocked from around her. Yrsa crossed her arms over her breasts to ward off the loss. It needled her that it was good to see him. Even after he'd so blatantly thrown her to the side.

"You scared me," she accused. "Aren't you supposed to be enjoying the festivities?"

"Aren't you supposed to be long gone?" he challenged.

Yrsa growled low in her throat. She couldn't reveal that she sought the gold hidden in the church. He'd never let her leave if he thought that she was planning thievery. And she wouldn't allow herself to admit that she lingered because leaving Ridley was...not something she wanted to do.

"I was on my way until you stopped me."

"Really? Because it seemed as if you were skulking behind the church."

"How would you know? You were well occupied."

"Occupied? Your golden hair was like a flag as you ran into the forest."

He pinched a few strands of her hair in his fingers and held them aloft before her eyes. She smacked his arm away.

"Go back to your party, Ridley. I am on my way, and you can return to your woman." She infused strength that she didn't feel into the words.

"You know not of what you speak. I have no woman." Ridley's tone was soft. He crowded her, his bulk eating up the village's spare light.

"Don't I? It looked as if you two were having an *intimate* moment alone. I am sorry to have disturbed you."

Though dressed in shadow, Yrsa could see Ridley's shoulders sag. He rocked back on his heels, shoved a hand through his hair, took a step toward Hyrstow, then came back to stand before her. The sound of damp earth hugged his steps.

"Yrsa..." he started then halted as if he wasn't sure if his next words would make her bolt. Her name dripped from his lips as if he was wrestling for control. Finally, he held his palm up toward her. "Would you come back to the hut, and we can discuss this?"

The suggestion was such a surprise, it filled Yrsa with such uncalled-for joy that she wanted to punch herself for being foolish. "No. I am not going back there."

"Please. You have my word that you will remain free. And you can leave in peace after we talk, but I cannot risk you being found out because we are arguing this close to Hyrstow."

The entreaty was so earnest, Yrsa found herself considering it when she should have been running in the other direction. After thrusting her small knife into Ridley's gut for his betrayal.

Nearby, a male laugh rumbled through the huts, followed by another. Ridley was right; they were too close to the village. If the men sought the river, she would be found out. It was either leave or follow. She knew she had to leave but her feet pulled her toward him.

"Fine," Yrsa hissed.

When she glared rather than take his outstretched hand, Ridley withdrew it and started toward the forest edge. She followed, easing her worn boots silently along the forest floor. Woodsmoke found her nose, and all at once she had the fleeting thought that it would be nice to return to the cozy hut rather than sleep on the chilled forest floor. It made the hair on the back of her neck stand up with worry. She should have craved the freedom of the wild forest, the ability to run until her chest ached. Instead, she felt a pleased flush every time Ridley looked back to make sure she still followed.

TWENTY-TWO

"I thought you had fled," he said. Only once Yrsa was inside his hut did Ridley release a breath of relief. The streak of golden hair that had disappeared into the trees had stirred hope so strong in Ridley, he wasted precious seconds with his mouth agape. He knew it to be Yrsa. And he disregarded every instinct that told him he should protect his people, the village. It could have been another raid and he would have followed Yrsa into the underbrush.

He'd advised Emma that he would check on the disturbance. She'd agreed, a strange look on her face when Ridley requested she tell no one of it. He only hoped she would stay true to her word and not raise the alarm.

Ridley could feel the tilt of Yrsa's chin, her wide-legged stance as he stared down at her in the dark. He'd crowded her against the closed door as soon as they entered, his hands hungry to hold her. He needed to distance himself to allow proper thought. Otherwise he would kiss Yrsa and not stop. And she would likely sink her fist into his gut.

He backed away and bent to light a fire among the stones. It was too dark. Ridley wished to gaze upon Yrsa's face, to trace the curve of her cheeks with his eyes. He had her again and was wasting her presence by not being able to look at her. The spark caught quick, as if heeding his impatience.

He blew on the small flame, adding pieces of wood as quickly as he could to bring light to the room. As the hut was illuminated, he was surprised to find that Yrsa hadn't upended anything in search of a weapon. The rope remained coiled on the floor. Yrsa stood in front of the door, small knife in hand, ready to either stab him or flee.

"I should have. I should be halfway to the sea by now."

"But you are not," he prompted. Though he should have cared what she'd been doing, he was too happy to see her. Even if she stared at him with a wariness that he didn't like. She was too still, too self-contained. Ridley had seen Yrsa angry, full of self-righteous fire, but there was a coldness to her surreptitious anger that rolled off her in waves. It made him desperate to not have her turn and run.

"I haven't been able to enjoy myself all night because I've been worried about you. Wondering if someone else caught you or if you made it away from here. Obviously not."

Yrsa scoffed. She toed the floor's straw with her boot, her fingers loosening then clenching the handle of the knife in a rhythmic pattern. Bathed in the fire's glow, Ridley's gaze roved up her leather boots, the length of her trouser-encased legs. They were sinfully long and toned, he knew. His tunic belled over her hips and gathered at her waist beneath the worn belt. As Ridley drank in the sight, he felt a rush thirst for her. No other woman called to him the way she did. Her eyes widened as he gazed up at her.

"What?" Yrsa demanded. "Why are you looking at me like that?"

"I am...happy to see you."

Yrsa leaned a shoulder against the wall, arms crossed. Ridley doubted she realized the movement molded the tunic to her breasts. His hands itched to yank her to him and not let her go.

"Are you drunk? You couldn't wait to be rid of me earlier."

"I was angry."

"Angry enough to free me? Angry enough to send me on my way forever?" Her voice wavered.

Ridley stood and moved around the fire, hand outstretched. Yrsa looked at him as if he had gone mad, then released a low chuckle. The sound was husky, tantalizing. Then she spread her arms wide, her gaze spinning around the hut, finally landing on him.

"Well, look at me now. I'm stupid enough to come back here. Without force, even! I've willingly come back into the wolf's den. So, what do you want of me, Ridley?

Because your pretty words and your smiles still don't tell me."

"You!" The word flew from his mouth before he could stop it. "I want you, princess."

The words landed as if he'd hit her.

"Impossible. You want to keep me as leverage or sell me to the highest bidder. You want me here, humiliated so that you feel like you've won against the Vikings that raided you."

The bite of guilt was bitter. More than anything he wanted to hold her, to kiss her senseless but knew that he was the cause of her misery. Seeing her again— arguing with her—made his heart pound and his breath catch.

He'd left Emma to chase her, not because she was Viking. She'd added color to the drab life he'd crafted himself. An empty life of obligation that had stretched before him during dinner. And he'd been satisfied with it. As a young man, he'd witnessed his mother's slaughter and revenge drove him. He'd grown with Lachlan's guidance and then the knighthood bestowed on him. After years of fighting, returning to Hyrstow had been enough.

Until her. The bane of his existence and the woman of his dreams.

His muscles tightened in protest as he kept himself from reaching for her. Ridley would not force Yrsa to stay but could try his damnedest to convince her not to leave. He allowed a smile to soften his lips.

"The first time I saw you, you looked like a fierce,

golden goddess. You were brave and terrifying and excellent with a sword."

She tossed her head to look at the fire. "I was captured."

The words that fell from his mouth were hoarse and true, some of the hardest he'd ever spoken. "You were injured. And though I didn't know it at the time, I wanted to keep you, Yrsa. I rarely take for myself, but you were the one thing I could salvage that day. You were too precious to me, even then, for me to let you go."

Yrsa sucked a breath through her teeth. She didn't look at him, though silver lined her eyes. Heart hammering to make her understand how much she mattered, he stepped into her space, and her juniper scent made him practically salivate. Slowly, Ridley hooked her chin with his finger to direct her gaze up.

"I've been a fool. You offended my pride when you said I was nothing but entertainment. After last night, I had thought we were more than that to each other. I care for you. And I hate myself for what I've done to you. I am sorry, Yrsa. For everything."

Yrsa's bottom lip trembled as he spoke. When he finished, she pressed her lips together, her eyes searching his, wonder and confusion and heat mixing in their depths. All he wanted was to press his forehead to hers, but instead, he released her. He knew he could no longer bend her to his will. That he never truly could. If he was to win her, she had to choose him herself.

Yrsa closed her eyes and drew a shaky breath. Ridley felt as if his entire future hung in the rise and fall of her chest. If she left now, they both knew where the other stood for eternity.

"What about Emma?" Yrsa asked, straightening her shoulders as if to not be dissuaded by Ridley's entreaty. Her lips folded downward around Emma's name, brows pinched. "You say you care for me, but what about her?"

If Ridley had been bashed over the head with a log, he couldn't have been more surprised. As annoyed as Yrsa was with him, she wanted to know his intentions toward Emma. He didn't bother to hide the smile that betrayed his pleasure. Gently, he ran a knuckle down her cheek.

"It is true that she is a kind woman. I respect her." Ridley bent to peer down into Yrsa's eyes so that she could see his conviction. "But Yrsa, she is not *you*. You are the one I think about all day. You are the one I want to spar with when I return home. You are the one I lust after to the point I think I may be mad."

A short laugh of disbelief escaped her. "Ridley...I... we...I am a Dane. And..."

Heedless of her rejection, Ridley stole a kiss from the corner of her mouth, tracing his finger along the back of her neck. Time with her was slipping away. When he pulled back, her blue-gray eyes glistened with unshed tears. She took hold of his wrist and brought it down. It caused frantic wings to take flight in his chest.

"I know I shouldn't feel this way for you, but Yrsa, you've become a part of me. Even if you leave after tonight, I will pine for you. I will think of your smart mouth and the trouble you cause me. Of your heart, because as much as you hide it, you are good. And worthy. You will be seared into my mind for the rest of my days."

Yrsa's grip on his wrist tightened, the strong pads of her fingers working their way beneath the soft wool of his tunic's sleeve. She stared at him, eyes wide, as if she'd never heard him speak until that moment.

Ridley's blood thrummed, his mouth dry, but he dared say what was on his heart. "I believe we were thrust together because you were made to be with me, and I you."

As the last word left his mouth Yrsa yanked on his wrist, her lips crashing to his, forceful and fervent, as if she thought he was going to leave her again. She tasted of hawthorn berries. Tart and sweet, like the woman herself. Before Ridley knew it, Yrsa dropped the knife to plunge her hand into the hair at his nape, securing him to her. He needed no further encouragement. Taking hold of her waist, he slid his hands around the curve of her ass to hoist her against him. To help, Yrsa locked her arm about his shoulders and fit herself to him. Their tongues clashed, warring for dominance.

He'd been so wrong before, thinking he could let her go.

Yrsa's tongue delved into his mouth, thrusting against his own, taking what she wanted. Ridley's lips answered hers greedily. He pushed her against the wall so that it could support the pressure building between their bodies as his hands roamed over her bottom, her thighs, any place he could grab and grind against her. A moan broke from her, and Ridley swallowed it, drinking her breath from her body as if it was the answer to life itself. He could have stood like that all night, reveling in the feel of Yrsa wrapped around him, her heart pounding alongside his.

"I thought you didn't want to be the one to introduce me to being a woman," she gasped as he ripped his mouth away to taste the skin of her throat. Ridley gripped her ass tighter, bringing her cheeks apart and sliding her core along his hard length. Yrsa growled low in her throat.

"True, but I cannot stand anyone else having that honor, either." He worked one hand beneath the hem of her tunic to splay it against the skin of her back. She felt like the finest silk. After thinking he'd never see her again to having her in his arms, Ridley's body thrummed with need. But he wouldn't take what she couldn't give. He forced his body to still. He would give her the choice if it killed him.

"Unless, you do not wish to have me," he said, ready to set her down. "I mean it, Yrsa, tell me, and I will stop."

Yrsa clamped her thighs around his hips, locking him in place.

"Put me down, and you will not see me again," she snarled, then stamped her lips upon his once more.

The kiss was all tongues and teeth. It would have hurt if not for the grins that had turned up their mouths. With the last of his concentration, Ridley steered them to the bed.

Yrsa pressed her hips into him, her lips moving from

his mouth to his neck, then ear and back to his mouth. It was as if he were a delicacy that she could not get enough of. He couldn't help the groan that worked up his throat as she nipped at the skin below his ear.

"Did I hurt you?" she asked as he knelt on the bed, the mattress sinking from their combined weight. Yrsa clung to him.

Ridley chuckled. "Only if pain is like heaven. Do it again."

Emboldened, Yrsa secured her teeth to the skin of his neck and bit down. The sting shot straight to his throbbing cock.

"Yrsa," he breathed, squeezing her ass.

Her hands were everywhere, moving around his neck, dipping beneath the collar of his tunic, skating up his back. It was as if she'd dreamt of all the ways she'd wanted to touch him but was too impatient to settle for one. He knew the feeling. Not wanting to release her but needing to touch her elsewhere, he loosened his grip on her backside, allowing her to prop up on her knees. Yrsa moved as if she read his mind, mouth fused to his, her hands securing themselves to his shoulders.

"Ridley," she breathed as she scraped her teeth along his bearded chin, "I want you."

Ridley tried for gentleness as he marveled at the feel of her ribcage beneath the breadth of his hands, his thumbs skating the sides of her breasts. Yrsa sucked a gasp through her teeth. Ridley grinned as he weighed them. The small peaks fit perfectly into his hands. Desire raced through him like a horse through a field. He needed to taste them.

"Yrsa, I want your clothes off."

"You do?" she teased.

Like lightning, it struck Ridley that Yrsa was a virgin. No matter how her kisses consumed him like fire, he pulled back with the reminder that he was about to ruin an unwed woman. Yrsa stared, her jeweled eyes unblinking. As she sensed his hesitation, her swollen lips curled upward in a devilish smile. Unbothered by his pause, she pressed her lips to his collarbone. He clenched his eyes shut at the pleasure that swamped him.

"Yrsa..." he began, leaning back to garner space. She moved with him, hands tightening around his neck.

"Don't," she whispered. "Don't say what you're about to say."

"What am I about to say?"

She moved against him like a cat along a person's leg when they want to be stroked.

"That you won't take my maidenhood. That your honor won't let you. That you won't be the monster of my life any more than you already have been. Am I right?"

Ridley couldn't help the smirk that formed. She knew him. Yet he also knew her. Yrsa would not stand to give herself to someone unwillingly, even if it were one of her own people.

"You are," he admitted, smoothing his hands down her sides to settle around her waist.

"If you are so concerned for me then heed my words

well, Saxon. I want a night with you. I want—no, need—you to quench the thirst I have for you."

Ridley's lips tipped upward, relief flooding him. He felt as if he'd wanted her for years. "Aye, I can do that. And, you should know, I will need you naked for how well I am about to enjoy you."

Yrsa's eyes filled with smoky heat. "Well then, show me, Ridley."

Ridley sat back between her legs and undid the belt at her waist. He gathered the material of her tunic in his hand. It scraped along her flesh, revealing her gloriously naked form as he pulled it over her head. She tossed her white-gold mane as her head was freed. It was all Ridley could do to not be struck dumb by her beauty. Somehow, the glow of the fire and the sweetness of her desire had sharpened her cheekbones, the underside of her chin. His thumb traced the welted scar that rose against the muscle of her shoulder. It had begun to heal well. Ridley leaned down and placed a kiss on the puckered tissue.

"Does it hurt?" he asked.

Yrsa swallowed heavily before answering. "Not any longer."

As if she knew he wanted to see more of her, she fell backwards on the mattress. The glow from the fire flickered, casting light and shadow along her body. She watched him as he devoured her breasts with his eyes. Her belly was taut and long, the skin delicate as silk. Unlike some of the Saxon women Ridley had been with in the past, Yrsa didn't cower or try to cover herself.

Instead, she propped herself on her elbows, leisurely waiting for him to do what he promised.

"You're perfect, princess," he muttered. Ridley's cock pushed at the confines of his trousers, needing to be unleashed.

"You mustn't be surprised. You saw me last night."

Ridley slowly shook his head as he traced his fingers up her sides to mold his hands to her breasts. He leaned down to tug one nipple into his mouth while he gently rolled the other between his deft fingers. Yrsa hissed through her teeth. He paused to answer her before switching sides.

"Yesterday..."

Yrsa clutched the back of his head as he scored her other nipple with his teeth. Her fingers threading through his hair urged him on.

"...was amazing. I've replayed it in my head a hundred times since. I will never get enough of seeing you."

Her lower legs clutched the sides of his knees, as if to lock him in place.

"I did not expect this to feel good," she admitted around a breathy chuckle.

Ridley grinned. He ran his fingers beneath the waistband of her trousers, slowly. She tensed. "Oh princess. We're just getting started."

Ridley made quick work of her clothing, stripping her bare, only to come to a halt at her boots. With impatience he unlaced the layers of leather, finally tossing the complicated thing at the door. Yrsa snickered, biting her lip as she watched him struggle. Her smile fled when he rose, and she saw the pure craving in his gaze.

Her hips flared over long shapely legs contoured with muscle. He appreciated that she wasn't soft like other women. Strong, stubborn, her beauty scored from pain and a life of training. Ridley was so hard for her his skin felt tight. All he wanted was to thrust inside of her. He couldn't. He'd always cared about his partner's pleasure, but with Yrsa, if he was to be her first, he yearned to be her best.

"Ridley." Yrsa sat up to reach for him. "This isn't fair. Your clothes are still on. I wish to see you."

With a grin she snatched the hem of his shirt and pulled upward, revealing the grooves of his stomach. Her progress was impeded by the belt slung along his waist. To help, Ridley grasped Yrsa's chin between his thumb and forefinger to pull her face up so that he could snatch a kiss. He undid his belt, dropped it on the floor then whipped his shirt over his head. As if she couldn't wait any longer to feel him, she began to press hot, wet kisses on the muscles there, trailing her lips across and up, over, and down. His cock throbbed, begging to slide into the hot cavern of her mouth.

Ridley didn't miss when Yrsa's eyes skittered over the dagger in the discarded belt's leather. But then she focused on the rest of him, eyes locked on his groin as he stood, thrust his pants down his thighs, and kicked them off. Her mouth opened as she stared at his length protruding before her. Ridley's pride came in like a bear.

A wide grin spread across his mouth. Yrsa's legs pressed together, as if for protection.

"That...is to go inside me?" She visibly gulped.

"It is," he replied gruffly, wrapping his hand around the base of his length. He eased his grip upward, squeezing his tip, then stroking down. Yrsa's hungry eyes followed his movement. "But I promise you will like it. You can touch it. Get to know the feel of it."

Never one to back down from a challenge, Yrsa reached a tentative hand out and curled it around his shaft. She kept her hand loose and ran her hand up, then down the length. Ridley cursed, his heart pounding. Yrsa stopped.

"I am sorry. I..."

"No. I like the look of you doing that to me. Here let me show you." Ridley took her hand within his and wrapped it snugly around himself. With a calming breath, he steered her hand downwards, around the base, then up. He let her circle her hand around the blunt head, showing her the pressure he craved, then down, all the while forcing himself to remain still rather than thrusting into her palm like an animal.

"Christ, woman, that feels good."

A smile curled her lips. Gaining confidence, she stroked him again, then took his bullocks in the other hand, testing the weight of them. Desire coiled in Ridley's lower stomach and trickled through his thighs. She glanced up at him from beneath her lashes as she circled his tip, licking her lips like she wanted to taste him but wasn't sure. The innocence in such a confident woman made Ridley's mind swim. He needed to touch her. Gently, he took her wrists, pulling her up to plant a kiss on her mouth.

"Now it is my turn to explore."

Yrsa's grin turned shy as Ridley guided her to lay back on the bed, his body following. Her body was stiff. Taking care not to crush her, he braced his arms on either side of her head.

"It's alright, princess," he murmured, placing a kiss on her neck then sucking the tender skin. She gasped, her hands flying to his sides.

"I know it is," she retorted, reverting to the tone she used when she thought he was being an idiot. Ridley grinned against her as he kissed his way to the slope of her breasts. He palmed the round flesh as he kissed and licked his way down her stomach to the dip of her naval. His fingers moved hungrily along her sides as he went, his ministrations eliciting all sorts of little pants and moans from Yrsa. Her skin tasted like warm wind and midnight air. Ridley wanted her in his bed forever.

The thought should have alarmed him. There could be no forever with Yrsa.

"Do you want me to stop?" he asked, to distract himself from thoughts of Yrsa splayed under him, over him, against the wall, for the rest of his life.

"Do not dare," she said, twisting her hand into his hair to hold him to her. He chuckled, moving lower to score his fingers along the sensitive flesh that connected her thigh. He planted a kiss in the wake of his finger.

Yrsa tensed. She pressed herself into the mattress,

trying to back away. He stamped a kiss on the inside of her leg and looked up at her, the length of her body splayed out like a map that he wanted to learn. His heart pounded. She was exquisite.

"Ridley..." she said, her tone thin, "I do not know... do you have to be down there for us to join?"

Ridley wasn't about to let uncertainty ruin her pleasure. He anchored his hands about her hips, yanking her closer to his face. With a grin he dipped his head to blow lightly on her. Yrsa gasped, mouth dropping open.

"Shhh. Lean back, princess. Let me feast on you."

She stared down at him with a question in her eyes. Her decision felt like an eternity as her sweet slit begged to be licked, with her bottom lip anchored between her teeth in a way that made Ridley's cock throb.

Finally, she nodded. Ridley dipped his head and touched his tongue to the sensitive skin before him. Yrsa tasted of musk and dawn and honey, a nectar that caused a burning need he'd never known to slam through him. He wanted more with this woman. Everything.

Yrsa sucked in a breath as his tongue sought out the sensitive nub between her legs. Hands still on her hips, he swirled the nub with his tongue then sucked it into his mouth.

She muttered what Ridley thought were Danish oaths as her hips jerked upward involuntarily, giving him better access. Ridley set to work, licking her softly then stronger, his tongue a weapon and Yrsa's body the battlefield. Soon she became greedy, thrusting herself into his face, eager to find release. Ridley had thought that pleasuring her would allow his body to calm, however her enjoyment only caused his blood to pound heavier through him. Impatient with himself, Ridley strangled the base of his cock and stroked, hard.

"Oh, Ridley," Yrsa moaned, as she melted into the mattress, "I like when you do that to yourself."

Ridley almost came in his hand. He hadn't been aware she was watching. Never had a woman he'd been with expressed such a thing. He pumped himself one more time, his eyes locked on hers, then halted. They only had tonight, and he'd be damned if he was going to put his own pleasure before hers. Gently, he sucked her bud into his mouth while he rimmed her entrance with the tip of a finger. He placed his other hand on top of her belly to steady the jolt of her hips. She panted as he flattened his tongue, giving several long licks upward, then crested her entrance with his finger, pausing to allow her to adjust, and pushed forward in search of the spot that would garner her the most pleasure.

"Oh, Ridley," Yrsa gasped as her inner muscles worked him. Ridley held a curse within his teeth; she was so damn responsive. Slowly at first to get her used to the feel, Ridley began to pump his finger in and out as he laved and sucked her. Yrsa's hips undulated, seeking her release with an urgency that made Ridley speed up.

Yrsa chanted 'yes' between bouts of foreign words inciting his own lust until he thought his heart would burst. Eyes closed, delicate brows tented, she chased her release. Ridley worked her until Yrsa sucked a breath through her teeth, pulsing around his finger. Gently, he pressed a kiss on the inside of her thigh as he withdrew, sitting back on his haunches to admire the view. Under the flickering glow of firelight, Yrsa splayed before him in all her golden-haired glory was a memory he wanted branded into him.

"That was..." She groaned, then threw back her head, an elated smile curling her lips. "Is it always like that? Is this why men like sex so much?"

Ridley shrugged as he slid his hands up her long thighs, savoring the feel of her skin. Placing his bent arms on either side of her head, he nipped a quick kiss before responding.

"It is for men. It's easy for us to come to completion though it takes more effort for a man to pleasure a woman properly. And often the man does not desire to take the time."

Yrsa raised a delicate eyebrow and snorted. "Men are pigs."

Ridley chuckled. "Aye, princess, you're probably right."

"But...maybe you're the exception." A wicked gleam twinkled in her eye as she reached between them and wrapped her hand around the insistent appendage that protruded from between his legs. With authority, she pumped him once, twice.

"Definitely not," he rasped. Her husky laughter enveloped them before she caught his mouth in another kiss. This one was slow, hypnotic torture that made him forget his need to thrust into her and instead demanded he focus on the softness of her mouth. It made his heart feel as if it were cracking open, swallowing him into the abyss that was Yrsa.

Yrsa released him, drawing her hand along the ridges of his stomach, ribcage, then around to his ass, urging him forward. "I want more from you, Ridley."

Ridley pulled back to look into her eyes. "I will go slow," he promised.

Yrsa bit her lip and nodded. Her trust was a heady elixir. Circling his hand around the base of his cock, he spread the evidence of her previous release along himself as he crested her entrance. Yrsa's legs quivered, the only sign of her nerves.

Dipping his head, Ridley secured his mouth to hers, inching himself forward. Yrsa clamped around him like a vice. He grimaced from the toll of restraint when his body begged for him to plunge forward. When he was half-way entrenched in her, Yrsa grasped his buttocks, urging him onward.

"I will not break, Ridley. I can take some pain. Now move," she commanded. The words were his undoing. His control shattered. He wanted Yrsa with every fiber of himself. Stamping a kiss on her mouth, he thrust home.

TWENTY-THREE

Yrsa had imagined the pain to be akin to the stab of a knife. It wasn't. Her inner muscles felt pinched and stretched but there was also a deep knowledge that if Ridley moved, the sensation would dissipate. Ridley had stalled as he pushed himself to the hilt, letting Yrsa adjust.

"Yrsa?" Ridley asked, strain lacing his words. "Are you alright?"

She nodded. Tears rushed to the corners of her eyes. Yrsa doubted anyone else would have bothered to check on how she felt. Yrsa knew the outcome would have been different with Aric, so emboldened by his own love of himself. Concern wouldn't combat lust like in Ridley's tawny gaze.

"Princess? I can stop." Ridley's arms vibrated with restraint beside her head, his belly quivering with the need to move. After everything, it struck her how utterly perfect this moment was and how deeply grateful she was that it was Ridley taking her maidenhood.

"I'm fine, Ridley. But I need all of you." Yrsa kissed him, full and hard, and as he dragged himself out of her and thrust inward, she knew that she would never be able to forget Ridley or this place or all that had happened to make her care for him.

Between one breath and the next, the sensation of her muscles stretching past their capacity eased. An echo of the feeling when Ridley's face was between her legs flickered low in her belly, promising more. Impatient, Yrsa dug her heels into the mattress and ground herself onto Ridley as he drove forward. A wicked grin spread over his mouth, one that made her heart flutter unsteadily. Even as she told herself that she was doing this for her, to choose who to give her maidenhood to, her feelings for Ridley kept getting in the way. He had been so courteous, so careful of lavishing her with affection, it was difficult to not feel the void of her heart burst with longing for more of him.

His eyes, like twin embers, burned with an intensity she hadn't seen before as he gripped her hips. She loved the pressure of his fingers. The sight of his arms bulging, sweat slicking his skin while he plunged in then out of her feathered the aching pulse between Yrsa's legs.

"Ridley, this is too good. It's..." Yrsa moaned, her words lost between snatches of breath. Tingles raced up and down her limbs, sparkling like firelight. Ridley called forth a magic in her, one that she now feared she would not be able to conjure without him.

"Harder," she gasped. She smoothed her hands along the hard bands of his stomach and up to his shoulders. Ridley growled deep in his chest as she kissed her way across his jaw then sunk her teeth gently into the skin below his ear. He seemed to enjoy that spot very much which made it Yrsa's new target. He withdrew then surged forward again, then again, each time slicing her to the quick.

"As you wish," Ridley gritted. He reared up on his knees causing him to hit a certain spot inside of her. Pleasure was like an arrow through her. All she could do was grasp the bedclothes beside her as she moaned.

"Yes, yes, Ridley..." Each time he sheathed himself, the pressure mounted. Yrsa chased it. She shoved her hips against his. She wanted the feeling, the release. And she wanted Ridley to experience the same pleasure with her. It hit her suddenly, like a lightning strike, how much she wanted to be the vessel of his pleasure.

"That's it, love. Let go," Ridley ground out.

Yrsa couldn't stop herself if she wanted to. Ridley drove into her, rutting her into the bed and suddenly Yrsa clenched around him in a flash of liquid heat. The world narrowed to a pinpoint of pleasure, then broke apart, throwing Yrsa into a gambit of stars. A moan of satisfaction spilled through her lips as she went limp.

Ridley surged into her twice more, before pulling out. Gipping his thick cock in hand, he stroked himself as milky liquid jetted onto the blanket beside her hip, his entire body jerking with the force of his release. It was the most arousing thing Yrsa had ever witnessed—this rugged, giant of a man coming undone. When he was finished, he rolled over top of her and settled on her other side.

They lay in silence, breaths sawing in and out as they stared at the thatched roof. Tingles of satisfaction warmed Yrsa's entire nether region. She was pure liquid, her body heavy with the weight of her bones. She considered never moving again. Ridley's bed seemed like the appropriate place to stay for the rest of her days if he agreed to do what he just did to her again. And again. And again.

Before Yrsa could reason out that her desire to stay was completely unjustified, Ridley turned to his side and secured his heavy arm around her middle, dragging her into the warmth of his body. He was damp with sweat and smelled of a heady musk that Yrsa considered her new favorite scent.

"How are you feeling?" he asked, nuzzling her ear. A smile spread her lips as effectively as Ridley had spread her legs. She reached back and wrapped a hand around the back of his neck. Idly, she wondered if sex turned all women into giddy puddles.

"Mmm. Very good."

She could feel his grin against her earlobe. "I'm glad."

Lazily, Ridley splayed his hand against her belly, his rough palm tracing a line to her breast, then down to her thigh and back.

"You have," he paused to dip a kiss to the skin of her neck. "the most perfect body."

Yrsa snorted. "I hardly think so. My mother always

told me I was too tall. With muscles like a boy and too small of breasts."

Ridley clasped her chin between his thumb and forefinger, tipping her face back to his for a kiss while he strummed her nipple. His chest hair tickled her back and the constant movement of his hands on her was like adding wood to the dying embers of a fire.

"Your mother didn't know what the hell she was talking about." There was an edge to his tone which Yrsa took as a compliment. She grinned into his mouth as he kissed her again.

"You are beautiful. And I love that you can fight, which molded your body into the perfect match for mine." His words were tiny treasures that Yrsa locked inside her heart. Indeed, Yrsa knew she had a pleasing face, but she also knew that most men preferred their women curvy.

"You are kind," she allowed with a dip of her chin.

Ridley laughed, teeth flashing as his head fell back. "Kindness has nothing to do with it." He flexed his hips forward into her. The movement caused a little thrill to settle down in her belly. She wanted him again.

"Even though I am Viking? The other Saxon women will be disappointed that you didn't remain at the celebration to court them."

The slow curl of Ridley's lips made Yrsa's heart flutter. "So, you admit your jealousy?"

Yrsa allowed a wry grin and met his eyes. She didn't blink so that he knew how serious she was. "Yes. And even now I battle with the knowledge that I must leave you tonight. But know that I am forever grateful to you for lying with me."

"Don't make it sound like I did it out of pity." He laughed. Satisfied, he brushed a kiss to the bridge of her nose then pushed off the bed to add a few logs to the fire. Yrsa stood to recover the tunic Ridley had given her and shrugged it on. The thing bagged on her but she loved how the soft fabric whispered against her skin. She pulled on her underclothes and trousers, but then Ridley caught her around the waist, lifting her to him for a kiss. She melded into him.

Instead of putting on her boots like she should have, Yrsa clung to Ridley as he brought them back to the bed. Darkness had fallen. She needed to leave under the cover of night. But it was as if her bones were made of oiled rope. All she wanted at that moment was to explore Ridley's body.

It was breathtaking. The muscles of his stomach begged to be licked and Yrsa yearned to drag her hands over the dusting of hair along his thighs. She didn't know if he would want to again, but she felt giddy and adventurous at the prospect of taking more time with Ridley. She had a shocking urge to please him. Never had she wanted to please a man. Or anyone, for that matter. She wished to watch Ridley come undone inside her again.

The urge should have propelled her out the door.

"You will make me blush if you keep staring at me like that, princess," Ridley said around a smile. Her grin was mischievous as he settled beside her and looped an arm about the top of her shoulders.

She settled back into him, relishing in the heat of his body. Greedy, she ran her hand through his chest hair and down his middle, brushing her fingers around his body until her hand reached the tip of the large scar at his hip. The skin was dented, the deep groove of folded tissue running from the top of his hip to the middle of his thigh.

"When did you get this? Was it in battle?" she whispered. Ridley had shared with her about his family though not much else. She knew him to be a warrior, though the scar looked old. Suddenly, she wanted to know him. Despite their intimacy, she was unsure if he'd be in the mood to discuss the past. He owed her nothing.

Ridley didn't speak. Instead, he caught her chin between his thumb and forefinger, rolling to his side so that he could press a feather-light kiss to her lips. When he pulled away, his ochre eyes were filled with grief.

"The man that invaded our hut gave me this. He was surprised that my mother and I were there. I'm not sure why. They raided under the cover of night, so we were caught off guard. There were many still in their homes. I wrestled out of my mother's grip and ran at him with one of my father's short swords. Got a good slice across his arm, too. But he shoved me back and stuck his sword in my leg. My mother, God rest her, tried to pull him away so the sword glanced around and up. He hobbled me, then finished off my mother."

Yrsa ran her fingers over the divots to the leg muscle and back. The sword had gone deep. And the thought of a dark haired, gangly little boy charging a man to protect his mother caused a lump like an egg to fill her throat.

"I'm sorry that you had to endure that," she murmured, snuggling closer. Guilt, heavy and laden with self-loathing, settled like a mantle on her shoulders. Her people had done the same. Ridley seemed to sense the way her thoughts delved. He ran his knuckles across her cheek and down her neck, clasping her shoulder.

"It is in the past. When I was older, I settled that blood feud."

"I'm glad. How?"

"When I was sixteen, a group of us banded together and hunted down the raiders. Some had already died. Most were from a village in the neighboring earldom of Bernira. When we'd rung from them what reasons we could, Bran, Grahame and I took the last living man to Lachlan, the Earl of Deircia. He'd only been in power for a short while, and it was the first time I'd met him." Ridley smiled, lost in the memory. "We were impudent brats at the time, demanding an audience when none was warranted. But Lachlan granted it. He got what he needed from our prisoner then allowed me to drive a sword through his gullet."

"What did he need?"

Ridley bounced a hand on his knee. When he peered down at her, she felt the weight of what he was about to tell her settle in her stomach.

"Confirmation. The men were sent by Eadric, the Earl of Bernira. He and the Earl of Deircia hate one another and, at that time, their skirmishes were at the verge of all out war. Lachlan was pleased by what we did and asked us to join his ranks."

Yrsa felt a glimmer of pride for the young orphan Ridley once was. "All of you?"

"Grahame was sent home. He was fourteen at the time. A small, rangy thing. His parents are shepherds. Lachlan knew not to embroil their only son in his own battles. Bran didn't want to stay. By that time, he'd fallen in love with Freda, Grahame's sister, and they had a child, Neil. He didn't want to be apart from them to fight a war that wasn't his."

"And you did?"

Ridley brushed his palm along her upper arm, the tips of his fingers tickling her scar. He pressed his lips together. There was a battle waging behind his eyes.

"I already know how it ends, Ridley," Yrsa said softly. She pressed a kiss to his shoulder and when she looked up, he was staring at her.

"I did," he said, his eyes liquid gold. His mouth folded into a line, disappearing beneath his beard before he said, "I remained with Lachlan for seven years. In that time, I learned weapons, strategy, and the most effective way to kill a man. And the best ways to make one suffer. I've done terrible things in the name of protecting my men and my mission, Yrsa."

"Do you think that scares me?" she breathed, holding his stare. "You are a warrior, made from nothing but your own will. Naught in this realm that calls to me more than that."

The way Ridley's features melted into a grin would

stick in her memory for the rest of her life. It was as if the boulder that had covered the cave to his spirit had been pushed open. He scrunched his nose at her as he molded a hand to her breast.

"Of course, you aren't fazed by my past, Viking princess. You've likely slain more than I." The words were said with mirth, yet they fell heavily against Yrsa's pride. Her throat felt too dry as she spoke.

"You are mistaken. I have not killed."

Ridley's brows shot to the roof. "You haven't?"

Yrsa ducked her head, embarrassed. "No. This was my first raid. I was put at the back. I had the chance to kill but didn't feel the need to take it. It shames me to say that I wished to slay you. Your death would have bestowed me with notoriety."

"Yrsa." Ridley sat up, causing her to straighten. She knew that he was about to tell her to leave. "You've been trying to kill me since you got here."

There was a teasing quality to the words. Yrsa looked over her shoulder at him to find him smiling. "In multiple ways."

The tightness in her chest eased. He wasn't going to kick her out right then. She didn't want to examine why that was such a relief. Instead, she twisted her mouth into a petulant scowl.

"And I've failed at that like I've failed at everything else," she retorted, tipping her nose into the air. Ridley barked out a laugh and took her by the waist, hauling her up and over him so that one of each of her legs was settled on either side of his. The pose left her open, her clothing the only barrier between them. She was happily surprised to feel Ridley's thick desire for her. Heat from the fire caressed her back. Ridley clamped his hands over her thighs, securing her in place. He pressed his lips to her forehead. Yrsa didn't think she'd ever felt more cherished.

The softness in Ridley's gaze made something inside her grow, like the stalk of a flower rising to the sun. "And what of your blood feud? You said you came here looking for the man that killed your father. How are you to find him?"

Yrsa searched the roof, as if the answer could be found there. She had no idea where to start looking. Naively, she had assumed searching for one tall, dark-haired Saxon in the coastal lands of Northumbria wouldn't be difficult. With Aric by her side and his knowledge of what the killer may have looked like, she would have been able to find him. But dark, gruff men were all she'd seen.

"My oath for vengeance is what brought me here. Aric and Harald were the ones who saw the man that did it. And they no longer live. But the years are long. Now, I won't be encumbered by marriage. Both my parents are dead. I've nothing to return to. First, I must see if my people are still shored at the river or if I've been abandoned. I can't very well go traipsing around Northumbria by myself, demanding to know who killed him. I will have to return. Maybe with my friend, Vidar. If he is still alive."

"What did he look like?"

"My height, light brown hair, crooked nose. He has a grin like a snake and moves like water." Affection rose in her as she thought of him.

"I don't remember him from the raid," Ridley said, his tone dismissive. His brows dropped. "Your camp is no longer. We've already searched there for the missing women." He swallowed, as if not finding those women caused him pain.

Yrsa's heart dipped. She had suspected that survivors would move on, but to hear the truth made her cold with abandonment.

Then Ridley's hands tightened on her legs, and he sucked a breath through his teeth. "You have nowhere to go. I worry."

Affection curled through her. She gave him a sad yet determined grin. "And yet I cannot stay."

Ridley nipped a kiss to her lips, then her neck, his hands roaming over the plane of her back as if to secure her to him. His breath ghosted along her neck as he spoke into her skin. "Yrsa, you are injured."

"Nearly healed." She laid a hand on his chest to push herself upward. His words of concern ate at her for they echoed her own doubt.

Eyes like pools of heated bronze stared back. "I would never force you to stay again. I know you can take care of yourself. Yet, I fear for you."

"Ridley..." She had no words of comfort. So she ran a hand through the hair of his chest, savoring the feel of the hard muscle beneath and planted a kiss on his mouth. He opened to her, tongue taking hers as if to slake his thirst before a long journey. She wove her hands through the hair at his nape and when she forced herself to pull away, she was dizzy with sheer want.

"I could help."

The words struck Yrsa mute. She opened her mouth, then closed it, shock ricocheting through her. She sat up, her tongue tripping over the question that Ridley rushed to answer.

"I do not think it was anyone from Hyrstow. The timing of your father's raid does not coincide with any I know of here. And I stand by my people. If I find out it was one of them, I cannot offer the man up for your vengeance, even though I understand it. But if it was someone from afar, another earldom...I could ask around, at least." Ridley's voice was soft, cupping the idea in invitation.

"You would do that?"

"I could inquire at the seasonal markets in Eoforwic. Maybe someone remembers something helpful. It would reduce bloodshed, I think, if you came to me first, and got whatever information I could supply."

Yrsa hadn't considered returning to Hyrstow or ever seeing Ridley again. But now that the prospect was put in front of her like a gift, she realized how much she would love the help of someone she could trust. Like a strike over the head, it dawned on Yrsa that she did trust him, that it was possible he was the man she trusted most in this world.

"It is a good idea. I could come under the cover of night and sneak back into Hyrstow without bloodshed."

Ridley's grin was one of relief as if he'd thought she'd turn him down. It made her feel giddy. A day ago, she would have. But in a matter of hours, with her freedom before her, Yrsa realized her feelings for the brawny Saxon had grown into something else. Something that mingled desire and understanding and respect. And with those feelings came a sense of duty toward him. It was one thing to be selfish, but another to risk him for her vengeance.

"Ridley, it will take months, possibly a year or longer for me to return. You have a life to live. And a future wife and children that you would risk by having me come back."

Ridley's frown was deep as he shook his head. He ran his knuckle down the side of her cheek before cupping her face. She leaned into it. He said softly, "There won't be a wife. Or children."

His words confused her. Ridley was a virile man, a man that needed a mate.

"Why not? You could marry Emma, or someone else and..."

"I will wait for you to come back to me, Yrsa," he replied, quietly. His thumb stroked her cheek. "If it takes years, I will wait. The risk is mine."

Yrsa's mouth dropped open as she absorbed what he was saying. To take no wife, to father no children because of *her*. Satisfaction was like a drum beat in her chest. Until she'd heard his words, she didn't realize how much she craved him to be hers. To know that he wasn't making a life with someone else, wasn't finding happiness in another woman's arms.

And as much as she didn't want to be with another man in the future, she couldn't doom him to a life of waiting.

"But Ridley, I would only be able to return for a night."

His arm settled around her waist, pulling her against his torso. Her breasts squashed into the muscle of his chest as he kissed her deep and long, tangling his tongue with hers as if she was made of the sweetest nectar. His hard length was insistent between her legs.

"Then one night we shall have. And I will continue to wait in case it strikes you to come back to me again. And if you marry, I will remain here, if one day you ever tire of your Viking husband and want to visit me again."

A thrill spun through Yrsa's belly at the depth of his promise. The word 'yes' pulled at her lips. She wanted Ridley to pine for her as she would him. She wanted to know that she could return to his bed, even just for stolen moments. The urge to bind Ridley to her so that their bond could not be broken was swift and sure and completely terrified her.

Before she could answer, the door was thrown open and chaos rained down upon them.

TWENTY-FOUR

"You knew this would happen, Rid." Branton tried to keep pace as Ridley shoved through the crowd that had formed around his hut. Bodies pressed in from all sides, men smelling of drink, women's eyes thirsty for a glance at the commotion. Ridley wanted to heave up his supper.

They'd come out of nowhere. Oswald, then Branton, had stormed in. Yrsa had just enough time to throw on her boots and belt before Oswald snatched her hands together with the length of rope on the floor. He didn't say a word to any of them. Oswald simply bound Yrsa, a smug grin of triumph curling his lips.

She hadn't put up a fight. That's what sent Ridley into a shouting match with Bran, shoving the other man into the wall, trying to get in front of her. It was too late. Fear was layered in the wide-eyed glance she threw him before she made her face a frozen mask and followed

Oswald out. A din had risen from outside, questions echoing into the night. Ridley somehow gained the presence of mind to yank on his own clothing.

Now, enclosed in people, Oswald jerked the rope that led Yrsa forward. The view of her tangled hair bobbed in and out of the swollen crowd. People rose on their toes as they followed the spectacle to the village square, severing Ridley's view. It was all he could do to not injure anyone as he shoved through.

"Oswald!" Ridley shouted. The depth of night was broken by the vermilion glow of the torches others held aloft. Oswald shot him a glare for the use of his first name in public, but Ridley's care of formalities had long fallen by the wayside. Yrsa's blonde head did not turn at his outcry. Her shoulders were straight, graceful neck tall.

He had to get to her. There had been enough ale consumed that night that everyone stunk with drink and bad judgment. Sweat slipped down Ridley's spine. A buzz of excited murmurs coursed through the crowd like a flock of birds taking flight. The scent of roast ham that hung in the air was cut with sour ale and close-knit bodies. The bonfire still burned bright, but against the flush of people learning there was a Viking present, it was more menacing than warm.

"Rid, listen to me." Someone strong grabbed his arm from behind, preventing him from plowing forward.

Without thought, Ridley closed his hand, reared back and let it fly. His fist landed squarely on Bran's jaw. The other man released him, hand to face, a look of pure incredulity smeared across his features. Ridley didn't stick around to see if Bran was going to fight him. Instead, he moved forward. Relentless fear for Yrsa chewed his gut.

Suddenly, someone threw a handful of dirt at Yrsa as Oswald pulled the rope past the tables offering remnants of food. Another picked up a mug and threw the dregs of the drink at her feet. Yrsa didn't react, though Ridley knew she must have been chomping at the bit to fight back. His only solace was that she knew she was outnumbered. A fight now would mean her certain death, but then, Yrsa had never been afraid of dying.

"Ridley!" Grahame pushed against the grain of bodies to get to Ridley. "People are saying you were keeping a Viking in your hut. Is it true?" Grahame's green eyes were wide, disbelief written on his face. Even in the black of night, his blonde hair was tousled, bits of straw clinging to the ends, as if he'd been rolling in it. If Ridley cared about anyone but Yrsa at that moment, he'd wonder with whom.

"It's true," Ridley replied with a clipped nod. He didn't have time to explain. He had to get to Yrsa before Oswald decreed her killed. It was in his power.

Another way he'd utterly failed. Lachlan had assigned him to Hyrstow in order to make inroads with the church. Oswald was gleaning too much authority. Ridley had been sent to garner the respect of the people for his earl. He'd tried. He'd allowed extra hunts on Lachlan's land and had spread the news that the wealth of harvest from the lands near Guston were to be for Hyrstow. But then the raid happened, and the capture of the Tanner sisters. His focus on Yrsa and the threat to Grahame's land...he'd been a terrible emissary to send in Lachlan's place.

The church rose like a tomb against the unending midnight sky. With what seemed like a deep breath drawn for performance, Oswald halted before the doors and turned to the crowd. In the firelight, his features were somber, his dark eyes flat, as if he'd expected such deceit from his brother and now had been tasked with teaching Ridley a lesson. He wrenched the rope binding Yrsa's hands so that she faced the crowd. It was the first time the people of Hyrstow were able to get a good look at her. Gasps flew. Someone swore at her; many others crossed themselves. Yrsa's gaze was wild yet wary as it scanned the surge of people before her. Though she held her shoulders straight and head high, her chin was tipped down in a manner of acceptance that Ridley couldn't reconcile.

With the patience a father has for a wayward child, Oswald held up his hands in a gesture for silence.

"People of Hyrstow! We have before us a Viking raider!"

He paused to allow shouted insults from the seething mass. A bread roll flew over heads and hit her in the cheek. Rage was as black as death as it shot through Ridley. He shoved his way to the front of the church and planted himself directly in front of Yrsa, legs braced, facing the crowd. Oswald continued as if he weren't there.

"She was found in Ridley Ward's home. Your chieftain. My brother." He paused for the collective gasp that went up like sparks drifting from a fire. "The Viking witch has seduced him!"

"Allow me an explanation," Ridley said, turning to his brother. Oswald stood at the mouth of his church, his hands loosely holding the end of the rope. As if the danger of Yrsa was the least of his worries.

"Let me explain!" Ridley turned back to the group, raising his voice to be heard. Narrowed eyes and contemptuous frowns locked on him. The people's anger at his betrayal was a wall that pressed his flesh, unwavering.

"No explanation is necessary," Oswald exclaimed with a crook of his brow. He spoke loudly so that the others could hear the exchange. "Were you not lying with the she-devil when I found you?"

Ridley gritted his teeth, angling himself in front of Yrsa so that he could speak to Oswald and the others. The denial of his actions would paint him in a worse light. He had broken trust. All he could do was tell them the truth.

"I was," he admitted. A flush burnt his neck and ears at having to reveal such intimacy with so many. Oswald nodded with pursed lips. "But—"

"Protest is for the weak. There is no order among men if they cannot trust their chieftain. How can you hope to guide your people if you have fallen prey to the woman who sacked their homes?"

An angry chorus of agreement and several nods wrought the crowd.

"You will do well to let me speak, Father," Ridley commanded. His voice rang out into the night, past the burnt glow from the bonfire. Oswald spread his hands before him in a gesture to indicate that Ridley should continue. His laconic grin gave no question as to who held the upper hand.

Ridley spoke around the dry lump in his throat, projecting his voice across the crowd: "It is true. Yrsa raided our village. She and I were in combat, and she was stabbed by His Holiness. She was helpless. I could not bring myself to deliver the death blow. Instead, I healed her. I planned to use her to negotiate if the Viking raiders returned. If they didn't, I would sell her in Eoforwic. No one knew."

The crowd buzzed like a beehive. Ridley desperately wanted to turn to look at Yrsa but knew it would show him as weak. Instead, he found the eyes of his friends. Branton stood with Freda at the rear of the crowd, both stoic and silent. Grahame was directly in the center, hands gesturing adamantly as he spoke to several people around him. Emma and Merthe stood huddled together near Joseph Cutter and his wife. Emma's eyes were locked on Ridley.

"You risked us! What if they raided again to find her?" a male shouted from the sea of faces. He raised the torch in his hand as he spoke.

"Indeed!" a woman's voice rang out.

"They can try!" Grahame shouted, a cocky grin spreading his mouth.

"And what of our blood feuds? We are entitled to justice!" said fourteen-year-old Robert, now an orphan.

"You've had your turn bedding her; turn her over to us!" another deep voice shouted.

Yrsa's low growl from behind made Ridley's stomach churn. He'd give anything to turn to her, but he had to stand his ground. He braced his hands on his hips, in an attempt to make himself bigger, to shield Yrsa further.

This was the true reason he'd been sent by Lachlan to gain the upper hand on the church. Oswald could work the people into a frenzy if he wanted, all in the name of securing their souls in heaven. But what of the decisions that were made in the present? He was chieftain. He should be able to decree Yrsa not be killed without argument. He'd not pushed hard enough when he'd come. He'd taken the gentle path of making friends and spreading wealth to those around him when he should have taken up residence in the mens' hall and ruled with an iron fist.

"Yrsa did not kill any of your fathers or husbands," Ridley bit out. He clenched his fists at his sides. "A blood feud is not her burden to bear."

"Isn't it?" Oswald chimed in from beside him. Ridley glanced at his brother whose gaze had locked on Yrsa, a sneer stretching his lips. His eyes gleamed like chips of polished stone. "Her people would do the same to any of us."

Ridley forced himself to swallow. His heart pounded in a frantic beat against his ribcage as the tide turned even further against him. Oswald had grown petulant over the years, but he wasn't so cruel as to insist upon Yrsa's abuse, was he? Bile clogged Ridley's throat at the thought. He'd seen the way Oswald had triumphed when he stabbed Yrsa during the raid. The slight comments he made about her feminine wiles. He was in his glory in front of the village, his piousness the only condemnation needed.

"God would dictate compassion," Ridley blurted, his palms sweaty. He wasn't well-versed in scripture, much to Oswald's chagrin. Oswald snapped his narrowed gaze to Ridley, but Ridley pressed on.

"Yrsa is kind and resourceful. She revealed where the Viking camp was so that I could look for the Tanner sisters."

"And did you find them?" Oswald asked, mirth flickering behind his solemn expression.

Ridley's heart stuttered. "No."

Another rush of words spread through the crowd. A sob rang up and Ridley knew it was Mrs. Tanner. Guilt ate at him. Some would have softness in their hearts for Yrsa as she was a woman, but others would not soon forgive the Viking raid. "Please. I ask as your chief, as a son of this village, to not condemn her for something for which she is not responsible."

A hard laugh cut through the sounds.

"Condemn a pagan?" Oswald stepped forward,

elevating his voice. "Only God can judge her for she has brought temptation and sin down upon you, Ridley."

"She is good-hearted! Indeed, I was tempted by her, and she by me. If you imply that she seduced me, you are wrong. We chose one another."

Ridley's voice felt raw as smoke. He bunched his hands into fists to ward off the craving for a blade. His taut hold on control was dripping through his fingers.

"How can you choose a pagan over your own people?" Oswald demanded. There was genuine shock in his tone, and Ridley felt a pang of regret that his brother was so out of touch with real life that he would not consider Ridley to have fallen in love with someone so unlike them.

"It is not one or the other." Ridley's eyes flew to the faces of his friends, silently begging for them to understand. "This land and its people are my blood. I would do anything to keep you safe."

"We were never safe," Branton's deep voice rang above the crowd.

Ridley's gaze snapped to where his friend stood with his giant arms crossed. His face was cloaked by shadow. Those around him had given a wide berth, as if Branton's anger was a tangible thing.

"There had been rumors for months. Ever since Lindisfarne. And Portland. We didn't do anything. We didn't prepare. Even more daft is how the earl put us at risk by handing us Guston land. A raid was going to come from somewhere."

Dozens of eyes flicked to Ridley. Despite Branton's

betrayal, the truth struck home. Hyrstow had been unprepared. It chafed Ridley's pride to know that he didn't do more to protect his people from the very real threat of Viking raiders. Even without the history of Lindisfarne's decimation hanging over their heads, they were destined for some type of retaliation from the Earl of Bernira because of Lachlan's theft.

Ridley nodded. He raised his gaze to Branton's in acceptance of his charges. "You're right."

People shifting from foot to foot was accompanied by murmurs of agreement. Bran's shoulders slumped. Freda clasped his shoulder, her head shaking back and forth in disagreement as she looked at Ridley.

"I should have prepared us. I was not expecting a Viking raid but the earl's decision to take land from Guston will impact us all. We will reap the reward of the land and must defend it."

Ridley couldn't stand it any longer. He stole a look behind him at Yrsa. She hadn't moved. Her back was straight, chin cut downward, staring unblinking at the ground. The thick tether of the rope bound her hand, but she did not struggle against its binding. Unshed tears pooled in her eyes.

"You are still under her spell," Oswald snorted. Ridley opened his mouth to retort but the rounded foreign sound of Yrsa's voice cut them off.

"My people will return," she said. Her words carried through the square, clear and strong. "It is not their way to stop, especially after being beaten by a village of peasants."

Exclamations of shock and outrage piled through the square. Joseph put a hand on Ewan's shoulder to stop the young man from charging forward. Oswald's smile turned from benevolent to downright gleeful. Ridley couldn't fathom what Yrsa was doing. Did she want to anger the mob? He turned to her, straightening his back so that his shoulders were as broad as they could be to block her from view, intent on making her quiet but she continued to shout.

"They want the treasure you hide."

"Princess, stop." Ridley tried to sound gruff, but the strength of his voice was driven out by the panic setting in.

"There is no treasure here!" someone that sounded like Grahame shouted. It was a feeble denial. His family would have been the best to raid. The townsfolk did not have much, but churches held goblets of silver and crosses of burnished gold.

"We killed most of 'em." Another shout from the middle, though the assertion tilted up at the end, as if unsure.

"My people have come for the church's riches. You must heed me! They will return and more of you will die." Yrsa's mouth moved quickly, her eyes wide. She didn't look at Ridley as she spoke. Instead her gaze met Oswald's.

"Enough!" Oswald shouted. "I decree this woman be put to death unless she humbles herself before God."

Ridley's stomach dropped. Sweat slicked his brow as he clenched his teeth against the protest that struggled to free itself. A murmur of agreement flickered through the crowd.

Yrsa's eyes were daggers that killed Oswald a thousand times over. As she opened her mouth in refusal, Ridley stole her chin, tipping it up to force her eyes to his. He spoke quickly, hoping to have her listen for once.

"Think, princess. Try to stay alive. I am doing what I can but you angering him doesn't help. If he puts you away for the night, I can try to break you out." An arm grabbed him from behind, pulling him back.

Yrsa spoke out of the side of her fixed teeth. "I am trying to warn them. My people will not stop. How many fled your village? Ten? Fifteen? More? We Vikings do not go easily. And I will humble myself to no one."

Oswald shoved himself between them, his face a sweaty red. Ridley pushed against his brother's hand on his chest but whoever held his arm tightened their punishing grip in warning. Unless he wanted to carve his way through his people, there was no easy escape. With a grimace, Ridley forced himself to relax.

"Easy Rid. I'm going to release you, but you have to keep your head," Grahame said near his ear.

Ridley nodded. He needed his arms free. Grahame eased off, and Ridley put his hands on his belt to control himself. There was a distinct gap where his dagger used to hang. His gaze shot to Yrsa. She lifted her chin ever so slightly.

The frantic, terrible knowledge that Yrsa took her dagger burned through him. She must have done so when she threw on her boots, as Ridley stood with the blanket bunched around his waist, shouting down the hut. He wanted to be sick. She would do something rash, he was sure.

"Humble yourself on your knees before God, or you shall face justice tonight," Oswald hissed, clamping rough fingers around her upper arm. It was her injured arm and Ridley caught the way her nose reared in pain. He wanted to slice his brother's hand off.

"I bet you'd like to see me on my knees, wouldn't you, priest?" Yrsa snarled. Despite her shackle, Oswald reared back, one jeweled hand flying to his mouth in shock. Grahame's boisterous laugh rumbled through the crowd, lightening Ridley's worry.

"I think we all might, Father," he shouted, causing a chuckle from many men, chased by scoffs from wives. Ridley sent up a silent prayer of thanks for his friend. If Grahame could lessen Yrsa as a threat, they'd all be better off.

"Father," Ridley tried to infuse authority he did not feel into his tone, "I am chief of Hystrow and your decree will not stand. I have the favor of the Earl of Deircia. Whatever you do tonight will follow you."

Ridley felt the ground wither beneath his feet as he was pierced by Oswald's hawkish gaze. He didn't have time to think about the claimed authority in his proclamation, but faced with Yrsa's execution, Ridley would say anything.

"You dare challenge the head of this church? With threats of power from mere mortals? Neither you, nor I, nor the rulers of this land are a match for the one true

King. Plus," Oswald lowered his voice so that only those close could hear, "whatever Lachlan brings down on my head will be long after maggots find a home in her."

Oswald turned back to glare at Yrsa with narrowed eyes. His lip curled back, hands fisting beneath the folds of his robe. Woodsmoke crackled beneath the silence that cloaked the square. Ridley's breaths sawed out of him, his innards clamping. Time to turn the tide was slipping away.

"There is drink and bloodlust about tonight. Please do not act in haste when Yrsa has done nothing," Ridley pleaded. He tried not to dwell on his inability to save her. Like his mother. Like the Tanner sisters. He brought death and destruction. Yrsa wouldn't be at risk if it weren't for him.

Oswald ignored his brother's plea. Instead, he turned, grinning, his hands aloft. "The Lord is merciful. I think that dread is as good a teacher as death itself. She will meet her fate at sunrise."

Several shouts sprang from the crowd: some in agreement, some indignant. Relief poured through Ridley, making his head feel light. She wouldn't be slain in mere moments. There was still time. For what, he wasn't sure.

Oswald turned to the church, and it dawned on Ridley that he intended for Yrsa to spend the night there. Fear surged. The men that lived in the barracks attached to the building did not have women in their presence for long periods. It was utter temptation for these men to keep a wildling in their hold. They could say, or do, whatever they wished to her before morning.

"At least put her in the jail!"

With a tight smile, Oswald turned, yanking on Yrsa's rope. He strode to the church, which must have been manned by eavesdropping priests because the doors opened at his approach. Stone faced, Yrsa followed him into the gaping cavern.

TWENTY-FIVE

The thick, cloying scent of incense made Yrsa want to gag. She could barely see in the dim light offered by the guttering candles. Her hackles rose at the whisper of the footsteps behind her. Oswald walked ahead, his strides quick. He tugged on the rope, at ease with her trailing behind him like an animal. She drew deep, even breaths through her mouth in an attempt to steady her heart.

Yrsa was led past the aisle of long benches, through the intersection of hallways. Rusty stains on the floor were the only proof of a previous conflict in the tidy church. Her palms slicked with sweat at the memory of Aric between the benches, bleeding, his skin ashen. After everything, it seemed too simple that the gods decree her to follow so closely in death.

To her surprise, Yrsa was led to the back room of the church where her journey had begun. As she entered, she half expected Oswald to whirl and sink a hidden blade into her belly. Though she guessed he was not the type to dirty his hands.

Two priests in the room held candles aloft, busily averting their eyes. The dim light revealed shelves filled with musty tapestries along the north wall. Nothing for Yrsa to defend herself with. No flame, no bit of iron left carelessly about nor tools scattered for her to use as a weapon. Yrsa's heart beat faster at the sight of the treasure chests, uncovered and pushed from the center of the room to squat beside the walls. Did these Saxons not learn the first time? Was their treasure of such little value to them that they risked leaving her trapped with it? Or did Ridley's brother view her as such a little threat?

"You shall remain here until we collect you in the morning," Oswald said, his tone lofty. He nodded at the men, a dismissal. One of them stepped forward, offering his candle to Oswald. They disappeared through the doorway, leaving Yrsa and the Reverend of Hyrstow in silence.

Sweat trickled down the center of her back as he turned to face her. His mouth morphed into what he probably thought was a benevolent smile. It made her skin itch.

"You will die tomorrow if you do not avail yourself to God," Oswald said, enunciating the words slowly, his deep-socketed brown eyes locked on her.

"Alright, then I avail myself to your God," Yrsa stated. She had no intention of dying tomorrow. She just had to figure out a way to stay alive. She'd succeeded so far. Though she doubted pretty words would sway this man.

Oswald's fleshy face broke into a wide grin. He spread his arms wide, jerking the rope that bound her hands. Yrsa was forced to take a step closer. "What excellent news. Being in the house of our Lord has been known to work miracles."

Just as quickly as his smile appeared, it vanished beneath a sneer. He lowered his voice. "You can trick my brother, but I am no fool. You cannot entice me with your serpent tongue. If you truly wish to prove your change of heart you will kneel before me."

If Yrsa could have killed him with a look, she would have. There was no way she was to kneel in front of this pig of a man. She would find another way. There were a good number of hours before morning. And Ridley wouldn't just leave her to her fate. He would try to intervene.

A pang hit her in the chest at the thought of Ridley. He'd deemed her worthy. A good person. Had admitted fault to his people when he could have easily thrown her to the wolves. She tried to block the memory of his panicked face as he fervently implored her to listen. Guilt threatened to swamp her. He'd given up so much. His people's trust, a bond with his brother.

Oswald seemed to know her thoughts. His wormy mouth slid upwards as he took another step toward her. The scent of fetid oats hung on his breath.

"Do you think that Ridley can do anything for you? He betrayed his people to keep you as a mistress..."

"That's not what happened," Yrsa interjected. She straightened to her full height, allowing her to look

310

down slightly at Oswald. This man knew nothing of Ridley.

"That is what they will remember. I speak over their souls every week, and they will believe what I tell them to. Ridley betrayed them to engage in immoral relations with a Viking. He shirked his responsibility."

"He did not! Ridley has been more than loyal to the village! He's rebuilt so much, laboring long hours, waking early to help others. He is chieftain. He could have doled out those duties yet he helped anyway. You should see how much he wrestles with—"

"Silence!" Oswald's voice sliced through Yrsa's protest. "The congregation's opinion of their chief will be decided by my good will. It's humorous, really. My own brother was assigned to lead Hyrstow when it already has the true leader of Christ. The earl has gone mad if he thinks his cherished knight will claim power in my stead. And you are his ruin and my key. So, when I tell you to kneel before me, you will kneel, or he will suffer."

Yrsa bit back a snarl. She had no idea what leadership the priest spoke of—Ridley was chieftain. He should have been able to claim her and overthrow the anger of the people. Dread solidified like a chunk of ice in her gut.

Oswald held more power.

"I will make his life hell. Get on your knees. Now."

The slice of his voice in the dim storage room caused Yrsa's rage to buck. She was tempted to kill this man and face whatever came next. The insults to herself she could take, for she already thought them. She was a failure. But she'd had no idea Ridley held such a precarious grasp on the village.

Something inside her felt as if it was breaking apart, little bits catching on the force that was Oswald's threat. Ridley had released her and she'd returned, only to land him in trouble. Slowly, glaring with all the hate she felt in her heart, she lowered to the floor at Oswald's feet. Grains of dirt bit into her knees.

A grin of pure satisfaction pressed the seam of Oswald's lips. Sweat made a home along her hairline. Yrsa wanted to look away but made herself speak.

"I cannot believe you would make your brother suffer by spreading lies."

"I ordered silence." Oswald's voice was suddenly thick. He regarded her, his chin folds glaring down over her his robe. A queer look lit his eyes. It was one Yrsa had seen before in men: a look of conquering.

"Filthy pagan," he spat.

Yrsa had to look away. She'd never considered that she would be wrong for believing in her thunderous, merciful, vengeful, heroic gods. But this man made her feel like less than refuse, perhaps because of the influence he wielded over Ridley. And she cared desperately what Ridley thought. After this was all over, whether she lived or died, would Ridley still care for her when his people turned on him at the instruction of his brother? Would he regret offering to wait for her when his church deemed her wrong?

A hollowness scraped a home for itself between her ribs. They were not wrong in their feelings for one another, that much she knew. Despite everything, the man that had held her captive had awakened a flame of something inside of her that she didn't think possible.

Oswald placed a heavy hand on the top of her head. It was hot against her hair. Yrsa bucked it off.

"Shhh," Oswald said. He tried again, this time dragging a bejeweled finger down her cheek and beneath her chin.

"Since you were so eager to bed my brother, you can show your appreciation of my generosity in the same manner," he hissed, his words thick.

Yrsa's blood went cold.

"I would rather die," she spat. Her muscles tensed, ready to pull out the dagger she had concealed within her clothes.

"Oh, you will," Oswald sneered, the stench of his sickly breath feathered over her lips as he dug his fingers into her cheeks so hard she was forced to open her mouth. Yrsa's hands fingered the hilt of the dagger swathed in her clothes. She had to call on all her strength to force herself still. If she slew him now, there would be no chance of escape. Instead, she glared into his beady eyes as he bent to hold the candle close to her face. Ropes of wax dripped about her knees.

"Scum like you are the reason our village must be protected. You are the same as those who ripped our parents from us. You are the monster that caused me to witness my father be strung up by his own entrails. You may have bewitched my brother but before this night is over, you will know the meaning of suffering." A glint of lust shone in Oswald's eyes as he released her chin and roughly grabbed Yrsa's breast and squeezed. Pain shot through her, causing her to curl into herself. Rage chased it. She would not allow herself to be raped. Her hands were tied but she had the element of surprise. Palming the handle of the concealed dagger with one hand, Yrsa clenched her teeth. She held her breath. She was ready for this fight to be her last.

A loud knock bounded around the room. Oswald, suddenly aware of others in the vicinity, released her and stood. He placed his hand on his chest, his eyes shifting from mad to calculating. "I will not have carnal relations with you, you demon!"

A sickly smile spread his lips as one of the monks appeared in the doorway, candle held aloft. Yrsa released her weapon and withdrew her tied hands from the folds of her tunic. She tried not to shake as she peered up at the priest. Oswald spat on the ground at her knees before he retreated from the room, muttering his concerns that she was beyond saving. The clang of the bar across the closed door caused Yrsa's shoulders to drop in relief.

Her wrists were raw from where the rope ate at them. Even so, she stood, peering around the blackened room. She waited for her eyes to adjust though, as time passed, darkness prevailed. She knew chests lined the walls of the room and the door to the outside stood directly behind her. Careful to shuffle so as not to trip, Yrsa turned and made her way to the rear door, tied hands out. Its roughly hewn surface held the scars of the hole that she had smashed though weeks ago. The inner door to the church was barred and probably guarded by priests. Or Oswald. She couldn't help the shudder that knocked along her spine. The revolting man was probably lying in wait for her to come out and beg for his mercy in exchange for her body. She had no idea how he and Ridley were brothers.

Her eyes pricked. Her heart felt as if it were being pulled apart by frothing horses. She had never cared for a man before. But she cared for Ridley. Deeply. When he'd told her he would wait for her, she wanted to take him up on his offer despite the knowledge that he deserved more. She wanted to be the only woman he cracked a rare smile for. To be the only one to rattle his ever-calm exterior with playful insults. Or practice combat or share a meal or enjoy the heat of his bed.

Yrsa dragged her sleeve over her cheeks to assuage the tears that had spilled from her eyes. Ridley had defended her in front of his people. Had risked his name. It would have been easier for him to claim her as a slave or that he was using her for her body. Instead, he told them of her goodness.

But was she good? She had raided an innocent village with the hopes of glory. She'd craved bloodshed to prove that she was worthy of being her father's only child, when he wasn't even in her life any longer. Vengeance had driven her, a nearly impossible task, she now understood. She needed to find out if Vidar still lived and return home, but what did she have when she got there? She'd failed to settle the blood feud. Her mother was long dead. No marriage. And no Ridley.

Thoughts of home sharpened her need to escape. The Saxons were to execute her in the morning. And, in spite of being held by the people of Hyrstow, she knew that her clansmen would not leave the country without spoils. If they were still alive, Danish dignity dictated they not fail again. They'd likely raided nearby settlements, slaking their desire for treasure.

Sweat trailed down her back as she thought of what her people would do. There were fewer of them, but Aric had made it clear that if the raid was to fail, they would be deemed cowards.

An image of pretty Emma, with her loaves of bread, then the beast Branton sprung to mind. They would have her die, yet somehow Yrsa knew it was because their dislike of her was rooted in their fear. And they should fear her clansmen.

Time constricted around her like a sheath. She needed to get out. With a taste of how sweet Ridley's affection was, she didn't want to die. His heat-filled glances and rough kindness had alluded that life could be more than vengeance and glory. That life could be worth living for the beauty nestled among the hardship.

Blind in the darkness, Yrsa carefully withdrew her father's dagger. During the commotion, while Ridley blustered and she scrambled for her boots, she'd yanked the knife from Ridley's discarded belt. Branton had entered just as she'd tied it beneath her clothes. She'd been careful to remain straight-backed as she walked. Careful so as not to drop it, she turned the hilt between her palms and went about sawing the rope.

The binding was thick and strong, and by the time Yrsa was free, she was drenched in a cold sweat. Every bump and murmur from the church door made her hackles rise. The sounds would approach then bleed away. Her shoulders ached. When finished she reached out to feel for the chest on her left. After pawing through empty air for several moments, Yrsa's hand finally contacted cool wood. Rivulets of a curling design had been carved into the lid. When her fingers brushed the empty holes of where a lock should be cradled, she stopped. She lifted the lid.

Instead of the smooth hardness of gold and silver, her hand met with a pebbled swath of leather. The sweet, musty scent of old paper reached her nostrils. Diving deeper, she touched cloth, and hard spines. Books. The chest was filled with them. Quick, she emptied handfuls, scattering them on the hard packed floor behind her. There had to be more; something else. Frantic, Yrsa yanked out several huge tombs, each surprisingly heavy. At the bottom, her hands met with cool planes of wood.

Six chests and the deep cut of sorrow later, Yrsa sat with her back to the last chest, empty-handed. She'd failed. Again. She'd been a fool. There wasn't any treasure. No jeweled goblets or gold coins. If there was such treasure, it wasn't in the storage room of the church. Like a simpleton, she'd believed it would be that easy. No part of her life was. Come morning, she was to face the executioner.

Fear wrung her gut. If she knew anything of Oswald,

it was that he wouldn't give her an honorable death. She'd be hung or cut down with no weapon. She'd be beaten, put on display, prey to those who wanted to warn off other Vikings. As much as Yrsa knew death would was painful, she wasn't sure if she was ready for the kind of indefensible pain she would have to endure.

As hopelessness swamped her, a plan weaseled its way into her mind.

If given any last words, she would demand death by combat. Maybe Ridley would be so kind as to fight her. She sniffed, shoving tears away with the heel of her hand. Ridley wouldn't want to, but a deathblow delivered by him would be quick. He would be merciful. He would be good to her.

The tears that she so desperately pushed back kept coming. Swordplay would be a good distraction in her last moments. She knew now what she didn't during the raid: she couldn't beat Ridley in a contest. He was needed. He was beloved by his people. She wouldn't put up much of a fight. It would be the last thing she demanded of her Saxon. If the man that she'd grown to care for so deeply would be the one to end her, she could die well. She only hoped that he would not carry the scar of her death for too long.

The scratching of a tool on wood broke through the cold spiral of her thoughts. Yrsa was on her feet in a flash, ear cocked toward the inner door. The sound stopped. She picked up the dagger from the floor beside her, tensing in anticipation of the priest she imagined coming in to demand her obedience. Whoever it was wasn't expecting her to brandish the dagger.

Yrsa held her breath. Her legs quivered with the need to run. After several heartbeats, scraping began again. Only it was at the rear door.

Yrsa scrambled on all fours toward the door and put her ear to the new wood. Pungent, freshly cut oak filled her nostrils. And deeper, the clawing noise permeated. Yrsa drew back, thinking it a rat, but the sound persisted, grinding through the aged panel above the repair. Curious, Yrsa drifted her fingers across the teeth of the old wood.

"Hello?" a female voice slipped through the cracks in the boards. Yrsa reared back. She had no female alliances in Hyrstow.

"Are you there?" the voice came again. It was soft yet urgent. When Yrsa didn't respond the clawing commenced with fervor.

"Yrsa, I am a friend of Ridley's. If you are unharmed, find a tool and help me dig the wood above the new brace. We must hurry."

CHAPTER
TWENTY-SIX

Yrsa tossed aside her suspicion. Whoever was on the other side of the door was preferred to the fate that awaited her inside the church. With a hard thrust, she struck the wood with her dagger beside where she guessed the other woman was chipping. Slowly, the wood flaked away in jagged swaths. Her tool was much smaller than the first time she'd broken into the building. It didn't help that the old boards weren't as rotted.

Time weighed heavy on her shoulders as she carved. More than once, the dagger slipped sideways, and her hands took the brunt of the slivers that seemed to reach for them. Sweat dove in rivulets down her back. By the time there was a hole large enough for Yrsa to stick her face through, her upper arms ached with fatigue, her injured shoulder screaming.

"Who are you?" Yrsa asked, wary.

A face surrounded by a cloud of dark hair popped up. "Emma. A friend of Ridley's. Are you hurt?"

All words left Yrsa's mouth as her mind scrambled for an answer. Why would Emma help her? As far as she knew, Emma had feelings for Ridley that extended further than the realm of friendship. If she wanted Ridley for herself, all she had to do was leave Yrsa in Oswald's captivity until morning, and Yrsa would be out of Ridley's life for good. Plus, helping a Viking escape must mean severe punishment if caught.

Emma didn't seem to notice Yrsa's pause. She continued chipping away at the wood with a small ax.

"Why are you helping me?"

Emma's small grunts of exertion filled in for an answer. Yrsa didn't press. Whether friend or foe, Emma was working to get Yrsa out of the church. If needed, she could evade Emma once she was free.

They carved at the wood for what felt like hours, limbs freezing every time they heard a noise. Each rustle from the trees, or shuffle of footsteps on the inside of the church made the hair on the back of Yrsa's neck stand on end. After it was nearly time for night to concede itself to day, the hole was large enough for Yrsa to push through.

She slung her dagger into her belt and stepped up onto the closest chest to hoist herself high enough to wiggle through the hole. Awkwardly, she had to pinch shoulders together while pressing her hands on the outside of the door. Her belly scraped along the wood, her feet swinging in the air behind her. Pain radiated from her shoulder as she gratefully accepted the outstretched arms of Emma. The slight woman was ready to catch her, and Yrsa couldn't help but lean into her so that she could bring her legs through. As she did so, their balance tipped, and the women thudded to the ground in a tangle of limbs. They rolled onto their backs and remained on the packed dirt for a few moments, breathing hard.

"Ridley cares deeply for you."

Emma's musical voice panted the words into the air, a statement, not a question.

Yrsa glanced sideways. The moon offered more light than the store room. It highlighted the curve of the other woman's pert nose and high, round cheeks. Her hair was a dark cloud that pillowed beneath her head. No wonder Yrsa had been so jealous of her mere hours ago. The woman was everything a man would like to look upon, and she was courageous enough to not heed for her own safety by helping Yrsa.

Yrsa held back from claiming Ridley's affection. She couldn't have it. "Why are you helping me?"

Emma sighed, the sound like worn cloth. They sat up, Emma turning to look at Yrsa. Her teeth flashed white in the darkness as she spoke, her tone even, voice quiet. "Ridley has the weight of the world on his shoulders. It's what makes him a good leader. Yet he's been different since you arrived."

Yrsa nodded. She knew Ridley was a good leader. It wasn't the time for dalliance, but she sensed Emma needed to say her piece.

"I was shocked, as many of us were, when you were

discovered. But he vouched for you. He's been tearing up the village, demanding his brother listen to him. He is the chief, and the Reverend Father not hearing him out is a grave insult."

"Ridley is stubborn," Yrsa allowed. Her palms itched with the need to push up and move. Every rustle from the forest behind her made her wince. For all she knew, Emma broke her out to have some other villager slit her throat.

"He is not the only reason I am here." Emma stood, wiping her hands along her skirt. She looked down at Yrsa. "The day of the raid, you encountered my daughter. Tonight, she told me that you stood face to face with her, weapon in hand, and did her no harm. You could have."

Yrsa cast her thoughts back to the morning of the raid and the girl in the doorway of the hut. She stood, adjusting her gaze to look down at the much shorter woman. "I did not come here to kill children. I came to avenge my father."

"You spared my entire life at that moment, so I thank you. My debt is now paid." Emma inclined her head and pointed to the trees. "We must go. I will lead you through the forest and away from here."

A thickness clogged Yrsa's throat at the simplicity of it all. That this tiny woman would risk herself to repay a debt...Yrsa shook her head and took up the small ax the woman had left on the ground.

They embarked on a thin deer trail that meandered to the south. Within moments, the abyss that was the forest swallowed them whole. The sky eased from pitch to lapis as they walked. Night creatures scurried through the under-bush, rustling the dried leaves of the forest floor. Yrsa was careful where she placed her feet yet still managed to trip over a log. She fell hard into Emma, nearly taking the shorter woman to the ground. As if to confirm she was made of kindness, Emma reached for Yrsa's hand and took it in her own, lacing her dainty fingers with Yrsa's calloused ones. Branches reached for their hair. Once, Emma's skirts got tangled in a knotted bush, but eventually, the forest spat them back out. Through the thick of it, Emma halted. Trees gave way to a clearing, empty but for a single figure on a horse.

The tall figure jumped from the beast and rushed toward them as they emerged. Yrsa's blood thrummed in anticipation of some sort of ambush. She tried to push Emma behind her as she held tightly to the small ax.

"It is Ridley," Emma hissed, her hand darting to Yrsa's arm to calm her.

Ridley. Relief and joy and the tart sense of home mingled in Yrsa's chest. Her knees buckled as she tried to move forward. Emma caught her around the waist.

Yrsa turned to Emma, a wide smile spreading her lips. "Thank you."

Emma inclined her head. "My debt to you for my daughter's life is paid. I will take my leave so that my absence is not noticed. Use your freedom well."

Infused with strength from unadulterated happiness, Yrsa made her way to Ridley, her feet devouring the ground between them. They crashed into one another, Ridley wrapping his arms around her waist and lifting her into him, while Yrsa threw her arms about his shoulders. She pressed her face to his neck to breathe in his smoked oak scent.

"Yrsa." He sowed her name into her hair between a dozen kisses. He was warm and sturdy, and he held her as if he would never let go. The realization struck that she never wanted him to. She could live in the cradle of Ridley's arms for the remainder of her life, however long it may be.

She began to tremble, her breaths unsteady against his neck as tears surged. Not until Ridley held her did she realize how inevitable she'd thought her demise. Even after Emma freed her, she had to blindly trust the woman not to lead her into a trap.

But Ridley had come for her. Like he said he would. Yrsa chastised herself for the shock she felt. She didn't think he would let her die without a fight, but she knew he wouldn't —couldn't—go against his own people.

The wet heat of her tears scored her cheeks and melted into the skin of Ridley's neck.

"Shh. You're safe. I have you," Ridley said into her hair as he placed her feet back on the ground, drawing her within the folds of his warm cloak. Yrsa wrapped her hands around his sides, skimming her fingers along the softness of his tunic before anchoring her hands against his lower back.

"Ridley. How?" She could barely form the words before he was nosing down to press a kiss to her upturned mouth. His lips moved over hers like a man starved, hands gripping her waist as if she were the most precious treasure. He dragged her bottom lip through his teeth. Greedy, she opened to him, taking as much as he gave. She palmed the planes of his chest, forcing her hands up into the hair at the nape of his neck to secure him to her. With a growl, Ridley scooped her up, securing her bottom in his hands and guiding her legs around his waist. Heat dipped between her legs at the feel of his big body against hers. Too soon, he tore away, breathless.

"You need to go," he rasped, easing her down.

Yrsa's heart felt as if it was being crushed in a fist. She knew she couldn't stay, and that he wouldn't leave.

Yrsa shook her head. "What will happen to you and Emma for freeing me?" She couldn't bear the thought of Ridley taking the brunt of the punishment for her freedom. Even Emma didn't deserve the inevitable shame that would come if she was found out. Guilt wormed a hole in Yrsa's belly.

"I will ensure Emma's safety. She insisted she help. I was crazed enough not to refuse." Ridley's calloused thumb caressed her cheek. The dawn cloaked his features in shadow, but Yrsa could make out the pinch of his brows, the grim set of his mouth. The cruelty of loss slammed into her all at once.

"I do not want to leave you." Her throat thickened. How could she leave this man who made desire swirl in her like a whirlwind and cause her heart to feel like bursting at the same time? Who made her feel protected yet strong? As if she had no idea what to do, her hands flitted across his shoulders, then down his arms to circle his wrists bringing each hand up for a kiss. With a sound more like a strangled sob than a sigh, he disengaged his hands and draped his arms around the top of her shoulders, remaining distanced enough to search the scatter of emotions across her face.

"Nor I you, princess. I will wait until the end of time to hold you again." The words seared themselves into her skin and wove between her bones. She didn't deserve his love, but she would not refuse it. Maybe she was as selfish as her mother had always said. Yrsa didn't care. Ridley had risked himself to free her. And because of that, she had to do her best to save him.

"If I come upon them, I will convince my people to never return. I will tell them that there is no treasure, that I killed the Saxons that kept me, that we must return home." Her tongue tripped over her words to get them out fast enough. Ridley's bronze eyes scoured hers, his brows tented with worry.

"Will you be safe?" His arms tensed around her, bringing her closer. She knew what he was asking. To return to a group of warriors, unharmed and spreading lies could cause her to meet her death just as quickly as at the end of Oswald's noose. Yrsa shoved down the fear of her own clan by burying her nose into the crook of Ridley's neck. When she looked up into his eyes, she had a stronger hold on her emotions.

"I will. I promise." She covered the lie with a smile.

Ridley's mouth brushed hers again. His beard scratched her, his lips soft. Yrsa molded herself to him. Her memories would be all she had. The impotent frustration that gathered like a storm quickly changed to anger. It shouldn't be the last time, but it would be. Ridley seemed to sense the shift in her because he grabbed her rougher than before, running his calloused hands down the back of her thighs, around her ass, up her back, settling around her nape. He plundered her mouth with his tongue, imparting as much of himself as he could. Meeting his ferocity, Yrsa ground herself against the hard length of him that pressed her core. Finally, Ridley broke away, panting.

"You must go," he said. As if it took all his self-control, he loosened his desperate grip and turned to the horse. They walked hand-in-hand to the huge animal. It grazed peacefully, oblivious to its master's fraught rush. Ridley scooped up the reins and held them out to her.

"Take it. There is bread, cheese, and water in a bundle on the back. Some gold in case you don't find your clan. Keep to the forest, trade. Stay out of trouble. I mean it, Yrsa. Stay safe. Please."

Yrsa nodded around the stone lodged in her throat. Everything in her wanted to stay but she knew that she had to do her part to keep Ridley safe. There were those in the village, like Emma and her child, who deserved to live in peace. Despite the urge to burn Oswald and his church to the ground, Yrsa believed in Ridley. In his patience and determination. He deserved to live a life of peace after a life of war.

She had to tell the others that Hyrstow was barren. And if her people were gone, Yrsa would find a way to survive. She'd gotten a taste of life and wanted to chase it.

Yrsa tore herself from Ridley's embrace and swung up to settle on the horse. The animal was wide and solid beneath her. Ridley caught hold of her foot, his fingers pressing into her boot to command her attention.

"If you can't find your clan, come back," Ridley urged, as if the words were a precious secret. He laid a hand along her lower leg and squeezed. His eyes were wide, crazed. "I promise you safety. I just need time to change their minds." Ridley's fevered eyes implored her.

Yrsa swallowed hard, her mouth dry. No one had ever wanted her the way Ridley had. She must have been mad. To be staring down death in Hyrstow and wanting to stay at the same time. It was a knife to the heart that she'd allowed herself to feel so deeply for Ridley and couldn't be with him.

She knew he would wait. Ridley was a man of his word. He would take no bride and sire no sons. The thought of dooming this magnificent man to a life of waiting struck her as the cruelest thing she could do.

Yrsa straightened, jutting her chin high as her heart shattered within her chest. "I will not return, Saxon. My place will never be here, and you would do well to forget me."

Without a further glance, Yrsa spurred the horse into a gallop across the open plain. She tucked her body close to its mane. She had to in order to keep herself from pulling on the reins and turning back.

She rode like that for a long time as tears of pain and regret streamed down her face.

TWENTY-SEVEN

"Admit you helped her escape. Tell me where she is!" Oswald thundered.

Ridley didn't bother hiding the smirk that had formed upon Oswald barging into his home. He was still abed, the blanket fallen to his waist. Oswald was a bear trapped in the cage of Ridley's hut, pacing around the fire, glaring into the corners of the room as if Yrsa was hidden in them.

"I do not know of what you speak, brother. I am as surprised and worried as you are that she is not where you left her."

"How could you do this? Was lying with her worth the risk to our village? To your own place in the kingdom of heaven?" The glare Oswald leveled at Ridley was loaded with accusation.

"Yes."

Oswald's eyes bulged at the plain truth.

The night previous, Ridley, frantic, had banged on

the door to Oswald's private quarters and tried to convince his brother that Yrsa was not a threat to the village. He had argued with a nightshirt-covered Oswald that he was the chieftain and would forbid Yrsa's death. Oswald, calm as an immovable rock, had simply grinned and told Ridley of the various ways that he'd betrayed his own people. How he'd failed to gain the upper hand in the village. Later, when Emma had approached him about a plan to free Yrsa, Ridley had returned, shouting and begging on his knees to drown out the sounds of Yrsa's escape. At least he'd been admitted into Oswald's private chambers. His brother had listened, cloaked in a finely spun tassel lined blanket, eyelids half closed.

Now Oswald huffed, turned to the table, stood straighter and swung back around.

"She will return, Ridley. She will bring with her the wrath of more Vikings who could decimate us."

With a sigh, Ridley hefted himself out of bed and pulled on his tunic. "That is untrue. Yrsa is not a killer. She doesn't care about Hyrstow. She was here for a blood feud. One I am confident we had nothing to do with. Her clan wanted to find treasure, and you said yourself that the chests had been opened and rifled through. She found the books the church was gifted. She won't return to the place where she was captive."

Oswald's eyebrow arched. "But would she return to the man?"

Ridley ran a hand over his unruly hair and covered his grief in a grimace. Yrsa's last words had cut through him. He knew they were said to free him of her, but the knowledge did not hurt his soul any less.

"No," he said with hollow finality. "She will not return to me."

Oswald snorted and came to stand in front of the bed. His usually tidy robe was wrinkled, the bottom singed with dirt as if he himself had sat on the dirt-packed floor of the storage room, sorting through the books Yrsa had carelessly discarded. The books were a treasure of sorts. Bestowed upon the church from the King's private library, they were rare and only a select few could read them.

"Get up and gather a search party."

Ridley ran his tongue over his teeth. "No. I'll post more sentries around the town. I will train the men for combat better than I have been. We will repair the church. But I will not help you hunt down my woman."

Oswald threw his hands up, snorting with exasperation. "Listen to yourself. She is a Viking. A Dane! She is just like those that killed our family, and she used you!" Oswald's robes thrashed around his wrists like sails through wind. He dropped his gaze back to Ridley, eyes flat with something Ridley couldn't place.

"Some leader you are. You are the worst thing to happen to this village."

The words were meant to hurt. To scar him. Ridley couldn't bring himself to care. They were true. He was a knight. A killer. Lachlan shouldn't have given him this station. And none of it mattered because his heart was riding south, away from him. He simply shrugged. The gesture made Oswald seethe.

"I expect immaculate repair of the church. Sentries doubled. We cannot afford another raid. So, help me, Ridley. I know what is best, and if she comes back here, I will see to it that she is cut down. And you will watch."

Ridley gripped his belt in a strangle hold as he readied to place it about his waist. "Over my rotting corpse will I allow that."

Oswald leveled one last glower before storming out.

Ridley's shoulders fell. It had taken all his energy to sit there and pretend as if he wasn't breaking in two. As if he didn't care that Yrsa was gone.

He diligently focused on each task—fastening his belt, absent of Yrsa's dagger, pulling on his worn leather boots, preparing one bowl of parritch—so as to not cast his eyes to the bed he and Yrsa had shared.

Had she gotten back to her clan? Did they believe her? The other outcome his mind kept chewing was of Yrsa wandering the countryside in search of a life. It's why he'd given her most of his personal income. When his mind dipped into the horrors that could meet a beautiful woman traveling alone, he grit his teeth and tried to think of ways to repair his relationships with the rest of the village.

Oswald had been right. He'd been a terrible leader. As much as he'd accomplished with building, searching for the Tanner sisters, and training men, it hadn't been enough. He'd failed Yrsa; he'd failed Lachlan, his adoptive father in every respect.

"Ridley!" Branton's shout came through the doorway seconds before the man himself. His chest heaved as if he'd been running. "Grahame spotted Viking rangers. Three miles out. To the south."

No. He'd sent Yrsa on her way that morning. Had she found them so fast? Unless they'd gotten answers from her and turned on her so quickly. Ridley was moving before he got his next word out. "When?"

Kneeling beside the table, Ridley unearthed his chainmail, shield and longsword from the hidden cellar beneath. Vikings must have had different holdings because Yrsa never found his compartments. His people stored food and grain and weapons beneath their floorboards. Even the few times she'd been free, he'd been surprised she hadn't discovered the straw covered door.

"Just now." Branton crossed his arms over his chest and leveled Ridley a look that could have spooked the devil. "There are rumors you freed your Viking. The Reverend storming out of here...my guess is they are right."

Ridley tunneled a hand through his hair, mind snagging on Yrsa's safety rather than his friend's reaction to his betrayal. "What of it?"

"Did she do this, Rid? Would the woman that you set free condemn us all?"

Bran's lips were pressed into an unforgiving line within his heavy beard but the shadows beneath his eyes were what shredded Ridley's resolve. He'd put that look in Bran's eyes.

Doubt ran fingers across the nape of his neck. Did

Yrsa gain her freedom only to give Hyrstow over to the wolves? Before the question finished forming, he was shaking his head.

"No," Ridley said as he stood. "I freed her. I admit it. But we did not know if her clan was in Northumbria anymore. I sent her away with the knowledge that she may never find them and that they could be gone, or dead. If she finds them, she swore to tell the others that there is no treasure. She was to warn them away from us. She did not do this, Bran."

"And if they didn't believe her?" Bran asked, plucking the question out of Ridley's mind.

Ridley expelled a shaky breath. "Then she's probably dead."

His voice cracked on the last word. He brought a fist to his mouth to bite back the lance of pain that burrowed its way into his side. To his surprise, Branton laid a heavy hand on his shoulder.

"I believe you," he said gruffly. He gave Ridley a strong pat on the upper arm. "If it were Freda, I would burn the whole world to the ground to make her safe."

Heartened by Bran's words, Ridley nodded. Whatever discord that lay between them had to be resolved later. Vikings on the perimeter would not wait. Ridley pulled the breastplate overhead. Tiny metal bearings were woven within the braiding. He then fastened his sword belt at his waist. It hugged him like a long-missed companion. His shortsword was cool in his palm, the grooves of the pommel nestling home. It distracted him from the worry that arched through him at a potential raid.

As he stalked to the door, Bran blocked the way, eyebrows pinched together. "Rid. If she is with them, you have to know that she won't come out of this."

Ridley clenched his teeth. Despite the praises he sang for her the night previous, he doubted the people of Hyrstow would spare any kindness for Yrsa if she was with her clan in an attack.

"I know."

Branton narrowed his eyes, as if in contemplation if Ridley would let Yrsa be cut down. He wouldn't. But until that decision had to be made, Ridley would give his best for his people.

As Ridley left the hut with Branton on his heels, he issued curt instruction. "Gather the men on the south-east side of the village. If you see Grahame, tell him to let the priests know to hunker down. The Vikings will make for the church."

The sun was strong over the rush of people. Several men walked toward the center of town, implements in hand. Women flocked toward the river with children and baskets of food or their family's wealth in bundles under their arms.

Branton nodded and took the quickest path south. Through the throng that passed north of his hut Ridley spotted Emma and Merthe.

"Emma," he said, raising a hand to catch her attention. Eyes wide, she searched for who called her name, unable to place the voice for a moment. Upon seeing Ridley, her pinched face brightened.

"Ridley!" she said, her voice burdened by fear. "Is it true? Are they back?"

"It appears so. Find Freda. Hide deep, away from the river, and do not come out until we come get you."

Emma nodded once, grasping Merthe's wrist tighter. "Be safe."

"Same to you."

The women ran to the forest beyond the village. Ridley could only pray the Viking scouts did not travel northwest through the woods. The women would fight to the death for their young, but he didn't know how many of Yrsa's clan were still alive.

Sword in hand, Ridley darted to the center of town. Tables from the previous night's feast were crooked teeth among the square after the night's commotion. In the middle of the group of fighting men, Grahame shouted instructions, sectioning off several according to ability and weapon. Whispers of indignation flew like a flame over dry kindling as Ridley made his way through the press of bodies. Awolf Tanner was angry enough to voice his outrage.

"Are you sure he is with us and not them?"

The immediate roll of Grahame's green eyes was paired with an easy smile. He hefted an ax overhead to pass into Awolf Tanner's big hand. Ridley couldn't help note that he moved well among the men, making jokes about defending the village again, as if it were an everyday occurrence. Like Freda, he held himself with an air of joviality that infused hope into those around him. Worry was a thorn in his side. Grahame was not a fighter. He trained and defended, but his friend was no warrior.

"Hey, Rid." Grahame gave Ridley a nod as he approached. His wide mouth turned downward as he relayed the news. "Saw three of them on horseback a ways down the south road. Like a patrol. They chased me for a quarter mile before turning around. I think they've gone back to get more."

Grahame inclined his head in deference to Ridley's lead.

"Thank you, Grahame." Doubt niggled in the back of Ridley's mind: would the men follow him, would they think him a traitor? But Grahame stood silent, expectant, hand on the pommel of the sword anchored at his side. Ridley felt the pull of command, the inexorable tight-ening of his muscles in preparation for battle.

"We'll station three men at each entrance. You and I will take five men and head south. If their intent is to raid again, they'll be easy to spot."

Ridley had no idea of their numbers. From what he'd gleaned from Yrsa there were originally near twenty-five men. Many had died, but more ships could have come to relieve them. Or they could be a small band of killers bent on revenge. Either way, it meant war for Hyrstow. And Ridley would not have his people be sitting ducks a second time.

Without hesitation, he shouted out a plan that detailed holding the Viking forces off until he could have words with the leader. His true hope was to avoid conflict altogether. Then he relayed a battle plan if it should come to that. Men beside him checked their weapons, fidgeting with belts and shields. Time pricked at the back of his neck. Ridley knew they had to move.

When Ridley spotted Bran at the rear of the crowd, relief pulled at his shoulders. At least he'd have his best with him. Suddenly, a younger man he recognized as Aeon Smith's son shouted from the rear of the crowd.

"We heard your Viking escaped." All eyes moved to the voice then fell back to Ridley.

Impatience made him grit his teeth. "Aye, she did."

"Is it her? Did she bring her men back here to get revenge?"

Ridley pressed a tight smile across his mouth. "It isn't. She was to stop her clan from returning. She wanted no part in harming us."

Awolf snorted. It was enough to cause a low laugh within the group.

"O'course she would say that to the man she was humping," another grumbled.

Ridley packed an angry retort down his throat. The others would forever doubt his leadership because he'd shown himself to be untrustworthy. And he was. There was no denying it. The truth tore at his pride and spurred his anger all at once.

"I know you do not trust me after the events of last night. How could you?"

The men shifted, weapons gripped in hands that looked like they wanted to fell Ridley instead of their enemy. He swallowed hard around the metallic taste of fear and frustration. He had to get his men back or they had no hope of winning this battle. A divided troop would not stand.

Ridley raised his voice to be heard throughout the square. "I hereby ask that you trust this: I am defender of this land, of your wives, of your children. I have the faith of the earl, but beyond that, Hyrstow raised me. This village is in my bones. I have sworn to defend it against all else. And I will shed more Viking blood in its honor!" Ridley threw his sword up, piercing the sky.

A roar started with Bran and Grahame then rolled through the others. It was the encouragement he needed to drive his point home. "I am Ridley of Hyrstow, and I will fight for my people until my dying breath. We will end these Viking scum! They will beg for mercy!"

Weapons were shoved into the air as hollers of agreement rang out. The air crackled with the promise of a fight, bloodlust reflecting in the men's eyes. It was good. They may not trust Ridley, but they would follow him into battle. He would fight his heart out for these men and their families. They were all he had left.

"For Hyrstow!" Ridley demanded.

"HYRSTOW!" the men shouted.

Ridley stalked to Bran, the crowd parting as he went. He felt Grahame flank his left. Bran grinned. He clapped Ridley on the back as the three of them moved through the village to horses that had been pulled around for them.

"Rid," Grahame said as they mounted their steeds, "what if she is with them?"

Ridley gnashed his teeth as he straightened in the saddle. "Then she is with them."

He didn't know what else to say. He didn't think that Yrsa would have gone back to her clan just to kill his people. Though, if it happened, he suspected because she was told to. He doubted the leader would accept any softening to the Saxons on her part. She would have had to rejoin her people and lie to live.

If she had to partake in battle, he had to somehow ensure her safety. Not knowing how or when, Ridley knew he had to be the one to get to her first.

TWENTY-EIGHT

"I'd always considered you a warrior. Now I see you are just a traitorous wench," Vidar snarled. His bent nose flared in disgust, teeth laid bare beneath his curled lip.

Yrsa's heartbeat pulsed in her neck as she stood amidst the watchful band of men that encircled her. Many still wore rust-coloured bandages, and the putrid scent of rot and unwashed body clung to them. Their eyes fixed on her as she stood her ground before her best friend. The man who was like a brother to her now looked at her with unveiled hate.

"I emptied the church's chests, Vidar. There is no treasure in Hyrstow. I searched high and low. We need to move on. Or return to Inivik." The sun pressed the top of her head through the dappled leaves above. Yrsa wished to turn her face to it.

"Home?" Vidar looked from her to the others, arching his eyebrow as if what she said was mirthful. "We did not sail for days to return home with our tail between our legs like dogs."

Brisk nods bobbed around her.

Yrsa had ridden across meadow and field and wound through a sparsely treed forest. When she'd heard a band of men coming through the woods, she'd tied her horse to a tree and climbed another to get out of harm's way. The band of men had tramped through, fifteen in all, hair braided or shorn to the sides of their heads. Various weapons decorated their battle-beaten bodies. There were two young women in tow. One was atop a horse, her body bracketed by the man saddled behind her; the other walked at the rear of the party, hands tied with a length of rope. Around the pounding in her ears, Yrsa heard the grumbles of their speech— different from the hard dialect of Northumbria. It sounded like home.

As the men came to a halt near her abandoned horse, Yrsa called out from her perch. The Danes scoured the trees and when Vidar's sights landed on her, a giant grin broke across his mouth. Her joyful greeting was in harsh contrast to the questioning she now received.

Yrsa issued a measured nod, keeping her eyes locked on Vidar. She moderated her words as if they were fine coins to be sparsely dealt. "Good. Let us raid elsewhere. We need not go back in search of death."

Vidar cocked a scabbed eyebrow as he anchored his hands to his hips. He smirked, though no warmth reached his eyes. "Why do you speak as if you have no heart behind your words? The Yrsa I grew up with would tear the hide off a boar with her insults and yet, here you stand, serving us neat lies about the Saxons."

Yrsa pressed her lips together. Not for the first time, she wondered how Vidar had earned command. He had raided before, but so had most of the others. Across from her glared Gunter, a neighbor of Aric's, and to her left was Ivar, who had been on many raids with her father. Vidar had always been well liked but a jovial man was not seen as a leader.

Yrsa hated that her friend was right. From the start she had taken the wrong approach by embracing Vidar, happy to see the men, ready to tell her story. The small party halted and had made a fire. Several had taken out waterskins and quenched their thirst as Yrsa spoke, though two of the men issued nods then peeled away from the group, riding the way Yrsa had come.

Upon a horse, Erik Ivarson held one of the females within the bracket of his arms. He dismounted, tossing his head to dislodge the bright blonde strands that fell across his forehead before cutting the woman a heart-stopping smile. Indeed, the women of Inivik loved Erik, though it didn't appear that the Saxon maiden did. He assisted her off the horse, ignoring her pursed-lipped glare as he brought her back to the woman at the rear of the party and tied the two together. As he remounted, he shot a deadly look to the men nearer the women before spurring the horse to catch up to the others.

These women, Yrsa assumed, were the Tanner sisters Ridley had been so fraught to find. As Yrsa related Hyrstow's lack of treasure, she evaluated their person, searching for evidence they had been maltreated. Both had brown hair and eyes though the one that had ridden with Erik had a smattering of freckles across the bridge of her nose. A crusted gash covered the bottom lip of the other, whose shrewd gaze appraised Yrsa with the same scrutiny she evaluated them. Her green dress had been ripped and hastily tied with what looked like a scrap of cloth so that her breasts wouldn't spill out. Yrsa breathed a slight sigh of relief that they were still capable of moving on their own.

"I do not lie. They are poor farmers..."

Vidar had grown restless during Yrsa's report of her captivity. He didn't ask after her struggle, just offered her a few slivers of meat and water, demanding information about Hyrstow's weaknesses. She told him what she thought he wanted: information on repairs, how many able-bodied men she guessed were left (a lie), and that the chests in the church held no treasure. Vidar had snorted, clenching, and unclenching his fists, a habit he had adopted when they were fourteen, and Yrsa had started beating him at swords.

As she spoke, the men around her began adjusting their axes and knives. They must have raided a settlement to have horses in their possession, but Yrsa didn't want to ask just yet.

They wouldn't believe she fought her way out. She decided to stick close to the truth and told Vidar that her captor grew in affection toward her and let her go. It was a grave mistake. Vidar didn't believe that a Saxon would chain her to his bed only to free her.

"With a church as large as theirs? It must have gold and silver."

"It has books," Yrsa said, her tone harsh enough to whittle bone. Vidar's disbelief wore at her thinning patience. She was free and with her people. Yrsa should have felt safe, elated that she'd happened upon them. Yet something was amiss.

With an exaggerated glance at the men that had closed in around them, Vidar grinned. "Well, I can understand if you were too busy humping Saxons to find anything other than books."

The red hand of rage shot so quickly through Yrsa that she didn't realize she'd slapped Vidar until he was holding his face. When he pulled his palm away, a crimson smear glared from the corner of his mouth.

Suddenly, the world shifted and, too late, Yrsa realized she was on the wrong end of it. Men shuffled inward, hands on their weapons. Vidar's smile was downright feline; the harsh glint in it made Yrsa want to cower. He'd never looked at her that way before.

"We go on as planned." Vidar's voice rose over the rest of the men. It was a loftier tone than she'd ever heard him use, one infused with authority. "These Saxons have sent a messenger to halt us! That is how weak they are!"

A rumble of agreement rose from the men. Too late, Yrsa noticed the wreath of weapons each man held, the shields they did not set down when she'd settled on the log to eat.

"Wait, what do you mean, 'go on'? What are you

planning?" Yrsa tried to snag Vidar's arm as he stalked to a group of horses. He snaked his arm forward, out of her reach.

"It ends today, Yrsa." Vidar threw the words over his shoulder. She stared at his retreating form, his dark hair braided tightly for luck. Like a fly in a web struggling to break free, Yrsa began to understand. The others had broken apart and were checking the weapons at their sides, some mounting horses.

Fear curled around the base of her spine. They were to raid? And she had just blundered her way upon them after all this time?

Yrsa clenched her shaking hands. She tried to rein in the quick breaths that flew from her. All at once, her mind felt like it was being boiled by the sun. "Vidar. Vidar Stop!"

She stomped behind Vidar until he whirled, bearing down on her with clenched teeth. "Yrsa, we are raiding Hyrstow. For our honor. For the treasure. The Saxons deserve our wrath, and we deserve our vengeance."

She couldn't let them. As much as she'd love to witness the horror on Oswald's smug face as her people spilled through the village, Yrsa didn't yearn for war. She didn't wish for Ridley to have to defend Hyrstow again, not when it was in upheaval because of her.

Yrsa grabbed for Vidar's arm again.

"Vidar, please. Don't do this." It struck her that she sounded desperate, like someone she would have despised mere weeks ago. Now her dignity was not worth the time. Ridley needed her.

And somehow, she had to salvage the last relationship she had. If not for Vidar, she was alone in the world. She clung to the hope that his coldness was a show of dominance. She had come upon them at the wrong time, and it was like seeing someone alive after they'd been thought dead.

Her hand on his arm, Yrsa hoped she could convince him that she was still his friend.

Vidar licked the side of his mouth where red still bloomed, then stepped close, bringing his nose to her ear. He smelled of old blood and unwashed hair. Yrsa held her breath as he spit words at her.

"Everyone always loved you best, Yrsa. Daughter of the great Arkyn Ironsword. Too good to stay home, you just had to raid with us men. Don't you realize what a laugh the rest of us had? Until now, we assumed you were dead. Never did we think you were even worse than dead—some Saxon's whore."

Like blows to the chest, his words were delivered to maim. It couldn't be true. Her heart scrambled to find purchase on the ledge that was their bond. The sweat along her nape slid down her back.

"Vidar. Why are you acting this way? We are friends."

Vidar raised an amused eyebrow. The men ignored them, weaving between trees to mount horses. Vidar jutted his chin to her horse, a command for one of the others to claim it.

"As children. But you outshined me, Yrsa. Though not in this. Raiding was mine. And you sought to take it from me."

He hit his chest with his fist. The smack of leather echoed around them. Yrsa winced. "Now I command. I will lead the men to riches, and they will see that loyalty to you will get them nowhere."

Yrsa's tongue felt thick. How could she have missed this side of Vidar? He'd never told her of a desire to lead a raid. When he came of age, he went and returned a little richer. When she'd declared that she would raid to settle her blood oath, he'd laughed, thinking it a joke. But he had stood by her when she'd petitioned Aric to join the group. Had treated her like any other raider.

"I don't want command of the men. You misunderstand. There is no use going back..."

"Gunter, take Yrsa to the fire and guard her until we come back." Vidar lifted his chin at the tall, sallow-haired Viking near the fire.

Gunter was quiet. He glanced from the two women who now huddled together on the ground against the trunk of a tree, back to Vidar and nodded. He came forward and clasped Yrsa's shoulder, blunt fingers digging hard into her injury. Pain shot through her, and suddenly, she was back in the church, helpless as the knife drove through her.

"Vidar! Do not put these men in danger for nothing!" Yrsa shouted as she was yanked over to a log.

Vidar leaned over the neck of the horse he'd mounted, his lip curling in disgust as he spoke. "Men have already left to patrol. It has been the plan all along. You showing up just delayed us a little. We raid today.

And I will do you the favor of returning with your Saxon lover's head on a pike."

Yrsa's stomach dropped out. Men on horses trotted around them, hooves crunching pine needles and the soft dirt of the forest floor. Others grimaced as they adjusted weapons to accommodate injuries. One man had bled through bandages that wrapped around his stomach; another's skin bore a sweaty, yellow tinge. Though they were small in number, Yrsa didn't like the deranged gleam in their eyes.

Panic made it hard for her to breathe. She'd only ever cared for her father, for Vidar. Had grown up striving for her father's recognition. And when he was no longer there, she shredded herself to prove to others that she could avenge him.

Her mother beat her. Her father left her. Her betrothed died. Ridley.

Now Vidar.

How much loss could she stand?

Yrsa spun the first lie that came to mind. "Vidar, you won't make it back. It is as if these Saxons are ten times stronger in number. Many men came from neighboring villages to aid them. My father, Aric...don't make their deaths mean nothing. They are powerful. Despite what you say to me now, I can't have you die too."

A smile sliced Vidar's mouth. The corners of his eyes crinkled, and for a sliver of a moment, Yrsa thought she'd gotten through to him. The tanned skin of his throat peered at her as he threw his head back and laughed. It was a hearty sound, as if she'd truly surprised him. The way it butted up against her urgency caused her gut to coil like a snake.

Vidar slipped down from the horse with lithe grace, still laughing. Her feet were stone as he came up, putting them chest to chest. A few of the others watched them over their shoulders, but most began to trot away, unperturbed by the disruption. Yrsa could feel the heavy stares of the women behind her.

The stench of venison on Vidar's breath mingled with his words. "I thought you had figured it out, but you're simpler than I thought."

"What?" Yrsa felt tears of frustration pool in her eyes. The sun baked her scalp. Vidar wasn't making sense. She wanted to scream.

"The man who killed your father and your dead betrothed are one in the same."

The words hit her in the teeth. Hard and blunt and brutal. She staggered back a step under the blow.

A grin of satisfaction painted the corner of Vidar's mouth as he witnessed it. His green eyes widened with his smirk, happy to tell the story. For some reason, his voice sounded muffled. A ringing overlaid what she heard next.

"I saw it. They quarreled over treasure. Aric thought he deserved more, and he did. On that raid, your father sat back and let us do all the work. He then demanded most of the silver. Aric beckoned him into the bush to meet his end. The few of us who saw it were sworn to secrecy. And given more than our share of plunder."

"It's not true!" Her voice was ragged, as if she'd been

screaming for days. Arkyn Ironsword was a shrewd leader. He was a tough warrior and prosperous raider. He wouldn't rob his own men of their riches. She looked to Gunter who stood beside her near the fire. His thin lips curled upward as his cold gaze landed on her.

"Oh, I assure you it is. Did you hear me, Yrsa? Your beloved Arkyn couldn't prevail against Aric. It was quick. He didn't expect it. You'll be glad to hear there was no begging. Now sit down. We'll be back."

CHAPTER
TWENTY-NINE

Heat flushed her limbs as if she were melting from the inside out. Vidar was wrong. Her father couldn't have been bested. Yet her betrothed had been young and strong. She shook her head against the image of fire-haired Aric plunging an ax into Arkyn's unaware back. The shock that would have overtaken his wrinkled, handsome face. Did his strong arms flail as he died?

Her father had been killed by a large, dark haired Saxon. It was what Aric had proclaimed upon his return to Inivik. It was asserted by Vidar and Aric's man, Harald. The image of the faceless dark-haired Saxon had fuelled her dreams of revenge. It's what drove her to conquer the savage Saxons, what had chased her into Ridley's village, intent on slaying him and any others like him...

Yrsa turned and heaved. Remnants of the bread that she'd eaten on the journey plopped wetly onto the grass.

The pain of her retching was a welcome respite to the knife-like ache of loss that filled her. It was all wrong. Her intentions, her hate, all of it. By the time she righted herself, wiping the back of her hand across her mouth, Vidar was on his mount. He ignored Yrsa's hoarse shout as he rode through the trees, the other men on his trail.

Yrsa bent over, hands on her knees and sucked in deep breaths, trying not to falter.

Her father, dead. Killed by her betrothed.

Spite curled within her, making a nest in the void left in her now emptied stomach. At least Aric had met his end. Not by her hand, as she had sworn, but an end nonetheless. Another boon from the Saxons.

"You best sit down," Gunter said. He'd moved over to the fire and poked at the coals with a long stick.

Yrsa obeyed, not because she accepted her renewed captivity, but because she was a wreck. Her mind scrambled over her interactions with Aric. Their marriage was arranged by her father because of the wealth and respect he'd gained as a raider. At the time, Yrsa had been pleased that Aric wasn't old and that he was fierce. She was indifferent to the men of the neighboring villages, and Aric would fit the mold for a suitable husband. He didn't seem to care that she wanted to raid one day or that she did a poor job of her womanly duties.

What if she had found out his secret? Was Aric unafraid to lay next to the woman whose father he killed? And what of allowing her to accompany the raid back to where he'd killed her father? Aric had known her intention to slake her blood feud. The questions that piled on one another made her want to gag again.

Unless...Ridley wasn't lying when he said there hadn't been a raid on Hyrstow. Aric could have told her anything he pleased when he announced her father's death, and she would have claimed vengeance rights. He could have pointed at any Saxon male and told her it was he, and Yrsa would have driven a sword through that man.

Yrsa closed her eyes against the headache that bloomed in the back of her skull. She sat heavily on a log that had been pulled near the fire. Aric would have looked the hero to everyone, her included, if he'd allowed her to kill an anonymous man and returned with treasure. Her craving to raid would have been subdued, and she might very well have been a good little wife.

As Yrsa tried to suck breaths through her nose, her mind shifted to Vidar. They were not the friends she thought they were. And where did that leave her? No family, prospects, or allies. Would Vidar even consider her a raider when he returned or was she to be killed? The other men had not spoken up for her, nor did they worry for her wellbeing. And what of Hyrstow? Ridley and his friends were no doubt dealing with the fallout of her escape. There was no way they would expect an attack from the Vikings so soon after she'd fled.

Ridley would fight to the death to protect his village. He was a brilliant warrior, but even he had limits against an unknown enemy. She couldn't let him perish. He was the one person who had proven himself genuine. She had to do something, anything to help.

Through a dry swallow Yrsa narrowed her eyes on Gunter. He was tall, with a deep forehead and jowls circling his frown. A crusty bandage wrapped his upper arm, though no other injuries decorated his body. A knife hung on his belt beside a short ax that boasted a red stained handle. His limbs were lanky, encased in sinewy muscle. When his sharp eyes fell on her, his frown deepened. Yrsa recalled that his sister used to tease her for her boyish ways, and he had a wife from a neighboring village.

Behind the fire, the Tanner sisters stared at her. The one with the split lip had her arm around her sister's shoulders. Her eyes were narrowed on Yrsa, as if she was just another Viking to hurt them. As if she didn't just witness Yrsa's own life being shattered. The other simply rested her head on her sister's chest, staring at Yrsa with vacant eyes.

Yrsa didn't know what to do with them. They were tied together, obviously too scared to realize that the three of them outnumbered Gunter. Perhaps they were hurt more than she realized because the freckled one quaked.

"Too bad you must miss the raid to guard me," Yrsa offered.

Gunter grunted, stirring the fire. She'd need him to put that stick down. No part of her wanted to be struck with the hot end of it.

"Where is there water? I'm parched."

Gunter lifted a heavy blonde brow. When she made to stand, he dropped the stick and strode to the bag tied to his horse. Yrsa's heart pulsed at her throat. She expelled a steady breath. This would be her only chance to free herself.

Yrsa tensed, hands flexing. Her blood surged as she unsheathed the dagger at her back. Without time to be silent, she ran at Gunter.

She kept her dagger aimed at the space between his shoulder blades. Her footfalls weren't muffled enough by the grass because he turned with a surprised oath, arms coming up between them. Yrsa managed a heavy slice to his forearm.

"You bitch!" Gunter howled, clutching his arm, rage coating his features.

Yrsa didn't stop. She ducked low, slicing at his legs with the dagger, the movement pushing him against his horse to avoid her. Her blade opened the skin along his upper thigh. His grunt of pain oiled her bones as she rolled upward. Her sense of victory was cut short.

Gunter kicked out at her leg. She turned to dodge it and he grabbed her hair to hold her in place. His fist connected with the back of her shoulder as she twisted away. The blow was hard enough to shove her to the ground. Gritting her teeth, Yrsa tossed her head to free her hair and dug her fingers into the soil, toes cutting against the dirt to push herself out of his grasp.

If Gunter pinned her down, the damage he could inflict would be monstrous.

He released her hair, but the snick of a sword through

leather made Yrsa's blood freeze. Dirt and leaves sprayed up as she scrambled back to the fire. She shoved her dagger into her belt. Getting to the ax that lay by the logs was her only hope.

"You'll pay for this, Yrsa. I doubt Vidar will care if you die at my hand."

Yrsa glanced back, panic clawing up her spine. Gunter gripped his sword in both hands, heedless of the blood that wept down his forearm. He strode to her, a limp hindering his steady progress. She rounded the fire, the hair on the back of her neck standing up as Gunter's steady footfalls ate the space between them.

Ahead, the ax leaned against a log. Yrsa lunged for it, her fingers wrapping around the handle. It was a satisfying, solid weight in her hand. She turned to face Gunter mere steps away.

"Vidar's a pup," she spat. "How quickly did the rest of you fall in line? Is he to claim leadership of Inivik as easily?"

"You're just like your father. Cocky. Selfish." The words stuck like barbs in Yrsa's heart. She had loved her father. He was a good man and brave leader. She couldn't let it show how it shook her to hear of his misdeeds.

"At least he is feasting in Valhalla looking down at the rest of you. Not likely you'll get there."

Gunter let loose a growl and lunged. The strike was sloppy, driven by frustration. Fire pinned them on one side, a pile of logs on the other and Gunter kept coming. Yrsa swung the ax at Gunter's belly. He jumped back, bringing his sword high. Yrsa spun away, hopping over discarded logs, breath in her throat. The strike cleaved its way into the ground where she'd stood a moment prior.

"Let me go," Yrsa said. She cast her gaze to the women. The stoic one stared at the horse, the other had her eyes shut. "Vidar is gone. You can say I got away. No one will know you freed me."

Gunter's lip curled to reveal missing teeth. He stepped over the logs so that she was within striking distance. With a toss of his lanky hair, he wiped a bloody hand along his leg, then drew the sword into a two-handed embrace.

"Scared, Saxon-lover?" Gunter snarled. "You'll never be free again. Should have sucked that Saxon's cock for the rest of your life; should have taken all the scum on at once because you won't make it back to Inivik. You think Vidar will let you live now that you know about Arkyn?"

Yrsa grit her teeth. She would have to kill him. She'd have to strike down one of her clansmen and wipe away any chance at rejoining her world. It should have bothered her more.

That life wasn't hers. Not anymore. Unknown to her at the time, the moment her father was slain by Aric, her entire path had changed.

The grain of the ax's handle dug into her palms, and Yrsa forced herself to loosen her grip. Sweat slicked her middle causing her tunic to stick to her. The weight of the weapon tugged at her injury.

Gunter's lips formed a thin line, brow drawn down as

he glared at her. His fingers flexed around his sword's handle. The wind, Gunter's hands, the nearby birds that peered down at them from the treetops, paused. There was a sway within time that Yrsa felt settle in her bones before everything sped up.

Yrsa swung the ax upward as Gunter thrust the sword at her chest. The blade ricocheted off the ax's head, the metal-on-metal clanging. Yrsa brought the ax down then back around, just as Gunter swung the sword in a sweeping arc at her legs. She dodged it with a slash of her own. He blocked it.

Yrsa growled and waited for him to swing at her. Gunter aimed for her neck. She ducked under the too wide arc and brought her ax up beneath his outstretched arm. It sunk into the flesh where his arm attached to his body. Gunter's grunt of pain rent the air, followed by the thump of his sword upon the ground. He loosed an inhuman howl as she yanked the ax's handle. It was stuck.

Before satisfaction could anchor itself within her, Gunter charged, screaming. He reached for her throat with his free hand, eyes wide. Surprised, Yrsa reared back, falling hard on her ass, hands outstretched behind her.

Gunter swung his fist. His aim was high but still hit her in the side of the head. Pain exploded behind her eyes. Still, she staggered upward. Not before Gunter threw a harsh, open handed slap that sent her to one knee. A punch to the gut had her curling into herself on the ground. The metallic tang of blood wound its way through her teeth.

Yrsa rolled, arms up to defend against another blow. Gunter kept coming. Even with the ax handle protruding from his chest. Yrsa kicked at the ax, but it was slick with blood. The hit glanced off but it took him to his knees over top of her. Her legs stuck beneath his, Yrsa reached up to shove the handle in further. He gave a savage groan as blood gushed from the wound. Mouth agape, Gunter half fell as he rammed himself atop her.

Yrsa couldn't get away. The air crushed from her lungs. His weight was like that of a horse. He was everywhere. She thrashed beneath him, trying to buck him off. Harsh, sucking breaths were all she could hear.

Gunter grinned, eyes unfocused as he brought his hand down on her neck. She had to get free. Gunter was heavy, the ax's handle pressing into her side as he covered her. Panic overrode her as the edges of her vision began to fray. With as much force as she could muster, Yrsa shoved the heel of her hand up into Gunter's windpipe. There was a sickly crunch as bones gave way beneath her palm. Gunter's head snapped up, then halted mid-air.

One of the Tanner sisters clutched his hair in both hands. Gunter's fist flew backward to get her off but she dug her fingers into the strands. Yrsa didn't think. She grabbed the dagger from her belt and shoved it into Gunter's side. Once, twice.

A terrible, inhuman moan escaped him as his life drained away. He slumped forward, against the pull of the woman holding his head. Yrsa shoved at him, digging her legs out as fast as she could while the Tanner sister gritted her teeth to hold him up. As Yrsa stood, the other woman let go and the body fell.

Silence descended with it.

There was a roar in her ears like the sound of waves crashing upon shore. Everything hurt.

The other woman stared at her, her own chest rising and falling rapidly. She wore no cloak, unlike her sister. Then she was a flurry of movement, scurrying to the top of Gunter's body. She snatched up the ax that had dislodged itself from his chest as he collapsed to the ground. The thing dripped with red gore but the sister didn't notice. She held the ax at an awkward angle in front of her, as if to ward off Yrsa.

Yrsa watched her, limbs tingling. Survival wasn't her only mission. She had to make it back to Hyrstow. Had to warn Ridley. Vidar and the others were so bent on revenge, all Yrsa could picture was Hyrstow in flames.

Yrsa yanked her dagger from Gunter's side. She didn't have time to feel the guilt that threatened when a memory surfaced of her clan around the fire, eating roasted rabbit the night before their raid. There had been laughter between greasy mouthfuls of venison. Gunter sang a song of luck. His blood was hers to carry.

Yrsa cleaned the dagger on her trousers, then slung it into her belt. She picked up the discarded sword and approached the Tanner women.

The one who'd helped her stood in front of the other. Her split lip looked angrier up close. She brandished the ax awkwardly, eyes cold as they fixed on Yrsa. Flecks of blood smeared her jaw. Yrsa allowed her lips to curl upward, hoping the women wouldn't be a problem.

"I will not harm you. I will return you to Hyrstow. We must be quick."

THIRTY

"You must be him," the crooked-nosed Viking that circled him spat.

"Who?"

Ridley heaved a deep breath through his nose, wincing at the shallow slice in his side. The sun baked him, heightening the scent of carnage that clogged the air. Viking bodies were strewn through the square as carrion birds cawed overhead, waiting for their meal.

A sparse group of Vikings had advanced from the south. Ridley, Bran, Grahame, and the others had been able to head them off in the field near Bran's home. It had been too easy. The battle-worn group was no match for Ridley's party.

Upon their return to Hyrstow, chaos reigned. In a blur of sweeping arms and glinting metal, Saxons outnumbered Vikings, but the invaders put up a fight worthy of their Valhalla. Riddled with injuries, they aimed to take a last stand for the village's riches or be cut down trying. Ridley had stopped two from breaking into the church. As he'd finished, a dark-haired man shouted at him and advanced from across the square, sword outstretched.

The man immediately thrust his sword at Ridley's chest. Ridley backpedaled to the church, nearly at the doors. He had reach, but the man had a shield. What he lacked in skill, he made up for in sheer will. And words.

"Yrsa spoke of you."

Ridley's heart stuttered. It was enough of a pause that the Viking slipped his weapon into Ridley's arm. A gash opened beneath his elbow. Pain radiated upward.

The Viking laughed. Paired with the bloodstains on his chest and neck, the sound was grotesque. He was shorter than Ridley, closer to Bran's height but not near his width. There was an oiliness about him that Ridley's mind tripped on.

"She tried to tell us there was nothing here. That she'd bedded a Saxon. She cried for you."

The Viking's smirk caused a darkness to slither through Ridley. His eyes were too bight, dancing with knowledge that Ridley wasn't privy to.

"You lie," Ridley shouted. He ducked to impart a blow to the man's side. The man hit it away with his shield and danced back, revealing blood-stained teeth as he grinned. Ridley swung again, his movement sloppy at the mention of Yrsa. Missed. Ridley shook his head to clear it. He couldn't think of her. Not during battle.

Without hesitation the Viking feigned to the right then struck. Ridley slipped out of the way just in time. He circled, putting the church at his front. He needed the man to drop the shield. Once, twice, Ridley thrust jagged swaths through the air, his sword barking against the shield each time.

"You must have been the one to bed her. Or was it all of you scum?" the man's grin widened. He dipped to the left, crouching, then slid back.

"Yrsa spurned me. She was a true Viking. Indeed, I let her go." As the words left his mouth, he drove his sword upward, beneath the safety of the shield. The tip of the weapon etched along the man's thigh. He grunted, baring teeth in anger.

"She was a whore. Darling Yrsa, betrayed."

Ridley shoved a breath through his nose. The man made no sense. He had to focus. Shouts of alarm rang out near him but he dared not look away from the Viking. His men still needed him.

"You must have been the one. Though, you are not the best fighter *I've* seen."

Ridley nearly tripped forward as the words he'd forced Yrsa to say slapped him. She must have been close enough to the man to share about her time in his hut. Unease clenched Ridley's gut in a fist and didn't let go.

Somewhere in the distance, Ridley heard Branton's raised voice. A man started to wail. The sorrow of it punctured the air. Female voices carried on the air, out of place.

The Viking came at him, weapon low. Ridley blocked the hit, but it cost him. The man swung his shield into Ridley's body. It hit his shoulder, forcing him to nearly drop his sword. Sweat stung his eyes as he righted himself.

"She called your name as her throat was cut."

Ridley's world halted.

A deep pain, one that had nothing to do with his injuries, ripped at Ridley's heart with claws. And behind it, an darkness that scared Ridley with its ferocity.

"She died the way her father did. Like a dog."

He failed to move as the man's sword came for him. He didn't care. Sorrow so deep, so blinding, carved its way into his soul.

"Ridley!" A voice peeled through the square.

It shook him enough to rear back just in time to avoid the Viking's blow.

His mind tripped over Yrsa, dead. She couldn't be. She was too vital, to crafty, too willful to simply be no more. Emptiness yawned before Ridley, swallowing him whole.

The Viking raised his sword. Ridley's shoulders sagged against the weight of his weapon. If she was dead, why bother to fight? He'd warred his entire life only to learn of his true love's death. There was nothing for him if Yrsa did not exist in the world. He watched, detached, as the Viking brought his blade toward him. Then, features twisted in surprise, the Viking halted in mid-swing. His sword was poised in the air above them as he looked down, eyes wide, shield arm falling.

The tip of a sword protruded from the center of the Viking's chest. His face contorted with shock then pain. Blood welled over his tongue.

Ridley came back to himself enough to thrust his own sword into the Viking's gut. That's when he saw her.

Over the dead man's shoulder, Yrsa held the sword that had pierced the man's back. Determination steeled her features. Her gorgeous mouth was curled with fury. It was the most beautiful sight Ridley had ever seen.

Yrsa's gaze caught his.

She was dressed in red, just like the first day he'd seen her. Blood coated her front. Ridley's worry spiked, but her blue eyes were bright and clear, feasting on him. As the body between them sagged to the ground, Ridley withdrew his sword, securing it in his belt.

A sob wrung its way past Ridley's dry lips as he reached for her. She stepped around the man between them and came into his arms. Hard. She slid her hands around his waist, nuzzled her face into his neck. The iron tang of blood and the scent of moist dirt marred her hair. Ridley didn't care. He showered kisses on the strands, her eyes, her lips. She blessed him with the same.

"Are you hurt?" he demanded, belatedly aware of how much blood covered her.

"I'm whole. I'm fine. Are you?" Her eyes skimmed his body, alighting on the red smear on his side, brows raising in question.

"Nothing serious," he replied. As quick and gentle as a small bird, her hands fell to his side and pressed along his tunic to stanch the trickle. Her mouth, a purplish bruise marring the corner, pinched together with worry.

A lump formed in his throat. Before he could speak, Yrsa's words rushed forth.

"I needed to get to you. I love you, Ridley. My heart belongs to you. I couldn't imagine a world where you were no longer." Her feverish words dissolved with hurried kisses.

"I was told..." he paused to gather the words that he could barely speak. "He told me you'd been killed."

She glanced at the body, her mouth trembling as her features collapsed with sorrow. "That was Vidar. He took command of our clansmen after Aric's death. He told me Aric killed my father—there had been greed during their last raid. He called me a Saxon whore, left me with a guard, and told me he'd be back with Hyrstow's riches."

Yrsa stared at the body for a long moment, her eyes glazing over. Ridley stroked her face as he ran a hand down her back, pulling her back to him. He wanted to erase all her pain.

"He wasn't who I thought. Nobody was. Not my father, not Aric, not Vidar. The only person I can trust is the one who kept me."

Yrsa's lips gave a wry twist as she spoke. As if needing to satisfy her own need for touch, she ran her free hand up his chest. She turned her face to his, the urgency in her tone laying her bare.

"I love you, Ridley. It was torture leaving you, but it was a thousand times worse knowing that you might die protecting Hyrstow. My worst fear was that I would come too late."

She drew his head down to her for a desperate kiss.

Their tongues clashed and wove, and they drank from one another as if parched. When she broke away, her grin was like the warmth of the sun.

"You test me and strengthen me. And if you never want to see me again after this day, I can accept that. But my hope is that you will allow me a life with you. Despite our differences, I know in my bones that my place is with you."

Pure, unadulterated elation galloped through Ridley. Her words were more than he could ever hope for. But with them, reality crashed down like a dungeon's door. He'd forced her into captivity once. He refused to do so again. Cupping her cheek, he feathered kisses on her lips, nose. He then dropped his forehead to hers.

"Yrsa, I love you with every part of myself. You are my match, and I will love you until I am in my grave and beyond, but I must ask: are you sure? You are free. There is no one to force your decision. Not your father or betrothed or friend. I will not hold you back from your destiny. I've heard of Viking settlements along the north coast. You could live with your people."

Yrsa pressed her lips together as she shook her head. A tear slipped down her cheek. Ridley brushed it away with his thumb, heart throbbing as he waited. Her gaze cut from him to Vidar's body then to the village square. A shy grin picked up the corners of her mouth at what she saw. Curious, Ridley turned to look.

The square was filled with bodies. Mostly Viking. One or two Saxons. Blood drenched the sun-baked ground.

Bran came from behind a hut, bloody but whole. A hint of a smile played on his lips. Against the backdrop of carnage, it painted him a madman.

"She came out of the west and helped dispatch them. The fighting's finished, Rid. And she brought the Tanner sisters with her."

Bran stepped back, palm spread wide to reveal Awolf Tanner embracing two women.

"The sisters..." Ridley could barely reconcile what he was seeing.

"I'm sorry," she murmured, her lips to his shoulder. "I meant to warn your people, but I was too late. I was put under guard and had to fight to get away. The sisters were there. I brought them back."

People had begun to gather, crowding into one another to catch their words. Some of the men must have sent for the women because a few of them emerged from behind huts. Others came up, still brandishing weapons, bloody, relief-filled faces staring. Suddenly, Grahame was there, shoving to the front to stand in front of Ridley and Yrsa. Somehow, only his hands were smeared with red, the rest of him clean, as if blood didn't dare touch his golden face.

"Hello, lady wolf," he said.

Yrsa gave a grin so beautiful with its timidness, Ridley's heart hurt. She inclined her head to Grahame as she wound her fingers through Ridley's.

"I saw you fight. Well done. And thank you."

A lump came to Ridley's throat. Grahame was Hyrstow's golden son, a poor merchant family turned prosperous. As much as he shrugged off his influence, others listened to him.

It was then that Ridley caught Bran's eye. Through the blood that decorated his face, Bran's gaze softened. He gave a begrudging nod, a small grin appearing, then raised his voice to be heard across the square.

"Yrsa the Viking came to our aid this morning! She tried to call off her clan! They did not heed her. Now they are food for the birds. Yrsa helped when she could have fled. She fought for Hyrstow!"

Bran threw his fist in the air with his last words, eliciting a few nods from those around them. Ridley shot him a heartfelt look of gratitude.

Awolf Tanner, at the edge of the square with his daughters, shouted his thanks, his arms around them. From behind the line of huts that created the village proper, women began to emerge. When they saw the sisters, they ran to them, hands to their mouths. Cries of relief decorated the square.

Yrsa's tug on his hand caused Ridley to turn back to her. She peered up at him, her face suddenly serious. He wanted to hold her for a fortnight. "If you would have me, Ridley of Hyrstow, I would stay, as your woman."

Ridley's smile was so wide he thought his face would split. He pulled Yrsa to him and planted his lips on hers in a kiss so searing, he thought they would melt the ground. A whistle sounded at their side, accompanied by a shout of approval. Yrsa smiled around his mouth, and Ridley felt as if he would float off the ground and be carried away on the wind.

A couple of claps sprang up. He broke the kiss and stood proudly before his people, Yrsa's hand in his.

"People of Hyrstow!" he shouted, loud enough for those in the back of the gathering to hear. "The Vikings have been vanquished! They will bother us no more!"

A triumphant shout rose from the battle-worn faces. He did not note any injury among his men. The luck of that sent his heart soaring.

If there was opposition, he was prepared to leave the village to be with Yrsa. He could go back to being a knight. They could settle somewhere else. He would move heaven and earth to claim a life with her.

"I was untruthful. I kept Yrsa Arkyndóttir in my home to heal her. She is a good, honorable woman. She is a true warrior and has pledged herself to Hyrstow! I implore you to welcome her, but if you don't, I understand. I am prepared to live elsewhere with the woman of my heart."

Ridley scoured the faces of the men and women he'd been chosen to steward. There were some confused, some angry, but most began to nod. Cheers and hollers started from Grahame's direction and rippled through the crowd. He spotted Emma and Merthe who were clapping, a smile brightening their faces. Ridley felt a surge of gratitude for her. She was one of the reasons Yrsa was standing beside him.

Ridley looked directly at her and mouthed the words 'thank you'. She inclined her head with a grin.

He could do this. With the Viking threat gone, he could continue to work with his people. For they were what mattered. Not Lachlan's agenda against the church, not Oswald's greed, but the good people of Hyrstow itself. With Yrsa by his side, he felt as if he had truly come home.

"What is the meaning of this?" Oswald's voice boomed from behind Ridley.

His good spirits were doused by his brother's frigid tone. Time seemed to slow as Oswald pushed between Yrsa and Ridley. Caught off guard, their hands broke apart. Oswald's face contorted into a mask of shock as he looked between them. The clapping stopped.

"The witch is back?"

No one spoke. Even Ridley was at a loss for words. Somehow, after all the killing, cocooned in his happiness, he'd forgotten Oswald's wrath. Ridley's hackles rose as he opened his mouth to speak, but Yrsa beat him to it.

"Yes," Yrsa answered, inching her chin upward. She stared into Oswald's eyes, meeting him head on. "I tried to warn my people away. When they didn't listen, I fought my way back to tell—"

"Silence her, Ridley! Does she not know to whom she speaks?" Oswald's eyes flashed with fury, as if he'd been slapped by Yrsa's entreaty.

Ridley spoke low and quick to silence his brother before he turned the tide against Yrsa once again. "I love her, brother. She has proven her loyalty to Hyrstow in the face of danger. She is my woman now. Please welcome her as partner of the chieftain."

Oswald's eyes widened as his mouth dropped open.

He cast his gaze about the crowd as if trying to peer into their souls. His attention caught and lingered on the Viking bodies sprawled throughout the square. His flinch was slight enough that Ridley guessed he was the only one who saw it. It was quickly covered with a sneer.

Whatever sympathy Ridley had for his brother's delicate sensibilities was smothered by the thought of him cowering inside the safety of the church with the other priests while a battle raged outside. Able-bodied men cowering like children while Yrsa cut through her own people struck him as a cruel twist of fate.

Oswald drew himself to his full height as he spit his words at Ridley. "I will not. I have looked out for you all your life, Ridley, and it looks as if I must do it again. She is a Viking. She will never belong."

"Not if you don't give her a chance."

But Oswald had heard enough. He stepped forward with his arms outstretched and used his preacher's voice. "I see before me many who have survived great struggles on this day. The Vikings sought to terrorize us—again—but we did not allow that to happen!"

There were several nods. Ridley stepped behind Oswald and grabbed Yrsa's hand. He didn't know what Oswald planned, but he knew that it would cast him in a poor light if he protested in the middle of the Reverend Father's speech. Yrsa arched an eyebrow at him, and Ridley gave a silent shake of his head for her to not interrupt. She squeezed his hand and shot an impatient look at Oswald's back.

"God has blessed us with victory on this day! And yet

there is still evil in our midst. This woman is of the clan that sought our deaths. She has bewitched our chief and twisted a tale of her innocence!"

Ridley pulled Yrsa into the shield of his body as Oswald stood back to level a finger at her. There were murmurs in the crowd, accompanied by the shuffling of bodies. Under the glaring heat of the sun, coupled with the stench of blood, Ridley felt the tide of approval shifting beneath his feet. Grahame slowly shook his head while Bran glared at Oswald.

"That is not true," Ridley said.

"Do you call me a liar?" Oswald demanded. His face twisted into exaggerated offense. Never had Ridley wanted to inflict so much harm to his brother.

Oswald had a long-held belief that pagans were less than dirt. And yet, his hate of Yrsa seemed more than that. It was as if he considered her a temptation; he'd admitted so himself. The finality of it fell on Ridley's shoulders like a sack of grain. Ridley knew that Oswald's hate for her would consume her chance of a life in Hyrstow. She was a risk to Oswald's own relationship with God and, therefore, could not remain.

"Of course not, Father," Ridley amended through the fence of his teeth. "May I suggest that you do not yet see the service that Yrsa has done for us today. She came into the fray and helped us defend against her own people."

"Ah, so she is a traitor to her own kind," Oswald said with a grin of satisfaction. Sweat snaked down Ridley's temple. The cold fingers of fear wiggled through his gut.

He could still lose her. After all that they'd fought for, she could still be ripped from him and butchered.

"Yrsa is strong, capable and knows the way of the Vikings. She is a defensive asset for Hyrstow. We can learn from her if she is willing to stay."

"I am," Yrsa said, releasing his hand and facing the crowd. "I do not know your customs and my tongue sounds strange to you. But I have found comfort and a home in this place, and I would like to pledge myself as an ally to you all."

Her voice rang clear and strong, her gaze touching on all of those who looked upon her. Despite Oswald flapping his arms and trying to speak over her, Yrsa prevailed. Even coated in crimson and grime, she commanded dignity and power.

Someone clapped and another whistled. Freda hollered, raising her hands above her head like a flag of welcome. It didn't take long for others to follow suit. Relief, sharp and clear, pierced Ridley. His people would not abandon him. He looked to Yrsa and she stared back at him, victory shining in her gaze. They could be together. After all of it, they could have the love they'd never expected to find.

"No!" Oswald shouted over the commotion. His face was puce as he lunged for Yrsa's dagger. She moved to step out of the way too late; Oswald caught hold of the handle and yanked it free. Yrsa's mouth made an 'O' of surprise as Oswald lunged.

THIRTY-ONE

Ridley's sword was in hand without him realizing he'd drawn it. The movement was crystalline in its finality. As the dagger was shoved at Yrsa with unpracticed vehemence, Oswald was halted by the tip of Ridley's blade poised at his neck.

A collective gasp escaped the villagers.

Ridley wanted to shake, to rage, to shout at his brother. But it was as if his limbs were a cool extension of his steady heart. A heart that pumped with the urge to drive the blade into the throat of the man that threatened Yrsa. His vision tunneled on the sweaty skin at the end of the sword.

"Ridley." A strong, slender hand settled on his forearm. "Lay down your sword. He is your brother."

Ridley slid his gaze to Yrsa, but he did not relax his stance. Her hand on his arm was like a warm brand. There was no fear in her gaze. Her blue eyes were steady, carrying such faith in him; she knew he was better than this. As if she could see their future, and this wasn't part of it. She was his strength. His constant. He wanted to wrap himself in her and never let go.

As the rage-fuelled haze lifted, Ridley's thoughts cleared. He was not a man to murder a priest, his own brother. He was a protector. Ridley released the sword as if it were a hot iron. It clattered to the dirt.

Oswald clutched at his throat as he sucked air, eyes bulging. He dropped Yrsa's dagger as if it had burned him. The dulled blade skittered toward Bran's feet.

The reality of what he'd almost done descended on Ridley. His people had witnessed him almost slay their priest. He was fit to be hung.

Ridley stumbled back a step under the weight of how close he'd come to destroying his life because Yrsa had been threatened. She moved with him, catching his arm in both her hands. He couldn't look anywhere but the blood-soaked ground. He was the Saxon monster she'd thought him to be.

"Ridley." His name was a caress. Yrsa wrapped her arm around his neck, pressing herself to his body, shielding him from the acrid fear that tinged the air. He didn't deserve her, but he would take her offering. He looped his arms around her back and held her, focusing on her rusty-scented hair. A silence from the depths of time careened around them.

"The Reverend owes Yrsa Arkyndóttir his life!" Bran's deep baritone came from the crowd.

"Here, here!" Awolf Tanner called.

In disbelief, Ridley watched nods of agreement dip

the heads of the spectators. The others witnessed Yrsa's goodwill. Ridley could have killed Oswald, and he would have been put to death. Yrsa saved them both.

"I owe this woman no such thing," Oswald spat. His frantic gaze bounced between Yrsa and Ridley and the people of Hyrstow. Chin wobbling, he blinked several times as he rubbed sweat from his forehead. In front of so many witnesses, it would be difficult for him to cast further judgment.

"She spared you," Grahame insisted. He began to push his way between Oswald and Yrsa, as if to shield his friends from Oswald's threats.

Oswald visibly gulped. He dragged an arm across the sweat on his brow. "That—that heathen woman is not allowed inside this holy church."

With a jeweled hand pressed to his throat, Oswald retreated to his sanctuary.

Ridley didn't look back. He held Yrsa to him tightly as he watched the crowd disperse. The feather-light caress of her chuckle in his ear reminded him to let her breathe.

"It's over," she said, pulling away to peer into his eyes. Ridley dropped his forehead to hers, eyes shut tight. Yrsa had proven she could take care of herself and him. The thought caused a rush of feeling so pure, it made him want to laugh.

"Love does not encompass all that I feel for you," he murmured. When he opened his eyes, he caught her biting her lip.

"Not bad flattery for a stupid Saxon," she teased. Her nose wrinkled in the most delectable way.

Ridley eased back as he saw Bran step forward. His brows were drawn tight. But his friend's next words were genuine.

"Yrsa. I want to welcome you, officially. Ridley is the best man I know, and I hope that you can become one of the best women."

Yrsa nodded, her grin unsure yet hopeful. "Thank you. I wish the same."

Bran offered his hand. Yrsa clasped it. They shook, each still wary of the other.

Grahame strode forward, slinging an arm around Yrsa's shoulders. Her eyes widened in surprise, hand fisting. "Come off it, Bran! She's already a good woman who could kick your ass all the way to Eoforwic."

Grahame ducked his chin, arching a golden brow at Yrsa's fist prepared to strike. "Looks like she'll do the same to me as well." With a loud laugh, he released her, hands up, eyes merry. "We'll leave you to it."

He shoved Bran, whose attention was locked wholly on his family.

Ridley threaded an arm around Yrsa's waist, bringing the other hand up to cup her face. He grazed his nose along hers. With her in his arms, he felt like he could breathe again.

"Thank you, Yrsa Arykdóttir. For having the strength to guide me even when I was intent on damning myself."

Yrsa's mouth curled around white teeth. In their time together, he'd grown accustomed to her glower, which he thought beautiful; however, her smile made him want to drop to his knees. His heart beat harder in his chest, and he knew that he would spend every day of the rest of his life trying to make her smile like that.

"You're welcome, Saxon. Now, I have a further request."

"What is that, princess?" Ridley couldn't help himself; he pressed a kiss to the corner of her lips.

"Take me to the river to wash." Yrsa's hands scored his shoulders and around his neck, pulling at the short hairs there. A wickedness flashed in her jeweled eyes that made Ridley's blood heat.

"Aye. Your hair looks tangled. I may have to help with that."

With a bite of her lower lip, Yrsa turned him in the direction of the river. "As long as you join me in the water, Saxon, you can help me in any way you see fit."

EPILOGUE

ne Month Later

YRSA CROUCHED in the sandy soil that bordered the river, damp earth pressing into her knees and palms. The rustle she'd heard in the bushes ahead had come from the northeast and whoever it was wasn't light on their feet. Yrsa shook her head at the ease with which she'd be able to pick them off with her bow. The instrument was new to her, but over the past month, she'd discovered she had a talent for it. The small quiver of arrows weighed against her back, and as the person approached, she slowly stood, pressing the pads of her fingers into the string, pulling back until it was taut. As her pursuer came into view, she released the cord absent of an arrow, the twang bursting through the woods.

Emma stopped in her tracks, searching for Yrsa, a hand to her heart. "Yrsa! Goodness! You scared me."

Grinning, Yrsa stepped out from her cover of dense bush. She picked her way through the bush to Emma and Merthe, reaching out to rustle the girl's gleaming auburn hair. Merthe batted her hand away, annoyed to be treated like a child.

Yrsa laughed. She'd learned a lot about the Saxons in her month with them, but one unexpected revelation was the bond that had grown between her and the girl. Merthe had become her shadow. Her daughter's curiosity had worried Emma at first, but Yrsa had worked hard to prove that she could be trusted with the child.

"You should have told me you were going hunting," Merthe complained.

Yrsa shrugged. "I wasn't hunting."

"You're going to be late for your wedding," Emma said. She smiled in that bashful way she had, as if holding herself in check. Yrsa still couldn't figure out if it was because she wanted to act proper in front of her daughter or if she was shy. Either way, Yrsa found that she liked the other woman more than she thought possible. Yrsa couldn't help but enjoy the sensible peace that emanated from Emma.

"I'm the bride. The ceremony won't start without me," Yrsa stated.

Emma rolled her eyes as she threaded her arm through Yrsa's. "Yes, but you will annoy your future brother-in-law further if you don't at least try to adhere to our traditions. He was generous enough to allow one of the other priests to perform the ceremony."

Yrsa nodded. Oswald had been sullen in the days following the raid. He didn't utter a word to Ridley for more than two weeks. Yrsa didn't mind. She hated the man who acted holier than his god. But their contempt for one another bothered Ridley. He never outright stated that he wanted them to get along, but he mentioned several times that Oswald's blessing would bode well for her welcome into Hyrstow. When Yrsa had protested, Ridley insisted, explaining it was to officially recognize their union, which would ensure Ridley's assets go to Yrsa upon his death. They'd had an explosive fight, followed by Ridley making up for his pigheadedness in bed.

Scrapping her pride, Yrsa went to Oswald to plead Ridley's case. Though Oswald refused to see her, he had one of the lesser priests listen to her concerns about the rift in Ridley's relationship with the Reverend Father and, after a few days of contemplation, was advised Oswald did not care how the wedding proceeded, which was a good enough 'yes' for Yrsa.

Merthe took Yrsa's hand and the three walked abreast out of the woods and into Hyrstow. The town bustled with activity. Fresh bread and fragrant flowers were set at each table in the town square. A light breeze brushed its fingers through the gauzy ivory panels that draped the willow arbor Bran had fashioned. It stood at the furthest point from the church steps, past the well. Everyone in town was invited but the group had decided to not push their luck with Oswald by demanding a traditional ceremony in or anywhere near the church. Ridley didn't seem to care. All he'd wanted was Yrsa protected by their union.

"There she is!" Freda said as the trio approached her hut. Her black curls had been secured in a haphazard bun at the base of her neck and her mossy coloured skirt brought out the paleness of her skin. Yrsa could see why Bran couldn't keep his hands off his wife. The bump of her pregnancy swelled her stomach further and had given her the glow of a goddess.

"Come on!" Freda gestured as she held the door open and ushered them inside.

Freda and Bran's home was every bit the warm center of family Yrsa had imagined. Colorful blankets and thick furs covered the beds and chairs. The scent of rosemary and mint were lent by the leafy arrangements that hung from the wall near the table on the left. Freda's youngest was there, running her hand over the long-paneled tunic that would serve as Yrsa's wedding attire.

Yrsa sifted the material through her fingers. It was a light, dreamy blend of thin-spun wool with long sleeves and a scooped neckline. The straight skirt fell to the floor and would be cinched by her belt, but there were long slits up the sides, which Yrsa had insisted upon since she'd be wearing trousers beneath.

"I still can't believe you didn't want skirts," Emma murmured behind her as she untied the leather that bound Yrsa's hair. Yrsa threw her a smile.

"How am I to defend the village in a dress?" she

asked. "I'd be no good to anyone if my movement was restricted."

"Mother, Yrsa is a sentry. If something happens, she needs to be able to run and ride and draw her sword..." Merthe added, eyes brightening.

"Alright, that's enough. There won't be any such disasters happening today," Freda said, her voice firm as she batted Merthe to the side to draw Yrsa's hunting tunic over head.

Over the next hour, Freda and Emma worked in sync to ready Yrsa for the ceremony. Yrsa did her best to heed their advice on where to stand or how to sit so that they could tie her hair back with a ribbon, but her locks were wild, she kept fidgeting, and soon, Freda decreed that her hair would remain loose. Yrsa was glad for it. She knew Ridley liked it when her hair tumbled down her back and the prospect of pleasing her soon-to-be husband was a novelty she didn't want to dismiss. When she reached for her dagger, Emma protested.

"I carry it with me always," Yrsa said simply as she slung the dented blade into the belt. The smith had offered to forge her new iron, but Yrsa wanted to keep it the way it was. It was her last Danish item, and though she felt as if she had been sewn into the fabric of Saxon life, there would always be a part of her that lusted for the wildness of discovery.

Thankfully, Ridley had noticed that her talents were not in keeping chickens or washing or cooking. Yrsa was made to wander, and he recognized that by giving her a position that would ensure her contribution to Hyrstow.

Gods, she loved the man.

As Freda pinched her cheeks for color and Emma handed her a ring of silver she was to give Ridley for her wedding present, there was a commotion outside before the groom-to-be entered the hut.

"Ridley! Get out of here! You'll see your bride soon enough," Freda chastised, flinging her hands in a gesture for him to leave.

Ridley was the picture of a gentleman. His hair had been combed back and he'd trimmed his beard. Yrsa very much enjoyed the clean, dark scruff around his chin and neck. A sage tunic brought out the bronze of his eyes and dark brown trousers with leather boots completed his attire.

"I know, but I have to see my wife-to-be. It's important."

Ridley's gaze found Yrsa and ate her up from the top of her head to the tips of her toes. She felt her cheeks burn at the blatant appraisal. Emma uttered a soft sound and scurried to leave while Freda remained in Ridley's way long enough to deliver a warning for him to be quick. She threw a glance at her bedroom, likely in the hope that Ridley and Yrsa would not make love in it. Her fear was not unfounded. Freda had caught Yrsa and Ridley bedding one another exactly three times in three different places. Yrsa grinned at the memory of her walking in on them in the timber shed, in the river, and up against a tree in the forest.

With the hut empty, Ridley strode to Yrsa, claiming her mouth with his own. Greedily, she opened to him, hands wandering over his tensed stomach. He groaned low in his throat while claiming a handful of her ass, pulling her against him.

"Freda thinks we're going to have sex on her bed." Yrsa giggled when they came up for air.

"Aren't we?" Ridley teased, wagging his eyebrows.

Yrsa laughed. She hadn't met much of the teasing, joyful man he was when she'd been his captive, though she'd been told that version of him didn't exist until she came along. She loved all facets of him though; moody, worried, teasing, stubborn, protective, and happy. They had what seemed rare in both his village and hers, a true partnership.

"What do you need, oh husband?"

Ridley bit his bottom lip and trailed his fingers through her hair. His lips quirked. "I like that. Husband."

Yrsa's own lips twitched.

Suddenly, his countenance shifted, his brows tenting. "The first night we were truly together, you had me undo your hair. I burned with desire for you and had no place to put those feelings."

Yrsa clasped her hand around his and guided it to her cheek. "And I you."

His handsome mouth dipped downward. "You've given up everything for me. Your home, your people. I want you to know how I am humbled by that decision. And so, you never doubt my intent to keep you against your will again, I've brought you your bride price."

Ridley loosened a bag from around his belt and placed the leather into her hand. It was heavy, nearly bursting with coins. Yrsa looked up, eyes wide with surprise. The package contained much more than a bride price.

"Ridley..." she said, her voice tender, "you don't have to make anything up to me. I want to be here. I know I could have sought out my own kind, but my people brought me nothing but strife. I love you. I want to stay with you. Please don't doubt that."

Ridley nodded, wrapping his hands around the outside of hers. "I know. I just need you to know that there is enough money there for you to live as you wish. It is your security and a symbol of my promise to never deny you again."

Tears itched the back of her eyes. Her throat felt swollen as she pressed her lips to his. She hoped that the passion of her kiss was enough to show him how much she appreciated the gesture. The kiss deepened and soon they were pulling hungrily at each other's clothes, seeking skin. Too soon, a woman cleared her throat outside, reminding them of their impending ceremony. With groans, they broke apart and straightened their clothing the best they could. Yrsa laughed when Ridley gave an exaggerated adjustment to his lower half. He then held his arm out for her to thread hers through.

"Let's be married so that I may take you to bed. My body is parched for you."

Yrsa grinned, feeling like the most beautiful, loved woman on earth.

"Yes. Let's."

DON'T MISS THE NEXT BOOK IN THE SAXONS OF HYRSTOW SERIES

From Amazon #1 Bestselling author, C.A. Fray, comes:

HIS SAXON WIFE

A marriage of convenience...

Heartbroken after his wife's death and overwhelmed by the needs of his children, Branton Cutter strikes a marriage bargain with widow Emma Baker. Despite his grief, Branton's life takes a chaotic turn when the attraction he feels toward Emma is more than that of their arrangement.

A temptation that cannot be ignored...

To escape the kingdom's widow tax, Emma agrees to Branton's proposal in order to save a proper dowry for her daughter. Little does she know that sharing a house with the broken man will test her patience as well as her desire.

While politics between the church and earldom unravel, peril linked to the past looms over the village of Hyrstow. Will Branton and Emma be able to reconcile their feelings in time to ensure their family's survival?

Releasing March 18th, 2024

And for author updates, musings, free snippets and more, sign up for my newsletter at cafrayauthor.com

Acknowledgments

To my husband, Mark. Thank you for supporting this dream of mine.

Next, my sister, Samantha, for being a sounding board and reading (several) drafts. Thank you to my soulmates, Jill and Robyn, for hyping me up and being the best friends a girl could ask for. *Boop boop boop*

My deepest gratitude goes to my beta readers, Lauren, May-Lin, and Heather. And Tracey, thank you for being a wonderful editor and a great friend in the writing trenches.

And thanks to my mom. For everything.

ACKNOWLEDGEMENTS

ABOUT THE AUTHOR

C.A. Fray is the Amazon #1 Bestselling Author of the steamy medieval romance, His Viking Captive.

C.A. grew up with her nose buried in romance books. She is a mother of three boys and maintains her sanity by writing tension-filled medieval romance. She has a house full of plants, runs a business with her husband, drinks too much coffee and still has her face buried in all kinds of books.

Find her at cafrayauthor.com to find out more about upcoming books.

instagram.com/cafrayauthor

www.ingramcontent.com/pod-product-compliance
Lightning Source LLC
Chambersburg PA
CBHW050856210726
48290CB00004B/1254